DEATH DU JOUR

Also by Kathy Reichs

DÉJÀ DEAD

DEATH DU JOUR

KATHY REICHS

William Heinemann : London

First published in the United Kingdom in 1999 by
William Heinemann

7 9 10 8 6

Published by arrangement with the original publisher, Scribner, an imprint of
Simon & Schuster Inc.

William Heinemann
The Random House Group Limited
20 Vauxhall Bridge Road, London, SW1V 2SA

Random House Australia (Pty) Limited
20 Alfred Street, Milsons Point, Sydney, New South Wales 2061, Australia

Random House New Zealand Limited
18 Poland Road, Glenfield
Auckland 10, New Zealand

Random House South Africa (Pty) Limited
Endulini, 5a Jubilee Road, Parktown, 2193, South Africa

The Random House Group Limited Reg. No. 954009

A CIP catalogue record for this book is available from the British Library

Papers used by Random House UK Limited are natural, recyclable products made
from wood grown in sustainable forests. The manufacturing processes conform to the
environmental regulations of the country of origin

Printed and bound in the United Kingdom by
Creative Print and Design (Wales), Ebbw Vale

ISBN 0 434 00736 6 Hardback
ISBN 0 434 00777 3 Paperback

To all who survived
the Great Quebec Ice Storm of 1998.

Nous nous souvenons.

The characters and events in this book are fictional and created out of the imagination of the author. The setting is in Montreal, Canada; Charlotte, North Carolina; and other locations. Certain real locations and institutions are mentioned, but the characters and events depicted are entirely fictional.

ACKNOWLEDGEMENTS

Grateful thanks are extended to Dr. Ronald Coulombe, specialiste en incendies; to Ms. Carole Péclet, specialiste en chimie; and to Dr. Robert Dorion, Responsable d'Odontologie, Laboratoire de Sciences Judiciaires et de Médecine Légale; and to Mr. Louis Metivier, Bureau du Coroner de la Province de Québec, for sharing their knowledge with me.

Dr. Walter Birkby, forensic anthropologist for the Office of the Medical Examiner of Pima County, Arizona, provided information on the recovery of burned remains. Dr. Robert Brouillette, Head of the Divisions of Newborn Medicine and of Respiratory Medicine at the Montreal Children's Hospital helped with data on infant growth.

Mr. Curt Copeland, the Beaufort County coroner; Mr. Carl McCleod, the Beaufort County sheriff; and Detective Neal Player of the Beaufort County sheriff's department were most helpful. Detective Mike Mannix of the Illinois State Police also answered many questions pertaining to the investigation of a homicide. Dr. James Tabor, Professor of Religious Studies at the University of North Carolina at Charlotte, supplied information on cults and religious movements.

Mr. Leon Simon and Mr. Paul Reichs provided information on Charlotte and its history. I am also indebted to the latter for his comments on the manuscript. Dr. James Woodward, chancellor at the University of North Carolina at Charlotte, supported me unquestioningly throughout the writing of this book.

Special thanks must go to three individuals. Dr. David Taub, mayor of Beaufort and primatologist extraordinaire, was steadfastly helpful despite the barrage of questions I sent his way. Dr. Lee Goff, Professor of Entomology at the University of Hawaii at Manoa, did not abandon me as I pestered him endlessly for advice on bugs. Dr. Michael Bisson, Professor of Anthropology at McGill University, was a resource on McGill University, on Montreal, and on basically anything I needed to know.

Two books were particularly useful in the writing of this story. *Plague: A Story of Smallpox in Montreal* (1991), by Michael Bliss, Harper Collins, Toronto; and *Cults in Our Midst: The Hidden Menace in Our Everyday Lives* (1995), by Margaret Thaler Singer with Janja Lalich, Jossey-Bass Publishers, San Francisco.

I am grateful for the loving care of my agent, Jennifer Rudolph Walsh, and my editors Susanne Kirk and Maria Rejt. Without them Tempe could not tell the stories that she does.

DEATH DU JOUR

IF THE BODIES WERE THERE, I COULDN'T FIND THEM.

Outside, the wind howled. Inside the old church, just the scrape of my trowel and the hum of a portable generator and heater echoed eerily in the huge space. High above, branches scratched against boarded windows, gnarled fingers on plywood blackboards.

The group stood behind me, huddled but not touching, fingers curled tightly in pockets. I could hear the shifting from side to side, the lifting of one foot, then the other. Boots made a crunching sound on the frozen ground. No one spoke. The cold had numbed us into silence.

I watched a cone of earth disappear through quarter-inch mesh as I spread it gently with my trowel. The granular subsoil had been a pleasant surprise. Given the surface, I had expected permafrost the entire depth of the excavation. The last two weeks had been unseasonably warm in Quebec, however, allowing snow to melt and ground to thaw. Typical Tempe luck. Though the tickle of spring had been blown away by another arctic blast, the mild spell had left the dirt soft and easy to dig. Good. Last night the temperature had dropped to seven degrees Fahrenheit. Not good. While the ground had not refrozen, the air was frigid. My fingers were so cold I could hardly bend them.

We were digging our second trench. Still nothing but pebbles and rock fragments in the screen. I didn't anticipate much at this depth, but you could never tell. I'd yet to do an exhumation that had gone as planned.

I turned to a man in a black parka and a tuque on his head. He wore leather boots laced to the knee, two pairs of socks rolled over the tops. His face was the color of tomato soup.

"Just a few more inches." I gave a palm-down gesture, like stroking a cat. Slowly. Go slowly.

The man nodded, then thrust his long-handled spade into the shallow trench, grunting like Monica Seles on a first serve.

"*Par pouces!*" I yelped, grabbing the shovel. By inches! I repeated the slicing motion I'd been showing him all morning. "We want to take it down in thin layers." I said it again, in slow, careful French.

The man clearly did not share my sentiment. Maybe it was the tediousness of the task, maybe the thought of unearthing the dead. Tomato soup just wanted to be done and gone.

"Please, Guy, try again?" said a male voice behind me.

"Yes, Father." Mumbled.

Guy resumed, shaking his head, but skimming the soil as I'd shown him, then tossing it into the screen. I shifted my gaze from the black dirt to the pit itself, watching for signs that we were nearing a burial.

We'd been at it for hours, and I could sense tension behind me. The nuns' rocking had increased in tempo. I turned to give the group what I hoped was a reassuring look. My lips were so stiff it was hard to tell.

Six faces looked back at me, pinched from cold and anxiousness. A small cloud of vapor appeared and dissolved in front of each. Six smiles in my direction. I could sense a lot of praying going on.

Ninety minutes later we were five feet down. Like the first, this pit had produced only soil. I was certain I had frostbite in every toe, and Guy was ready to bring in a backhoe. Time to regroup.

"Father, I think we need to check the burial records again."

He hesitated a moment. Then, "Yes. Of course. Of course. And we could all use coffee and a sandwich."

The priest started toward a set of wooden doors at the far end of the abandoned church and the nuns followed, heads down, gingerly navigating the lumpy ground. Their white veils spread in identical arcs across the backs of their black wool coats. Penguins. Who'd said that? The Blues Brothers.

I turned off the mobile spotlights and fell in step, eyes to the ground, amazed at the fragments of bone embedded in the dirt floor. Great. We'd dug in the one spot in the entire church that didn't contain burials.

Father Ménard pushed open one of the doors and, single file, we exited to daylight. Our eyes needed little adjustment. The sky was leaden and seemed to hug the spires and towers of all the buildings in the convent's compound. A raw wind blew off the Laurentians, flapping collars and veils.

Our little group bent against the wind and crossed to an adjacent building, gray stone like the church, but smaller. We climbed steps to an ornately carved wooden porch and entered through a side door.

Inside, the air was warm and dry, pleasant after the bitter cold. I smelled tea and mothballs and years of fried food.

Wordlessly, the women removed their boots, smiled at me one by one, and disappeared through a doorway to the right just as a tiny nun in an enormous ski sweater shuffled into the foyer. Fuzzy brown reindeer leaped across her chest and disappeared beneath her veil. She blinked at me through thick lenses and reached for my parka. I hesitated, afraid its weight would tip her off balance and send her crashing to the tile. She nodded sharply and urged me with upturned fingertips, so I slipped the jacket off, laid it across her arms, and added cap and gloves. She was the oldest woman that I had ever seen still breathing.

I followed Father Ménard down a long, poorly lit hallway into a small study. Here the air smelled of old paper and schoolhouse paste. A crucifix loomed over a desk so large I wondered how they'd gotten it through the door. Dark oak paneling rose almost to the ceiling. Statues stared down from the room's upper edge, faces somber as the figure on the crucifix.

Father Ménard took one of two wooden chairs facing the desk, gestured me to the other. The swish of his cassock. The click of his beads. For a moment I was back at St. Barnabas. In Father's office. In trouble again. Stop it, Brennan. You're over forty, a professional. A forensic anthropologist. These people called you because they need your expertise.

The priest retrieved a leather-bound volume from the desktop, opened it to a page with a green ribbon marker, and positioned the book between us. He took a deep breath, pursed his lips, and exhaled through his nose.

I was familiar with the diagram. A grid with rows divided into rectangular plots, some with numbers, some with names. We'd spent hours poring over it the day before, comparing the descriptions and records for the graves with their positions on the grid. Then we'd paced it all off, marking exact locations.

Sister Élisabeth Nicolet was supposed to be in the second row from the church's north wall, third plot from the west end. Right next to Mother Aurélie. But she wasn't. Nor was Aurélie where she should have been.

I pointed to a grave in the same quadrant, but several rows down and to the right. "O.K. Raphael seems to be there." Then down the row. "And Agathe, Véronique, Clément, Marthe, and Eléonore. Those are the burials from the 1840s, right?"

"*C'est ça.*"

I moved my finger to the portion of the diagram corresponding to the southwest corner of the church. "And these are the most recent graves. The markers we found are consistent with your records."

"Yes. Those were the last, just before the church was abandoned."

"It was closed in 1914."

"Nineteen fourteen. Yes, 1914." He had an odd way of repeating words and phrases.

"Élisabeth died in 1888?"

"*C'est ça,* 1888. Mère Aurélie in 1894."

It didn't make sense. Evidence of the graves should be there. It was clear that artifacts from the 1840 burials remained. A test in that area had produced wood fragments and bits of coffin hardware. In the protected environment inside the church, with that type of soil, I thought the skeletons should be in pretty good shape. So where were Élisabeth and Aurélie?

The old nun shuffled in with a tray of coffee and sandwiches. Steam from the mugs had fogged her glasses, so she moved with short, jerky steps, never lifting her feet from the floor. Father Ménard rose to take the tray.

"*Merci,* Sister Bernard. This is very kind. Very kind."

The nun nodded and shuffled out, not bothering to clear her lenses. I watched her as I helped myself to coffee. Her shoulders were about as broad as my wrist.

"How old is Sister Bernard?" I asked, reaching for a croissant. Salmon salad and wilted lettuce.

"We're not exactly sure. She was at the convent when I first started coming here as a child, before the war. World War II, that is. Then she went to teach in the foreign missions. She was in Japan for a long time, then Cameroon. We think she's in her nineties." He sipped his coffee. A slurper.

"She was born in a small village in the Saguenay, says she joined the order when she was twelve." Slurp. "Twelve. Records weren't so good in those days in rural Quebec. Not so good."

I took a bite of sandwich then rewrapped my fingers around the coffee mug. Delicious warmth.

"Father, are there any other records? Old letters, documents, anything we haven't looked at?" I wriggled my toes. No sensation.

He gestured to the papers littering the desk, shrugged. "This is everything Sister Julienne gave me. She is the convent archivist, you know."

"Yes."

Sister Julienne and I had spoken and corresponded at length. It was she who had initially contacted me about the project. I was intrigued from the outset. This case was very different from my usual forensic work involving the recently dead who end up with the coroner. The archdiocese wanted me to exhume and analyze the remains of a saint. Well, she wasn't really a saint. But that was the point. Élisabeth Nicolet had been proposed for beatification. I was to find her grave and verify that the bones were hers. The saint part was up to the Vatican.

Sister Julienne had assured me that there were good records. All graves in the old church were cataloged and mapped. The last burial had taken place in 1911. The church was abandoned and sealed in 1914 following a fire. A larger one was built to replace it, and the old building was never used again. Closed site. Good documentation. Piece of cake.

So where was Élisabeth Nicolet?

"It might not hurt to ask. Perhaps there's something Sister Julienne didn't give you because she thought it unimportant."

He started to say something, changed his mind. "I'm quite sure she's given me everything, but I'll ask. Sister Julienne has spent a great deal of time researching this. A great deal."

I watched him out the door, finished my croissant, then another. I crossed my legs, tucked my feet under me, and rubbed my toes. Good. Feeling was returning. Sipping my coffee, I lifted a letter from the desk.

I'd read it before. August 4, 1885. Smallpox was out of control in Montreal. Élisabeth Nicolet had written to Bishop Édouard Fabre, pleading that he order vaccinations for parishioners who were well, and use of the civic hospital by those who were infected. The handwriting was precise, the French quaint and outdated.

The Convent Notre-Dame de l'Immaculée-Conception was absolutely silent. My mind drifted. I thought of other exhumations. The policeman in St-Gabriel. In that cemetery the coffins had been stacked three deep. We'd finally found Monsieur Beaupré four graves from his recorded location, bottom position, not top. And there was the man in Winston-Salem who wasn't in his own coffin. The occupant was a woman in a long floral dress. That had left the cemetery with a double problem. Where was the deceased? And who was the body in the coffin? The family never was able to rebury Grandpa in Poland, and the lawyers were girding for war when I left.

Far off, I heard a bell toll, then, in the corridor, shuffling. The old nun was heading my way.

"*Serviettes,*" she screeched. I jumped, rocketing coffee onto my sleeve. How could so much volume come from so small a person?

"*Merci.*" I reached for the napkins.

She ignored me, closed in, and began scrubbing my sleeve. A tiny hearing aid peeked from her right ear. I could feel her breath and see fine white hairs ringing her chin. She smelled of wool and rose water.

"Eh, *voilà*. Wash it when you get home. Cold water."

"Yes, Sister." Reflex.

Her eyes fell on the letter in my hand. Fortunately, it was coffee-free. She bent close.

"Élisabeth Nicolet was a great woman. A woman of God. Such purity. Such austerity." *Pureté. Austérité.* Her French sounded as I imagined Élisabeth's letters would if spoken.

"Yes, Sister." I was nine years old again.

"She will be a saint."

"Yes, Sister. That's why we're trying to find her bones. So they can receive proper treatment." I wasn't sure just what proper treatment was for a saint, but it sounded right.

I pulled out the diagram and showed it to her. "This is the old church." I traced the row along the north wall, and pointed to a rectangle. "This is her grave."

The old nun studied the grid for a very long time, lenses millimeters from the page.

"She's not there," she boomed.

"Excuse me?"

"She's not there." A knobby finger tapped the rectangle. "That's the wrong place."

Father Ménard returned at that moment. With him was a tall nun with heavy black eyebrows that angled together above her nose. The priest introduced Sister Julienne, who raised clasped hands and smiled.

It wasn't necessary to explain what Sister Bernard had said. Undoubtedly they'd heard the old woman while in the corridor. They'd probably heard her in Ottawa.

"That's the wrong place. You're looking in the wrong place," she repeated.

"What do you mean?" asked Sister Julienne.

"They're looking in the wrong place," she repeated. "She's not there."

Father Ménard and I exchanged glances.

"Where is she, Sister?" I asked.

She bent to the diagram once again, then jabbed her finger at the southeast corner of the church. "She's there. With Mère Aurélie."

"But, Sis—"

"They moved them. Gave them new coffins and put them under a special altar. There."

Again she pointed at the southeast corner.

"When?" we asked simultaneously.

Sister Bernard closed her eyes. The wrinkled old lips moved in silent calculation.

"Nineteen eleven. The year I came here as a novice. I remember, because a few years later the church burned and they boarded it up. It was my job to go in and put flowers on their altar. I didn't like that. Spooky to go in there all alone. But I offered it up to God."

"What happened to the altar?"

"Taken out sometime in the thirties. It's in the Holy Infant Chapel in the new church now." She folded the napkin and began gathering coffee things. "There was a plaque marking those graves, but not anymore. No one goes in there now. Plaque's been gone for years."

Father Ménard and I looked at each other. He gave a slight shrug.

"Sister," I began, "do you think you could show us where Élisabeth's grave is?"

"*Bien sûr.*"

"Now?"

"Why not?" China rattled against china.

"Never mind the dishes," said Father Ménard. "Please, get your coat and boots on, Sister, and we'll walk over."

Ten minutes later we were all back in the old church. The weather had not improved and, if anything, was colder and damper than in the morning. The wind still howled. The branches still tapped.

Sister Bernard picked an unsteady path across the church, Father Ménard and I each gripping an arm. Through the layers of clothing, she felt brittle and weightless.

The nuns followed in their spectator gaggle, Sister Julienne ready with steno pad and pen. Guy hung to the rear.

Sister Bernard stopped outside a recess in the southeast corner. She'd added a hand-knitted chartreuse hat over her veil, tied under her chin. We watched her head turn this way and that, searching for markers, getting her bearings. All eyes focused on the one spot of color in the dreary church interior.

I signaled to Guy to reposition a light. Sister Bernard paid no attention. After some time she moved back from the wall. Head left, head right, head left. Up. Down. She checked her position once more, then gouged a line in the dirt with the heel of her boot. Or tried to.

"She's here." The shrill voice echoed off stone walls.

"You're sure?"

"She's here." Sister Bernard did not lack self-assurance.

We all looked at the mark she'd made.

"They're in little coffins. Not like regular ones. They were just bones, so everything fit into small coffins." She held her tiny arms out to indicate a child-size dimension. An arm trembled. Guy focused the light on the spot at her feet.

Father Ménard thanked the ancient nun and asked two of the sisters to help her back to the convent. I watched their retreat. She looked like a child between them, so small that the hem of her coat barely cleared the dirt floor.

I asked Guy to bring the other spotlight to the new location. Then I retrieved my probe from the earlier site, positioned the tip where Sister Bernard had indicated, and pushed on the T-bar handle. No go. This spot was less defrosted. I was using a tile probe to avoid damaging anything underground, and the ball-shaped tip did not pass easily through the partially frozen upper layer. I tried again, harder.

Easy, Brennan. They won't be happy if you shatter a coffin window. Or poke a hole through the good sister's skull.

I removed my gloves, wrapped my fingers around the T-bar, and thrust again. This time the surface broke, and I felt the probe slide into the subsoil. Suppressing the urge to hurry, I tested the earth, eyes closed, feeling for minute differences in texture. Less resistance could mean an airspace where something had decomposed. More could mean that a bone or artifact was present underground. Nothing. I withdrew the probe and repeated the process.

On the third try I felt resistance. I withdrew, reinserted six inches to the right. Again, contact. There was something solid not far below the surface.

I gave the priest and nuns a thumbs-up, and asked Guy to bring the screen. Laying aside the probe, I took up a flat-edged shovel and began to strip thin slices of earth. I peeled soil, inch by inch, tossing it into the screen, my eyes moving from the fill to the pit. Within thirty minutes I saw what I was looking for. The last few tosses were dark, black against the red-brown dirt in the screen.

I switched from shovel to trowel, bent into the pit, and carefully scraped the floor, removing loose particles and leveling the surface. Almost immediately I could see a dark oval. The stain looked about three feet long. I could only guess at its width since it lay half hidden under unexcavated soil.

"There's something here," I said, straightening. My breath hung in front of my face.

As one, the nuns and priest moved closer and peered into the pit. I outlined the oval with my trowel tip. At that moment Sister Bernard's escort nuns rejoined the flock.

"It could be a burial, though it looks rather small. I've dug a bit to the left, so I'll have to take this portion down." I indicated the spot where I was squatting. "I'll excavate outside the grave itself and work my way down and in. That way we'll have a profile view of the burial as we go. And it's easier on the back to dig that way. An outside trench will also allow us to remove the coffin from the side if we have to."

"What is the stain?" asked a young nun with a face like a Girl Scout.

"When something with a high organic content decays, it leaves the soil much darker. It could be from the wooden coffin, or flowers that were buried with it." I didn't want to explain the decomposition process. "Staining is almost always the first sign of a burial."

Two of the nuns crossed themselves.

"Is it Élisabeth or Mère Aurélie?" asked an older nun. One of her lower lids did a little dance.

I raised my hands in a "beats me" gesture. Pulling on my gloves, I started troweling the soil over the right half of the stain, expanding the pit outward to expose the oval and a two-foot strip along its right.

Again, the only sounds were scraping and screening. Then,

"Is that something?" The tallest of the nuns pointed to the screen.

I rose to look, grateful for an excuse to stretch.

The nun was indicating a small, reddish-brown fragment.

"You bet your a—. That sure is, Sister. Looks like coffin wood."

I got a stack of paper bags from my supplies, marked one with the date, location, and other pertinent information, set it in the screen, and laid the others on the ground. My fingers were now completely numb.

"Time to work, ladies. Sister Julienne, you record everything we find. Write it on the bag, and enter it in the log, just as we discussed. We're at"—I looked into the pit—"about the two-foot level. Sister Marguerite, you're going to shoot some pictures?"

Sister Marguerite nodded, held up her camera.

They flew into action, eager after the long hours of watching. I troweled, Sisters Eyelid and Girl Scout screened. More and more fragments appeared, and before long we could see an outline in the stained soil. Wood. Badly deteriorated. Not good.

Using my trowel and bare hands, I continued to uncover what I hoped was a coffin. Though the temperature was below freezing and all feeling had left my fingers and toes, inside my parka I sweated. Please let this be her, I thought. Now who was praying?

As I inched the pit northward, exposing more and more wood, the object expanded in breadth. Slowly, the contour emerged: hexagonal. Coffin shape. It took some effort not to shout "Hallelujah!" Churchy, but unprofessional, I told myself.

I teased away earth, handful by handful, until the top of the object was fully exposed. It was a small casket, and I was moving from the foot toward the head. I put down my trowel and reached for a paintbrush. My eyes met those of one of my screeners. I smiled. She smiled. Her right lid did a jitterbug.

I brushed the wooden surface again and again, teasing away decades of encrusted soil. Everyone stopped to watch. Gradually, a raised object emerged on the coffin lid. Just above the widest point. Exactly where a plaque would be. My heart did its own fast dance.

I brushed dirt from the object until it came into focus. It was oval, metallic, with a filigreed edge. Using a toothbrush, I gently cleaned its surface. Letters emerged.

"Sister, could you hand me my flashlight? From the pack?"

Again, they leaned in as one. Penguins at a watering spot. I shone the beam onto the plaque. "Élisabeth Nicolet—1846–1888. *Femme contemplative*."

"We've got her," I said to no one in particular.

"Hallelujah!" shouted Sister Girl Scout. So much for church etiquette.

For the next two hours we exhumed Élisabeth's remains. The nuns, and even Father Ménard, threw themselves into the task like undergraduates on their first dig. Habits and cassock swirled around me as dirt was screened, bags were filled, labeled, and stacked, and the whole process was captured on film. Guy helped, though still reluctant. It was as odd a crew as I've ever directed.

Removing the casket was not easy. Though it was small, the wood was badly damaged and the coffin interior had filled with dirt, increasing the weight to about ten tons. The side trench had been a good call, though I'd underestimated the space we'd need. We had to expand outward by two feet to allow plywood to slide under the coffin. Eventually, we were able to raise the whole assemblage using woven polypropylene rope.

By five-thirty we were drinking coffee in the convent kitchen, exhausted, fingers, toes, and faces thawing. Élisabeth Nicolet and her casket were locked in the back of the archdiocese van, along with my equipment. Tomorrow, Guy would drive her to the Laboratoire de Médecine Légale in Montreal, where I work as Forensic Anthropologist for the Province of Quebec. Since the historic dead do not qualify as forensic cases, special permission had been obtained from the Bureau du Coroner to perform the analysis there. I would have two weeks with the bones.

I set down my cup and said my good-byes. Again. The sisters thanked me, again, smiling through tense faces, nervous already about my findings. They were great smilers.

Father Ménard walked me to my car. It had grown dark and a light snow was falling. The flakes felt strangely hot against my cheeks.

The priest asked once more if I wouldn't prefer to overnight at the convent. The snow sparkled behind him as it drifted in the porch light. Again, I declined. A few last road directions, and I was on my way.

Twenty minutes on the two-lane and I began to regret my decision. The flakes that had floated lazily in my headlights were now slicing across in a steady diagonal curtain. The road and the trees to either side were covered by a membrane of white that was growing more opaque by the second.

I clutched the wheel with both hands, palms clammy inside my gloves. I slowed to forty. Thirty-five. Every few minutes I tested the brakes. While I have been living in Quebec off and on for years, I have never grown accustomed to winter driving. I think of myself as tough, but put me on wheels in snow and I am Princess Chickenheart. I still have the typical Southern reaction to winter storms. Oh. Snow. Then we won't be going out, of course. Les québécois look at me and laugh.

Fear has a redeeming quality. It drives away fatigue. Tired as I was, I stayed alert, teeth clenched, neck craned, muscles rigid. The Eastern Townships Autoroute was a bit better than the back roads, but not much. Lac Memphrémagog to Montreal is normally a two-hour drive. It took me almost four.

Shortly after ten, I stood in the dark of my apartment, exhausted, glad to be home. Quebec home. I'd been away in North Carolina almost two months. *Bienvenue.* My thought process had already shifted to French.

I turned up the heat and checked the refrigerator. Bleak. I microzapped a frozen burrito and washed it down with room temperature root beer. Not haute cuisine, but filling.

The luggage I'd dropped off Tuesday night sat unopened in the bedroom. I didn't consider unpacking. Tomorrow. I fell into bed, planning to sleep at least nine hours. The phone woke me in less than four.

"*Oui,* yes," I mumbled, the linguistic transition now in limbo.

"Temperance. It is Pierre LaManche. I am very sorry to disturb you at this hour."

I waited. In the seven years I'd worked for him, the lab director had never called me at three in the morning.

"I hope things went well at Lac Memphrémagog." He cleared his throat. "I have just had a call from the coroner's office. There is a house fire in St-Jovite. The firefighters are still trying to get it under control. The arson investigators will go in first thing in the morning, and the coroner wants us there." Again the throat. "A neighbor says the residents are at home. Their cars are in the driveway."

"Why do you need me?" I asked in English.

"Apparently the fire is extremely intense. If there are bodies, they will be badly burned. Perhaps reduced to calcined bone and teeth. It could be a difficult recovery."

Damn. Not tomorrow.

"What time?"

"I will come for you at six A.M.?"

"O.K."

"Temperance. It could be a bad one. There were children living there."

I set the alarm for five-thirty.

Bienvenue.

I HAVE LIVED IN THE SOUTH ALL OF MY ADULT LIFE. IT CAN NEVER be too hot for me. I love the beach in August, sundresses, ceiling fans, the smell of children's sweaty hair, the sound of bugs at window screens. Yet I spend my summers and school breaks in Quebec. Most months during the academic year, I fly from Charlotte, North Carolina, where I am on the anthropology faculty at the university, to work at the medicolegal lab in Montreal. This is a distance of approximately twelve hundred miles. Due north.

When it is deep winter, I often have a talk with myself before deplaning. It will be cold, I remind myself. It will be very cold. But you will dress for it and be ready. Yes. I will be ready. I never am. It's always a shock to leave the terminal and take that first, startling breath.

At 6 A.M., on the tenth day of March, the thermometer on my patio read two degrees Fahrenheit. Seventeen below, Celsius. I was wearing everything I possibly could. Long underwear, jeans, double sweaters, hiking boots, and woolen socks. Inside the socks, I had sparkly insulated liners designed to keep astronaut feet toasty on Pluto. Same provocative combo as the day before. I'd probably stay just as warm.

When LaManche honked, I zipped my parka, pulled on gloves and ski hat, and bolted from the lobby. Unenthused as I was for the day's outing, I didn't want to keep him waiting. And I was extremely overheated.

I had expected a dark sedan, but he waved at me from what would probably be called a sport utility vehicle. Four-wheel drive, bright red, with racing stripes.

"Nice car," I said as I climbed in.

"*Merci.*" He gestured to a center rack. It held two Styrofoam cups and a Dunkin' Donuts bag. Bless you. I chose an apple crunch.

On the drive to St-Jovite, LaManche related what he knew. It went little beyond what I'd heard at 3 A.M. From across the road a neighbor couple saw occupants enter the residence at nine in the evening. The neighbors left after that and visited friends some distance away, where they stayed late. When they were returning around two they noted a glow from down the road, and then flames shooting from the house. Another neighbor thought she'd heard booming sounds sometime after midnight, wasn't sure, and went back to sleep. The area is remote and sparsely populated. The volunteer fire brigade arrived at two-thirty, and called in help when they saw what they had to deal with. It took two squads over three hours to put out the flames. LaManche had talked to the coroner again at five forty-five. Two deaths were confirmed, others anticipated. Some areas were still too hot, or too dangerous, to search. Arson was suspected.

We drove north in the predawn darkness, into the foothills of the Laurentian Mountains. LaManche talked little, which was fine with me. I am not a morning person. He is an audio junkie, however, and kept an unbroken succession of cassettes playing. Classics, pop, even C&W, all converted to easy listenin'. Perhaps it was meant to calm, like the numbing music piped to elevators and waiting rooms. It made me jittery.

"How far is St-Jovite?" I picked a double-chocolate honey-glazed.

"It will take us about two hours. St-Jovite is about twenty-five kilometers this side of Mont Tremblant. Have you skied there?" He wore a knee-length parka, army green with a fur-lined hood. From the side, all I could see was the tip of his nose.

"Um. Beautiful."

I nearly got frostbite on Mont Tremblant. It was the first time I'd skied in Quebec, and I was dressed for the Blue Ridge Mountains. The wind at the summit was cold enough to freeze liquid hydrogen.

"How did things go at Lac Memphrémagog?"

"The grave wasn't where we expected, but, what's new? Apparently she was exhumed and reburied in 1911. Odd that there was no record of it." Very odd, I thought, taking a sip of tepid coffee. Instrumental Springsteen. "Born in the U.S.A." I tried to block it. "Anyway, we found her. The remains will be delivered to the lab today."

"It is too bad about this fire. I know you were counting on a free week to concentrate on that analysis."

In Quebec, winters can be slow for the forensic anthropologist. The temperature rarely rises above freezing. The rivers and lakes ice over, the ground turns rock hard, and snow buries everything. Bugs disappear, and many scavengers go underground. The result: Corpses do not putrefy in the great outdoors. Floaters are not pulled from the St. Lawrence. People, too, burrow in. Hunters, hikers, and picnickers quit roaming the woods and fields, and some of last season's dead are not found until the spring melt. The cases that are assigned to me, the faceless in need of a name, decline in number between November and April.

The exception is house fires. During the cold months, these increase. Most burned bodies go to the odontologist and are identified by dental records. The address and its occupant are generally known, so antemortem files can be pulled for comparison. It is when charred strangers turn up that my help may be requested.

Or in difficult recovery situations. LaManche was right. I'd been counting on an open agenda, and did not appreciate having to go to St-Jovite.

"Maybe I won't be involved in the analysis." A million and one strings began "I'm Sitting on Top of the World." "They'll probably have records on the family."

"Probably."

We arrived in St-Jovite in less than two hours. The sun had risen and was painting the town and countryside in icy, dawn tones. We turned west onto a winding two-lane. Almost immediately two flatbeds passed us, heading in the opposite direction. One carried a battered gray Honda, the other a red Plymouth Voyager.

"I see they have impounded the cars," said LaManche.

I watched the vehicles disappear in the side mirror. The van had infant carriers in the backseat and a yellow smiley face on the rear bumper. I pictured a child in the window, tongue out, fingers in ears, mugging at the world. Googly eyes, my sister and I had called it. Perhaps that child lay charred beyond recognition in an upstairs room ahead.

Within minutes we saw what we were looking for. Police cruisers, fire engines, utility trucks, mobile press units, ambulances, and unmarked cars lined the road and flowed up either side of a long, gravel driveway.

Reporters stood in clusters, some talking, some adjusting equipment. Others sat in cars, keeping warm while waiting out the story. Thanks to the cold and the early hour, there were surprisingly few sightseers. Now and then a car passed, then returned slowly for a second sweep. Round-trip gawkers. Later, there would be many more.

LaManche signaled a turn and angled onto the drive, where a uniformed officer waved us to a stop. He wore an olive green jacket with black fur collar, dark olive muffler, and olive hat, earflaps tied in the up position. His ears and nose were raspberry red, and when he spoke, a cloud of vapor billowed from his mouth. I wanted to tell him to cover his ears, immediately felt like my mother, and didn't. He's a big boy. If his lobes crack off, he'll deal with it.

LaManche showed ID, and the guard waved us in, indicating we should park behind the blue crime scene recovery truck. SECTION D'IDENTITÉ JUDICIAIRE it said in bold black letters. The Crime Scene Recovery unit was already here. The arson boys, too, I suspected.

LaManche and I tugged on hats and gloves and got out. The sky was azure now, the sunlight dazzling off last night's snow. The air was so frigid it felt crystalline and made everything look sharp and clear. Cars, buildings, trees, and utility poles cast dark shadows on the snowy ground, clean-edged, like images on high-contrast film.

I looked around. The blackened remains of a house, as well as an intact garage and a smaller outbuilding of some sort clustered at the head of the drive, all done in cheap Alpine style. Footpaths formed a triangle in the snow, linking the three buildings. Pines circled what was left of the house, their branches so laden with snow that the tips bowed downward. I watched a squirrel scamper along a limb, then retreat to the safety of the trunk. In its wake, clumps of snow cascaded down, pockmarking the white below.

The house had a high-pitched roof of red-orange tile, partially standing but darkened now and coated in ice. That portion of the exterior surface which had not burned was covered in cream-colored siding. The windows gaped black and empty, the glass shattered, the turquoise trim burned or darkened with soot.

The left half of the house was charred, its rear largely destroyed. On the far side I could see blackened timbers where roof and walls had once met. Wisps of smoke still rose from somewhere in the back.

The front was less badly damaged. A wooden porch ran its length, and small balconies jutted from upstairs windows. The porch and balconies were constructed of pink pickets, round at the top, with heart-shaped cutouts at regular intervals.

I looked behind me, down the drive. Across the road sat a similar chalet, this one trimmed in red and blue. A man and woman stood in front, arms folded, mittened hands tucked under armpits. They watched silently, squinting into the morning glare, their faces grim below identical orange hunting caps. The neighbors who had reported the fire. I scanned the road. There were no other homes within visual distance. Whoever thought she had heard muffled booms must have good ears.

LaManche and I started toward the house. We passed dozens of firefighters, colorful in their yellow suits, red hard hats, blue utility belts, and black rubber boots. Some wore oxygen tanks strapped to their backs. Most seemed to be gathering equipment.

We approached a uniformed officer standing by the porch. Like the driveway guard, he was Sûreté du Québec, probably from a post in St-Jovite or a nearby town. The SQ, or Quebec Provincial Police, have jurisdiction everywhere off the island of Montreal, except in towns that maintain their own police. St-Jovite would be too small for that, so the SQ had been called, maybe by the fire chief, maybe by the neighbor. They, in turn, had called the arson investigators from our lab. Section d'Incendie et Explosif. I wondered who had made the decision to call the coroner. How many victims would we find? In what condition would they be? Not good, I was sure. My heart stepped up its tempo.

Again LaManche held up his badge, and the man inspected it.

"*Un instant, Docteur, s'il vous plaît,*" he said, holding up a gloved palm. He called to one of the firefighters, said something, and pointed at his head. In seconds we had hard hats and masks. We put on the former, hung the latter over our arms.

"*Attention!*" said the officer, inclining his head toward the house. Then he stepped aside to let us pass. Oh yes. I'd be careful.

The front door was wide open. When we crossed the threshold out of the sunshine the temperature dropped twenty degrees. The air inside felt damp and smelled of charred wood and soggy plaster and fabric. A dark goo covered every surface.

Straight ahead a staircase rose to a second story, to the left and right gaped what must have been the living and dining rooms. What remained of the kitchen was in back.

I'd been to other fire scenes, but few as devastated as this. Charred boards lay everywhere, like debris hurled against a seawall. They crisscrossed on top of tangled chair and sofa frames, angled against stairs, and trellised against walls and doors. Remnants of household furnishings lay in blackened heaps. Wires dangled from walls and ceilings, and pipes twisted inward from their points of attachment. Window frames, stair rails, boards, everything was edged in black icicle lace.

The house was crawling with people in hard hats, talking, taking measurements, photos, and videos, collecting evidence, and scribbling on clipboards. I recognized two arson investigators from our lab. They held a measuring tape between them and one squatted at a fixed point while the other circled, recording data every few feet.

LaManche spotted a member of the coroner's staff, and began picking his way forward. I followed, snaking between twisted metal shelving, broken glass, and what looked like a tangled red sleeping bag, its stuffing spewed like charcoal innards.

The coroner was very fat and very flushed. He straightened slightly when he saw us, blew a puff of air, pooched out his lower lip, and gestured an upturned mitten at the devastation around us.

"So, Monsieur Hubert, there are two dead?"

LaManche and Hubert were design opposites, like contrasting

shades on a color wheel. The pathologist was tall and rangy, with a long, bloodhound face. The coroner was round in every way. I thought of Hubert in horizontals, LaManche in verticals.

Hubert nodded, and three chins rippled above his muffler. "Upstairs."

"Others?"

"Not yet, but they haven't finished in the lower level. The fire was much more intense in the back. They think it probably started in a room off the kitchen. That area burned completely, and the floor collapsed into the basement."

"Have you seen the bodies?"

"Not yet. I'm waiting for clearance to go upstairs. The fire chief wants to be sure it's safe."

I shared the chief's sentiment.

We stood in silence, surveying the mess. Time passed. I curled and uncurled my fingers and toes, trying to keep them flexible. Eventually three firemen descended. They wore hard hats and goggle masks, and looked as if they'd been rummaging for chemical weapons.

"It's O.K.," said the last fireman, unsnapping and removing his mask. "You can go up now. Just watch your step and keep the hard hats on. That whole damn ceiling could come down. But the floors look O.K." He continued toward the door, then turned back. "They're in the room on the left."

Hubert, LaManche, and I worked our way up the stairs, shards of glass and charred rubble crunching under our feet. Already my stomach was tightening and a hollow feeling was building in my chest. Though it is my business, I have never grown immune to the sight of violent death.

At the top a door opened to the left, another to the right, there was a bath straight ahead. Though badly smoke damaged, compared with the downstairs, things seemed to be reasonably intact at this level.

Through the left doorway I could see a chair, a bookcase, and the end of a twin bed. On it was a pair of legs. LaManche and I entered the left-hand room, Hubert went to check the one on the right.

The back wall was partially burned, and at places two-by-fours were exposed behind the flowered wallpaper. The beams were charcoal black, their surfaces rough and checked, like the skin on a croc. "Alligatored," the arson boys would write. Charred and frozen debris lay underfoot, and soot covered everything.

LaManche took a long look around, then pulled a tiny Dictaphone from his pocket. He recorded the date, time, and location, and began describing the victims.

The bodies lay on twin beds that formed an L in the far corner of the room, a small table between them. Strangely, both individuals appeared to be fully clothed, though smoke and charring had obscured all indicators of style or gender. The victim along the back wall wore sneakers, the one on the side had died in stocking feet. I noticed that one athletic sock was partly off, exposing a smoke-stained ankle. The tip of the sock hung limply over the toes. Both victims were adult. One appeared more robust than the other.

"Victim number one . . ." continued LaManche.

I forced myself to take a closer look. Victim number one held its forearms high, flexed as if ready to fight. Pugilistic pose. While not long enough or hot enough to consume all the flesh, the fire that raced up the back wall had produced sufficient heat to cook the upper limbs and cause the muscles to contract. Below the elbows the arms were stick-thin. Clumps of scorched tissue clustered along the bones. The hands were blackened stumps.

The face reminded me of Rameses' mummy. The lips had burned away, exposing teeth with dark and cracked enamel. One incisor was delicately outlined in gold. The nose was burned and squashed, the nostrils pointing upward like the snout of a fruit bat. I could see individual muscle fibers circling the orbits and streaming across the cheekbones and mandible, like a line drawing in an anatomy text. Each socket held a dried and shriveled eyeball. The hair was gone. So was the top of the head.

Victim number two, though equally dead, was more intact. Some of the skin was blackened and split, but in most places it was merely smoked. Tiny white lines radiated from the corners of the eyes, and the ears were pale on the insides and underneath the lobes. The hair had been reduced to a frizzled cap. One arm lay flat, the other was flung wide, as if reaching for its partner in death. The outstretched hand had been reduced to a bony, blackened claw.

LaManche's somber monotone droned on, describing the room

and its lifeless occupants. I half listened, relieved that I wouldn't be needed. Or would I? There were supposed to be kids. Where were they? Through the open window I could see sunshine, pine trees, and glistening white snow. Outside, life went on.

Silence interrupted my thoughts. LaManche had stopped dictating and replaced wool gloves with latex. He began to examine victim number two, lifting the eyelids and observing the inside of the nose and mouth. Then he rolled the body toward the wall and raised the shirttail.

The outer layer of skin had split and the edges were curling back. The peeling epidermis looked translucent, like the delicate film inside an egg. Underneath, the tissue was bright red, mottled white where it had lain in contact with the crumpled sheets. LaManche pressed a gloved finger into the back muscle and a white spot appeared in the scarlet flesh.

Hubert rejoined us as LaManche was returning the body to its supine position. We both looked a question at him.

"Empty."

LaManche and I did not change expression.

"There are a couple of cribs in there. Must be the kids' room. Neighbors say there were two babies." He was breathing hard. "Twin boys. They're not in there."

Hubert took out a hankie and wiped his chapped face. Sweat and arctic air are not a good combination. "Anything here?"

"Of course this will require a full autopsy," answered LaManche in his melancholy bass. "But based on my preliminary, I would say that these people were alive when the fire broke out. At least this one was."

He indicated body number two.

"I'll be here another thirty minutes or so, then you may remove them."

Hubert nodded and left to tell his transport team.

LaManche crossed to the first body, then returned to the second. I watched in silence, breathing warmth onto my mittened fingers. Finally, he finished. I didn't have to ask.

"Smoke," he said. "Around the nostrils, in the nose and air passages." He looked at me.

"They were still breathing during the fire."

"Yes. Anything else?"

"The lividity. The cherry red color. That suggests carbon monoxide in the blood."

"And . . . ?"

"The blanching when you applied pressure. Livor isn't fixed yet. Blanching only occurs for a matter of hours after lividity first develops."

"Yes." He looked at his watch. "It's just past eight now. This one could have been alive as late as three or four A.M." He pulled off the latex gloves. "*Could* have been, but the fire brigade got here at two-thirty, so death was before that. Livor is extremely variable. What else?"

The question went unanswered. We heard commotion below, then feet pounded up the stairs. A fireman appeared in the doorway, flushed and breathing hard.

"*Estidecolistabernac!*"

I ran through my québécois lexicon. Not there. I looked at LaManche. Before he could translate the man went on.

"Someone here named Brennan?" he asked LaManche.

The hollow feeling spread to my innards.

"We've got a body in the basement. They say we're going to need this Brennan guy."

"I'm Tempe Brennan."

He looked at me for a long time, helmet under one arm, head tipped. Then he wiped his nose with the back of his hand, and looked back at LaManche.

"You can go down there as soon as the chief clears you through. And better bring a spoon. There's not much left of this one."

THE VOLUNTEER FIREMAN LED US DOWN THE STAIRS AND INTO THE back of the house. Here, most of the roof was gone and sunlight poured into the gloomy interior. Particles of soot and dust danced on the wintry air.

We stopped at the entrance to the kitchen. On the left I could make out the remains of a counter, sink, and several large appliances. The dishwasher was open, its contents black and melted. Charred boards lay everywhere, the same giant pickup sticks I'd seen in the front rooms.

"Keep back by the walls," said the fireman, gesturing with his arm as he disappeared around the doorjamb.

He reappeared seconds later, working his way along the west side of the room. Behind him, the countertop curled upward like a giant licorice twist. Embedded in it were fragments of shattered wine bottles and unidentifiable globs of various sizes.

LaManche and I followed, sliding along the front wall, then rounding the corner and moving down the counter. We stayed as far from the center of the room as possible, picking our way through burned rubble, imploded metal containers, and scorched propane tanks.

I stopped next to the fireman, back to the counter, and surveyed the damage. The kitchen and an adjacent room were incinerated. The ceilings were gone, the separating wall reduced to a few charred timbers. What had been the floor was now a yawning black hole. An extension ladder angled from it in our direction. Through the opening I could see men in hard hats lifting debris and either flinging or carrying it out of sight.

"There is a body down there," said my guide, tipping his head at the opening. "Found it when we began to clear rubble from the floor collapse."

"Just one, or more?" I asked.

"Hell if I know. It doesn't hardly look human."

"Adult or child?"

He gave me a "lady, are you stupid?" look.

"When can I get down there?"

His eyes slid to LaManche, back to me. "That's up to the chief. They're still clearing the area. We wouldn't want anything to split your pretty skull."

He gave me what he no doubt felt was an engaging smile. He probably practiced it in the mirror.

We watched as firemen below pitched boards and tramped back and forth with loads of debris. From out of sight I could hear banter and the sound of things being dislodged and dragged.

"Have they considered that they might be destroying evidence?" I asked.

The fireman looked at me as if I'd suggested the house had been hit by a comet.

"It's just floorboards and shit that fell down from this level."

"That 'shit' may help establish sequence," I said, my voice as chilly as the icicles on the counter behind us. "Or body position."

His face went rigid.

"There could still be hot spots down there, lady. You don't want one flaring up in your face, do you?"

I had to admit I didn't.

"And that guy's past caring."

Inside my hard hat I could feel a throbbing along the side of my pretty skull.

"If the victim is as burned as you suggest, your colleagues could be obliterating major body parts."

His jaw muscle bunched as he looked past me for support. LaManche said nothing.

"The chief's probably not gonna let you in there, anyway," he said.

"I need to get in now to stabilize what's there. Especially the teeth." I thought of baby boys. I hoped for teeth. Lots of them. All adult. "If there are any left."

The fireman gave me a head to toe, sizing up my five-foot-five, one-hundred-twenty-pound frame. Though the thermal outfitting disguised my shape and the hard hat hid my long hair, he saw enough to convince himself I belonged elsewhere.

"She's not really going down there?" He looked to LaManche for an ally.

"Dr. Brennan will be doing the recovery."

"*Estidecolistabernac!*"

This time I didn't need translation. Fireman Macho thought the job required testicles.

"Hot spots are no problem," I said, looking him dead in the eye. "In fact, I usually prefer to work right in the flames. I find it warmer."

With that he gripped the side rails, swung onto the ladder, and slid down, never touching the rungs with his feet.

Great. He also does tricks. I could imagine what he was scripting for the chief.

"These are volunteers," said LaManche, almost smiling. He looked like Mr. Ed in a hard hat. "I must finish upstairs, but I will rejoin you shortly."

I watched him weave a path to the door, his large, hooded frame hunched in concentration. Seconds later the chief emerged on the ladder. It was the same man who'd directed us to the upstairs bodies.

"You're Dr. Brennan?" he asked in English.

I nodded once, ready for a fight.

"Luc Grenier. I head up the St-Jovite volunteer squad." He unsnapped his chin strap and let it dangle. He was older than his misogynous teammate.

"We're going to need another ten, fifteen minutes to secure the lower level. This was the last section we put down, so there could still be hot spots." The strap jumped as he talked. "This was a pisser, and we don't want a flare-up." He pointed behind me. "See how that pipe's deformed?"

I turned to look.

"That's copper. To melt copper you've got to get up over eleven hundred degrees centigrade." He shook his head, and the strap swung back and forth. "This was a real pisser."

"Do you know how it started?" I asked.

He pointed to a propane tank near my feet. "So far we've counted twelve of those suckers. Either someone knew exactly what he was doing, or he really fucked up the family barbecue." His face reddened slightly. "Sorry."

"Arson?"

Chief Grenier shrugged both shoulders and raised his eyebrows. "Not my call." He snapped his chin strap and gripped the sides of the ladder. "All we're doing is moving debris to be sure the fire's completely cold. This kitchen was full of junk. That's what provided the fuel to burn right through the floor. We'll take extra care around the bones. I'll give a whistle when it's safe."

"Don't spray any water on the remains," I said.

He gave a hand salute and disappeared down the ladder.

It took thirty minutes before I was allowed into the basement. During that time I went to the crime scene truck to collect my equipment and arrange for a photographer. I located Pierre Gilbert and asked to have a screen and spotlight set up below.

The basement was one large open space, dark and damp and colder than Yellowknife in January. At the far end loomed a furnace, its pipes rising, black and gnarled, like the limbs of a giant dead oak. It reminded me of another cellar I'd visited not long ago. That one had hidden a serial killer.

The walls were cinder block. Most of the large debris had been cleared and heaped against them, exposing a dirt floor. In places the fire had turned it reddish brown. In others it was black and rock-hard, like ceramic tile fired in an oven. Everything was covered by a thin membrane of frost.

Chief Grenier took me to a spot on the right edge of the floor collapse. He said that no victims had been found elsewhere. I hoped he was right. The thought of sifting the entire basement almost made me weep. Wishing me good luck, he left to rejoin his men.

Little of the kitchen sun made it this far back, so I took a high-powered flashlight from my kit and shone it around me. One look caused adrenaline to report for duty. This was not what I'd expected.

The remains were strewn over an area at least ten feet in length. They were largely skeletonized, and showed varying degrees of heat exposure.

In one cluster I could see a head surrounded by fragments of differing shapes and sizes. Some were black and shiny, like the skull. Others were chalky white and looked ready to crumble. Which is exactly what they would do if not handled properly. Calcined bone is featherlight and extremely fragile. Yes. This would be a difficult recovery.

Five feet south of the skull an assortment of vertebrae, ribs, and long bones lay in rough anatomical position. Also white and fully calcined. I noted the orientation of the vertebrae and the position of the arm bones. The remains were lying faceup, one arm crossing the chest, the other flung above the head.

Below the upper arms and chest lay a heart-shaped black mass with two fractured long bones projecting distally. The pelvis. Beyond this, I could see the charred and fragmented bones of the legs and feet.

I felt relief, but some confusion. This was a single, fully grown victim. Or was it? Infant bones are tiny and extremely fragile. They could easily be hidden below. I prayed I'd find none when I sifted through the ash and sediment.

I made notes, took Polaroids, then began to sweep away soil and ash using a soft-bristle paintbrush. Slowly, I exposed more and more bone, carefully inspecting the displaced debris, collecting it for later screening.

LaManche returned as I was clearing the last of the muck that lay in direct contact with the bones. He watched silently as I took four stakes, a ball of string, and three retractable measuring tapes from my kit.

I hammered a stake into the ground just above the cranial cluster, and hooked the ends of two tapes onto a nail I'd driven into the top. I ran one tape ten feet south and pounded in a second stake.

LaManche held that tape at the second stake while I went back to the first and ran the other tape perpendicular, ten feet toward the east. Using the third tape, I measured off a hypotenuse of fourteen feet one and three-quarter inches from LaManche's stake to the northeast corner. Where the second and third tapes met, I hammered in a third stake. Thanks to Pythagoras, I now had a perfect right triangle with two ten-foot sides.

I unhooked the second tape from the first stake, hooked it to the northeast stake, and ran it ten feet south. LaManche brought his tape ten feet east. Where these tapes met I hammered in the fourth stake.

I ran a string around the four stakes, enclosing the remains in a ten-by-ten-foot square with ninety-degree corners. I would triangulate from the stakes when taking measurements. If needed, I could divide the square into quadrants, or break it into grid units for more precise observations.

Two evidence recovery techs arrived as I was placing a north arrow near the cranial cluster. They wore dark blue arctic suits, SECTION D'IDENTITÉ JUDICIAIRE stamped on their backs. I envied them. The damp cold in the basement was like a knife, cutting right through my clothes and into my flesh.

I'd worked with Claude Martineau before. The other tech was new to me. We introduced ourselves as they set up the screen and portable light.

"It's going to take some time to process this," I said, indicating the staked-out square. "I want to locate any teeth that might have survived, and stabilize them if necessary. I may also have to treat the pubes and rib ends if I find any. Who's going to shoot pics?"

"Halloran is coming," said Sincennes, the second tech.

"O.K. Chief Grenier says there's nobody else down here, but it wouldn't hurt to walk off the basement."

"There were supposed to be kids living in this house," said Martineau, his face grim. He had two of his own.

"I'd suggest a grid search."

I looked to LaManche. He nodded agreement.

"You've got it," said Martineau. He and his partner flicked on the lights on their hard hats, then moved to the far end of the basement. They would walk back and forth in parallel lines, first proceeding north to south, then crisscrossing east to west. When they'd finished, every inch of floor would have been searched twice.

I took several more Polaroids, then began to clear the square. Using a trowel, a dental pick, and a plastic dustpan, I loosened and dislodged the filth that encased the skeleton, leaving each bone in place. Every pan of dirt went into the screen. There I separated silt, cinders, fabric, nails, wood, and plaster from bone fragments. The latter I placed on surgical cotton in sealed plastic containers, noting their provenance in my notes. At some point, Halloran arrived and began shooting.

Now and then I glanced at LaManche. He watched silently, his face its usual solemn mask. In the time I'd known the chief, I'd rarely seen him express emotion. LaManche has witnessed so much over the years, perhaps sentiment is just too costly for him. After some time, he spoke.

"If there is nothing for me to do here, Temperance, I will be upstairs."

"Sure," I responded, thinking of the warming sun. "I'll be at this awhile."

I looked at my watch. Ten past eleven. Behind LaManche I could see Sincennes and Martineau, creeping along shoulder to shoulder, heads down, like miners seeking a rich vein.

"Do you require anything?"

"I'm going to need a body bag with a clean white sheet inside. Be sure they put a flat board or a gurney tray under it. Once I get these fragments out I don't want everything slumping together in transport."

"Of course."

I went back to troweling and screening. I was so cold I was shaking all over, and had to stop now and then to warm my hands. At one point the morgue transport team brought the tray and body bag. The last firemen left. The basement grew quiet.

Eventually, I had exposed the entire skeleton. I made notes and sketched its disposition, while Halloran took photos.

"Mind if I grab a coffee?" he asked when we'd finished.

"No. I'll holler if I need you. I'll just be transferring bones for a while."

When he left I began to move the remains to the body bag, starting at the feet and working toward the head. The pelvis was in good condition. I picked it up and placed it on the sheet. The pubic symphyses were embedded in charred tissue. They would not need stabilizing.

The leg and arm bones I left encased in sediment. It would hold them together until I could clean and sort them in the autopsy room. I did the same with the thoracic region, carefully lifting out sections with a flat-blade shovel. Nothing of the anterior rib cage had survived, so I did not have to worry about damaging the ends. For now I left the skull in place.

When I had removed the skeleton, I began to screen the top six inches of sediment, starting at the southwest stake and working northeast. I was finishing the last corner of the square when I spotted it, approximately a foot and a half east of the skull, at a depth of two inches. My stomach did a little flip. Yes!

The jaw. Gingerly, I teased away soil and ash to reveal a complete right ascending ramus, a fragment of the left ramus, and a portion of the mandibular body. The latter contained seven teeth.

The outer bone was checked by a latticework of cracks. It was thin and powdery white. The spongy interior looked pale and brittle, as if each filament had been spun by a Lilliputian spider then left to air dry. The enamel on the teeth was already splintering, and I knew the whole thing would crumble if disturbed.

I took a bottle of liquid from my kit, shook it, and checked to be sure no crystals remained in the solution. I dug out a handful of five-milliliter disposable pipettes.

Working on hands and knees, I opened the bottle, unwrapped a pipette, and dipped it in. I squeezed the bulb to fill the pipette with solution, then allowed the fluid to drip onto the jaw. Drop by drop I soaked each fragment, watching to be sure I was getting good penetration. I lost all track of time.

"Nice angle." English.

My hand jumped, splattering Vinac on the sleeve of my jacket. My back was stiff, my knees and ankles locked, so lowering my rear quickly was not an option. Slowly, I sat back on my haunches. I didn't have to look.

"Thank you, Detective Ryan."

He circled to the far side of the grid and looked down at me. Even in the dim light of the basement I could see that his eyes were as blue as I remembered. He wore a black cashmere coat and a red wool muffler.

"Long see, no time," he said.

"Yes. No time. When was it?"

"The courthouse."

"The Fortier trial." We'd both been waiting to testify.

"Still dating Perry Mason?"

I ignored the question. The previous fall I'd briefly dated a defense attorney I'd met through my Tai Chi course.

"Isn't that fraternizing with the enemy?"

I still didn't answer. Obviously my sex life was a topic of interest to the homicide squad.

"How have you been?"

"Great. You?"

"Can't complain. If I did, no one would listen."

"Get a pet."

"Could try that. What's in the eyedropper?" he asked, pointing a leather-gloved finger at my hand.

"Vinac. It's a solution of a polyvinyl acetate resin and methanol. The mandible is toast and I'm trying to keep it intact."

"And that will do it?"

"As long as the bone is dry this will penetrate and hold things together pretty well."

"And if it's not dry?"

"Vinac won't mix with water, so it'll just stay on the surface and turn white. The bones will come out looking like they've been sprayed with latex."

"How long does it take to dry?"

I felt like Mr. Wizard.

"It dries quickly through evaporation of the alcohol, usually in thirty to sixty minutes. Although being in the subarctic won't speed things up."

I checked the jaw fragments, hit one with a few more drops, then rested the pipette on the solution jar cover. Ryan came around and held out a hand. I took it and rose to my feet, wrapping my arms around my middle and tucking my hands under my pits. I could feel nothing in my fingers, and suspected my nose was the shade of Ryan's scarf. And running.

"It's colder than a witch's tit down here," he agreed, surveying the basement. He held one arm behind him at an odd angle. "How long have you been down here?"

I looked at my watch. No wonder I was hypothermic. One-fifteen.

"Over four hours."

"Che-rist. You're going to need a transfusion."

It suddenly dawned. Ryan worked homicide.

"So it's arson?"

"Probably."

He pulled a white bag from behind his back, withdrew a Styrofoam cup and a machine sandwich, and waggled them in front of me.

I lunged. He backed up.

"You'll owe me."

"It's in the mail."

Soggy bologna and lukewarm coffee. It was wonderful. We talked while I ate.

"Tell me why you think it's arson," I said as I chewed.

"Tell me what you've got here."

O.K. He was a sandwich up.

"One person. Could be young, but it's not a little kid."

"No babies?"

"No babies. Your turn."

"Looks like someone used the old tried and true. The fire burned in trails way down between the floorboards. Where there still *are* floorboards, that is. That means liquid accelerant, probably gasoline. We found dozens of empty gas cans."

"That's it?" I finished the sandwich.

"The fire had more than one point of origin. Once it started it burned like a son of a bitch, because it set off the world's largest indoor collection of propane tanks. Big boom every time one went. Another tank, another big boom."

"How many?"

"Fourteen."

"It started in the kitchen?"

"And the adjoining room. Whatever that was. Hard to tell now."

I thought it over.

"That explains the head and jaw."

"What about the head and jaw?"

"They were about five feet away from the rest of the body. If a propane tank fell through with the victim and exploded later, that could have caused the head to relocate after it burned away from the trunk. Same with the jaw."

I finished the coffee, wishing I had another sandwich.

"Could the tanks have ignited accidentally?"

"Anything's possible."

I flicked crumbs from my jacket and thought of LaManche's doughnuts. Ryan fished in the bag and handed me a napkin.

"O.K. The fire had multiple points of origin and there's evidence of an accelerant. It's arson. Why?"

"Got me." He gestured at the body bag. "Who's this?"

"Got me."

Ryan headed upstairs, and I went back to the recovery. The jaw was not quite dry, so I turned my attention to the skull.

The brain contains a large amount of water. When exposed to fire, it boils and expands, setting up hydrostatic pressure inside the head. Given enough heat, the cranial vault may crack or even explode. This person was in pretty good shape. Though the face was gone and the outer bone was charred and flaking, large segments of the skull were intact. I was surprised, given the intensity of this fire.

When I cleaned away the mud and ash and looked closely, I saw why. For a moment I just stared. I rolled the skull over and inspected the frontal bone.

Sweet Jesus.

I climbed the ladder and poked my head into the kitchen. Ryan stood by the counter talking with the photographer.

"You'd better come down," I said.

They both raised eyebrows and pointed to their chests.

"Both of you."

Ryan set down the Styrofoam cup he was holding.

"What?"

"This one may not have lived to see the fire."

It was late afternoon before the last of the bone was packaged and ready for transport. Ryan watched as I carefully extracted and wrapped the skull fragments and placed them in plastic containers. I would analyze the remains at the lab. The rest of the investigation would be his baby.

Dusk was easing in when I emerged from the basement. To say I was cold would be like saying Lady Godiva was underdressed. For the second day in a row I finished the afternoon with no feeling in any digit. I hoped amputation would not be necessary.

LaManche was gone, so I rode to Montreal with Ryan and his partner, Jean Bertrand. I sat in back, shivering and asking for more heat. They sat up front, sweating, now and then removing an article of outerwear.

Their conversation wafted in and out of my consciousness. I was fully drained and just wanted to take a hot bath and crawl into my flannel nightgown. For a month. My mind drifted. I thought about bears. There was an idea. Curl up and sleep until spring.

Images floated in my head. The victim in the basement. A sock dangling over singed and stiffened toes. A nameplate on a tiny casket. A happy-face sticker.

"Brennan."

"What?"

"Good morning, starshine. Earth says 'Hello.'"

"What?"

"You're home."

I'd been sound asleep.

"Thanks. Talk to you on Monday."

I stumbled from the car and up the stairs of my building. A light snow was topping the neighborhood like frosting on a sticky bun. Where did so much snow come from?

The grocery situation had not improved, so I ate soda crackers spread with peanut butter and washed them down with clam chowder. I found an old box of Turtles in the pantry, dark chocolate, my favorite. They were stale and hard, but I was not in a position to be choosy.

The bath was all I'd hoped it would be. Afterward, I decided to light a fire. I was finally warm, but felt very tired and very alone. The chocolate had been some comfort, but I needed more.

I missed my daughter. Katy's school year was divided into quarters, my university was on a semester system, so our spring breaks did not coincide. Even Birdie had stayed south this trip. He hated air travel and voiced that opinion loudly through each flight. Since I'd be in Quebec less than two weeks this time, I'd decided to spare both the cat and the airline.

As I held the match to the starter log I considered fire. *Homo erectus* first tamed it. For almost a million years we'd been using it to hunt, cook, keep warm, and light our way. That had been my last lecture before break. I thought of my students in North Carolina. While I'd been searching for Élisabeth Nicolet, they'd been taking their midterm exam. The little blue books would arrive here tomorrow by overnight delivery, while the students split for the beaches.

I turned off the lamp and watched the flames lick and twist among the logs. Shadows danced around the room. I could smell pine and hear moisture hiss and pop as it boiled to the surface. That's why fire has such appeal. It involves so many senses.

I synapsed back to childhood Christmases and summer camps. Such a dicey blessing, fire. It could give solace, rekindle gentle memories. But it could also kill. I did not want to think about St-Jovite anymore tonight.

I watched snow gather on the windowsill. My students would be planning their first beach day by now. While I was fighting frostbite, they were preparing for sunburn. I didn't want to think about that, either.

I considered Élisabeth Nicolet. She'd been a recluse. "*Femme contemplative*," the plaque had said. But she hadn't done any contemplating for over a century. What if we had the wrong casket? Something else I didn't want to think about. At least for tonight, Élisabeth and I had little in common.

I checked the time. Nine-forty. Her sophomore year Katy was voted one of the "Beauties of Virginia." Though she maintained a grade point average of 3.8 while working on dual degrees in English and psychology, she'd never been a slouch socially. Not a chance she'd be home on a Friday night. Ever the optimist, I brought the phone to the hearth and dialed Charlottesville.

Katy answered on the third ring.

Expecting her voice mail, I stuttered something unintelligible.

"Mom? Is that you?"

"Yes. Hello. What are you doing home?"

"I've got a zit on my nose the size of a hamster. I'm too ugly to go out. What are you doing home?"

"There is no way you are ugly. No comment on the zit." I settled against a cushion and put my feet up on the hearth. "I've spent two days digging up dead people and I'm too tired to go out."

"I won't even ask." I heard cellophane crinkle. "This zit is pretty gross."

"It, too, will pass. How is Cyrano?" Katy had two rats, Templeton and Cyrano de Bergerat.

"He's better. I got some medicine at the pet store and I've been giving it to him with an eyedropper. He's pretty much stopped that sneezing thing."

"Good. He's always been my favorite."

"I think Templeton knows that."

"I'll try to be more discreet. What else is new?"

"Not much. Went out with a guy named Aubrey. He was pretty cool. Sent me roses the next day. And I'm going on a picnic tomorrow with Lynwood. Lynwood Deacon. He's first-year law."

"Is that how you pick them?"

"What?"

"The names."

She ignored that. "Aunt Harry called."

"Oh?" My sister's name always made me slightly apprehensive, like a bucket of nails balanced too close to an edge.

"She's selling the balloon business or something. She was actually calling to find you. Sounded a little weirded out."

"Weirded out?" On a normal day my sister sounded a little weirded out.

"I told her you were in Quebec. She'll probably call tomorrow."

"O.K." Just what I needed.

"Oh! Dad bought a Mazda RX-7. It is so sweet! He won't let me drive it, though."

"Yes, I know." My estranged husband was undergoing a mild midlife crisis.

There was a slight hesitation. "Actually, we were just going out to grab a pizza."

"What about the zit?"

"I'm going to draw ears and a tail on it and claim it's a tattoo."

"Should work. If caught, use a false name."

"Love you, Mom."

"I love you, too. Talk to you later."

I finished the rest of the Turtles and brushed my teeth. Twice. Then I fell into bed and slept eleven hours.

I spent the rest of the weekend unpacking, cleaning, shopping, and grading exams. My sister called late Sunday to say she'd sold her hot air balloon. I felt relieved. I'd spent three years inventing excuses to keep Katy on the ground, dreading the day she'd finally go up. That creative energy could now be turned elsewhere.

"Are you at home?" I asked.

"Yep."

"Is it warm?" I checked the drift on the windowsill. It was still growing.

"It's always warm in Houston."

Damn her.

"So why are you selling the business?"

Harry has always been a seeker, though her grail has never been in focus. For the past three years she'd been gung-ho buggers over ballooning. When not floating safaris over Texas, she and her crew packed an old pickup and zigzagged the country to balloon rallies.

"Striker and I are splitting."

"Oh."

She'd also been gung-ho buggers over Striker. They met at a rally in Albuquerque, married five days later. That had been two years ago.

For a long time no one spoke. I cracked first.

"What now?" I asked.

"I may go into counseling."

That surprised me. My sister rarely did the obvious.

"It might help you get through this."

"No. No. Striker's got Kool-Aid for brains. I'm not crying over him. That just makes me puffy." I heard her light a cigarette, draw deeply, exhale. "There's this course I've heard about. You take it, then you can advise people on holistic health and stress relief and stuff. I've been reading about herbs and meditation and metaphysics and it's pretty cool. I think I'll be good at this."

"Harry. That sounds a little flaky." How many times had I said that?

"Duh. Of course I'll check it out. I'm not flat-ass stupid."

No. She was not stupid. But when Harry wants something, she wants it intensely. And there is no dissuading her.

I hung up feeling a little shaken. The thought of Harry advising people with problems was unnerving.

Around six I made myself a dinner of sautéed chicken breast, boiled red potatoes with butter and chives, and steamed asparagus. A glass of Chardonnay would have made it perfect. But not for me. That switch had been in the off position for seven years and it was staying there. I'm not flat-ass stupid either. At least not when I'm sober. The meal still beat the hell out of last night's soda crackers.

As I ate, I thought about my baby sister. Harry and formal education have never been compatible. She married her high school sweetheart the day before graduation, three others after that. She's raised Saint Bernards, managed a Pizza Hut, sold designer sunglasses, led tours in the Yucatán, done PR for the Houston Astros, started and lost a carpet-cleaning business, sold real estate, and, most recently, taken up riders in hot air balloons.

When I was three and Harry was one, I broke her leg by rolling over it with my tricycle. She never slowed down. Harry learned to walk while dragging a cast. Unbearably annoying and totally endearing, my sister offsets with pure energy what she lacks in training or focus. I find her thoroughly exhausting.

At nine-thirty I turned on the hockey game. It was the end of the second period and the Habs were losing four-zip to St. Louis. Don Cherry blustered about the ineptness of the Canadiens management, his face round and flushed above his high-collar shirt. He looked more like a tenor in a barbershop quartet than a sports commentator. I watched, bemused that millions listened to him every week. At ten-fifteen I turned off the TV and went to bed.

The next morning I got up early and drove to the lab. Monday is a busy day for most medical examiners. The random acts of cruelty, senseless bravado, lonely self-loathing, and wretched bad timing that result in violent death accelerate on weekends. The bodies arrive and are stored in the morgue for Monday autopsy.

This Monday was no exception. I got coffee and joined the morning meeting in LaManche's office. Natalie Ayers was at a murder trial in Val-d'Or, but the other pathologists were present. Jean Pelletiér had just returned from testifying in Kuujjuaq, in far northern Quebec. He was showing snapshots to Emily Santangelo and Michael Morin. I leaned in.

Kuujjuaq looked as if it had been flown in and assembled the night before.

"What's that?" I asked, indicating a prefab building with a plastic outer layer.

"The aqua center." Pelletiér pointed to a red hexagonal sign with unfamiliar characters above, *Arrêt* below in bold white letters. "All the signs are in French and Inuktitut." His upriver accent was so heavy, to my ear he might have been speaking the latter. I'd known him for years and still had trouble understanding his French.

Pelletiér pointed at another prefab building. "That's the courthouse."

It looked like the pool, sans plastic. Behind the town, the tundra stretched gray and bleak, a Serengeti of rocks and moss. A bleached caribou skeleton lay by the roadside.

"Is that common?" asked Emily, studying the caribou.

"Only when they're dead."

"There are eight autopsies today," said LaManche, handing out the roster. He went over them all. A nineteen-year-old male had been hit by a train, his torso bisected. It happened on a barricaded trestle frequented by teens.

A snowmobile had gone through the ice on Lac Megantic. Two bodies recovered. Alcohol intoxication suspected.

An infant had been found dead and putrefied in its bed. Mama, who was downstairs watching a game show when authorities arrived, said ten days earlier God told her to stop feeding the baby.

An unidentified white male was found behind a Dumpster on the McGill campus. Three bodies were recovered from a house fire in St-Jovite.

Pelletiér was assigned the infant. He indicated that he might request an anthropology consult. While the baby's identity was not in question, cause and time of death would be tough.

Santangelo got the bodies from Lac Megantic, Morin the train and Dumpster cases. The victims from the bedroom in St-Jovite were intact enough for normal autopsy. LaManche would perform them. I would do the bones from the basement.

After the meeting, I went to my office and opened a dossier by transferring the information from the morning etiquette sheet onto an anthropology case form. Name: *Inconnu*. Unknown. Date of birth: blank. Laboratoire de Médecine Légale number: 31013. Morgue number: 375. Police incident number: 89041. Pathologist: Pierre LaManche. Coroner: Jean-Claude Hubert. Investigators: Andrew Ryan and Jean Bertrand, Escouade de Crimes Contre la Personne, Sûreté du Québec.

I added the date and slipped the form into a file folder. Each of us uses a different color. Pink is Marc Bergeron, the odontologist. Green is Martin Levesque, the radiologist. LaManche uses red. A bright yellow jacket means anthropology.

I keyed in and rode the elevator to the basement. There I asked an autopsy technician to place LML 31013 in room three, then went to change into surgical scrubs.

The four autopsy rooms of the Laboratoire de Médecine Légale are adjacent to the morgue. The LML controls the former, the

Bureau du Coroner the latter. Autopsy room two is large and contains three tables. The others have one each. Number four is equipped with special ventilation. I often work there since many of my cases are less than fresh. Today I left room four to Pelletiér and the baby. Charred bodies do not have a particularly offensive odor.

When I got to room three, a black body bag and four plastic containers lay on a gurney. I peeled the lid from a tub, removed the cotton padding, and checked the skull pieces. They had weathered the trip without damage.

I filled out a case identification card, unzipped the body bag, and pulled back the sheet that wrapped the bones and debris. I took several Polaroids, then sent everything for X-rays. If there were teeth or metal objects, I wanted to pinpoint them before disturbing the fill.

As I waited I thought of Élisabeth Nicolet. Her coffin was locked in a cooler ten feet from me. I was anxious to see what was in it. One of my messages this morning had been from Sister Julienne. The nuns were impatient, too.

After thirty minutes Lisa wheeled the bones back from radiography and handed me an envelope of films. I popped several onto a view box, starting with the foot end of the body bag.

"They're O.K.?" asked Lisa. "I wasn't sure what setting to use with all that rubble in there, so I did several exposures of each."

"They're good."

We were looking at an amorphous mass surrounded by two tiny white railroad tracks: the bag's contents and metal zipper. The fill was speckled with construction debris, and here and there, a particle of bone appeared pale and honeycombed against the neutral background.

"What's that?" Lisa pointed to a white object.

"Looks like a nail."

I replaced the first films with three more. Soil, pebbles, scraps of wood, nails. We could see the leg and hip bones with attached charred flesh. The pelvis looked intact.

"Looks like metallic fragments in the right femur," I said, indicating several white spots in the thigh bone. "Let's be careful when we handle that. We'll get another shot later."

The next films showed the ribs to be as fragmented as I remembered. The arm bones were better preserved, though fractured and badly jumbled. Several vertebrae looked salvageable. Another metal object was visible to the left of the thorax. It didn't look like a nail.

"Let's watch for that, too."

Lisa nodded.

Next we examined the X-rays of the plastic tubs. They showed nothing unusual. The mandible had held together well, the slender tooth roots still solidly encased in bone. Even the crowns were intact. I could see bright blobs in two of the molars. Bergeron would be pleased. If there were dental records, the fillings would be useful in establishing positive ID.

Then I noticed the frontal bone. It was speckled with tiny white dots, as though someone had seasoned it with salt.

"I'm going to want another shot of that, too," I said softly, staring at the radiopaque particles near the left orbit.

Lisa gave me an odd look.

"O.K. Let's get him out," I said.

"Or her."

"Or her."

Lisa spread a sheet over the autopsy table and set a screen across the sink. I took a paper apron from one of the stainless steel counter drawers, slipped it over my head, and tied it around my waist. Then I placed a mask over my mouth, pulled on surgical gloves, and unzipped the body bag.

Starting at the feet and working north, I removed the largest and most easily identifiable objects and pieces of bone. Then I went back and sifted the fill to locate any small items or bone fragments I might have missed. Lisa screened each handful under gently running water. She washed and placed artifacts on the counter, while I arranged skeletal elements in anatomical order on the sheet.

At noon Lisa broke for lunch. I worked through, and by two-thirty the painstaking process was done. A collection of nails, metal caps, and one exploded cartridge lay on the counter, along with a small plastic vial containing what I thought could be a scrap of fabric. A charred and disconnected skeleton lay on the table, the skull bones fanning out like petals on a daisy.

It took over an hour to do an inventory, identifying each bone and determining if it came from the left or right side. Then I turned my attention to the questions Ryan would ask. Age. Sex. Race. Who is it?

I picked up the mass that contained the pelvis and thigh bones. The fire had cooked the soft tissue, turning it black and leathery hard. A mixed blessing. The bones had been protected, but it might be a bitch getting them out.

I rotated the pelvis. The flesh on the left had burned away, causing the femur to split. I could see a perfect cross section of the ball-and-socket hip joint. I measured the diameter of the femoral head. It was tiny, falling on the low end of the female range.

I studied the internal structure of the head, just below the articular surface. The spicules of bone showed the typical honeycombed pattern of an adult, with no thick line to indicate a recently fused growth cap. That was consistent with the completed molar roots I'd noticed earlier in the jaw. This victim was not a kid.

I looked at the outer edges of the cup that formed the hip socket, and at the lower border of the femoral head. On both the bone seemed to drip downward, like wax overflowing a candle. Arthritis. The individual was not young.

I already suspected the victim was a woman. What remained of the long bones were small in diameter, with smooth-muscle attachments. I shifted my attention to the cranial fragments.

Small mastoids and brow ridges. Sharp orbital borders. The bone was smooth at the back of the skull and in all the places male bone would be rough and bumpy.

I examined the frontal bone. The upper ends of the two nasal bones were still in place. They met at a high angle along the midline, like a church steeple. I found two pieces of maxilla. The lower border of the nasal opening ended in a sharp ledge with a spike of bone projecting upward at its center. The nose had been narrow and prominent, the face straight when viewed from the side. I located a fragment of temporal bone and shone a flashlight into the ear opening. I could see a tiny round opening, the oval window to the inner ear. All good Caucasoid traits.

Female. White. Adult. Old.

I returned to the pelvis, hoping it would allow me to confirm the sex and be more precise about the age. I was particularly interested in the region where the two halves meet in front.

Gently, I teased away charred tissue, revealing the joint between the pubic bones, the pubic symphysis. The pubes themselves were wide, the angle below them broad. Each had a raised ridge angling across its corner. The lower branch of each pubic bone was gracile and gently recurved. Typical female features. I noted them on my case form and took more Polaroid close-ups.

The intense heat had shrunk the connective cartilage and pulled the pubic bones apart along the midline. I twisted and turned the charred mass, trying to peer into the gap. It looked like the symphyseal surfaces were intact, but I couldn't make out any detail.

"Let's take the pubes out," I said to Lisa.

I smelled burned flesh as the saw buzzed through the wings connecting the pubic bone to the rest of the pelvis. It took just seconds.

The symphyseal joint was singed, but easily readable. There were no ridges or furrows on either surface. In fact, both faces were porous, their outer edges irregularly lipped. Erratic threads of bone projected from the front of each pubic element, ossifications into the surrounding soft tissue. The lady had lived a long time.

I turned the pubes over. A deep trench scarred the belly side of each. And she had given birth.

I reached again for the frontal bone. For a moment I stood there, the fluorescent light showing in harsh detail what I'd first suspected in the basement, and what the metallic scatter on the X-ray had confirmed.

I'd held my feelings at bay, but now I allowed myself to grieve for the ravaged human being on my table. And to puzzle over what had happened to her.

The woman had been at least seventy, undoubtedly a mother, probably a grandmother.

Why had someone shot her in the head and left her to burn in a house in the Laurentians?

5

By noon on Tuesday I was finishing my report. I'd worked past nine the night before, knowing Ryan would want answers. Surprisingly, I'd yet to see him.

I read what I'd written, checking for errors. Sometimes I think gender agreements and accent marks are Francophone curses specifically designed for my torment. I try my best, but I always blow a few.

In addition to a biological profile of the unknown, the report included an analysis of trauma. On dissection I found the radiopaque fragments in the femur were the result of postmortem impact. The small bits of metal were probably blasted into the bone by the explosion of a propane tank. Most of the other damage was also due to the fire.

Some was not. I read my summary.

> Wound A is a circular defect, of which only the superior half is preserved. It is localized to the midfrontal region, lying approximately 2 centimeters above glabella and 1.2 centimeters to the left of midline. The defect measures 1.4 centimeters in diameter and presents characteristic beveling of the inner table. Charring is present along the margins of the defect. Wound A is consistent with a gunshot entrance wound.
>
> Wound B is a circular defect with characteristic beveling of the

> outer table. It measures 1.6 centimeters in diameter endocranially, and 4.8 centimeters in diameter ectocranially. The defect is localized to the occipital bone, 2.6 centimeters superior to opisthion and 0.9 centimeters to the left of the midsagittal line. There is focal charring of the left, right, and inferior margins of the defect. Wound B is consistent with a gunshot exit wound.

While fire damage made a complete reconstruction impossible, I was able to piece together enough of the vault to interpret the fractures lacing between the exit and entrance holes.

The pattern was classic. The old woman had suffered a gunshot wound to the head. The bullet entered the middle of her forehead, traversed her brain, and exited at the back. It explained why the skull had not shattered in the flames. A vent for intracranial pressure had been created before heat became a problem.

I walked the report to the secretarial pool and returned to find Ryan sitting across from my desk, gazing out the window behind my chair. His legs stretched the length of my office.

"Nice view." He spoke in English.

Five floors down the Jacques Cartier Bridge arched across the St. Lawrence River. I could see minuscule cars crawling across its back. It *was* a nice view.

"It distracts me from thinking about how small this office is." I slipped past him, around the desk, and into my chair.

"A distracted mind can be dangerous."

"My bruised shins bring me back to reality." I swiveled sideways and propped my legs on the ledge below the window, ankles crossed. "It's an old woman, Ryan. Shot in the head."

"How old?"

"I'd say she was at least seventy. Maybe even seventy-five. Her pubic symphyses have a lot of miles on them, but folks are variable up in that range. She has advanced arthritis and she's osteoporotic."

He dipped his chin and raised his brows. "French or English, Brennan. Not doctor talk." His eyes were the shade of blue on the Windows 95 screen.

"Os-te-o-po-ro-sis." I spoke each syllable slowly. "I can tell from the X-rays that her cortical bone is thin. I can't see any fractures, but I only had parts of the long bones. The hip is a common site for breaks in older women because a lot of weight is transferred there. Hers were O.K."

"Caucasian?"

I nodded.

"Anything else."

"She probably had several kids." The laser blues were fixed on my face. "She has a trench the size of the Orinoco on the back of each pubic bone."

"Great."

"Another thing. I think she was already in the basement when the fire started."

"How's that?"

"There was absolutely no floor debris below the body. And I found a few tiny scraps of fabric embedded between her and the clay. She must have been lying directly on the floor."

He thought for a moment.

"So you're telling me someone shot Granny, dragged her down to the basement, and left her to fry."

"No. I'm saying Granny took a bullet in the head. I don't have a clue who fired it. Maybe she did. That's your job, Ryan."

"Did you find a gun near her?"

"No."

Just then Bertrand appeared in the doorway. While Ryan looked neat and pressed, his partner's creases were sharp enough to cut precious gems. He wore a mauve shirt keyed to the tones of his floral tie, a lavender and gray tweed jacket, and wool trousers a precise half note down from shade four in the tweed.

"What have you got?" Ryan asked his partner.

"Nothing we didn't already know. It's like these people were beamed down from space. No one really knows who the hell was living in there. We're still trying to track down the guy in Europe that owns the house. The neighbors across the road saw the old lady from time to time, but she never spoke to them. They say the couple with the kids had only been there a few months. They rarely saw them, never learned their names. A woman up the road thought they were part of some sort of fundamentalist group."

"Brennan says our Doe is a Jane. As in Baby Jane. A septuagenarian."

Bertrand looked at him.

"In her seventies."

"An old lady?"

"With a bullet in her brain."

"No shit?"

"No shit."

"Someone shot her and torched the place?"

"Or Granny pulled the trigger after having lit the barbecue. But, then, where's the weapon?"

When they'd gone I checked my consult requests. A jar of ashes had arrived in Quebec City, the cremains of an elderly man who died in Jamaica. The family was accusing the crematory of fraud, and had brought the ashes to the coroner's office. He wanted to know what I thought.

A skull was found in a ravine outside the Côte des Neiges Cemetery. It was dry and bleached, and had probably come from an old grave. The coroner needed confirmation.

Pelletiér wanted me to look at the baby for evidence of starvation. That would require microscopy. Thin sections of bone would have to be ground down, stained, and placed on slides so I could examine the cells under magnification. While high turnover of bone is typical of infants, I'd look for signs of unusual porosity and abnormal remodeling in the microanatomy.

Samples had been sent to the histology lab. I'd also study the X-rays and the skeleton, but that was still soaking to remove the putrefied flesh. A baby's bones are too fragile to risk boiling.

So. Nothing urgent. I could open Élisabeth Nicolet's coffin.

After a refrigerated sandwich and a yogurt in the cafeteria, I rode down to the morgue, asked to have the remains brought to room three, then went to change.

The coffin was smaller than I remembered, measuring less than three feet in length. The left side had rotted, allowing the top to collapse inward. I brushed off loose soil and took photos.

"Need a crowbar?" Lisa stood in the doorway.

Since this was not an LML case, I was to work alone, but I was getting a lot of offers. Apparently I was not the only one fascinated by Élisabeth.

"Please."

It took less than a minute to remove the cover. The wood was soft and crumbly, and the nails gave easily. I scooped dirt from the interior to reveal a lead liner containing another wood coffin.

"Why are they so little?" asked Lisa.

"This isn't the original casket. Élisabeth Nicolet was exhumed and reburied around the turn of the century, so they just needed enough space for her bones."

"Think it's her?"

I drilled a look at her.

"Let me know if you need anything."

I continued scooping dirt until I had cleared the lid of the inner casket. It bore no plaque, but was more ornate than the outer, with an elaborately carved border paralleling the hexagonal outside edge. Like the exterior coffin, the one inside had collapsed and filled with dirt.

Lisa returned in twenty minutes.

"I'm free for a while if you need X-rays."

"Can't do it because of the lead liner," I said. "But I'm ready to open the inner casket."

"No problem."

Again the wood was soft and the nails slipped right out.

More dirt. I'd removed only two handfuls when I spotted the skull. Yes! Someone was home!

Slowly, the skeleton emerged. The bones were not in anatomical order, but lay parallel to one another, as though tightly bound when placed into the coffin. The arrangement reminded me of archaeological sites I'd excavated early in my career. Before Columbus, some aboriginal groups exposed their dead on scaffolds until the bones were clean, then bundled them for burial. Élisabeth had been packed like this.

I'd loved archaeology. Still did. I regretted doing so little of it, but over the past decade my career had taken a different path. Teaching and forensic casework now occupied all my time. Élisabeth Nicolet was allowing me a brief return to my roots, and I was enjoying the hell out of it.

I removed and arranged the bones, just as I had the day before. They were dry and fragile, but this person was in much better shape than yesterday's lady from St-Jovite.

My skeletal inventory indicated that only a metatarsal and six phalanges were missing. They did not show up when I screened the soil, but I did locate several incisors and a canine, and replaced them in their sockets.

I followed my regular procedure, filling out a form just as I would for a coroner case. I started with the pelvis. The bones were those of a female. No doubt there. Her pubic symphyses suggested an age of thirty-five to forty-five years. The good sisters would be happy.

In taking long-bone measurements I noted an unusual flattening on the front of the tibia, just below the knee. I checked the metatarsals. They showed arthritis where the toes join the feet. Yahoo! Repeated patterns of movement leave their marks on the skeleton. Élisabeth was supposed to have spent years in prayer on the stone floor of her convent cell. In kneeling, the combination of pressure on the knees and hyperflexion of the toes creates exactly the pattern I was seeing.

I remembered something I'd noticed as I removed a tooth from the screen, and picked up the jaw. Each of the lower central incisors had a small but noticeable groove on the biting edge. I found the uppers. Same grooves. When not praying or writing letters, Élisabeth sewed. Her embroidery still hung in the convent at Lac Memphrémagog. Her teeth were notched from years of pulling thread or holding a needle between them. I was loving this.

Then I turned the skull faceup and did a double take. I was standing there, staring at it, when LaManche entered the room.

"So, is this the saint?" he asked.

He came up beside me and looked at the skull.

"*Mon Dieu.*"

"Yes, the analysis is going well." I was in my office, speaking with Father Ménard. The skull from Memphrémagog sat in a cork ring on my worktable. "The bones are remarkably well preserved."

"Will you be able to confirm that it's Élisabeth? Élisabeth Nicolet?"

"Father, I wanted to ask you a few more questions."

"Is there a problem?"

Yes. There may be.

"No, no. I'd just like a little more information."

"Yes?"

"Do you have any official document stating who Élisabeth's parents were?"

"Her father was Alain Nicolet, and her mother was Eugénie Bélanger, a well-known singer at that time. Her uncle, Louis-Philippe Bélanger, was a city councilman and a very distinguished physician."

"Yes. Is there a birth certificate?"

He was silent. Then,

"We have not been able to locate a birth certificate."

"Do you know where Élisabeth was born?"

"I think she was born in Montreal. Her family was here for generations. Élisabeth is a descendant of Michel Bélanger, who came to Canada in 1758, in the last days of New France. The Bélanger family was always prominent in city affairs."

"Yes. Is there a hospital record, or a baptismal certificate, or anything that officially records her birth?"

More silence.

"She was born more than a century and a half ago."

"Were records kept?"

"Yes. Sister Julienne has searched. But things can be lost over such a long time. Such a long time."

"Of course."

For a moment we were both silent. I was about to thank him when,

"Why are you asking these questions, Dr. Brennan?"

I hesitated. Not yet. I could be wrong. I could be right but it meant nothing.

"I just wanted a bit more background."

I'd hardly replaced the receiver when the phone rang.

"*Oui*, Dr. Brennan."

"Ryan." I could hear tension in his voice. "It was arson all right. And whoever planned it made sure the place went up. Simple but effective. They hooked a heat coil to a timer, same kind you use to turn on your lamps when you go off to the spa."

"I don't go to spas, Ryan."

"Do you want to hear this?"

I didn't answer.

"The timer turned on the hot plate. That set off a fire which ignited a propane tank. Most of the timers were destroyed, but we recovered a few. Looks like they were set to go off at intervals, but once the fire spread it was bombs away."

"How many tanks?"

"Fourteen. We found one undamaged timer out in the yard. Must have been a dud. It's the kind you can buy in any hardware store. We'll try for prints, but it's a long shot."

"The accelerant?"

"Gasoline, as I suspected."

"Why both?"

"Because someone friggin' wanted the place destroyed big time and didn't want a screw-up. Probably figured there wouldn't be a second chance."

"How do you know that?"

"LaManche was able to draw fluid samples from the bodies in the bedroom. Toxicology found celestial levels of Rohypnol."

"Rohypnol?"

"I'll let him tell you about it. It's called the date rape drug or something because it's undetectable to the victim and knocks you flat on your ass for hours."

"I know what Rohypnol is, Ryan. I'm just surprised. It's not so easy to come by."

"Yeah. That could be a break. It's banned in the U.S. and Canada."

So is crack, I thought.

"Here's another weird thing. It wasn't Ward and June Cleaver up in that bedroom. LaManche says the guy was probably in his twenties, the woman closer to fifty."

I knew that. LaManche had asked my opinion during the autopsy.

"Now what?"

"We're heading back out there to take the other two buildings apart. We're still waiting for word from the owner. He's some kind of hermit buried in the Belgian boonies."

"Good luck."

Rohypnol. That kindled something way down in my memory cells, but when I tried to bring it up the spark went out.

I checked to see if the slides for Pelletiér's malnourished baby case were finished. The histology tech told me they'd be ready tomorrow.

I then spent an hour examining the cremains. They were in a jelly jar with a handwritten label stating the name of the decedent, the name of the crematorium, and the date of cremation. Not typical packaging for North America, but I knew nothing of practices in the Caribbean.

No particle was over a centimeter in size. Typical. Few bone fragments survive the pulverizers used by modern crematoriums. Using a dissecting scope, I was able to identify a few things, including a complete ear ossicle. I also located some small bits of twisted metal that I thought might be parts of a dental prosthesis. I saved them for the dentist.

Typically, an adult male will be reduced by firing and pulverization to about 3,500 cc's of ash. This jar contained about 360. I wrote a brief report stating that the cremains were those of an adult human, and that they were incomplete. Any hope at personal identification would lie with Bergeron.

At six-thirty I packed up and went home.

ÉLISABETH'S SKELETON TROUBLED ME. WHAT I'D SEEN JUST couldn't be, but even LaManche had spotted it. I was anxious to resolve the question, but the next morning a set of tiny bones by the sink in the histo lab commanded my attention. The slides were also ready, so I spent several hours on Pelletiér's baby case.

Finding no other requisition on my desk, at ten-thirty I phoned Sister Julienne to find out as much as I could about Élisabeth Nicolet. I asked her the same questions I'd posed to Father Ménard, with similar results. Élisabeth was "*pure laine*." Pure-wool québécoise. But no papers directly establishing her birth or parentage.

"What about outside the convent, Sister? Have you checked other collections?"

"Ah, *oui.* I've researched all the archives in the archdiocese. We have libraries throughout the province, you know. I've gotten materials from many convents and monasteries."

I'd seen some of this material. Most was in the form of letters and personal journals containing references to the family. A few were attempts at historical narrative, but were not what my dean would call "peer reviewed." Many were purely anecdotal accounts, made up of hearsay on top of hearsay.

I tried a different tack. "Until recently, the church was responsible for all birth certificates in Quebec, correct?" Father Ménard had explained that.

"Yes. Until just a few years ago."

"But none can be found for Élisabeth?"

"No." There was a pause. "We've had some tragic fires over the years. In 1880 the Sisters of Notre Dame built a beautiful motherhouse on the side of Mount Royal. Sadly, it burned to the ground thirteen years later. Our own motherhouse was destroyed in 1897. Hundreds of priceless documents were lost in those fires."

For a moment neither of us spoke.

"Sister, can you think of anywhere else I might find information on Élisabeth's birth? Or on her parents?"

"I . . . well, you could try the secular libraries, I suppose. Or the historical society. Or perhaps one of the universities. The Nicolet and Bélanger families have produced several important figures in French Canadian history. I'm certain they are discussed in historical accounts."

"Thank you, Sister. I'll do that."

"There's a professor at McGill who's done research in our archives. My niece knows her. She studies religious movements, but she's also interested in Quebec history. I can't remember if she's an anthropologist, or a historian, or what. She might be able to help." She hesitated. "Of course, her references would be different from ours."

I was certain of that, but said nothing.

"Do you remember her name?"

There was a long pause. I could hear others on the line, far away, like voices carrying across a lake. Someone laughed.

"It's been a long time. I'm sorry. I could ask my niece if you wish."

"Thank you, Sister. I'll follow up your lead."

"Dr. Brennan, when do you think you'll finish with the bones?"

"Soon. Unless something comes up, I should be able to complete my report on Friday. I'll write up my assessments of age, sex, and race, and any other observations I've made, and comment on how my findings compare to the facts known about Élisabeth. You can include whatever you feel is appropriate with your application to the Vatican."

"And you will call?"

"Of course. As soon as I'm done." Actually, I was done, and I had little doubt what my report would say. Why didn't I just tell them now?

We exchanged good-byes, then I disconnected, waited for the tone, and dialed again. A phone rang across town.

"Mitch Denton."

"Hi, Mitch. Tempe Brennan. Are you still head honcho at your place?"

Mitch was the anthropology chair who'd hired me to teach part-time when I first came to Montreal. We'd been friends ever since. His specialty was the French Paleolithic.

"Still stuck. Want to do a course for us this summer?"

"No, thanks. I've got a question for you."

"Shoot."

"Do you remember the historic case I told you about? The one I'm doing for the archdiocese?"

"The saint wanna-be?"

"Right."

"Sure. Beats the hell out of most of the stuff you work on. Did you find her?"

"Yes. But I've noticed something a bit odd, and I'd like to learn more about her."

"Odd?"

"Unexpected. Listen, one of the nuns told me someone at McGill does research involving religion and Quebec history. Does that ring a bell?"

"Dong! That would be our own Daisy Jean."

"Daisy Jean?"

"Dr. Jeannotte to you. Professor of Religious Studies and students' best friend."

"Back up, Mitch."

"Her name is Daisy Jeannotte. Officially she's on the Faculty of Religious Studies, but she also teaches some history courses. 'Religious Movements in Quebec.' 'Ancient and Modern Belief Systems.' That sort of thing."

"Daisy Jean?" I repeated the question.

"Just an in-house endearment. It's not for direct address."

"Why?"

"She can be a bit . . . odd, to use your expression."

"Odd?"

"Unexpected. She's from Dixie, you know."

I ignored that. Mitch was a transplanted Vermonter. He never let up on my Southern homeland.

"Why do you say she's the students' best friend?"

"Daisy spends all her free time with students. She takes them on outings, advises them, travels with them, has them to the house for dinner. There's a constant line of needy souls outside her door seeking solace and counseling."

"Sounds admirable."

He started to say something, caught himself. "I suppose."

"Would Dr. Jeannotte know anything about Élisabeth Nicolet or her family?"

"If anyone can help you it will be Daisy Jean."

He gave me her number and we promised to get together soon.

A secretary told me Dr. Jeannotte would be holding office hours between one and three, so I decided to drop in after lunch.

It takes analytical skills worthy of a degree in civil engineering to understand when and where one is allowed to leave a car in Montreal. McGill University lies in the heart of Centre-Ville, so even if one is able to comprehend where parking is permitted, it is almost impossible to find a space. I found a spot on Stanley that I interpreted to be legal from nine to five, between April 1 and December 31, except from 1 to 2 P.M. on Tuesdays and Thursdays. It did not require a neighborhood permit.

After five reversals of direction and much manipulation of the steering wheel, I managed to wedge the Mazda between a Toyota pickup and an Oldsmobile Cutlass. Not a bad job on a steep grade. When I got out I was sweating despite the cold. I checked the bumpers. I had at least twenty-four inches to spare. Total.

The weather was not as frigid as it had been, but the modest rise in temperature had come with an increased dampness. A cloud of cold, moist air pressed down on the city, and the sky was the color of old tin. A heavy, wet snow began to fall as I walked downhill to Sherbrooke and turned east. The first flakes melted when they touched the pavement, then others lingered and threatened to accumulate.

I trudged uphill on McTavish and entered McGill through the west gate. The campus lay above and below me, the gray stone buildings climbing the hill from Sherbrooke to Docteur-Penfield. People hurried about, shoulders rounded against the cold and damp, books and packages shielded from the snow. I passed the library and cut behind the Redpath Museum. Exiting the east gate, I turned left, and headed uphill on rue Universitie, my calves feeling as though I'd done three miles on a Nordic Track. Outside Birks Hall I nearly collided with a tall young man walking head down, his hair and glasses coated with snowflakes the size of luna moths.

Birks is from another time, with its Gothic exterior, carved oak walls and furniture, and enormous cathedral windows. It is a place that inspires whispering, not the chatting and swapping of notes that occurs in most university buildings. The first-floor lobby is cavernous, its walls hung with portraits of grave men looking down in scholarly self-importance.

I added my boots to the row of footwear trickling melted snow onto the marble floor, and stepped over for a closer look at the august artworks. *Thomas Cranmer, Archbishop of Canterbury.* Good job, Tom. *John Bunyan, Immortal Dreamer.* Times had changed. When I was a student abstract reverie in class, if detected, got you called on and humiliated for being inattentive.

I climbed a winding staircase, past two sets of wooden doors on the second floor, one to the chapel, the other to the library, and continued to the third. Here the elegance of the lobby gave way to signs of aging. Patches of paint peeled from walls and ceiling, and here and there a tile was missing.

At the top of the stairs I paused to get my bearings. It was strangely quiet and gloomy. On my left I could see an alcove with double doors opening on to the chapel balcony. Two corridors flanked the alcove, with wooden doors set at intervals along each hall. I passed the chapel and started up the far corridor.

The last office on the left was open but unoccupied. A plaque above the door said "Jeannotte" in delicate script. Compared with my office, the room looked like St. Joseph's Oratory. It was long and narrow, with a bell-shaped window at the far end. Through the leaded glass I could see the administration building and the drive leading up to the Strathcona Medical-Dental Complex. The floor was oak, the planks buffed yellow by years of studious feet.

Shelves lined every wall, filled with books, journals, notebooks, videotapes, slide carousels, and stacks of papers and reprints. A wooden desk sat in front of the window, a computer workstation to its right.

I looked at my watch. Twelve forty-five. I was early. I moved back up the hall and began to examine the photos lining the corridor. School of Divinity, Graduating Class of 1937, and 1938, and 1939. Stiff poses. Somber faces.

I had worked my way to 1942 when a young woman appeared. She wore jeans, a turtleneck, and a wool plaid shirt that hung to her knees. Her blond hair was cut blunt at the jawline, and thick bangs covered her eyebrows. She wore no makeup.

"May I help you?" she asked in English. She tipped her head and the bangs fell sideways.

"Yes. I'm looking for Dr. Jeannotte."

"Dr. Jeannotte's not here yet, but I expect her any time. Can I do something for you? I'm her teaching assistant." With a quick gesture, she tucked hair behind her right ear.

"Thank you, I'd like to ask Dr. Jeannotte a few questions. I'll wait, if I may."

"Uh, oh, well. O.K. I guess that's O.K. She's just, I'm not sure. She doesn't allow anyone in her office." She looked at me, glanced through the open door, then back at me. "I was at the copy machine."

"That's fine. I'll wait out here."

"Well, no, she could be a while. She's often late. I . . ." She turned and scanned the corridor behind her.

"You could sit in her office." Again the hair gesture. "But I don't know if she'll like that."

She seemed unable to make a decision.

"I'm fine here. Really."

Her eyes moved past me, then back to my face. She bit her lip and did another hair tuck. She didn't seem old enough to be a college student. She looked about twelve.

"What did you say your name is?"

"Dr. Brennan. Tempe Brennan."

"Are you a professor?"

"Yes, but not here. I work at the Laboratoire de Médecine Légale."

"Is that the police?" A crease formed between her eyes.

"No. It's the medical examiner."

"Oh." She licked her lips, then checked her watch. It was the only jewelry she wore.

"Well, come in and sit down. I'm here, so I think it's O.K. I was just at the copy machine."

"I don't want to cause . . ."

"No. It's no problem." She gave a follow-me jerk of her head and entered the office. "Come in."

I entered and took a seat on the small sofa she indicated. She moved past me to the far end of the room and began reshelving journals.

I could hear the hum of an electric motor, but couldn't see the source. I looked around. I'd never seen books take up so much space in a room. I scanned the titles immediately across from me.

The Elements of Celtic Tradition. The Dead Sea Scrolls and the New Testament. The Mysteries of Freemasonry. Shamanism: Archaic Techniques of Ecstasy. The Kingship Rituals of Egypt. Peake's Commentary on the Bible. Churches That Abuse. Thought Reform and the Psychology of Totalism. Armageddon in Waco. When Time Shall Be No More: Prophecy Belief in Modern America. An eclectic collection.

Minutes dragged by. The office was uncomfortably warm, and I felt a headache begin at the base of my skull. I removed my jacket.

Hmmmmmm.

I studied a print on the wall to my right. Naked children warmed themselves at a hearth, skin glowing in firelight. Below was written *After the Bath*, Robert Peel, 1892. The picture reminded me of one in my grandmother's music room.

I checked the time. One-ten.

"How long have you worked for Dr. Jeannotte?"

She was bending over the desk but straightened quickly at the sound of my voice.

"How long?" Bewildered.

"Are you one of her graduate students?"

"Undergraduate." She stood silhouetted by the light from the window. I couldn't see her features, but her body looked tense.

"I hear she is very involved with her students."

"Why are you asking me?"

Strange answer. "I was just curious. I never seem to have enough time to see my students outside the classroom. I admire her."

That seemed to satisfy her.

"Dr. Jeannotte is more than a teacher to many of us."

"How did you come to major in religious studies?"

For a while she didn't answer. When I thought she wasn't going to, she spoke slowly.

"I met Dr. Jeannotte when I signed up for her seminar. She . . ." Another long pause. It was hard to see her expression because of the backlighting. ". . . inspired me."

"How so?"

Another pause.

"She made me want to do things right. To learn how to do things right."

I didn't know what to say, but this time no prompt was necessary to keep her talking.

"She made me realize that a lot of the answers have already been written, we just have to learn to find them." She took a deep breath, let it out. "It's hard, it's really hard, but I've come to understand what a mess people have made of the world, and that only a few enlightened . . ."

She turned slightly, and I could see her face again. Her eyes had widened and her mouth was tense.

"Dr. Jeannotte. We were just talking."

A woman stood in the doorway. She was no more than five feet tall, with dark hair pulled tightly back from her forehead and knotted at the back of her head. Her skin was the same eggshell color as the wall behind her.

"I was at the copy machine before. I was only out of the office for a few seconds."

The woman remained absolutely still.

"She wasn't in here by herself. I wouldn't allow that." The student bit her lip and dropped her eyes.

Daisy Jeannotte never wavered.

"Dr. Jeannotte, she wants to ask you a few questions so I thought it would be O.K. if she came in to wait. She's a medical examiner." Her voice was almost trembling.

Jeannotte did not look in my direction. I had no idea what was going on.

"I . . . I'm shelving the journals. We were just making conversation." I could see drops of sweat on her upper lip.

For a moment Jeannotte continued her gaze, then, slowly, she turned in my direction.

"You have chosen a slightly inconvenient time, Miss . . . ?" Soft. Tennessee, maybe Georgia.

"Dr. Brennan." I stood.

"Dr. Brennan."

"I apologize for coming unannounced. Your secretary told me that this is your time for office hours."

She took a long time to look me over. Her eyes were deep-set, the irises so pale they were almost without color. Jeannotte accentuated this by darkening her lashes and brows. Her hair, too, was an unnatural, dense black.

"Well," she said finally, "since you are here. What is it you are seeking?" She remained motionless in the doorway. Daisy Jeannotte was one of those people who possess an air of total calm.

I explained about Sister Julienne, and about my interest in Élisabeth Nicolet, without revealing the reasons for my interest.

Jeannotte thought a moment, then shifted her gaze to the teaching assistant. Without a word the young woman laid down the journals and hurried from the office.

"You'll have to excuse my assistant. She's very high-strung." She gave a soft laugh and shook her head. "But she is an excellent student."

Jeannotte moved to a chair opposite me. We both sat.

"This time of the afternoon I normally reserve for students, but today there seem to be none. Would you like some tea?" Her voice had a honeyed quality, like the country club ladies back home.

"No, thank you. I've just had lunch."

"You are a medical examiner?"

"Not exactly. I'm a forensic anthropologist, on the faculty at the University of North Carolina at Charlotte. I consult to the coroner here."

"Charlotte is a lovely city. I've visited there often."

"Thank you. Our campus is quite different from McGill, very modern. I envy you this beautiful office."

"Yes. It is charming. Birks dates to 1931 and was originally called Divinity Hall. The building belonged to the Joint Theological Colleges until McGill acquired it in 1948. Did you know that the School of Divinity is one of the oldest faculties at McGill?"

"No, I didn't."

"Of course, today we call ourselves the Faculty of Religious Studies. So, you are interested in the Nicolet family." She crossed her ankles and settled back. I found the lack of color in her eyes unsettling.

"Yes. I'd particularly like to know where Élisabeth was born and what her parents were doing at the time. Sister Julienne has been unable to locate a birth certificate, but she's certain the birth was in Montreal. She felt you might be able to lead me to some references."

"Sister Julienne." She laughed again, a sound like water running over rocks. Then her face sobered. "There's been a great deal written about and by members of the Nicolet and Bélanger families. Our own library has a rich archive of historic documents. I'm sure you will find many things there. You could also try the Archives of the Province of Quebec, the Canadian Historical Society, and the Public Archives of Canada." The soft, Southern tones assumed an almost mechanical quality. I was a sophomore on a research project.

"You could check journals such as the *Report of the Canadian Historical Society*, the *Canadian Annual Review*, the *Canadian Archives Report*, the *Canadian Historical Review*, the *Transactions of the Quebec Literary and Historical Society*, the *Report of the Archives of the Province of Quebec*, or the *Transactions of the Royal Society of Canada.*" She sounded like a tape. "And, of course, there are hundreds of books. I myself know very little about that period in history."

My face must have reflected my thoughts.

"Don't look so daunted. It just takes time."

I'd never find enough hours to wade through that volume of material. I decided to try another tack.

"Are you familiar with the circumstances surrounding Élisabeth's birth?"

"Not really. As I said, that's not a period for which I've done research. I do know who she is, of course, and of her work during the smallpox epidemic of 1885." She paused a moment, choosing her words carefully. "My work has focused on messianic movements and new belief systems, not on the traditional ecclesiastical religions."

"In Quebec?"

"Not exclusively." She circled back to the Nicolets. "The family was well known in its day, so you might find it more interesting to go through old newspaper stories. There were four English language dailies back then, the *Gazette, Star, Herald,* and *Witness.*"

"Those would be in the library?"

"Yes. And, of course, there was the French press, *La Minerve, Le Monde, La Patrie, L'Etendard,* and *La Presse.* The French papers were a bit less prosperous and somewhat thinner than the English, but I believe they all carried birth announcements."

I hadn't thought of press accounts. Somehow that seemed more manageable.

She explained where the newspapers were stored on microfilm, and promised to draw up a list of sources for me. For a while we spoke of other things. I sated her curiosity about my job. We compared experiences, two female professors in the male-dominated world of the university. Before long a student appeared in the doorway. Jeannotte tapped her watch and held up five fingers, and the young woman disappeared.

We both stood at the same time. I thanked her, slipped on my jacket, hat, and scarf. I was halfway through the door when she stopped me with a question.

"Do you have a religion, Dr. Brennan?"

"I was raised Roman Catholic, but currently I don't belong to a church."

The ghostly eyes looked into mine.

"Do you believe in God?"

"Dr. Jeannotte, there are some days I don't believe in tomorrow morning."

After I left, I swung by the library and spent an hour browsing the history books, skimming indexes for Nicolet or Bélanger. I found several in which one or the other name was listed, and checked them out, thankful I still had faculty privileges.

It was growing dark when I emerged. Snow was falling, forcing pedestrians to walk in the street or follow narrow trails on the sidewalks, carefully placing one foot in front of the other to keep out of the deeper snow. I trudged behind a couple, girl in front, boy behind, his hands resting on her shoulders. Ties on their knapsacks swung back and forth as hips swiveled to keep feet inside the snow-free passage. Now and then the girl stopped to catch a snowflake on her tongue.

The temperature had dropped as daylight had faded, and when I got to the car, the windshield was coated with ice. I dug out a scraper and chipped away, cursing my migratory instincts. Anyone with any sense would be at the beach.

During the short drive home I replayed the scene in Jeannotte's office, trying to figure out the curious behavior of the teaching assistant. Why had she been so nervous? She seemed in awe of Jeannotte, beyond even the customary deference of an undergraduate. She mentioned her trip to the copy machine three times, yet when I'd met her in the hall she had nothing in her hands. I realized I'd never learned her name.

I thought about Jeannotte. She'd been so gracious, so totally composed, as if used to being in control of any audience. I pictured the penetrating eyes, such a contrast to the tiny body and soft, gentle drawl. She'd made me feel like an undergraduate. Why? Then I remembered. During our conversation Daisy Jean's gaze didn't leave my face. Never once did she break eye contact. That and the eerie irises made a disconcerting combination.

I arrived home to find two messages. The first made me mildly anxious. Harry had enrolled in her course and was becoming a guru of modern mental health.

The second sent a chill deep into my soul. I listened, watching snow pile up against my garden wall. The new flakes lay white atop the underlying gray, like newborn innocence on last year's sins.

"*Brennan, if you're there, pick up. This is important.*" Pause. "*There's been a development in the St-Jovite case.*" Ryan's voice was tinged with sadness. "*When we tossed the outbuildings we found four more bodies behind a stairway.*" I could hear him pull smoke deep into his lungs, release it slowly. "*Two adults and two babies. They're not burned, but it's grisly. I've never seen anything like it. I don't want to go into details, but we've got a whole new ball game, and it's a shit-pot. See you tomorrow.*"

RYAN WASN'T ALONE IN HIS REVULSION. I HAVE SEEN ABUSED AND starved children. I have seen them after they were beaten, raped, smothered, shaken to death, but I had never seen anything like what had been done to the babies found in St-Jovite.

Others had received calls the night before. When I arrived at eight-fifteen several press vans had taken up stations outside the SQ building, windows fogged, exhaust billowing from tailpipes.

Although the workday normally begins at eight-thirty, activity already filled the large autopsy room. Bertrand was there, along with several other SQ detectives and a photographer from SIJ, La Section d'Identité Judiciare. Ryan hadn't arrived.

The external exam was under way, and a series of Polaroids lay on the corner desk. The body had been taken to X-ray, and LaManche was scribbling notes when I entered. He stopped and looked up.

"Temperance, I am glad to see you. I may need help in establishing the age of the infants."

I nodded.

"And there may be an unusual"—he searched for a word, his long, basset face tense—". . . tool involved."

I nodded and went to change into scrubs. Ryan smiled and gave a small salute as I passed him in the corridor. His eyes were teary, his nose and cheeks cherry red, as though he'd walked some distance in the cold.

In the locker room I steeled myself for what was to come. A pair of murdered babies was horror enough. What did LaManche mean by an unusual tool?

Cases involving children are always difficult for me. When my daughter was young, after each child murder I'd fight an urge to tether Katy to me to keep her in sight.

Katy is grown now, but I still dread images of dead children. Of all victims, they are the most vulnerable, the most trusting, and the most innocent. I ache each time one arrives in the morgue. The stark truth of fallen humanity stares at me. And pity provides small comfort.

I returned to the autopsy room, thinking I was prepared to proceed. Then I saw the small body lying on the stainless steel.

A doll. That was my first impression. A life-size latex baby that had grayed with age. I'd had one as a child, a newborn that was pink and smelled rubbery sweet. I fed her through a small, round hole between her lips, and changed her diaper when the water flowed through.

But this was no toy. The baby lay on its belly, arms at its sides, fingers curled into the tiny palms. The buttocks were flattened, and bands of white crisscrossed the purple livor of the back. A cap of fine red down covered the little head. The infant was naked save for a bracelet of miniature blocks circling the right wrist. I could see two wounds near the left shoulder blade.

A sleeper lay on the adjacent table, blue and red trucks smiling from the flannel. Spread next to it were a soiled diaper, a cotton undershirt with crotch snaps, a long-sleeved sweater, and a pair of white socks. Everything was bloodstained.

LaManche spoke into a recorder.

"*Bébé de race blanche, bien développé et bien nourri. . . .*"

Well developed and well nourished but dead, I thought, the outrage beginning to build.

"*Le corps est bien préservé, avec une légère macération épidermique. . . .*"

I stared at the small cadaver. Yes, it was well preserved, with only slight skin slippage on the hands.

"Guess he won't have to check for defense wounds."

Bertrand had come up beside me. I didn't respond. I was not in the mood for morgue humor.

"There's another one in the cooler," he continued.

"That's what we'd been told," I said crisply.

"Yeah, but, Christ. They're babies."

I met his eyes and felt a stab of guilt. Bertrand was not trying to be funny. He looked as if his own child had died.

"Babies. Someone wasted them and stashed them in a basement. That's about as cold as a drive-by. Worse. The bastard probably knew these kids."

"Why do you say that?"

"Makes sense. Two kids, two adults who are probably the parents. Someone wiped out the whole family."

"And burned the house as a cover?"

"Possible."

"Could be a stranger."

"Could be, but I doubt it. Wait. You'll see." He refocused on the autopsy proceeding, hands clutched tightly behind his back.

LaManche stopped dictating and spoke to the autopsy technician. Lisa took a tape from the counter and stretched it the length of the baby's body.

"*Cinquante-huit centimètres.*" Fifty-eight centimeters.

Ryan observed from across the room, arms crossed, right thumb grating the tweed on his left bicep. Now and then I saw his jaw tense and his Adam's apple rise and fall.

Lisa wrapped the tape around the baby's head, chest, and abdomen, calling out after each measurement. Then she lifted the body and laid it in a hanging scale. Normally the device is used to weigh individual organs. The basket swung slightly and she placed a hand to steady it. The image was heartrending. A lifeless child in a stainless steel cradle.

"Six kilos."

The baby had died weighing only six kilos. Thirteen pounds.

LaManche recorded the weight, and Lisa removed the tiny corpse and placed it on the autopsy table. When she stepped back my breath froze in my throat. I looked at Bertrand, but his eyes were now fixed on his shoes.

The body had been a little boy. He lay on his back, legs and feet splayed sharply at the joints. His eyes were wide and button round, the irises clouded to a smoky gray. His head had rolled to the side, and one fat cheek rested against his left collarbone.

Directly below the cheek I saw a hole in the chest approximately the size of my fist. The wound had jagged edges, and a deep purple collar circled its perimeter. A star burst of slits, each measuring one to two centimeters in length, surrounded the cavity. Some were deep, others superficial. In places one slit crossed another, forming L- or V-shaped patterns.

My hand flew to my own chest and I felt my stomach tighten. I turned to Bertrand, unable to form a question.

"Do you believe that?" he said dismally. "The bastard carved his heart out."

"It's gone?"

He nodded.

I swallowed. "The other child?"

He nodded again. "Just when you think you've seen it all, you learn that you haven't."

"Christ." I felt cold all over. I hoped fervently the children were unconscious when the mutilation took place.

I looked across at Ryan. He was studying the scene on the table, his face without expression.

"What about the adults?"

Bertrand shook his head. "Looks like they were stabbed repeatedly, throats slashed, but nobody harvested their organs."

LaManche's voice droned on, describing the external appearance of the wounds. I didn't have to listen. I knew what the presence of hematoma meant. Tissue will bruise only if blood is circulating. The baby had been alive when the cut was made. Babies.

I closed my eyes, fought the urge to run from the room. Get a grip, Brennan. Do your job.

I crossed to the middle table to examine the clothing. Everything was so tiny, so familiar. I looked at the sleeper with its attached footies and soft, fleecy collar and cuffs. Katy had worn a dozen of them. I remembered opening and closing the snaps to change her diaper, her fat little legs kicking like mad. What were these things called? They had a specific name. I tried to recall but my mind refused to focus. Perhaps it was protecting me, urging me to stop personalizing and get back to business before I began to weep or simply went numb.

Most of the bleeding had been while the baby lay on his left side. The right sleeve and shoulder of the sleeper were spattered, but blood had soaked the left side, darkening the flannel to shades of dull red and brown. The undershirt and sweater were similarly stained.

"Three layers," I said to no one in particular. "And socks."

Bertrand crossed to the table.

"Someone took care that the child would be warm."

"Yeah, I guess," Bertrand agreed.

Ryan joined us as we stared at the clothing. Each garment displayed a jagged hole surrounded by a star burst of small tears, replicating the injuries on the baby's chest. Ryan spoke first.

"The little guy was dressed."

"Yeah," said Bertrand. "Guess clothing didn't interfere with his vicious little ritual."

I said nothing.

"Temperance," said LaManche, "please get a magnifying glass and come here. I've found something."

We clustered around the pathologist, and he pointed to a small discoloration to the left and below the hole in the infant's chest. When I handed him a glass, he bent close, studied the bruise, then returned the lens to me.

When I took my turn I was stunned. The spot did not show the disorganized mottling characteristic of a normal bruise. Under magnification I could see a distinct pattern in the baby's flesh, a cruciate central feature with a loop at one end like an Egyptian ankh or Maltese cross. The figure was outlined by a crenulated rectangular border. I handed the glass to Ryan and looked a question at LaManche.

"Temperance, this is clearly a patterned injury of some kind. The tissue must be preserved. Dr. Bergeron is not here today, so I would appreciate your assistance."

Marc Bergeron, odontologist to the LML, had developed a technique for lifting and fixing injuries in soft tissue. Initially he'd devised it to remove bite marks from the bodies of victims of violent sexual assault. The method had also proved useful for excising and preserving tattoos and patterned injuries on skin. I'd seen Marc do it in hundreds of cases, had assisted him in several.

I got Bergeron's kit from a cabinet in the first autopsy room, returned to room two, and spread the equipment on a stainless steel cart. By the time I'd gloved, the photographer had finished and LaManche was ready. He nodded that I should go ahead. Ryan and Bertrand watched.

I measured five scoops of pink powder from a plastic bottle and placed it in a glass vial, then added 20 cc's of a clear liquid monomer. I stirred and, within a minute, the mixture thickened until it resembled pink modeling clay. I formed the dough into a ring, and placed it on the tiny chest, completely encircling the bruise. The acrylic felt hot as I patted it into place.

To accelerate the hardening process, I placed a wet cloth over the ring, then waited. In less than ten minutes the acrylic had cooled. I reached for a tube and began squeezing a clear liquid around the edges of the ring.

"What's that?" asked Ryan.

"Cyanoacrylate."

"Smells like Krazy Glue."

"It is."

When I thought the glue was dry, I tested by tugging gently on the ring. A few more dabs, more waiting, and the ring held fast. I marked it with the date, and case and morgue numbers, and indicated top, bottom, right, and left relative to the baby's chest.

"It's ready," I said, and stepped back.

LaManche used a scalpel to dissect free the skin outside the acrylic doughnut, cutting deep enough to include the underlying fatty tissue. When the ring finally came free, it held the bruised skin tightly in place, like a miniature painting stretched on a circular pink frame. LaManche slid the specimen into the jar of clear liquid that I held ready.

"What's that?" Ryan again.

"A solution of ten percent buffered formalin. In ten to twelve hours the tissue will be fixed. The ring will ensure that there's no distortion, so later, if we get a weapon, we'll be able to compare it to the wound to see if the patterns match. And, of course, we'll have the photos."

"Why not just use the photos?"

"With this we can do transillumination if we have to."

"Transillumination?"

I wasn't really in the mood for a science seminar, so I kept it simple. "You can shine a light up through the tissue and see what's going on under the skin. It often brings out details not visible on the surface."

"What do you think made it?" Bertrand.

"I don't know," I said, sealing the jar and handing it to Lisa.

As I was turning away I felt a tremendous sadness, and couldn't resist lifting the tiny hand. It felt soft and cold in my fingers. I rotated the blocks circling the wrist. M-A-T-H-I-A-S.

I'm so sorry, Mathias.

I looked up to see LaManche gazing at me. His eyes seemed to mirror the despair I was feeling. I stepped back, and he began the internal exam. He would excise and send upstairs the ends of all bones cut by the killer, but I wasn't optimistic. Though I'd never looked for tool marks on a victim this young, I suspected that an infant's ribs would be too tiny to retain much detail.

I stripped off my gloves and turned to Ryan as Lisa made a Y-shaped incision on the infant's chest.

"Are the scene photos here?"

"Just the backups."

He handed me a large brown envelope containing a set of Polaroids. I took them to the corner desk.

The first showed the largest of the outbuildings at the chalet in St-Jovite. The style was that of the main house: Alpine Tacky. The next photo was taken inside, shot from the top of a staircase looking downward. The passage was dark and narrow, with walls on both sides, wooden handrails on the walls, and junk heaped at both ends of each step.

There were several pictures of a basement taken from different angles. The room was dim, the only light coming from small rectangular windows close to the ceiling. Linoleum floor. Knotty pine walls. Washtubs. A hot water heater. More junk.

Several photos zoomed in on the water heater, then on the space between it and the wall. The niche was filled with what looked like old carpets and plastic bags. The next pictures showed these objects lined up on the linoleum, first unopened, then laid out to expose their contents.

The adults had been wrapped in large pieces of clear plastic, then rolled in rugs and stacked behind the water heater. Their bodies showed abdominal bloating and skin slippage, but were well preserved.

Ryan came and stood over me.

"The water heater must have been off," I said, handing him the picture. "If it was running the heat would have caused more decomposition."

"We don't think they were using that building."

"What was it?"

He shrugged.

I went back to the Polaroids.

The man and woman were both fully dressed, though barefoot. Their throats had been cut and blood saturated their clothing and stained the plastic shrouds. The man lay with one hand thrown back, and I could see deep slashes across his palm. Defense wounds. He had tried to save himself. Or his family.

Oh, God. I closed my eyes for a moment.

With the infants the packaging had been simpler. They were bundled in plastic, placed in garbage bags, then stuffed in above the adults.

I looked at the little hands, the dimpled knuckles. Bertrand was right. There would be no defense wounds on the babies. Grief and anger merged in my mind.

"I want this son of a bitch." I looked up into Ryan's eyes.

"Yeah."

"I want you to get him, Ryan. I mean it. I want this one. Before we see another baby butchered. What good are we to anyone if we can't stop this?"

The electric blues stared straight back. "We'll get him, Brennan. No doubt about that."

I spent the rest of the day riding the elevator between my office and the autopsies. It would take at least two days to complete them since LaManche was doing all four victims. This is standard procedure in multiple homicides. Using one pathologist provides coherence in a case, and ensures consistency in testimony if it goes to trial.

When I looked in at one o'clock Mathias had been rolled back to the morgue cooler and the autopsy of the second infant was under way. The scene we'd played out in the morning was taking place again. Same actors. Same setting. Same victim. Except this one wore a bracelet that spelled out M-A-L-A-C-H-Y.

By four-thirty Malachy's belly had been closed, his tiny skullcap replaced, his face repositioned. Save for the Y-incisions and the mutilation to their chests, the babies were ready for burial. As yet we had no idea where that would be. Or by whom.

Ryan and Bertrand had also spent the day coming and going. Prints had been taken from both boys' feet, but the smudges on hospital birth records are notoriously unreadable, and Ryan was not optimistic about a match.

The bones in the hand and wrist represent over 25 percent of those in the skeleton. An adult has twenty-seven in each hand, an infant far fewer, depending on its age. I'd examined X-rays to see which bones were present and how well they were formed. According to my estimate, Mathias and Malachy were about four months old when they were killed.

This information was released to the media, but, aside from the usual loonies, there was little response. Our best hope lay with the adult bodies in the cooler. We were sure that when the identities of the adults were established, those of the children would follow. For the present the infants remained Baby Malachy and Baby Mathias.

ON FRIDAY I SAW NEITHER RYAN NOR BERTRAND. LAMANCHE spent all day downstairs with the adult corpses from St-Jovite. I had the babies' ribs soaking in glass vials in the histology lab. Any grooves or striations that might be present would be so tiny I didn't want them damaged by boiling or scraping, and I couldn't risk introducing nicks with a scalpel or scissors, so all I could do at that point was periodically change the water and tease off flesh.

I was glad for the temporary lull in the level of activity, and was using the time to finalize my report on Élisabeth Nicolet, which I'd promised that day. Since I had to return to Charlotte on Monday, I planned to examine the ribs over the weekend. If nothing else came up, I thought I could get everything that was pressing done before Monday. I had not counted on the call I took at ten-thirty.

"I am very, very sorry to call you like this, Dr. Brennan." English, spoken slowly, each word chosen with care.

"Sister Julienne, it's nice to hear from you."

"Please. I apologize for the calls."

"The calls?" I riffled through the pink slips on my desk. I knew she'd phoned back Wednesday, but thought it was a follow-up on our earlier conversation. There were two other slips with her name and number.

"I'm the one who should apologize. I was tied up all day yesterday, and didn't check my messages. I'm sorry."

There was no response.

"I'm writing the report now."

"No, no, it's not that. I mean, yes, of course, that is terribly important. And we are all anxious . . ."

She hesitated, and I could picture her dark brows deepening the perpetual frown she wore. Sister Julienne always looked worried.

"I feel very awkward, but I don't know where to turn. I've prayed, of course, and I know God is listening, but I feel *I* should be doing something. I devote myself to my work, to keeping God's archives, but, well, I have an earthly family too." She was forming her words precisely, shaping them like a baker molding dough.

There was another long pause. I waited her out.

"He does help those who help themselves."

"Yes."

"It's about my niece, Anna. Anna Goyette. She's the one I spoke of on Wednesday."

"Your niece?" I couldn't imagine where this was going.

"She's my sister's child."

"I see."

"She's . . . We're not sure where she is."

"Uh-huh."

"She's normally a very thoughtful child, very reliable, never stays out without calling."

"Uh-huh." I was beginning to get the drift.

Finally, she blurted it out. "Anna didn't come home last night and my sister is frantic. I've told her to pray, of course, but, well . . ." Her voice trailed off.

I wasn't sure what to say. This was not where I'd expected the conversation to go.

"Your niece is missing?"

"Yes."

"If you're worried, perhaps you should contact the police."

"My sister called twice. They told her that with someone Anna's age their policy is to wait forty-eight to seventy-two hours."

"How old is your niece?"

"Anna is nineteen."

"She's the one studying at McGill?"

"Yes." Her voice sounded tense enough to saw metal.

"Sister, there's really noth . . ."

I heard her choke back a sob. "I know, I know, and I apologize for bothering you, Dr. Brennan." Her words came out between sharply inhaled breaths, like hiccups. "I know you are busy, I know that, but my sister is hysterical and I just don't know what to tell her. She lost her husband two years ago and now she feels that Anna is all she has. Virginie is calling me every half-hour, insisting I help her find her daughter. I know this is not your job, and I would never call you unless I was desperate. I've prayed, but, oh . . ."

I was startled to hear her burst into tears. They engulfed her speech, obliterating her words. I waited, my mind in a muddle. What should I say?

Then the sobs receded and I heard the sound of tissues pulled from a box, then a nose being blown.

"I . . . I . . . Please forgive me." Her voice was trembling.

Counseling has never been my strong point. Even with those close to me, I feel awkward and inadequate in the face of emotion. I focus on the practical.

"Has Anna taken off before?" Solve the problem.

"I don't think so. But my sister and I don't always . . . communicate well." She had calmed somewhat and was back to word sifting.

"Has she been having problems at school?"

"I don't think so."

"With friends? A boyfriend, perhaps?"

"I don't know."

"Have you noticed any changes in her behavior lately?"

"What do you mean?"

"Has she changed her eating habits? Is she sleeping more or less than usual? Has she become less communicative?"

"I . . . I'm sorry. Since she's been in university I haven't seen as much of Anna as I used to."

"Is she attending her classes?"

"I'm not sure." Her voice faded on the last word. She sounded completely drained.

"Does Anna get along with her mother?"

There was a very long pause.

"There is the usual tension, but I know Anna loves her mother."

Bingo.

"Sister, your niece might have needed some time to herself. I'm sure if you wait a day or two she'll either show up or call."

"Yes, I suppose you're right, but I feel so helpless for Virginie. She is totally distraught. I can't reason with her, and I thought if I could tell her the police were checking, she might be . . . reassured."

I heard another tissue pull and feared a second round of tears.

"Let me make a call. I'm not sure it will do any good, but I'll give it a try."

She thanked me and we hung up. For a moment I sat there, running through my options. I thought of Ryan, but McGill is located on the island of Montreal. Communauté Urbaine de Montréal Police. CUM. I took a deep breath and dialed. When the receptionist answered, I made my request.

"Monsieur Charbonneau, *s'il vous plaît.*"

"*Un instant, s'il vous plaît.*"

She came back shortly and said Charbonneau was out for the afternoon.

"Do you want Monsieur Claudel?"

"Yes." Like I wanted anthrax. Damn.

"Claudel," said the next voice.

"Monsieur Claudel. It's Tempe Brennan."

As I listened to empty air, I pictured Claudel's beak nose and parrot face, usually set with disapproval of me. I enjoyed talking to this detective as much as I enjoyed boils. But since I didn't deal with juvenile runaways, I wasn't sure whom else to ask. Claudel and I had worked CUM cases before, and he had come to tolerate me, so I hoped he would at least tell me where to turn.

"*Oui?*"

"Monsieur Claudel, I have a rather odd request. I realize this isn't exactly you—"

"What is it, Dr. Brennan?" Abrupt. Claudel was one of the few who could make the French language sound cold. Just the facts, ma'am.

"I've just had a call from a woman who is concerned about her niece. The girl is a student at McGill and she didn't return home last night. I was wond—"

"They should fill out a missing person report."

"The mother was told that nothing could be done for forty-eight to seventy-two hours."

"Age?"

"Nineteen."

"Name."

"Anna Goyette."

"Does she live on campus?"

"I don't know. It didn't sound like it. I think she lives with the mother."

"Did she attend her classes yesterday?"

"I don't know."

"Where was she last seen?"

"I don't know."

Another pause. Then,

"There is a great deal you do not know, it appears. This may not be a CUM case, and, at this point, it is definitely not a homicide matter." I could picture him tapping something against something, his face pinched with impatience.

"Yes. I would simply like to know who I could contact," I spat. He was making me feel unprepared, which was making me irritable. And screwing up my grammar. As usual, Claudel did not bring out the best in me, particularly when his criticism of my methodology was in part legitimate.

"Try missing persons."

I listened to a dial tone.

I was still fuming when the phone rang again.

"Dr. Brennan," I barked.

"Is this a bad time?" The soft, Southern English was a sharp contrast to Claudel's clipped, nasal French.

"Dr. Jeannotte?"

"Yes. Please call me Daisy."

"Please excuse me, Daisy. I—it's been a rough couple of days. What can I do for you?"

"Well, I have found some interesting Nicolet materials for you. I hate to send them by courier, since some items are quite old and probably valuable. Would you like to drop by and pick them up?"

I looked at my watch. It was after eleven. Hell, why not. Maybe while on campus I might ask about Anna. At least I'd have something to tell Sister Julienne.

"I could come by about noon. Would that be convenient?"

"That would be just fine."

Again, I arrived early. Again, the door was open and the office empty except for a young woman shelving journals. I wondered if it was the same stack Jeannotte's assistant had been clearing on Wednesday.

"Hi. I'm looking for Dr. Jeannotte."

The woman turned and her large loop earrings swung and caught the light. She was tall, perhaps six feet, with dark hair shaved close to her head.

"She's gone downstairs for a minute. Do you have an appointment?"

"I'm a bit early. No problem."

The office was just as warm and just as cluttered as on my first visit. I took off my jacket and stuffed my mittens into the pocket. The woman indicated a wooden hall tree, and I hung the jacket there. She watched me wordlessly.

"She does have a lot of journals," I said, indicating the stack on the desk.

"I think I spend my life sorting these things." She reached up and slid a journal onto a shelf above her head.

"Helps to be tall, I guess."

"Helps with some things."

"I met Dr. Jeannotte's TA on Wednesday. She was reshelving, too."

"Um-hum." The young woman picked up another journal and examined its spine.

"I'm Dr. Brennan," I offered.

She slipped the journal into a row at eye level.

"And you are . . . ?" I coaxed.

"Sandy O'Reilly," she said without turning. I wondered if my height remark had offended her.

"Nice to meet you, Sandy. After I left on Wednesday I realized I'd never asked the other assistant her name."

She shrugged. "I'm sure Anna didn't care."

The name hit me like a spitball. I couldn't be that lucky.

"Anna?" I asked. "Anna Goyette?"

"Yeah." Finally she turned to face me. "Know her?"

"No, not really. A student by that name is related to an acquaintance of mine, and I wondered if it might be the same person. Is she here today?"

"No. I think she's sick. That's why I'm working. I'm not scheduled on Fridays, but Anna couldn't, so Dr. Jeannotte asked me to fill in today."

"She's sick?"

"Yeah, I guess. Actually, I don't know. All I know is she's out again. It's O.K. I can use the money."

"Again?"

"Well, yeah. She misses quite a bit. I usually fill in. The extra money's nice, but it isn't helping my thesis get written." She gave a short laugh, but I could detect annoyance in her voice.

"Does Anna have health problems?"

Sandy tilted her head and looked at me. "Why are you so interested in Anna?"

"I'm not really. I'm here to pick up some research that Dr. Jeannotte has for me. But I am a friend of Anna's aunt, and I know that her family is worried because they haven't seen her since yesterday morning."

She shook her head and reached for another journal. "They ought to worry about Anna. She is one weird cookie."

"Weird?"

She shelved the journal then turned to face me. Her eyes rested on mine for a long time, assessing.

"You're a friend of the family?"

"Yes." Sort of.

"You're not an investigator or reporter or something?"

"I'm an anthropologist." True, though not fully accurate. But an image of Margaret Mead or Jane Goodall might be more reassuring. "I'm only asking because Anna's aunt called me this morning. Then when it developed that we were talking about the same person . . ."

Sandy crossed the office and checked the corridor, then leaned against the wall just inside the door. It was obvious that her height did not embarrass her. She held her head high and moved with long, languid strides.

"I don't want to say anything that will cost Anna her job. Or me mine. Please don't tell anyone where this came from, particularly Dr. Jeannotte. She would not like me talking about one of her students."

"You have my word."

She took a deep breath. "I think Anna's really messed up and needs help. And it's not just because I have to cover for her. Anna and I were friends, or at least we hung out a lot last year. Then she changed. Zoned out. I've been thinking of calling her mother for a while now. Someone should know."

She swallowed and shifted weight.

"Anna spends half her time over at the counseling center because she's so unhappy. She goes missing for days on end, and when she is around she doesn't seem to have any life, just hangs here all the time. And she always looks edgy, like she's ready to jump off a bridge."

She stopped, her eyes riveted on mine, deciding. Then,

"A friend told me Anna is involved in something."

"Yes?"

"I have absolutely no idea if this is true, or if I should even say it. It's not my style to pass on gossip, but if Anna is in trouble, I'd never forgive myself for keeping quiet."

I waited.

"And if it is true she could be at risk."

"What is it you think Anna is involved in?"

"This sounds so bizarre." She shook her head and the earrings tapped her jaw. "I mean, you hear about these things, but it's never someone you know."

She swallowed again and glanced over her shoulder out the door.

"My friend told me that Anna joined a cult. A group of Satan worshipers. I don't know if . . ."

On hearing the creak of floorboards, Sandy crossed to the far end of the office and picked up several journals. She was busy shelving when Daisy Jeannotte appeared in the doorway.

"I AM SO SORRY," DAISY SAID, SMILING WARMLY. "I SEEM TO ALWAYS be keeping you waiting. Have you and Sandy introduced yourselves?" Her hair was in the same impeccable bun.

"Yes, we have. We've been talking about the joys of shelving."

"I do ask them to do a lot of that. Copying and shelving. Very tedious, I know. But a great deal of real research is just plain tedious. My students and helpers are very patient with me."

She turned her smile on Sandy, who gave her own brief version and returned to the journals. I was struck by how differently Jeannotte interacted with this student compared with what I'd seen with Anna.

"Now, then, let me show you what I've found. I think you'll like it." She gestured toward the sofa.

When we'd settled she lifted a stack of materials from a small brass table to her right, and looked down at a two-page printout. Her part was a stark white line bisecting the crown of her head.

"These are titles of books about Quebec during the nineteenth century. I'm sure you'll find mention of the Nicolet family in many of them."

She gave it to me and I glanced down the list, but my mind was not on Élisabeth Nicolet.

"And this book is about the smallpox epidemic of 1885. It may contain some mention of Élisabeth or her work. If nothing else, it will give you a sense of the times and the enormity of suffering in Montreal in those days."

The volume was new and in perfect condition, as though no one had ever read it. I flipped a few pages, seeing nothing. What had Sandy been about to say?

"But I think you're especially going to like these." She handed me what looked like three old ledgers, then leaned back, the smile still on her lips, but watching me intently.

The covers were gray, with deep burgundy binding and trim. Gingerly, I opened the top one and turned several pages. It smelled musty, like something kept for years in a basement or attic. It was not a ledger, but a diary, handwritten in a bold, clear script. I glanced at the first entry: January 1, 1844. I flipped to the last: December 23, 1846.

"They are written by Louis-Philippe Bélanger, Élisabeth's uncle. It is known that he was a prodigious journal keeper, so, on a hunch, I checked with our rare documents section. Sure enough, McGill owns part of the collection. I don't know where the rest of the journals are, or if they've even survived, but I could try to find out. I had to pledge my soul to get these." She laughed. "I borrowed the ones that date to the period of Élisabeth's birth and early infancy."

"This is too good to be true," I said, momentarily forgetting Anna Goyette. "I don't know what to say."

"Say you will take exceedingly good care of them."

"May I actually take them with me?"

"Yes. I trust you. I'm sure you appreciate their value and will treat them accordingly."

"Daisy, I'm overwhelmed. This is more than I'd hoped for."

She raised a hand in a gesture of dismissal, then refolded it quietly in her lap. For a moment neither of us spoke. I couldn't wait to get out of there and into the journals. Then I remembered Sister Julienne's niece. And Sandy's words.

"Daisy, I wonder if I could ask you something about Anna Goyette."

"Yes." She was still smiling, but her eyes grew wary.

"As you know I've been working with Sister Julienne, who is Anna's aunt."

"I didn't know they were kin."

"Yes. Sister Julienne called to tell me that Anna hasn't been home since yesterday morning, and her mother is very worried."

Throughout our conversation I'd been aware of Sandy's movements as she sorted journals and placed them on shelves. The far end of the office now grew very still. Jeannotte noticed, too.

"Sandy, you must be quite tired. You go on now and take a little break."

"I'm fi—"

"Now, please."

Sandy's eyes met mine as she slipped past us and out the office door. Her expression was unreadable.

"Anna is a very bright young woman," Jeannotte continued. "A bit skittish, but a good intellect. I'm sure she's fine." Very firm.

"Her aunt says it isn't typical for Anna to take off like this."

"Anna probably needed some time to reflect. I know she's had some disagreements with her mama. She's probably gone off for a few days."

Sandy had hinted that Jeannotte was protective of her students. Was that what I was seeing? Did the professor know something she wasn't telling?

"I suppose I'm more of an alarmist than most. In my work I see so many young women who *aren't* just fine."

Jeannotte looked down at her hands. For a moment she was absolutely still. Then, with the same smile, "Anna Goyette is trying to extract herself from the influence of an impossible home situation. That's all I can say, but I assure you she is well and happy."

Why so certain? Should I? What the hell. I threw it out to see her reaction.

"Daisy, I know this sounds bizarre, but I've heard that Anna is involved in some kind of satanic cult."

The smile disappeared. "I won't even ask where you picked up that information. It doesn't surprise me." She shook her head. "Child molesters. Psychopathic murderers. Depraved messiahs. Doomsday prophets. Satanists. The sinister neighbor who feeds arsenic to trick-or-treaters."

"But those threats do exist." I raised my eyebrows in question.

"Do they? Or are they just urban legends? Memorates for modern times?"

"Memorates?" I wondered how this concerned Anna.

"A term folklorists use to describe how people integrate their fears with popular legends. It's a way to explain bewildering experiences."

My face told her I was still confused.

"Every culture has stories, folk legends that express commonly held anxieties. The fear of bogeymen, outsiders, aliens. The loss of children. When something happens we can't understand, we update old tales. The witch got Hansel and Gretel. The man in the mall got the child who wandered off. It's a way to make confusing experiences seem credible. So people tell stories of abductions by UFO's, Elvis sightings, Halloween poisonings. It always happened to a friend of a friend, a cousin, the boss's son."

"Aren't the Halloween candy poisonings real?"

"A sociologist reviewed newspaper accounts from the 1970s and 1980s and found that during that time only two deaths could be shown to have occurred due to candy tampering, both by family members. Very few other incidents could be documented. But the legend grew because it expresses deep-seated fears: loss of children, fear of the night, fear of strangers."

I let her go on, waiting for the link to Anna.

"You've heard of subversion myths? Anthropologists love to discuss these."

I dug back to a grad school seminar on mythology. "Blame giving. Stories that find scapegoats for complicated problems."

"Exactly. Usually the scapegoats are outsiders—racial, ethnic, or religious groups that make others uneasy. Romans accused early Christians of incest and child sacrifice. Later Christian sects accused one another, then Christians pointed the same finger at Jews. Thousands died because of such beliefs. Think of the witch trials. Or the Holocaust. And it's not just old news. After the student uprising in France in the late sixties, Jewish shopkeepers were accused of kidnapping teenage girls from boutique dressing rooms."

I vaguely remembered that.

"And most recently it's been Turkish and North African immigrants. Several years ago hundreds of French parents claimed children were being abducted, killed, and eviscerated by them, even though virtually no children had been reported missing in France.

"And that myth continues, even here in Montreal, only now there's a new bogeyman practicing ritual child killing." She leaned forward, widening her eyes, and almost hissing the last word. "Satanists."

It was the most animated I'd seen her. Her words caused an image to take shape in my mind. Malachy lying on stainless steel.

"Not surprising, really," she continued. "Preoccupation with demonology always intensifies during periods of social change. And toward the end of millennia. But now the threat is from Satan."

"Hasn't Hollywood created a lot of that?"

"Not intentionally, of course, but it has certainly contributed. Hollywood just wants to make commercially successful films. But that's an age-old question: Does art shape the times or merely reflect them? *Rosemary's Baby, The Omen, The Exorcist.* What do these movies do? They explain social anxieties through the use of demonic imagery. And the public watches and listens."

"But isn't that just part of the increasing interest in mysticism in American culture over the past three decades?"

"Of course. And what's the other trend that has taken place during the last generation?"

I felt as if I was being quizzed. What did all this have to do with Anna? I shook my head.

"The rise in popularity of fundamentalist Christianity. The economy had a lot to do with it, of course. Layoffs. Plant closings. Downsizing. Poverty and economic insecurity are very stressful. But that isn't the only source of worry. People at every economic level are feeling anxiety due to shifting social norms. Relations have changed between men and women, within families, between generations."

She ticked the points off on her fingers.

"The old explanations are breaking down and new ones haven't been established yet. The fundamentalist churches provide solace by presenting simple answers to complex questions."

"Satan."

"Satan. All the world's evil is due to Satan. Teenagers are being recruited to devil worship. Children are being abducted and killed in demonic rituals. Satanic livestock killing is spreading across the country. The Proctor and Gamble logo contains a secret satanic symbol. Grass roots frustration locks on to these rumors and feeds them so they grow."

"So, are you suggesting that satanic cults don't exist?"

"I'm not saying that. There are a few, what shall we say, high-profile, organized Satanist groups, like that of Anton LaVey."

"The Church of Satan, out in San Francisco."

"Yes. But they're a small, small group. Most 'Satanists'"—she hooked both index fingers in the air, placing the term in quotation marks—"are probably just white, middle-class kids playing at devil worship. Occasionally these kids get out of line, of course, vandalize churches or cemeteries, or torture animals, but mostly they perform a lot of rituals, and go off on legend trips."

"Legend trips?"

"I believe that term came from the sociologists. Visits to spooky sites, like cemeteries or haunted houses. They light bonfires, tell ghost stories, cast spells, maybe do some vandalism. That's about it. Later, when police find graffiti, an overturned gravestone, a campfire site, maybe a dead cat, they assume the local youth are all in a satanic cult. The press picks it up, the preachers sound the alarm, and another legend takes flight."

She was, as usual, totally composed, but her nostrils dilated and contracted as she spoke, betraying a tension I hadn't seen before. I said nothing.

"I am suggesting that the threat of Satanism is vastly overblown. Another subversion myth, as your colleagues would say."

Without warning her voice rose and sharpened, causing me to jump.

"David! Is that you?"

I hadn't heard a sound.

"Yes, ma'am." Muffled.

A tall figure appeared in the doorway, his face concealed by the hood of his parka and an enormous muffler wrapped around his neck. The hunched form looked vaguely familiar.

"Excuse me a moment."

Jeannotte rose and disappeared through the doorway. I caught little of their conversation, but the man sounded agitated, his voice rising and falling like a whining child's. Jeannotte interrupted him frequently. She spoke in short bursts, her tone as steady as his was volatile. I could make out only one word. "No." She repeated it several times.

Then there was silence. In a moment, Jeannotte returned, but did not sit.

"Students," she said, laughing and shaking her head.

"Let me guess. He needs more time to finish his paper."

"Nothing ever changes." She looked at her watch. "So, Tempe, I hope your visit has been helpful. You will take care of the diaries? They are very dear." I was being dismissed.

"Of course. I'll return them by Monday at the latest." I rose, slid Jeannotte's materials into my briefcase, and collected my jacket and purse.

She smiled me out of the room.

In winter, the Montreal sky displays mainly gray tones, shifting from dove, to iron, to lead, to zinc. When I stepped out of Birks Hall moist clouds had turned the day a dull pewter.

I slung my purse and briefcase over my shoulder, stuffed my fists into my pockets, and turned downhill into a raw, damp wind. Before I'd taken twenty steps tears filled my eyes, making it hard to see. As I walked, an image of Fripp Island flashed across my mind. Palmetto palms. Sea oats. Sunlight glinting on the marsh.

Knock it off, Brennan. March is windy and cold in many parts of the planet. Stop using the Carolinas as a baseline against which to measure the weather of the world. It could be worse. It could be snowing. With that, the first fat flake struck my cheek.

As I opened the car door, I looked up to see a tall young man staring at me from the far side of the street. I recognized the parka and muffler. The hunched form was that of David, Jeannotte's unhappy visitor.

Our gazes locked for a moment, and the raw anger in his eyes startled me. Then, without a word, the student turned and hurried off down the block. Unnerved, I climbed into the car and locked the doors, thankful he was Jeannotte's problem and not mine.

On the drive back to the lab my mind went through its usual paces, rehashing the immediate, and worrying about things undone. Where was Anna? Should Sandy's concerns about a cult be seriously considered? Was Jeannotte right? Were satanic cults little more than youth clubs? Why had I not asked Jeannotte to elaborate on her remark that Anna was safe? Our conversation had gotten so fascinating I'd been sidetracked from asking further about Anna. Was that deliberate? Was Jeannotte purposefully concealing something? If so, what and why? Was the professor merely shielding her student from outsiders prying into a personal matter? What was Anna's "impossible home situation"? Why did David's behavior seem so sinister?

How would I ever get through the ledgers by Monday? My flight was at 5 P.M. Could I finish the Nicolet report today, do those for the babies tomorrow, and work through the ledgers on Sunday? No wonder I had no social life.

By the time I got to rue Parthenais, steadily falling snow was sticking to the street. I found a parking spot just outside the door, and said a prayer that the car wouldn't be plowed in when I came back.

The air in the lobby felt steamy and smelled of wet wool. I stomped my boots, contributing to the slick, shallow pool of melted snow spreading across the floor, and punched for an elevator. On the ride up I tried to clean streaked mascara from my lower lids.

There were two pink message slips on my desk. Sister Julienne had called. No doubt she wanted reports on Anna and Élisabeth. I wasn't ready on either. Next. Ryan.

I dialed and he answered.

"Long lunch."

I checked my watch. One forty-five.

"I'm paid by the hour. What's up?"

"We've finally tracked down the owner of the house in St-Jovite. Guy's name is Jacques Guillion. He's from Quebec City, but moved to Belgium years ago. His whereabouts remain unknown, but a Belgian neighbor says Guillion has been renting the St-Jovite place to an old lady named Patrice Simonnet. She thinks the tenant is Belgian, but isn't sure. She says Guillion also provides the tenant with cars. We're running a check."

"Pretty well-informed neighbor."

"Apparently they were close."

"The burned body from the basement could be Simonnet."

"Could be."

"We got good dental X-rays during the post. Bergeron has them."

"We've given the name to the RCMP. They're working with Interpol. If she's Belgian, they'll track her."

"What about the other two bodies in the main house and the two adults with the babies?"

"We're working on it."

We both thought for a moment.

"Pretty big place for one old lady."

"Looks like she wasn't all that alone."

I spent the next two hours in the histology lab teasing the last of the tissue from the babies' ribs and examining them under the microscope. As I'd feared, there were no unique nicks or patterns in the bone. There was nothing I could say except that the killer had used a very sharp knife with a blade which was not serrated. Bad for the investigation. Good for me. The report would be brief.

I'd just returned to my office when Ryan called back.

"How about a beer?" he asked.

"I don't keep beer in my office, Ryan. If I did, I'd drink it."

"You don't drink."

"Then why are you asking me for beer?"

"I'm asking if you'd like one. Could be green."

"What?"

"Aren't you Irish, Brennan?"

I glanced at my wall calendar. March 17. The anniversary of some of my best performances. I didn't want to remember.

"Can't do it anymore, Ryan."

"It's a generic way of saying 'Let's take a break.'"

"Are you asking me for a date?"

"Yes."

"With you?"

"No, with my parish priest."

"Wow. Does he cheat on his vows?"

"Brennan, do you want to meet me for a beverage this evening? Alcohol-free?"

"Ryan, I—"

"It's St. Paddy's Day. It's Friday night and snowing like a sonofabitch. Got a better offer?"

I didn't. In fact, I had no other offers. But Ryan and I often investigated the same cases, and I'd always had a policy of keeping work and home separate.

Always. Right. I'd been separated and living on my own less than two years of my adult life. And they hadn't been banner ones for male companionship.

"I don't think it's a good idea."

There was a pause. Then,

"We got a break on Simonnet. She popped right up on the Interpol search. Born in Brussels, lived there until two years ago. Still pays taxes on a piece of property in the countryside. Loyal old gal, went to the same dentist her whole life. The guy's been in practice since the Stone Age, keeps everything. They're faxing the records. If it looks like a match, we'll get the originals."

"When was she born?"

I heard a paper flip.

"Nineteen-eighteen."

"That fits. Family?"

"We're checking."

"Why did she leave Belgium?"

"Maybe she needed a change of scenery. Look, champ, if you decide *you* do, I'll be at Hurley's after nine. If there's a line, use my name."

I sat awhile, thinking about why I'd said no. Pete and I had reached an accord. We still loved each other, but couldn't live together. Separated, we were once again able to be friends. Our relationship hadn't been as good in years. Pete was dating, I was free to do the same. Oh, God. Dating. The word raised images of acne and braces.

To be honest, I found Andrew Ryan extremely attractive. No zits or orthodontics. A definite plus. And technically we didn't work together. But I also found him extremely annoying. And unpredictable. No. Ryan is trouble.

I was finishing my report on Malachy and Mathias when the phone rang again. I smiled. O.K., Ryan. You win.

The voice of a security guard told me I had a visitor in the downstairs lobby. I looked at my watch. Four-twenty. Who would be coming this late? I didn't remember making any appointments.

I asked for the name. When he told me, my heart sank.

"Oh no." I couldn't help myself.

"*Est-ce qu'il y a un problème?*"

"*Non. Pas de problème.*" I told him I'd be right down.

No problem? Who was I kidding?

I said it again in the elevator.

Oh no.

10

"WHAT ARE YOU DOING HERE?"

"Well, you could look glad to see me, big sister."

"I—of course I'm glad to see you, Harry. I'm just surprised." I couldn't have been more astounded if the guard had announced Teddy Roosevelt.

She snorted. "That's about as heartfelt as grits."

My sister sat in the lobby of the SQ building surrounded by shopping bags from Nieman Marcus and canvas packs of varying shapes and sizes. She wore red cowboy boots engraved with black and white loops and swirls and a matching leather jacket with fringe. When she stood I could see jeans tight enough to cut off blood flow. We all could.

Harry hugged me, fully aware of but completely unself-conscious about her effect on others. Especially the others with Y chromosomes.

"Whew, it is bad-ass cold out there! I'm iced enough to freeze tequila." She hunched her shoulders and wrapped her arms around her rib cage.

"Yes." I didn't get the analogy.

"My flight was supposed to touch down at noon, but the pissant snow held us up. Oh well, here I am, big sister."

She dropped her shoulders and held out her arms, causing the jacket fringe to shimmy. Harry looked so out of place it was surreal. Amarillo comes to the tundra.

"O.K. Great. What a surprise. Well. I— What brings you to Montreal?"

"I'll tell you all about it. It's awesome. When I heard about it I just couldn't believe my ears. I mean, right here in Montreal and all."

"What is 'it,' Harry?"

"The seminar I'd done. I told you about it, Tempe, when I called last weekend. I did it. I signed up for that training course in Houston and now I'm mainlinin' this stuff. I have never been so pumped. I cruised the first level. I mean cruised it. Some people take years to realize their own reality and I just whupped that puppy in a few weeks. I mean I am learning some powerful therapeutic strategies, and I am taking hold of my life. So when they invited me to this level-two workshop, and right here where my big sister lives, well, I packed my bags and pointed my nose north."

Harry beamed at me with clear, blue eyes surrounded by gobs of mascara.

"You're here for a workshop?"

"Exactamundo. All expenses paid. Well, almost all."

"I want to hear all about it," I said, hoping the course was short. I was unsure if Quebec Province and Harry could survive each other.

"This shit is awesome," she said, rephrasing her initial assessment, but adding little additional information.

"Let's go upstairs and I'll wrap up. Or would you rather wait here?"

"Hell, no. I want to see where the great cadaver doctor works. Lead on."

"You'll have to submit a photo ID to get a visitor's pass," I said, indicating the guard at the security desk.

He was observing the scene, a half smile on his face, and spoke before either of us could make a move.

"*Vôtre sœur?*" he bellowed across the lobby, exchanging looks with the other guards.

I nodded. Obviously everyone now knew that Harry was my sister, and found it terribly amusing.

The guard gave a sweeping gesture toward the elevators.

"*Merci,*" I mumbled, and shot him a withering glance.

"Mercy," Harry drawled, giving each guard a radiant smile.

We gathered her bundles and rode to the fifth floor, where I stacked everything in the hall outside my office. No way to fit it inside. The quantity of her gear raised apprehension as to the likely length of her stay.

"Hell, this office looks like a twister just traveled through here." Though she was only five feet nine and thin as a fashion model, Harry seemed to fill the small space.

"It's a little messy right now. Let me shut down the computer and collect a few things. Then we'll head out."

"Take your time, I'm in no hurry. I'll just chat with your friends." She was looking up at a row of skulls, her head tipped back so that the ends of her hair brushed the bottom fringe on her jacket. It looked blonder than I remembered it.

"Howdy," she said to the first, "decided to quit while you're a head, did you?"

I couldn't help but smile. Her cranial friend did not. While Harry worked her way along the shelf, I logged off and gathered the ledgers and books from Daisy Jeannotte. I planned to be back first thing in the morning, so I didn't pack my unfinished reports.

"So, what's new with you?" Harry spoke to the fourth skull. "Not talking? Oh, you're so sexy when you're moody."

"She's always moody." Andrew Ryan stood in the doorway.

Harry turned and looked the detective up and down. Slowly. Then blue eyes met blue eyes.

"What the hey?"

My sister's smile for the security guards was nothing compared with the one she now beamed at Ryan. In that moment I knew calamity was predestined.

"We were just leaving, " I said, zipping my computer case.

"Well?"

"Well what, Ryan?"

"Out-of-town company?"

"A good detective always notices the obvious."

"Harriet Lamour," said my sister, sticking out her hand. "I'm Tempe's younger sister." As usual, she emphasized the birth order.

"Reckon you're not from around these parts," Ryan drawled. The fringe went to town as they shook hands.

"Lamour?" I asked, incredulous.

"Houston. That's in Texas. Ever been there?"

"Lamour?" I repeated. "What happened to Crone?"

"Once or twice. Mighty pretty country." Ryan was still doing Brett Maverick.

"Or Dawood?"

That got her attention.

"Now why would I ever go back to using that retard's name? Do you *remember* Esteban? The only human being ever fired for being too dumb to stock the 7-Eleven?"

Esteban Dawood had been her third husband. I couldn't summon an image of his face.

"Are you and Striker divorced already?"

"No. But I have dumped his ass and scrapped that ridiculous name. Crone? What was I thinking? Who'd ever choose a handle like Crone? What kinda name is that for your descendants? Missus Crone? Cousin Crone? Great-granddaddy Crone?"

Ryan joined in. "Not bad if you're a lone Crone."

Harry giggled. "Yeah, but I don't ever want to be an old Crone."

"That's it. We're outta here." I reached for my jacket.

"Bergeron says we've got a positive," said Ryan.

I stopped and looked at him. His face had gone serious.

"Simonnet?"

He nodded.

"Anything on the bodies from upstairs?"

"Bergeron thinks they're probably European, too. Or at least they got drilled and filled over there. Something about their dental work. We had Interpol run a search in Belgium, because of the Simonnet link, but they came up empty. The old lady had no family, so that's a dead end. The RCMP got no hits in Canada. Same for NCIC. No matches in the States."

"Rohypnol's pretty hard to get here, and those two were loaded. A European connection might explain that."

"Might."

"LaManche says the bodies in the outbuilding were negative for drugs and alcohol. Simonnet was too badly burned to test."

Ryan knew this. I was thinking aloud.

"Jesus, Ryan, it's been a week and we still have no idea who these people are."

"Yip." He smiled at Harry, who was listening closely. Their flirting was starting to annoy me.

"You haven't found any leads in the house?"

"You may have heard about a little altercation on the West Island Tuesday? The Rock Machine blew the lights out on two Hell's Angels. The Angels returned fire and left one of the Machine dead and three others bleeding bad. So I've been otherwise engaged."

"Patrice Simonnet took a bullet in the head."

"The biker boys also took out a twelve-year-old kid who happened to be on his way to hockey practice."

"Oh, God. Look, I'm not suggesting you're dragging your feet, but surely someone must miss these people. We're talking about a whole damn family. Plus two others. There must be *something* in that house that provides a clue."

"Recovery took forty-seven cartons of crap out of there. We're sifting through it, but so far zippo. No letters. No checks. No photos. No shopping lists. No address books. The utility and phone bills are paid by Simonnet. Heating oil is delivered once a year, she pays in advance. We can't find anyone who's been into the place since Simonnet's been renting."

"What about property taxes?"

"Guillion. Pays by an official check drawn on Citicorp in New York."

"Were any weapons recovered?" I asked.

"Nope."

"Pretty much rules out suicide."

"Yeah. And it isn't likely Granny slashed the family."

"Did you run a history on the address?"

"It was negative. The police were never called there."

"Have you gotten the phone records?"

"They're coming."

"What about the cars? Weren't they registered?"

"Both to Guillion. At the St-Jovite address. He also pays the insurance by official check."

"Does Simonette have a driver's license?"

"Yeah, Belgian. Clean record."

"Health insurance card?"

"No."

"Anything else?"

"Nothing comes up."

"Who serviced the cars?"

"Apparently Simonnet took them to a station in town. The description matches. She paid cash."

"And the house? A woman that age couldn't do her own repairs."

"Obviously there were other people living there. The neighbors say the couple with the babies had been around for several months. They'd seen other cars pull in, sometimes in large numbers."

"Maybe she took in boarders?"

We both turned to Harry.

"You know. Maybe she rented out rooms."

Ryan and I let her go on.

"You could check the newspapers for ads. Or church bulletins."

"She doesn't seem to have been a churchgoer."

"Maybe she ran a drug ring. With this dude Guillion. That's why she got killed. That's why there are no records or anything." Her eyes were round with excitement. She was getting into it. "Maybe she was hiding out there."

"Who is this Guillion?" I asked.

"He's got no police record here or there. The Belgian cops are checking him out. The guy kept to himself, so nobody knows much about him."

"Like the old lady."

Ryan and I stared at her. Good point, Harry.

A phone shrilled, indicating the lines had been switched to the night service. Ryan glanced at his watch.

"Well, I hope I'll see y'all this evening." Maverick was back.

"Probably not. I've got to get through this Nicolet report."

Harry opened her mouth, but seeing my look, closed it.

"Thanks anyway, Ryan."

"*Enchanté,*" he said to Harry, then turned and headed up the hall.

"That's one good-looking cowboy."

"Don't train your scope on him, Harry. His little black book has more entries than the Omaha white pages."

"Just lookin', darlin'. That's still free."

* * *

Though it was only five, we walked out into deep dusk. Headlights and streetlamps shone through falling snow. I unlocked and started the car, then spent several minutes cleaning the windows and windshield while Harry scanned the radio choices. When I got in, my usual Vermont Public Radio had been replaced by a local rock station.

"That is so cool." Harry voiced her approval of Mitsou.

"She's a québécoise," I said, shifting between drive and reverse to rock the Mazda out of the snow rut. "Been big here for years."

"I mean, rock and roll in French. That is too cool."

"Yeah." The front wheels caught pavement, and I joined the flow of traffic.

Harry listened to the lyrics as we wound our way west toward Centre-Ville.

"Is she singing about a cowboy? *Mon* cowboy?"

"Yes," I said, turning onto Viger. "I think she likes the guy."

We lost Mitsou when we entered the Ville-Marie Tunnel.

Ten minutes later I unlocked the door to my condo. I showed Harry the extra bedroom and went to the kitchen to check my food stock. Since I'd planned to hit the Atwater Market over the weekend, there wasn't much. When Harry joined me I was rummaging in the tiny closet I call a pantry.

"I'm taking you out to dinner, Tempe."

"You are?"

"Actually, Inner Life Empowerment is taking you to dinner. I told you. They're paying all my expenses. Well, at least up to twenty dollars for dinner tonight. Howie's Diners Club card will pick up the rest."

Howie was her second husband, and probably the source of whatever had been in the Nieman Marcus bags.

"Why is Inner Life whatever paying for this trip?"

"Because I did so well. Actually, it's a special deal." She gave an exaggerated wink, opening her mouth and scrunching the right side of her face. "They don't usually do that, but they really want me to go on with this."

"Well, if you're sure. What do you feel like?"

"Action!"

"I meant food."

"Anything but barbecue."

I thought a minute. "Indian?"

"Shawnee or Paiute?"

Harry hooted. She always loved her own jokes.

"The Etoile des Indes is just a few blocks from here. They make a great khorma."

"Yippee. I don't think I've ever eaten an Indian. And I know I've never eaten a French Indian. Anyway, I don't think you can eat karma."

I could only shake my head.

"I look like forty miles of bad road," said Harry, singling out several long strands for inspection. "I'm going to do a few repairs."

I went to my bedroom, changed into jeans, then got pen and paper and propped myself against the pillows on my bed. I opened the first ledger and noted the date of the earliest entry: January 1, 1844. Selecting one of the library books, I flipped to the section on Élisabeth Nicolet and checked the day of her birth. January 18, 1846. Her uncle had begun this volume two years before she was born.

Though Louis-Philippe Bélanger wrote with a strong hand, time had faded his entries. The ink was a dull brown, and at places the words were too blurry to read. In addition, the French was antiquated and replete with unfamiliar terms. After thirty minutes my head was pounding and I'd taken few notes.

I lay back and closed my eyes. I could still hear water running in the bathroom. I was tired and discouraged and pessimistic. I'd never get through this in two days. I'd do better to spend a few hours at the copy machine, then work through the ledgers at my leisure. Jeannotte hadn't said anything about *not* copying the material. And it was probably safer for the originals, I reasoned.

And I didn't have to find the answer right away. After all, my report didn't require an explanation. I saw what I saw in the bones. I would report my findings, and let the good sisters come to me with theorizations. Or questions.

Perhaps they wouldn't understand. Perhaps they wouldn't believe me. They probably wouldn't welcome the news. Or would they? Would it affect their application to the Vatican? I couldn't help that. I was certain I was right about Élisabeth. I just couldn't imagine what it meant.

TWO HOURS LATER HARRY SHOOK ME AWAKE. SHE HAD FINISHED bathing, blow drying, and whatever else the repair process required. We bundled up and headed out, winding our way to rue Ste-Catherine. The snow had stopped, but a layer blanketed everything, slightly muffling the city clamor. Signs, trees, mailboxes, and parked cars wore fluffy caps of white.

The restaurant was not crowded and we were seated immediately. When we'd ordered, I asked about her workshop.

"It's awesome. I've learned whole new ways of thinking and being. I don't mean some kinda Eastern mysticism cow flop. And I'm not talking about potions or crystals or that astral projection shit. I mean I am learning how to take control of my life."

"How?"

"How?"

"How."

"I'm learning self-identity, I'm undergoing empowerment through spiritual awakening. I'm gaining internal peace through holistic health and healing."

"Spiritual awakening?"

"Now don't get me wrong, Tempe. This isn't some rebirthing thing like the damn evangelists preach down home. There's none of that repenting, and making a joyful noise unto the Lord, and the righteous walking through flames and all."

"How is it different?"

"That all has to do with damnation, and guilt, and accepting your lot as a sinner, and turning yourself over to the Lord so He'll take care of you. I didn't buy that agenda from the nuns, and thirty-eight years of living haven't changed my mind."

Harry and I had spent our early days in Catholic schools.

"This has to do with me taking care of myself." She stabbed a manicured finger at her chest.

"How?"

"Tempe, are you trying to ridicule me?"

"No. I'd like to know how one does this."

"It's a matter of interpreting your own mind and body, then purifying yourself."

"Harry, you're just giving me jargon. How do you do this?"

"Well, you eat right and you breathe right and—did you notice that I passed up the beer? That's part of purifying."

"Did you pay a lot of money for this seminar?"

"I told you. They waived my fees and they flat out gave me the plane ticket."

"What about in Houston?"

"Well, yeah, of course I paid some fees. They have to charge something. These are very prominent people."

Just then our food arrived. I'd ordered lamb khorma. Harry had vegetable curry and rice.

"See?" She pointed to her dish. "No more dead carcasses for me. I am getting clear."

"Where did you find this course?"

"At the North Harris County Community College."

That sounded legit.

"When do you start here?"

"Tomorrow. The seminar goes for five days. I'll tell you all about, it, really I will. I'll come home every night and fill you in on exactly what we did. It's O.K. if I stay with you, isn't it?"

"Of course. I truly am glad to see you, Harry. And I'm very curious about what you're doing. But I'm leaving for Charlotte on Monday." I rummaged in the back pocket of my purse for the emergency keys I keep there, and handed them to her. "You're more than welcome to stay as long as you need the place."

"No wild parties," she said, leaning forward and pointing a stern finger at me. "I have a lady watching the house."

"Yes, Mom," I answered. The fictitious house watcher was perhaps our oldest family joke.

She gave me a brilliant Harry smile and slid the keys into her jeans pocket.

"Thanks. Now, enough about me, let me tell you what Kit's up to."

For the next half-hour we talked about my nephew's latest scheme. Christopher "Kit" Howard had resulted from her second marriage. He'd just turned eighteen, and come into a sizable sum of money from his father. Kit had bought, and was renovating, a forty-eight-foot sailboat. Harry was unsure as to why.

"Tell me again how Howie got his name?" I knew the story, but loved to hear her tell it.

"Howie's mama took off right after he was born, and his daddy had left well before then. She left Howie on the steps of an orphanage in Basic, Texas, with a note pinned to his blanket. It said she'd be back, and that the baby's name was Howard. The folks at the orphanage weren't sure if Mama meant his first name or his family name, so they took no chances. They baptized him Howard Howard."

"What's Howie doing now?"

"Still bringing in gushers and chasing every skirt in West Texas. But he's generous to me and Kit."

When we'd finished, the waiter cleared the dishes and I ordered coffee. Harry passed, because stimulants interfered with her purification process.

We sat in silence awhile, then,

"So where's this cowboy want you to meet him?"

I stopped stirring, and my mind scanned for a connection. Cowboy?

"The cop with the great ass."

"Ryan. He's going to a place called Hurley's. Today is St. Pat—"

"Hell, yes." Her face went serious. "I feel we owe it to our heritage to join in the recognition of a truly great patron saint, in whatever small way we can."

"Harry, I've had a long—"

"Tempe, but for St. Pat snakes would have eaten our ancestors and we would never have been."

"I'm not suggesting—"

"And right now, at a time when the Irish people are in such turmoil—"

"That's not the point and you know it."

"How far is Hurley's from here?"

"A few blocks."

"No-brainer." She spread her hands, palms up. "We go over, we listen to a few songs, we leave. We're not committing to a night at the opera."

"I've heard that before."

"No. I promise. As soon as you're ready, we're outta there. Hey, I've got an early morning, too."

That argument did not impress me. Harry is one of those people who can go days with no sleep.

"Tempe. You've got to make some effort at a social life."

That argument did.

"All right. But—"

"Hee. Haw. May the saints preserve ye, ye rascal."

As she waved for the check, I was already feeling the knot below my sternum. There was a time I loved Irish pubs. Pubs of any kind. I didn't want to open that scrapbook, and had no intention of making new entries.

Lighten up, Brennan. What are you afraid of? You've been to Hurley's and you didn't drown yourself in beer. True. So why the trepidation?

Harry chatted amiably as we walked back up Ste-Catherine to Crescent. At nine-thirty the sidewalk crowd was already thick, the couples and cruisers mingling with the last of the shoppers and sightseers. Everyone wore heavy coats with hats and mufflers. People looked thick and bulky, like shrubbery wrapped and tied for winter.

The portion of Crescent above Ste-Catherine is the Anglo "Street of Dreams," lined on both sides with singles bars and trendy restaurants. The Hard Rock Café. Thursdays. Sir Winston

Churchill's. In summer, the balconies are filled with spectators sipping drinks and watching the dance of romance below. In winter, the action moves inside.

Few but the Hurley's regulars frequent Crescent below Ste-Catherine. Except on St. Patrick's Day. When we arrived, the line from the entrance stretched up the steps and halfway to the corner.

"Oh hell, Harry. I don't want to stand out here freezing my butt." I didn't want to mention Ryan's offer.

"Don't you know anyone who works here?"

"I'm not a regular."

We joined the queue and stood in silence, shifting our feet to keep warm. The movement reminded me of the nuns at Lac Memphrémagog, which made me think of the unfinished Nicolet report. And the ledgers on my bedside table. And the report on the dead babies. And the classes I had to teach in Charlotte next week. And a paper I planned to present at the Physical Anthropology meeting. I felt my face grow numb from the cold. How did I let Harry talk me into these things?

There is little patron exodus from pubs at 10 P.M. After fifteen minutes we'd advanced about two feet.

"I feel like one of those flash-frozen deserts," said Harry. "Are you sure you don't know someone inside?"

"Ryan did say I could use his name if there was a wait." My egalitarian principles were being sorely tested by encroaching hypothermia.

"Big sister, what are you thinking?" Harry had no qualms about exploiting any available advantage.

She shot up the sidewalk and disappeared into the head of the line. Moments later I saw her at a side door, flanked by a particularly large representative of the Irish National Football Club. They were both gesturing to me. Avoiding eye contact with those remaining in line, I scurried down the steps and slipped inside.

I followed Harry and her guardian through the labyrinth of rooms that make up Hurley's Irish Pub. Every chair, ledge, table, bar stool, and square inch of floor was filled with green-clad patrons. Signs and mirrors advertised Bass, Guinness, and Kilkenny Cream Ale. The place smelled of beer, and the smoke was thick enough to rest your elbows on.

We wormed our way along stone walls, between tables, leather armchairs, and kegs, and eventually around an oak and brass bar. The sound level exceeded that permitted on airport runways.

As we rounded the main bar I could see Ryan seated on a tall wooden stool outside a back room. He had his back to a brick wall, one heel hooked on the stool's bottom rung. The other leg stretched across the seats of two empty stools to his right. His head was framed by a square opening in the brick bordered with carved green wood.

Through the opening I could see a trio playing fiddle, flute, and mandolin. Tables ringed the room's perimeter, and five dancers cavorted in an impossibly small space in the middle. Three women did passable jigs, but the young men just hopped from foot to foot, sloshing beer on anything within a five-foot radius. No one seemed to care.

Harry hugged the footballer, and he melted back into the crowd. I wondered how Ryan had managed to keep two stools free. And why. I couldn't decide whether his confidence annoyed or pleased me.

"Well, bless my heart," said Ryan when he spotted us. "Glad you could make it, podnas. Sit down and rest a spell." He had to yell to be heard.

Ryan hooked his free foot around one of the empty stools, pulled it out, and patted the cushion. Without hesitation Harry slipped off her jacket, draped it across the seat, and settled herself.

"On one condition," I yelled back.

He raised his eyebrows and focused the blues on me.

"Lose the wrangler routine."

"That's about as kind as gravel in peanut butter." Ryan spoke so loud the veins stood out in his neck.

"I mean it, Ryan." I'd never be able to keep up this volume.

"O.K. O.K. Sit down."

I moved toward the end stool.

"And I'll buy you a soda pop, ma'am."

Harry hooted.

I felt my mouth open, then Ryan was up and unzipping my jacket. He laid it on the stool and I sat.

Ryan flagged a waitress, ordered Guinness for himself and a Diet Coke for me. Again, I felt pique. Was I *that* predictable?

He looked at Harry.

"I'll have the same."

"Diet Coke?"

"No. The other."

The waitress disappeared.

"What about the purification?" I bellowed in Harry's ear.

"What?"

"The purification?"

"One beer won't poison me, Tempe. I'm not a zealot."

Since conversation required screaming, I focused on the band. I grew up with Irish music, and the old songs always summon childhood memories. My grandmother's house. Old ladies, brogue, canasta. The roll-away bed. Danny Kaye on the black-and-white TV. Falling asleep to John Gary L.P.'s. I suspected these musicians were a bit loud for Gran's taste. Too much amplification.

The lead singer began a ballad about a wild rover. I knew the song and braced myself. At the chorus hands slammed in a five-strike staccato. Bam! Bam! Bam! Bam! Bam! The waitress arrived at the last pounding.

Harry and Ryan chatted, their words lost to the din. I sipped my drink and looked around. High on the wall I could see a row of carved wooden shields, totems of the old-line families. Or were they clans? I looked for one named Brennan, but it was too dark and smoky to read most of them. Crone? No.

The group began a tune Gran would have liked. It was about a young woman who wore her hair tied up with a black velvet band.

I studied a series of photographs in oblong oval frames, close-up portraits of men and women in their Sunday best. When had they been taken—1890? 1910? These faces looked as grim as those in Birks Hall. Maybe the high collars were uncomfortable.

Two schoolhouse clocks gave the time in Dublin and Montreal. Ten-thirty. I checked my watch. Yip.

Several songs later Harry got my attention by waving both arms. She looked like a referee signaling an incomplete pass. Ryan was holding up his empty mug.

I shook my head. He spoke to Harry, then raised two fingers above his head.

Here we go, I thought.

As the band began a reel, I noticed Ryan pointing in the direction from which we'd entered. Harry slid off her stool and disappeared into the mass of bodies. The price of tight jeans. I didn't want to think about how long her wait would be. Just another gender inequality.

Ryan lifted Harry's jacket, slid onto her stool, and placed the jacket where he'd been sitting. He leaned close and shouted in my ear.

"Are you sure you two have the same mother?"

"And father." Ryan smelled of something like rum and talcum powder.

"How long has she lived in Texas?"

"Since Moses led the Exodus."

"Moses Malone?"

"Nineteen years." I swirled and stared at the ice in my Coke. Ryan had every right to talk to Harry. Conversation was impossible anyway, so why was I pissed off?

"Who is this Anna Goyette?"

"What?"

"Who is Anna Goyette?"

The band stopped in midsentence, and the name boomed out in the relative quiet.

"Jesus, Ryan, why don't you take out an ad?"

"We're a little jumpy tonight. Too much caffeine?" He grinned.

I glared at him.

"It's not good at your age."

"It's not good at any age. How do you know about Anna Goyette?"

The waitress brought the drinks and showed Ryan as many teeth as my sister at her friendliest. He paid and winked at her. Spare me.

"You're not exactly poetry to be with," he said after placing one of the beers on the ledge above Harry's jacket.

"I'll work on it. How do you know about Anna Goyette?"

"I ran into Claudel on this biker thing, and we talked about it."

"Why in the world would you do that?"

"He asked me."

I could never figure out Claudel. He blows me off, then discusses my phone call with Ryan.

"So who is she?"

"Anna is a McGill student. Her aunt asked me to locate her. It's not the Hoffa case."

"Claudel says she's a very interesting young lady."

"What the hell does that mean?"

Harry chose that moment to rejoin us.

"Whoa, little buckaroos. If you have to pee you'd better plan ahead."

She took in the altered seating arrangement and slid onto the stool to Ryan's left. As if on cue the band began singing about whiskey in a jug. Harry swayed and clapped along until a geezer in a checkered cap and green suspenders jigged over and took her by the hand. She jumped up and followed him to the back room, where two young men were once again doing egret imitations. Harry's partner had a substantial belly and a soft, round face. I hoped she wouldn't kill the guy.

I looked at my watch. Eleven-forty. My eyes burned from smoke and my throat was scratchy from shouting.

And I was enjoying myself.

And I wanted a drink.

Seriously.

"Look, I've got a headache. As soon as Ginger Rogers gets off the dance floor I'm going to cut out."

"Suit yourself, bucko. You've done very well for your first session."

"Jesus, Ryan. I've been here before."

"For the storyteller?"

"No!" I had thought about that. I love Irish folklore.

I watched Harry hop and twist, her long blond hair flying. Everyone watched her. After a while I shouted in Ryan's ear.

"Does Claudel know where Anna is?"

He shook his head.

I gave up. The potential for conversation was zero.

Harry and the geezer danced on. His face was red and covered with sweat, and his clip-on tie hung at an odd angle. When Harry's jig brought her round to face me I pantomimed a finger across the throat. Cut. Wrap.

She waved gaily.

I jabbed my thumb toward the exit, but she'd already rotated out of eye contact.

Oh, God.

Ryan watched me, an amused smile on his face.

I gave him a look that could freeze El Niño, and he slouched back and held both hands in a palms-out gesture.

The next time Harry circled toward me I gestured again, but she was staring at something over my shoulder, an odd look on her face.

At twelve-fifteen my prayers were answered as the band took a break. Harry returned, flushed but beaming. Her partner looked like he needed a resuscitator.

"Whew! I feel rode hard and put away wet."

She ran a finger around her collar, hopped onto her stool, and chugged the beer Ryan had ordered. When the geezer made a move to settle next to her, she patted him on his cap.

"Thanks, big guy. I'll see y'all later."

He tipped his head and gave her a puppy look.

"Bye-bye."

Harry wriggled her fingers, and the geezer shrugged and blended back into the crowd.

Harry leaned across Ryan. "Tempe, who's that over there?" She tipped her head toward the bar behind us.

I started to turn.

"Don't look now!"

"What?"

"The tall skinny dude with the glasses."

I rolled my eyes, which didn't help my headache. Harry would use this routine in junior high when I wanted to leave and she wanted to stay.

"I know. He's cute and he's really interested in me. Only he's shy. Been there, done that, Harry."

The band started another reel. I stood and put on my jacket.

"Bedtime."

"No. Really. This guy was scoping you the whole time I was dancing. I could see him through the window."

I looked in the direction she'd indicated. No one fit her description.

"Where?"

She scanned the faces around the bar, then looked over her shoulder in the other direction.

"Really, Tempe." She shrugged. "I can't spot him now."

"He's probably one of my students. They're always amazed to see me out without a walker."

"Yeah, I guess. The guy looked pretty young for you."

"Thanks."

Ryan watched like Gramps observing the young 'uns.

"Are you ready?" I buttoned my jacket and pulled on my mittens.

Harry looked at her Rolex, then said exactly what I expected.

"It's just past midnight. Couldn't we—"

"I'm heading out, Harry. The condo's only four blocks from here and you've got a key. You can stay if you want."

For a moment she looked undecided, then she turned to Ryan.

"Are you going to be here awhile?"

"No problema, kiddo."

She gave me the same puppy look the geezer had used.

"You're sure you don't mind?"

"Of course not." Like hell.

I explained the keys and she gave me a hug.

"Let me walk you back," said Ryan, reaching for his jacket. My protector.

"No, thanks. I'm a big girl."

"Then let me call a taxi for you."

"Ryan, I am allowed to travel unaccompanied."

"Suit yourself." He settled back, shaking his head.

The cold air felt good after the heat and smoke of the pub. For about a millisecond. The temperature had dropped and the wind had picked up, plunging the chill factor to a billion degrees below zero.

Within steps my eyes were tearing and I could feel ice forming around the edges of my nostrils. I drew my muffler across my mouth and nose, and tied it in a big knot at the back of my head. I looked like a geek, but at least my orifices wouldn't freeze over.

I stuffed my hands deep into my pockets, lowered my head, and trudged on. Warmer, but barely able to see, I angled across Crescent and up to Ste-Catherine. There wasn't a soul in sight.

I'd just crossed MacKay when I felt my scarf tighten, and my feet go out from under me. At first I thought I'd slipped on ice but then I realized I was being pulled backward. I had passed the old York Theater and I was being dragged toward the side of the building. Hands spun me and shoved me face first against the wall. My own were still trapped in my pockets. As my face struck the brick I slid downward. When my knees hit the ground, I was shoved facedown into the snow. A heavy blow struck my back, as though a large person had dropped knees first onto my thoracic spine. Pain shot down my back and my breath exploded outward through my muffler. I was pinned to the ground in a prone position. I couldn't see, I couldn't move, and I couldn't breathe! I felt panic and air hunger. Blood pounded in my ears.

I closed my eyes and concentrated on turning my mouth to the side. I pulled a shallow breath. Then another. And another. The burning subsided and I began to exchange air.

I felt pain in my jaw and face. My head was locked at an awkward angle, my right eye pressed against the frozen snow. I felt a bulkiness below me and knew it was my purse. It had helped knock the wind out of me.

Give him the purse!

I wriggled to free myself, but my jacket and scarf still bound me like a straitjacket. I felt his body move. He seemed to stretch out on top of me. Then his breathing in my ear. Though muffled by the scarf, it sounded heavy and rapid, desperate, animal-like in its intensity.

Don't lose consciousness. Unconscious means dead in this weather. Move! Do something!

Under my heavy clothing I was covered in sweat. I inched my hand around inside my pocket, searching. My fingers felt slick inside the wool mitten.

There!

I gripped my keys. The instant he let up I'd be ready. Helpless, I waited for an opening.

"Leave it alone," a voice hissed in my ear.

He'd spotted the movement!

I froze.

"You don't know what you're doing. Back off!"

Back off what? Who did he think I was?

"Leave it alone," he repeated, his voice trembling with emotion.

I couldn't speak, and he didn't seem to expect an answer. Was it a madman and not a mugger?

We lay there for what seemed eternity. Cars whooshed past. I'd lost all feeling in my face, and my neck vertebrae felt as if they would crack. I breathed with my mouth open, saliva freezing on my muffler.

Stay calm. Think!

My mind raced through possibilities. Was he drunk? Stoned? Undecided? Was he savoring some sick fantasy that would trigger him to action? My heart pounded so loud I feared it would be the catalyst.

Then I heard footsteps. He must have heard them, too, for he tightened his grip on my scarf and placed a gloved hand over my face.

Scream! Do something!

I couldn't see him and it made me crazy.

"Get off me you goddamn dirtbag!" I yelled through my muffler.

But my voice came from a million miles away, smothered by the thick layer of wool.

I held the keys in a death grip, my hand slippery inside the mitten and tensed to drive them into his eye if I got an opening. Suddenly, I felt the scarf tighten and his body shift. He rose to his knees again, concentrating all of his weight in the center of my back. His weight and my purse compressed my lungs, making me gasp for air.

Using the scarf he lifted my head, then drove it down with his hand. My ear slammed into ice and gravel, and a cloud of sparks burst behind my eyes. He lifted and slammed down again and the sparks began to coalesce. I could feel blood on my face and taste it in my mouth. I thought I felt something snap in my neck. My heart thundered inside my rib cage.

Get off me you demented piece of shit!

I felt light-headed. My tortured brain foresaw the autopsy report. *My* autopsy. *Nothing under her nails. No defense wounds.*

Don't pass out!

I squirmed and tried to scream, but again my voice was barely audible.

Suddenly, the pounding stopped and my attacker leaned close

again. He spoke, but I caught only garbled sounds through the ringing in my ears.

Then I felt his hands press against my back and his weight lifted. Boots crunched on gravel, and he was gone.

Dazed, I pulled my hands free, pushed myself to all fours, and rolled to a seated position. A wave of dizziness washed over me, and I raised my knees and lowered my head between them. My nose was running and either blood or saliva was oozing from my mouth. My hands trembled as I wiped my face with the end of my muffler, and I knew I was a hair away from tears.

Wind rattled the broken windows in the abandoned theater. What was the name? Yale? York? It seemed terribly important. I knew it before, so why couldn't I remember it now? I felt disoriented, and began shivering uncontrollably, from cold, from fear, and perhaps from relief.

When the dizziness passed I rose, inched my way along the building, and peeked around the corner. There was no one in sight.

I stumbled home on rubbery legs, looking over my shoulder every other step. The few pedestrians I passed looked away and gave me a wide berth. Just another drunk.

Ten minutes later I sat on the edge of my bed, checking myself for injuries. My pupils were even and coordinated. No numbness. No nausea.

The scarf had been a mixed blessing. While it provided my attacker a convenient handle, it had also cushioned the blows. I had a few cuts and abrasions on the right side of my head, but I believed I had not sustained a concussion.

Not bad for a mugging survivor, I thought as I slipped between the sheets. But had it been a mugging? The guy hadn't stolen anything. Why did he run? Did he panic and give up? Was he just a drunk? Did he figure out I wasn't who he thought I was? Subzero cold rarely inspires sexual assaults. What was his motive?

I tried to sleep but my mind was still on an adrenaline high. Or was it post-traumatic stress syndrome? My hands still shook and I jumped at every sound.

Should I call the cops? What for? I wasn't hurt much and nothing was stolen. And I never got a look at the guy. Should I tell Ryan? Not a chance in hell after my cocky departure. Harry? No way.

Oh, God. What if Harry walks home alone? Could he still be out there?

I rolled over and looked at the clock. Two thirty-seven. Where the hell was Harry?

I touched my broken lip. Would she notice? Probably. Harry had instincts like a wildcat. She missed nothing. I thought of cover stories. Doors are always good, or face-first falls on the ice while your hands are deep in your pockets.

My eyes drifted shut, then flew open as I felt the knee on my back and heard the rasping breath.

I checked the clock again. Three-fifteen. Did Hurley's stay open this late? Had Harry gone home with Ryan?

"Where are you, Harry?" I said to the glowing green digits.

I lay there, wishing she'd come home, not wanting to be alone.

I WOKE TO BRIGHT SUNLIGHT AND TOTAL SILENCE, HAVING SLEPT fitfully. My brain cells had called an all-night meeting to organize input from the past few days. Missing students. Muggers. Saints. Murdered babies and grandmas. Harry. Ryan. Harry and Ryan. They broke around dawn, having accomplished little.

I rolled over on my back and a burst of pain in my neck reminded me of last night's adventure. I flexed and extended my neck and each arm and leg. Pretty good. In the morning light the attack seemed illogical and imaginary. But the memory of fear was very real.

I lay still for a while, exploring for damage to my face and listening for signs of my sister. Tender areas on the face. No noise from the sister.

At seven-forty I hauled myself out of bed and grabbed my ratty old robe and slippers. The guest room door was open, the bed made. Had Harry been home last night?

I found a Post-it on the refrigerator explaining the absence of two cartons of yogurt and saying she'd be back after seven. O.K. She'd come in, but had she slept here?

"Who cares," I said, reaching for the coffee beans.

Just then the phone rang.

I slammed down the canister and padded to the living room phone.

"Yeah."

"Hey, Mom. Rough night?"

"Sorry, honey. What's up?"

"Are you going to be in Charlotte the week after next?"

"I get in Monday and I'll be there until early April, when I go to the Physical Anthropology meetings in Oakland. Why?"

"Well, I thought I'd come home for a few days. This beach trip isn't working out."

"Great. I mean, great that we can spend some time together. Sorry your trip went bust." I didn't ask why. "Will you be staying with me or with Dad?"

"Yes."

"O.K. O.K. Classes going all right?"

"Yeah. I'm really enjoying the abnormal psych. The prof is so cool. And criminology's pretty good, too. We never have to turn anything in on time."

"Hm. How's Aubrey?"

"Who?"

"Guess that answers my question. How's the zit?"

"Gone."

"Why are you up so early on a Saturday?"

"I've got to write a paper for my crim class. I'm going to do something on profiling, maybe bring in stuff from abnormal psych."

"I thought you never had to hand anything in on time."

"It was due two weeks ago."

"Oh."

"Can you help me think of a project for my anthro class?"

"Sure."

"Nothing too elaborate. It's supposed to be something I can do in one day."

I heard a beep.

"I've got another call, Katy. I'll think about the project. Let me know when you're arriving in Charlotte."

"Will do."

I clicked over and was amazed to hear Claudel's voice.

"Claudel *ici.*"

As usual there was no greeting, and he did not apologize for phoning me on Saturday morning. He dove straight to the point.

"Has Anna Goyette returned home?"

My chest went hollow. Claudel had never called me at home. Anna must be dead.

I swallowed and answered. "I don't think so."

"She is nineteen."

"Yes."

I saw Sister Julienne's face. I couldn't bear to think of telling her.

"*. . . caractéristiques physiques?*"

"I'm sorry. What was that?"

Claudel repeated the question. I had no idea if Anna had any unusual physical features.

"I don't know. I'd have to ask the family."

"When was she last seen?"

"Thursday. Monsieur Claudel, why are you asking me these questions?"

I waited out a Claudel pause. I could hear commotion in the background and guessed he was calling from the homicide squad room.

"A white female was found early this morning, naked, with no identification."

"Where?" The hollow feeling pushed against my sternum.

"Île des Sœurs. At the back of the island there is a wooded area and a pond. The body was found"—he hesitated—"on the water's edge."

"Found how?" He was holding back.

Claudel considered my question for a moment. I could picture his beak nose, his close-set eyes narrowed in thought.

"The victim was murdered. The circumstances are . . ." Again the hesitation. ". . . unusual."

"Tell me." I shifted the phone to my other hand and wiped my palm on my robe.

"The body was found in an old steamer trunk. There were multiple injuries. LaManche is doing the autopsy today."

"What kinds of injuries?" I stared at a pattern of spots on my robe.

He took a deep breath. "There are multiple stab wounds and ligature marks around the wrists. LaManche suspects there has also been an animal attack."

I found Claudel's habit of depersonalizing annoying. A white female. The victim. The body. The wrists. Not even a personal pronoun.

"And the victim may have been burned," he continued.

"Burned?"

"LaManche will know more later. He is going to do the post today."

"Jesus." Though one pathologist from the lab is on call at all times, rarely is an autopsy carried out on a weekend. I knew the murder had to be extraordinary. "How long has she been dead?"

"The body wasn't fully frozen, so it was probably outside less than twelve hours. LaManche will try to narrow the time of death."

I didn't want to ask the next question.

"Why do you think it could be Anna Goyette?"

"The age and description fit."

I felt a little weak.

"What physical characteristic were you referring to?"

"The victim has no lower molars."

"Were they extracted?" I felt stupid as soon as the question was out.

"Dr. Brennan, I am not a dentist. There is also a small tattoo on the right hip. Two figures holding a heart between them."

"I'll call Anna's aunt and get back to you."

"I can—"

"No. I'll do it. I have something else to discuss with her."

He gave me his beeper number and hung up.

My hand trembled as I punched the digits for the convent. I saw frightened eyes gazing from below blonde bangs.

Before I could think of how to frame my questions, Sister Julienne was on the line. I spent several minutes thanking her for sending me to Daisy Jeannotte, and telling her about the journals. I was evading what I had to do, and she saw right through me.

"I know something bad has happened." Her voice was soft, but I could hear tension just below the surface.

I asked if Anna had turned up. She had not.

"Sister, a young woman has been found—"

I heard the swish of fabric and knew she was crossing herself.

"I need to ask a few personal questions about your niece."

"Yes." Barely audible.

I asked about the molars and tattoo.

The line was quiet only a second, then I was surprised to hear her laugh.

"Oh my, no, no, that isn't Anna. Oh heavens, no, she'd never allow herself to be tattooed. And I'm certain Anna has all of her teeth. In fact she often mentions her teeth. That's how I know. She has a lot of trouble with them, complains about pain when she eats something cold. Or hot."

The words flew in such a torrent I could almost feel her relief rush across the line.

"But, Sister, it's possible—"

"No. I know my niece. She has all of her teeth. She isn't happy with them, but she has them." Again the nervous laugh. "And no tattoos, thank the Lord."

"I'm glad to hear that. This young woman is probably not Anna, but perhaps it would be best to have your niece's dental records sent over, just to be sure."

"I am sure."

"Yes. Well, perhaps to assure Detective Claudel. It can't hurt."

"I suppose. And I will pray for that poor girl's family."

She gave me the name of Anna's dentist and I called Claudel back.

"She's sure Anna didn't have a tattoo."

"Hi, Auntie nun! Guess what? I had my ass tattooed last week!"

"I agree. Not likely."

He snorted.

"But she's absolutely certain Anna has all of her teeth. She remembers her niece complaining about toothaches."

"Who has extractions?"

My thought precisely.

"It's usually not people with happy teeth."

"Yes."

"And this aunt also believes Anna never went off without telling her mother, right?"

"That's what she said."

"Anna Goyette has a better act than David Copperfield. She disappeared seven times in the last eighteen months. At least that's how many reports the mother filed."

"Oh." The hollowness spread from my breastbone to the pit of my stomach.

I asked Claudel to keep me informed, and hung up. I doubted he would.

I was showered, dressed, and in my office by nine-thirty. I finished my report on Élisabeth Nicolet, describing and explaining my observations, just as I would with any forensic case. I wished I could have included information from the Bélanger journals, but there just hadn't been time to go through them.

After printing the report, I spent three hours photographing. I was tense and clumsy, and had trouble positioning the bones. At two I grabbed a sandwich from the cafeteria, and ate it as I proofed my findings on Mathias and Malachy. But my mind was focused on the phone and wouldn't concentrate on the work at hand.

I was at the copy machine with the Bélanger journals when I looked up to see Claudel.

"It is not your young lady."

I stared into his eyes. "Really?"

He nodded.

"Who is she?" I asked.

"Her name was Carole Comptois. When the dentals excluded Goyette we ran the prints and got a hit. There were a couple of arrests for soliciting."

"Age?"

"Eighteen."

"How did she die?"

"LaManche is finishing the post now."

"Any suspects?"

"Many." He stared at my face a moment, said nothing, and left.

I continued photocopying, a robot with emotions swirling inside. The relief I'd felt at learning it wasn't Anna had immediately turned to guilt. There was still a girl on a table downstairs. A family to be told.

Lift the cover. Turn the page. Lower the cover. Push the button. Eighteen.

I had no desire to see the autopsy.

* * *

At four-thirty I finished with the journals and returned to my office. I dropped the babies' reports in the secretarial office then left a note on LaManche's desk explaining about the photocopies. When I reentered the corridor LaManche and Bergeron stood talking outside the dentist's office. Both men looked tired and grim. As I approached they took in my face, but didn't inquire.

"Bad one?" I asked.

LaManche nodded.

"What happened to her?"

"What didn't," said Bergeron.

I shifted my gaze from one to the other. Even stooped the dentist was over six feet tall, and I had to look up to meet his eyes. His white frizz was backlit by a fluorescent ceiling light. I remembered Claudel's comment about an animal attack and suspected why Bergeron's Saturday had also been spoiled.

"It looks like she was hung by her wrists and beaten, then attacked by dogs," said LaManche. "Marc thinks there were at least two."

Bergeron nodded. "One of the larger breeds. Maybe shepherds or Dobermans. There are over sixty bite wounds."

"Jesus."

"A boiling liquid, probably water, was poured on her while she was naked. Her skin is badly scalded, but I couldn't find traces of anything identifiable," LaManche continued.

"She was still alive?" My gut recoiled at the thought of her pain.

"Yes. She finally died as a result of multiple stab wounds to the chest and abdomen. Do you want to see the Polaroids?"

I shook my head.

"Were there defense wounds?" I recalled my own ordeal with the mugger.

"No."

"When did she die?"

"Probably late yesterday."

I didn't want to know the details.

"One other thing." LaManche's eyes were full of sadness. "She was four months pregnant."

I moved past them quickly and slipped into my office. I don't know how long I sat there, my eyes moving over the familiar objects of my trade, not seeing them. Though I had some emotional immunity, inoculated by years of exposure to cruelty and violence, some deaths still broke through. The recent onslaught of horrors seemed uglier than most I could remember. Or were my circuits simply overloaded to the point that I could not absorb more heinousness?

Carole Comptois was not my case, and I'd never laid eyes on her, but I couldn't control the visions surfacing from the darkest depths of my mind. I saw her in her last moments, her face contorted in pain and terror. Did she beg for her life? For her unborn baby? What kind of monsters were afoot in the world?

"Damn it to hell!" I said to the empty office.

I shoved my papers into my briefcase, grabbed my gear, and slammed the door behind me. Bergeron said something as I passed his office, but I didn't stop.

The six o'clock news began as I drove under the Jacques Cartier Bridge, the Comptois murder the lead story. I jammed the button, repeating my last thought.

"Damn it to hell!"

By the time I got home my anger had cooled. Some emotions are too intense to persist without ebbing. I phoned Sister Julienne and assured her about Anna. Claudel had already called, but I wanted to make personal contact. She will turn up, I said. Yes, she agreed. Neither of us fully believed it anymore.

I told her Élisabeth's skeleton was packed and ready, and that the report was being typed. She said the bones would be picked up first thing Monday morning.

"Thank you so much, Dr. Brennan. We await your report with great anticipation."

I did not avail myself of the opening. I had no idea how they'd react to what I'd written.

I changed to jeans, then prepared dinner, refusing to allow myself to think about what had been done to Carole Comptois. Harry arrived at half past seven and we ate, commenting on little but the pasta and zucchini. She seemed tired and distracted, and willing to accept my explanation of having fallen face forward on the ice. I was completely drained by the day's events. I didn't ask about the night before, or about the seminar, and she didn't offer. I think we both were glad to neither listen nor respond.

After dinner Harry read her workshop material and I started with the diaries again. My report to the sisters was complete, but I wanted to know more. The photocopying had not improved the technical quality, and I found it just as discouraging as I had on Friday. Besides, Louis-Philippe was not the most exciting chronicler. A young medical doctor, he wrote long accounts of his days at the Hôtel Dieu Hospital. In forty pages I came across only a few references to his sister. It seemed he was concerned about Eugénie continuing to sing in public after her marriage to Alain Nicolet. He also disliked her hairdresser. Louis-Philippe sounded like a real prig.

Sunday Harry was gone again before I got up. I did laundry, worked out at the gym, and updated a lecture I planned to give in my human evolution class on Tuesday. By late afternoon I felt reasonably caught up. I lit a fire, made myself a cup of Earl Grey, and curled up on the couch with my books and papers.

I started where I'd left off in the Bélanger diary, but after about twenty pages I shifted to the smallpox book. It was as fascinating as Louis-Philippe was dull.

I read about the streets I walk every day. Montreal and its surrounding villages had over two hundred thousand inhabitants in the eighteen-eighties. The city stretched from Sherbrooke Street on the north to the port along the river on the south. To the east it was bounded by the industrial town of Hochelaga, and to the west by the working-class villages of Ste-Cunégonde and St-Henri, which lay just above the Lachine Canal. Last summer I'd pedaled the length of the canal bike path.

Then, as now, there was tension. Though most of Montreal west of rue St-Laurent was English-speaking, by the eighteen-eighties the French had become a clear majority in the city as a whole. They dominated municipal politics, but the English ruled in commerce and in the press.

The French and Irish were Catholic, the English, Protestant. The groups remained largely separate, both in life and in death. Each had its own cemetery high on the mountain.

I closed my eyes and thought about that. Even today language and religion determined so much in Montreal. The Catholic schools. The Protestant schools. The Nationalists. The Federalists. I wondered where Élisabeth Nicolet's loyalties would lie.

The room dimmed and the lamps clicked to life. I read on.

In the late nineteenth century Montreal was a major commercial hub, boasting a magnificent harbor, huge stone warehouses, tanneries, soapworks, factories. McGill was already a leading university. But, like other Victorian cities, it was a place of contrasts, with the huge mansions of the merchant princes overshadowing the hovels of the working poor. Just off the wide, paved avenues, beyond Sherbrooke and Dorchester, lay hundreds of dirt lanes and unpaved alleys.

The city then was poorly drained, with garbage and animal carcasses rotting in vacant lots, and excrement everywhere. The river was used as an open sewer. Though frozen in winter, the offal and refuse rotted and reeked in the warmer months. Everyone complained of the foul odors.

My tea had grown cold so I uncurled, stretched, and made a fresh cup. When I reopened the book, I skipped ahead to a section on sanitation. It had been one of Louis-Philippe's recurring gripes about the Hôtel Dieu Hospital. Sure enough, there was a reference to the old boy. He'd gone on to become a member of the Health Committee of the City Council.

I read an engrossing account of the council discussing human waste. Disposal was chaotic at the time. Some Montrealers flushed excrement into city sewers that led into the river. Some used earth closets, sprinkling dirt over their deposits then putting them out for garbage collectors. Others defecated into outdoor privy pits.

The city's medical officer reported that inhabitants produced approximately 170 tons of excrement each day, or over 215,000 tons per year. He warned that the 10,000 privy pits and cesspools in the city were the primary source of zymotic diseases, including typhoid, scarlet fever, and diphtheria. The council decided in favor of a system of collection and incineration. Louis-Philippe voted yea. It was January 28, 1885.

The day after the vote, Grand Trunk Railway's western train pulled into Bonaventure Station. A conductor was ill and the railroad's doctor was called. The man was examined and diagnosed as having smallpox. Being Protestant, he was taken to the Montreal General Hospital, but was refused admission. The patient was allowed to wait in an isolated room in the contagious diseases wing. Finally, at the railroad doctor's pleading, he was grudgingly admitted to the Catholic Hôtel Dieu Hospital.

I got up to stoke the fire. As I rearranged the logs I pictured the rambling, gray-stone building that stood at avenue des Pins and rue St-Urbain. The Hôtel Dieu was still a functioning hospital. I'd driven past it many times.

I went back to the book. My stomach was growling, but I wanted to read until Harry arrived.

The doctors at the Montreal General thought those at the Hôtel Dieu had reported the smallpox to public health authorities. Those at the Hôtel Dieu thought the converse. No one told the authorities, and no one told the medical staff at either hospital. By the time the epidemic ended, over three thousand people were dead, most of them children.

I closed the book. My eyes were burning and my temples throbbed. The clock said seven-fifteen. Where was Harry?

I went to the kitchen, took out and rinsed the salmon steaks. As I mixed dill sauce I tried to picture my neighborhood a century earlier. How did one face smallpox in those days? To what home remedies did one turn? Over two thirds of the dead were children. What was it like to see your neighbors' children die? How did one deal with the helplessness of caring for a doomed child?

I scrubbed two potatoes and put them in the toaster oven, then washed lettuce, tomatoes, and cucumbers. Still no Harry.

Though the reading had taken my mind off Mathias and Malachy and Carole Comptois, I was still tense and my head hurt. I ran a hot bath and added aromatherapy ocean mineral salts. Then I put on a Leonard Cohen CD and slipped in for a long soak.

I used Élisabeth to keep my mind off my recent homicide cases. The trip through history had been fascinating, but I hadn't learned what I needed to know. I was already familiar with Élisabeth's work during the epidemic through the volumes of information Sister Julienne had sent before the exhumation.

Élisabeth had been a recluse for years, but when the epidemic raged out of control she became an advocate for medical modernization. She wrote letters to the Provincial Board of Health, to the Health Committee of the City Council, and to Honoré Beaugrand, mayor of Montreal, begging for improved sanitation. She bombarded the French- and English-language papers, demanding the reopening of the city smallpox hospital and arguing for public vaccination.

She wrote to her bishop, pointing out that the fever was spread in places where crowds gathered, and begging him to temporarily close the churches. Bishop Fabre refused, stating that to close the churches would be to laugh at God. The bishop urged his flock to church, telling them that united prayer was more powerful than prayer in isolation.

Good thinking, Bishop. That's why French Catholics were dying and English Protestants were not. The heathens got inoculated and stayed home.

I added hot water, imagining Élisabeth's frustration and how much tact I would have used.

O.K. I knew about her work, and I knew about her death. The nuns had gone to town on that. I'd read reams on her final illness and the public funeral that followed.

But I needed to know about her birth.

I took the soap and worked up a lather.

There was no avoiding the journals.

I ran the bar over my shoulders.

But I had the photocopies, so that could wait until I got to Charlotte.

I washed my feet.

Newspapers. That had been Jeannotte's suggestion. Yes. I'd use the time I had on Monday to view old newspapers. I had to go to McGill anyway to return the diaries.

I slid back into the hot water and thought about my sister. Poor Harry. I'd pretty much ignored her yesterday. I'd been tired, but was that it? Or was it Ryan? She had every right to sleep with him if she wanted. So why had I been so cold? I resolved to be more friendly tonight.

* * *

I was toweling off when I heard the beep of the security alarm. I dug out a flannel Disney nightshirt Harry had given me one Christmas, and pulled it over my head.

I found her standing in the living room, still wearing her jacket, gloves, and hat, her eyes fixed on something a million miles away.

"Long day, I'd say."

"Yeah." She refocused on the present, and gave me a half smile.

"Hungry?"

"I guess. Just let me have a few minutes." She threw her pack onto the couch and flopped down beside it.

"Sure. Take your coat off and stay awhile."

"Right. Damn, it gets cold here. I feel like a Popsicle just walking from the metro."

A few minutes later I heard her in the guest room, then she joined me in the kitchen. I grilled the salmon and tossed the salad while she set the table.

When we sat down to eat I asked about her day.

"It was fine." She cut her potato, squeezed it, and added sour cream.

"Fine?" I encouraged.

"Yeah. We covered a lot."

"You look like you covered forty miles of bad road."

"Yeah. I'm pretty beat." She didn't smile at my use of her expression.

"So what did you do?"

"Lots of lectures, exercises." She spooned sauce onto her fish. "What are these little green threads?"

"Dill. What kinds of exercises?"

"Meditation. Games."

"Games?"

"Storytelling. Calisthenics. Whatever they tell us to do."

"You just do whatever they say?"

"I do it because I choose to do it," she snapped.

I was taken aback. Harry rarely barked at me like that.

"Sorry. I'm just tired."

For a while we ate in silence. I didn't really want to hear about her touchy-feely therapy, but after a few minutes I tried again.

"How many people are there?"

"Quite a few."

"Are they interesting?"

"I'm not doing this to make new friends, Tempe. I'm learning to be accountable. To be responsible. My life sucks, and I'm trying to figure out how to make it work."

She stabbed at her salad. I couldn't remember when I'd seen her so down.

"And these exercises help?"

"Tempe, you just have to try it for yourself. I can't tell you exactly what we do or how it works."

She scraped off the dill sauce and picked at her salmon.

I said nothing.

"I don't think you'd get it anyway. You're too frozen."

She picked up her plate and carried it to the kitchen. So much for my resolve to be interested.

I joined her at the sink.

"I think I'm just going to turn in," she said, laying a hand on my shoulder. "I'll talk to you tomorrow."

"I'm leaving in the afternoon."

"Oh. I'll call you."

In bed, I replayed the conversation. I'd never seen Harry so listless, or so snappish when approached. She must have been exhausted. Or maybe it was the thing with Ryan. Or her breakup with Striker.

Later, I'd wonder why I hadn't seen the signs. It might have changed so much.

ON MONDAY I GOT UP AT DAWN, PLANNING TO MAKE BREAKFAST for Harry and myself. She declined, saying it was a fast day. She left before seven, wearing sweats and no makeup, a sight I had never expected to experience.

There are records identifying the coldest spot on earth, the driest, the lowest. The gloomiest is without doubt the serials and microform department of McGill's McLennan Library. It is a long narrow room on the second floor done in poured cement and fluorescent lighting, set off smartly by a bloodred floor.

Following the librarian's instructions, I worked my way past the stacks of serials and newspapers to rows of metal shelves holding tiny cardboard boxes and round metal tins. I found the ones I wanted and took them to the reading room. Deciding to start with the English press, I withdrew a roll of microfilm and wound it onto the reading machine.

In 1846 the *Montreal Gazette* was published triweekly, with a format like today's *New York Times.* Narrow columns, few pictures, numerous ads. My viewer was bad and so was the film. It was like trying to read under water. The print kept moving in and out of focus, and hairs and particles of debris migrated across the screen.

Ads extolled fur caps, British stationery, untanned sheepskins. Dr. Taylor wanted you to buy his balsam liverwort, Dr. Berlin, his antibilious pills. John Bower Lewis promoted himself as a worthy barrister and attorney-at-law. Pierre Grégoire would be pleased to do your hair. I read the ad:

> Gentleman can accommodate respectable male and female clients. Will render hair soft and glossy, however harsh. Will use admirable preparations to produce beautiful curls and do excellent restoration. Reasonable prices. Select clients only.

And now for the news.

Antoine Lindsay died when his neighbor hit him in the head with a piece of wood. Coroner's finding: Willful Murder.

A young English girl, Maria Nash, lately landed in Montreal, was victim of an abduction and betrayal. She died in a state of madness at the Emigrant Hospital.

When Bridget Clocone gave birth to a male child at the Women's Lying-In Hospital, doctors found that the forty-year-old widow had recently delivered another child. Police searched her employer's home and found the body of a second male infant hidden under clothes in a box. The baby showed ". . . marks of violence as though occasioned by the strong pressure of fingers on the neck." Coroner's finding: Willful Murder.

Jesus. Does anything ever change?

I shifted gears and scanned a list of ships that had cleared the port, and a list of ocean passengers leaving Montreal for Liverpool. Pretty dry stuff.

Fares for the steamboat. Stagecoach service to Ontario. Notices of removal. Not many folks moving that week.

Finally I found it. Births, Marriages, Deaths. In this city on the seventeenth, Mrs. David Mackay, a son. Mrs. Marie-Claire Bisset, a daughter. No mention of Eugénie Nicolet and her baby.

I noted the position of the birth notices within each paper, and fast-forwarded through the next several weeks, going right to that section. Nothing. I checked every paper on the reel. Through the end of 1846 there was no notice of Élisabeth's birth.

I tried the other English papers. Same story. No mention of Eugénie Nicolet. No birth of Élisabeth. I shifted to the French press. Still nothing.

By ten o'clock my eyes were throbbing and pain had spread throughout my back and shoulders. I leaned back, stretched, and rubbed my temples. Now what?

Across the room someone at another machine hit the rewind knob. Good idea. Good as anything. I'll go backward. Élisabeth was born in January. Let's check the period when the little sperm and egg were introducing themselves to each other.

I got the boxes and wound a film through the spools. April 1845. Same ads. Same notices of removal. Same passenger lists. English press. French press.

By the time I got to *La Presse* my eyes would hardly focus. I looked at my watch. Eleven-thirty. Twenty minutes more.

I rested my chin on my fist and hit rewind. When the film stopped I was in March. I was advancing manually, stopping here and there to scan down the middle of the screen, when I spotted the Bélanger name.

I sat up and brought the article into focus. It was brief. Eugénie Bélanger was off to Paris. The noted singer and wife of Alain Nicolet would be traveling with a company of twelve and would return after the season. Except for some verbiage saying how much she'd be missed, that was it.

So Eugénie had left town. When had she returned? Where was she in April? Did Alain go with her? Did he join her there? I looked at my watch. Shit.

I checked my wallet, dug into the bottom of my purse, then printed as many pages as my coins would allow. I rewound and returned the films and hurried across campus to Birks Hall.

Jeannotte's door was closed and locked, so I found the department office. The secretary dragged her eyes from her computer screen long enough to assure me that the journals would be delivered safely. I attached a note of thanks and left.

Walking back to the condo, my mind was still on history. I imagined the grand old homes I was passing as they'd been a century ago. What had the occupants seen when they looked out across Sherbrooke? Not the Musée des Beaux-Arts or the Ritz-Carlton. Not the latest offerings of Ralph Lauren, Giorgio Armani, and the atelier of Versace.

I wondered if they would have liked such trendy neighbors.

Surely the boutiques were more uplifting than the smallpox hospital that had reopened not far from their backyards.

At home I checked the answering machine, afraid that I'd missed Harry's call. Nothing. I quickly made a sandwich, then drove to the lab to sign reports. When I left I placed a note on LaManche's desk reminding him of my date of return. As a rule I spend most of April in Charlotte, with the understanding that I'd return to Montreal immediately for court appearances or urgent matters. Come May and the end of spring semester, I'm back for the summer.

Home again, I spent an hour packing and organizing work materials. While I am not exactly a light traveler, clothes are not the problem. After years of commuting between countries, I've found it's easier to keep two sets of everything. I have the world's largest suitcase on wheels, and I load it with books, files, journals, manuscripts, lecture notes, and anything else on which I'm working. This trip it held several pounds of Xerox copies.

At three-thirty I took a taxi to the airport. Harry had not called.

I live in perhaps the most unique apartment in Charlotte. Mine is the smallest unit in a complex known as Sharon Hall, a two-and-a-half-acre property situated in Myers Park. Deeds don't record the original function of the little structure, and today, for lack of a better label, the residents call it the Coach House Annex, or just the Annex.

The main house at Sharon Hall was built in 1913 as home for a local timber magnate. On the death of his wife in 1954, the 7,500-square-foot Georgian was donated to Queens College. The buildings housed the college's music department until the mid-eighties, when the property was sold and the mansion and coach house were converted to condos. At that time wings and annexes with an additional ten town houses were added, all conforming to the style of the original home. Old brick from a courtyard wall was incorporated into the new buildings, and windows, moldings, and hardwood floors were made as similar to the 1913 style as possible.

In the early sixties a gazebo was built next to the Annex, and the tiny building served as a sort of summer kitchen. It eventually fell into disuse, then served as a storage shed for the next two decades.

In 1993 a NationsBank executive bought the Annex and converted it into the world's smallest town house, incorporating the gazebo as part of the main living area. He was transferred just as my deteriorating marital situation sent me into the market for alternative living arrangements. I have a little over eight hundred square feet on two floors and, though cramped, I love it.

The only sound in the town house was the slow, steady ticking of my schoolhouse clock. Pete had been there. How like him to wind it for me. I called Birdie's name, but he didn't appear. I hung my jacket in the hall closet and muscled the suitcase up the narrow staircase to my bedroom.

"Bird?"

No answering meow and no furry white face appearing around a corner.

Downstairs, I found a note on the kitchen table. Pete still had Birdie, but he was going to Denver on Wednesday for a day or two, and wanted the cat picked up no later than tomorrow. The answering machine was blinking like a hazard light, and appropriately so, I thought.

I looked at my watch. Ten-thirty. I really didn't want to go back out.

I dialed Pete's number. My number for so many years. I could picture the phone on the kitchen wall, the V-shaped nick in the right-side casing. We'd had good times in that house, especially in that kitchen, with its walk-in fireplace and huge old pine table. Guests always drifted to that room, no matter where I tried to steer them.

The machine came on and Pete's voice asked for a short message. I left one. I tried Harry. Same routine, my voice.

I played my own messages. Pete. My department chair. Two students. A friend inviting me to a party the previous Tuesday. My mother-in-law. Two hang-ups. My best friend, Ann. No land mines. Always a relief when the series of monologues runs its course without describing catastrophies concluded or in the making.

I'd zapped and eaten a frozen pizza, and was almost finished unpacking when the phone rang.

"Good trip?"

"Not bad. Same old."

"Bird says he's bringing suit."

"For?"

"Abandonment."

"He may have a case. Will you represent him?"

"If he can come up with the retainer."

"What's in Denver?"

"A deposition. Same old."

"Could I get Birdie tomorrow? I've been up since six and I'm really exhausted."

"I understand Harry paid you a visit."

"That's not it," I snapped. My sister had always been a source of friction with Pete.

"Hey, hey. Ease down. How is she?"

"She's terrific."

"Tomorrow is fine. What time?"

"It's my first day back, so I know I won't get away until late. Probably six or seven."

"No problem. Come after seven and I'll feed you."

"I—"

"For Birdie. He needs to see that we're still friends. I think he feels it's all his fault."

"Right."

"You don't want him in veterinary therapy."

I smiled. Pete.

"O.K. But I'll bring something."

"Fine with me."

The next day was even more hectic than I'd anticipated. I was up by six, on campus by seven-thirty. By nine I'd checked my e-mail, sorted my snail mail, and reviewed my lecture notes.

I handed back exams in both my classes, so I had to extend office hours well beyond the normal time. Some students wanted to discuss their grades, others needed clemency for missing the test. Relatives always die during exams, and all manner of personal crises incapacitate the test takers. This midterm had been no exception.

At four I attended a College Course and Curriculum Committee meeting where we spent ninety minutes discussing whether the philosophy department could change the name of an upper-level course on Thomas Aquinas. I returned to my office to find my phone light blinking. Two messages.

Another student with a dead aunt. A taped message from campus security warning of break-ins in the Physical Sciences Building.

Next I turned to collecting diagrams, calipers, casts, and a list of materials I planned to have my assistant lay out for a lab exercise the next day. Then I spent an hour in the lab assuring that the specimens I'd chosen were appropriate.

At six I locked all the cabinets and the outer lab door. The corridors of the Colvard Building were deserted and quiet, but when I turned the corner toward my office I was surprised to see a young woman leaning against my doorway.

"Can I help you?"

She jumped at the sound of my voice.

"I— No. Sorry. I knocked." She spoke without turning, making it hard to see her face. "I have the wrong office." With that she bolted around the corner beyond my office and disappeared.

I suddenly recalled the message about break-ins.

Chill, Brennan. She was probably just listening to see if someone was inside.

I turned the handle and the door opened. Damn. I was sure I'd locked it. Or had I? My arms were so full I had pulled the door closed with my foot. Maybe the latch hadn't caught.

I did a quick inventory of the room. Nothing looked disturbed. I pulled my purse from the bottom file drawer and checked. Money. Keys. Passport. Credit cards. Everything worth taking was there.

Maybe she *had* been at the wrong place. Maybe she'd looked in, realized her mistake, and was leaving. I hadn't actually seen her open the door.

Whatever.

I packed my briefcase, turned the key and tested the lock, then headed for the parking deck.

Charlotte is as different from Montreal as Boston is from Bombay. A city suffering from multiple personality disorder, it is at once the graceful Old South and also the country's second-largest financial center. It is home to the Charlotte Motor Speedway and to NationsBank and First Union, to Opera Carolina and Coyote Joe's. It is churches on every corner, with a few titty bars around the corner. Country clubs and barbecue joints, crowded expressways and quiet cul-de-sacs. Billy Graham grew up on a dairy farm where a shopping center now stands, and Jim Bakker had his start in a local church and his finish in a federal courthouse. Charlotte is the place where mandatory busing to achieve racial balance in public schools began, and the home of numerous private academies, some with a religious orientation, others entirely secular.

Charlotte was a segregated city going into the 1960s, but then an extraordinary group of black and white leaders began to work to integrate restaurants, public lodging, recreation, and transportation. When Judge James B. McMillan handed down the mandatory busing order in 1969, there were no riots. The judge took a lot of personal heat, but his order stood, and the city complied.

I have always lived in the southeast part of town. Dillworth. Myers Park. Eastover. Foxcroft. Though a long way from the university, these neighborhoods are the oldest and prettiest, labyrinths of winding streets lined with stately homes and large lawns canopied by huge elms and willow oaks older than the pyramids. Most of Charlotte's streets, like most of Charlotte's people, are pleasant and graceful.

I cracked the car window and breathed in the late March evening. It had been one of those transitional days, not quite spring but no longer winter, when you slip your jacket on and off at least a dozen times. Already the crocuses were pushing through the earth, and soon the air would be lush with the smell of dogwoods, redbuds, and azaleas. Forget Paris. In spring, Charlotte is the most beautiful city on the planet.

I have several choices of routes going home from campus. Tonight I decided to take the highway, so I used the back exit to Harris Boulevard. Highways I-85 and I-77 were moving well, so in fifteen minutes I had cut through uptown and was heading southeast on Providence Road. I stopped at the Pasta and Provisions Company for spaghetti, Caesar salad, and garlic bread, and shortly after seven I was ringing Pete's doorbell.

He answered wearing faded jeans and a yellow and blue rugby shirt, open at the neck. His hair stuck up as though he'd just combed it with his fingers. He looked good. Pete always looks good.

"Why didn't you use your key?"

Why didn't I?

"And find a blonde in spandex in the den?"

"Is she here now?" he said, whipping around as if seriously searching.

"You wish. Here, boil water." I held out the pasta.

As Pete took the bag, Birdie made his appearance, stretching first one hind leg, then the other, then sitting with all four feet in a neat square. His eyes locked onto my face, but he did not approach.

"Hey, Bird. Did you miss me?"

The cat didn't move.

"You're right. He's pissed," I said.

I threw my purse onto the couch and followed Pete to the kitchen. The chairs on each end of the table were filled with stacks of mail, most unopened. The same was true of the buggy seat beneath the window and the wooden shelf below the phone. I said nothing. It was no longer my problem.

We passed a pleasant hour eating spaghetti and discussing Katy and other family. I told him his mother had called complaining of neglect. He said he'd represent her and Birdie in a package deal. I told him to call her. He said he would.

At eight-thirty I carried Birdie to the car, Pete following with the paraphernalia. My cat travels with more baggage than I do.

As I opened the door Pete placed his hand over mine.

"You're sure you don't want to stay?"

He tightened his fingers and, with the other hand, gently stroked my hair.

Did I? His touch felt so good, and dinner had seemed so normal, so comfortable. I felt something inside me start to melt.

Think, Brennan. You're tired. You're horny. Get your ass home.

"What about Judy?"

"A temporary disturbance in the cosmic order."

"I don't think so, Pete. We've been over this. I enjoyed the dinner."

He shrugged and dropped his hands.

"You know where I live," he said, and walked back to the house.

* * *

I've read that there are ten trillion cells in the human brain. All of mine were awake that night, engaged in frenzied communication on one topic: Pete.

Why *hadn't* I used my key?

Boundaries, the cells agreed. Not the old "here's a line in the dirt, don't cross it" challenge, but the establishing of new territorial limits, both real and symbolic.

Why the breakup at all? There was a time I wanted nothing more than to marry Pete and live with him the rest of my life. What had changed between the me then and the me now? I was very young when I married, but was the me in the making so very different from the me today? Or had the two Petes diverged course? Had the Pete I married been so irresponsible? So unreliable? Had I once thought that was part of his charm?

You are starting to sound like a Sammy Cahn song, the cells piped up.

What along the way had led to our present separateness? What choices had we made? Would we make those choices now? Was it me? Pete? Fate? What had gone wrong? Or had it gone right? Was I now on a new but correct path, the road of my marriage having led as far as it was going to take me?

Tough ones, the brain cells said.

Did I still want to sleep with Pete?

A unanimous yes from the cells.

But it's been a lean year for sex, I argued.

Interesting choice of words, the id guys pointed out. Lean. No meat. Implies hunger.

There was that lawyer in Montreal, I protested.

That's not it, the higher centers said. That guy hardly jiggled the needle. The voltage is in the red zone with this one.

There's no arguing with the brain when it's in that mood.

WEDNESDAY MORNING I HAD JUST ARRIVED AT THE UNIVERSITY when my office phone rang. Ryan's voice took me by surprise.

"I don't want a weather report," he said by way of greeting.

"Low sixties and I'm wearing sunblock."

"You really do have a vicious streak, Brennan."

I said nothing.

"Let's talk about St-Jovite."

"Go ahead." I picked up a pen and began drawing triangles.

"We've got names on the four in back."

I waited.

"It was a family. Mother, father, and twin baby boys."

"Hadn't we already figured that out?"

I heard the rustle of paper.

"Brian Gilbert, age twenty-three, Heidi Schneider, age twenty, Malachy and Mathias Gilbert, age four months."

I connected my base series to a set of secondary triangles.

"Most women would be impressed with my detecting."

"I'm not most women."

"Are you pissed off at me?"

"Should I be?"

I unclenched my molars and filled my lungs with air. For a long time he didn't reply.

"Bell Canada was unhurried as usual, but the phone records

finally came on Monday. The only nonlocal number called during the past year was to an eight-four-three area code."

I stopped in mid-triangle.

"Seems you're not the only one whose heart's in Dixie."

"Cute."

"Old times there are not forgotten."

"Where?"

"Beaufort, South Carolina."

"Are you on the level?"

"The old lady was a great dialer, then the calls stopped last winter."

"Where was she calling?"

"It's probably a residence. The local sheriff's going to check it out today."

"That's where this young family lived?"

"Not exactly. The Beaufort link started me thinking. The calls were pretty regular, then they stopped on December twelfth. Why? That's about three months before the fire. Something kept bugging me about that. The three-month part. Then I remembered. That's how long the neighbors said the couple and the babies had been at St-Jovite. You had said the babies were four months old, so I figured maybe those kids were born in Beaufort, and the calls stopped when they arrived in St-Jovite."

I let him go on.

"I called Beaufort Memorial, but there'd been no twin boys delivered there in the past year. Next I tried the clinics and hit pay dirt. They remembered the mother at . . ." More paper rustling. ". . . Beaufort-Jasper Comprehensive Health Clinic out on Saint Helena. That's an island."

"I know that, Ryan."

"It's a rural health clinic, mostly black doctors, mostly black patients. I spoke to one of the OB-GYNS, and, after the usual patient privacy bullshit, she admitted she treated a prenatal that fit my description. The woman had come in four months pregnant, carrying twins. Her due date was late November. Heidi Schneider. The doctor said she remembered Heidi because she was white, and because of the twins."

"So she delivered there?"

"No. The other reason the doctor remembered her was because

she'd disappeared. The woman kept her appointments through her sixth month, then never went back."

"That's it?"

"That's all she'd give up until I faxed her the autopsy photo. I suspect she'll be seeing that in her sleep for a while. When she phoned back she was more cooperative. Not that the chart info was all that helpful. Heidi wasn't exactly forthcoming when she filled out the forms. She listed the father as Brian Gilbert, gave a home address in Sugar Land, Texas, and left the boxes for local address and phone number blank."

"What's in Texas?"

"We're checkin', ma'am."

"Don't start, Ryan."

"How schooled are the Beaufort boys in blue?"

"I don't really know them. Anyway, they wouldn't have jurisdiction out on Saint Helena. It's unincorporated, so it's the sheriff's turf."

"Well, we're going to meet him."

"We?"

"I'm flying in on Sunday and I could use a local guide. You know, someone who speaks the language, knows local protocol. I have no idea how you eat grits."

"Can't do it. Katy's coming home next week. Besides, Beaufort is perhaps my favorite spot on the planet. If I ever do give you a tour, which I probably won't, it will not be while you're taking care of business."

"Or why."

"Why what?"

"Why anyone would eat grits."

"Ask Martha Stewart."

"Think about it."

No need. I had as much intention of meeting Ryan in Beaufort as I did of registering myself as an available single person in the People Meeting People section of my local paper.

"What about the two charred bodies upstairs?" Back to St-Jovite.

"We're still working on it."

"Has Anna Goyette turned up?"

"No idea."

"Any developments on Claudel's homicide?"

"Which one?"

"The scalded pregnant girl."

"Not that I'm aware of."

"You've been a fountain of information. Let me know what you find in Texas."

I hung up and got myself a Diet Coke. I didn't know at that point, but it was going to be a phone-intensive day.

All afternoon I worked on a paper I planned to present at the American Association of Physical Anthropology meetings in early April. I felt the usual stress from having left too much until the last minute.

At three-thirty, as I was sorting photos of CAT scans, the phone rang again.

"You ought to get out more."

"Some of us work, Ryan."

"The address in Texas is the Schneider home. According to the parents, who, by the way, aren't ever going to win Final Jeopardy, Heidi and Brian showed up sometime in August and stayed until the babies were born. Heidi refused prenatal care and delivered at home with a midwife. Easy birth. No problems. Happy grandparents. Then a man visited the couple in early December, and a week later an old lady drove up in a van and they split."

"Where did they go?"

"The parents have no idea. There was no contact after that."

"Who was the man?"

"No clue, but they say this guy scared the crap out of Heidi and Brian. After he left they hid the babies and refused to go out of the house until the old lady got there. Papa Schneider didn't like him much either."

"Why?"

"Didn't like his looks. Said he brought to mind a . . . Let me get this exactly." I could picture Ryan flipping pages in his notebook. ". . . 'goddam skunk.' Kinda poetic, don't you think?"

"Dad's a regular Yeats. Anything else?"

"Talking to these folks is like talking to my parakeet, but there was one other thing."

"You have a bird?"

"Mama said Heidi and Brian had been members of some sort of group. That they'd all been living together. Ready for this?"

"I just swallowed four Valium. Hit me."

"In Beaufort, South Carolina."

"That fits."

"Like O.J.'s Bruno Maglis."

"What else did they say?"

"Nothing useful."

"What about Brian Gilbert?"

"He and Heidi met at college two years ago, both dropped out shortly after that. Mama Schneider thought he came from Ohio. She said he talked funny. We're checking it out. "

"Did you tell them?"

"Yes."

For a moment neither of us spoke. Breaking the news of a murder is the worst part of a detective's job, the one they all dread the most.

"I still could use you in Beaufort."

"I still am not coming. This is detective work, not forensics."

"Knowing the hood speeds the process."

"I'm not sure Beaufort has hoods."

Ten minutes later the phone rang again.

"*Bonjour,* Temperance. *Comment ça va?*"

LaManche. Ryan had wasted no time, and had argued his case well. Could I possibly help Detective Lieutenant Ryan on the matter in Beaufort? This was a particularly sensitive investigation, and the media were becoming restive. I could bill my time and my expenses would be covered.

The message light came on as we were speaking, indicating I'd missed a call. I promised LaManche I'd see what I could work out, and hung up.

The message was from Katy. Her plans for next week had recrystallized. She'd still come home for the weekend, but then wanted to join friends on Hilton Head Island.

As I sat back to organize, my eyes drifted to the computer screen with its unfinished paper. Katy and I *could* go to Beaufort for the weekend, and I *could* work on it there. Then she'd move on to Hilton Head and I'd stay to help Ryan. LaManche would be happy. Ryan would be happy. And God knew I could use the extra income.

I also had reasons for not going.

Since Ryan's call an image of Malachy had been floating through my mind. I saw his half-open eyes and mangled chest, his tiny fingers curled in death. I thought of his dead sibling and his dead parents and his grieving grandparents. Thinking about that case plunged me into melancholy, and I wanted to get away from it for a while.

I checked my course syllabi for the next week. I had a film scheduled for Thursday in the human evolution course. I could switch that. Don Johanson would be just as enlightening on Tuesday.

A bone quiz in the osteology course, then open lab. I made a quick call. No problem. Alex would proctor if I organized everything for her.

I checked my agenda book. No more committee meetings this month. After tomorrow, no student appointments until late the following week. How could there be? I was sure I'd seen every student in the university yesterday.

It could work.

And the real truth was I had a duty to help if I could. No matter how small the contribution. I couldn't bring color back to Malachy's cheeks, or close the terrible wound in his chest. And I couldn't erase the older Schneiders' pain, or give them back their child and grandchildren. But I just might be able to help rein in the psychopathic mutant who had killed them. And maybe save a future Malachy.

If you're going to do this kind of work, Brennan, just do it.

I phoned Ryan and told him he could have me Monday and Tuesday. I'd let him know where I would stay.

I had another idea, so I made a second call, then dialed Katy. I explained my plan, and she was all for it. She'd meet me at home on Friday and we'd go down in my car.

"Go to the health clinic right now and get a TB test," I told her. "Subdermal, not just the scratch thing. Then have it read on Friday before you leave."

"Why?"

"Because I have a great idea for your project, and that's a prerequisite. And while you're at the clinic get a photocopy of your immunization record."

"My what?"

"A record of all your shots. You had to put it on file to register at the university. And bring everything the professor handed out for the field project assignment."

"Why?"

"You'll see."

15

THURSDAY PASSED IN A BLUR OF TEACHING AND STUDENT ADVISING. After dinner I called to ask Pete to check on Birdie over the weekend. Harry phoned around ten to say that the seminar had ended. She'd been singled out to meet the professor, and would be dining at his home on Friday. She wanted to use the condo through the weekend.

I told her to stay as long as she wanted. I didn't ask where she'd been all week, or why she hadn't phoned. I'd called several times and never gotten an answer, including twice after midnight. I didn't point that out, either.

"You're meeting Ryan in the Land of Cotton next week?" she asked.

"It looks that way." I felt my molars reach for each other. How did she know that?

"Should be fun."

"It's strictly work, Harry."

"Right. He's still cute as a bean bug."

"His ancestors were bred to root truffles."

"What?"

"Never mind."

Friday morning I selected bone fragments, wrote out questions, and set the assemblage up on trays. Alex, my teaching assistant, would arrange the cards and specimens in numerical order, and time the students as they moved from station to station. The ever-popular bone quiz.

Katy showed up right on time, and by noon we were cruising south. The temperature was in the high sixties, the sky the color portrayed in Grand Strand promotional posters. We put on our shades and rolled the windows down to let our hair blow. I drove and Katy chose the rock and roll.

We took I-77 south through Columbia, cut southeast on I-26, and south again on I-95. At Yemassee we left the interstate and flew along narrow low-country roads. We talked and laughed and stopped when we wanted. Barbecue at Maurice's Piggy Park. A snapshot at the Old Sheldon-Prince Williams Church ruins, burned by Sherman after his march to the sea. It felt wonderful to be schedule-free, and with my daughter, and heading for the place I love most on earth.

Katy told me about her classes, and about the men she was dating. In her words, no keepers. She shared the story of the rift, now patched, that had threatened her plans for spring break. She described the girls with whom she'd be sharing the Hilton Head condo, and I laughed until I hurt. Yes, this was my daughter, with a humor dark enough to house vampires. I'd never felt closer to her, and for a while I was young and free, and forgot about murdered babies.

In Beaufort we passed the marine air station, made a quick stop at the Bi-Lo, then wound our way through town and over the Woods Memorial Bridge to Lady's Island. At the top I turned and looked back at the Beaufort waterfront, a sight that always lifts my spirits.

I spent my childhood summers near Beaufort, and most of those as an adult, the chain being broken only recently, when I began my work in Montreal. I witnessed the mushrooming of fast-food strips and the construction of the county government center, dubbed the "Taj Mahal" by the locals. The roads have been widened, the traffic is heavier. The islands are now home to golf resorts and condos. But Bay Street remains unchanged. The mansions still stand in antebellum grandeur, shaded by water oaks draped in Spanish moss. So little in life is constant; I find reassurance in the languid pace of life in Beaufort. The tide of time itself ebbs tardily to the eternal sea.

As we descended the far side of the bridge, ahead and to the left I could see a colony of boats docked on Factory Creek, a small loop of water off the Beaufort River. The late-afternoon sun glinted off their windows and glowed white on masts and decks. I drove another half mile on Highway 21, then turned into the parking area at Ollie's Seafood restaurant. Winding my way through live oaks, I headed to the back of the lot and pulled in at the water's edge.

Katy and I gathered our groceries and duffel bags and crossed a walkway from Ollie's to the Lady's Island Marina. To either side lay mudflats, the new spring shoots green among last year's dark stubble. Marsh wrens rasped complaints at our passing, and darted in and out among the cordgrass and cattails. I breathed the gentle blend of brackish water, chlorophyll, and decaying vegetation, and felt glad to be back in the low country.

The walkway from the shore led like a tunnel through the marina headquarters, a square white building with a narrow third story running the length of its roof, and an open passage on the first floor. On our right, doors opened to washrooms and a laundry. The offices of Apex Realty, a sail maker, and the harbormaster occupied the space to our left.

We passed through the tunnel, descended a floating gangplank with horizontal wooden risers, and crossed to the farthest of the docks. As we walked its length, Katy scanned each of the boats we passed. The *Ecstasy,* a forty-foot Morgan out of Norfolk, Virginia. The *Blew Palm,* a custom-built fifty-three-footer with a steel hull and enough sail to go round the world. The *Hillbilly Heaven,* a classic nineteen-thirties power yacht, once elegant, now weathered and no longer seaworthy. The *Melanie Tess* was the last boat on the right. Katy eyed the forty-two-foot Chris Craft, but said nothing.

"Hold here a second," I said, dropping my bundles onto the dock.

I stepped onto the stern, climbed to the bridge, and worked the combination on a toolbox to the right of the captain's chair. Then I dug out a key, unlocked and opened the aft entrance, slid back the hatch, and lowered myself the three steps to the main cabin. Inside, the air was cool and smelled of wood and mildew and pine disinfectant. I unlocked the port-side entrance and Katy handed me our food and duffels, then came aboard.

Without a word my daughter and I left everything in the main salon, then darted around the boat, snooping out the decor. It was a habit we'd started when she was very young, and no matter how old I live to be, it will remain my favorite part of stays in unknown places. The *Melanie Tess* wasn't exactly unknown, but I hadn't been on her in five years, and was curious to see the changes Sam had described.

Our survey revealed a galley one step down and forward from the main salon. It had a two-burner stove, a sink, and a wooden refrigerator with an old-style icebox handle. The floor was parquet, the walls, as everywhere, teak. On the starboard side was a dining nook, its cushions covered in bold pinks and greens. Forward of the galley were a pantry, a head, and a V-berth large enough to sleep two.

Aft lay the master stateroom with its king-size bed and mirrored closets. As in the main salon and dining nook, it was done in teak and bright cotton foliage. Katy looked relieved to see a shower in the master head.

"This is so cool," said Katy. "Can I have the V-berth?"

"Are you sure?" I asked.

"Totally. It looks so snug I'm going to make a little nest up there, put all my *stuff* along those shelves." She mimed lining up and straightening small objects.

I laughed. George Carlin's "stuff" routine was one of our favorite comedy bits.

"Besides, I'm only going to be here two nights, you take the large bed."

"O.K."

"Look, a communiqué with your name on it." She took an envelope from the table and handed it to me.

I tore the flap and shook out a note.

The water and electricity are hooked up so you should be set. Give me a call when you're settled. I want to take you out to feed. Enjoy.

Sam

We stowed the groceries, then Katy went to arrange her stuff while I dialed Sam.

"Hey, hey, darlin', you're all tucked in?"

"We've been here about twenty minutes. She looks beautiful, Sam. I can't believe it's the same boat."

"Nothing a little money and muscle can't accomplish."

"It shows. Do you ever stay on board?"

"Oh, yeah. That's why the phone and answering machine are there. It's a bit over the top for a boat, but I can't afford to miss messages. You feel free to use that number."

"Thanks, Sam. I really appreciate this."

"Hell, I don't use her enough. Someone ought to."

"Well, thanks again."

"How about dinner?"

"I really don't want to impose on—"

"Hell, I need to eat, too. I'll tell you what. I'm going out to the Gay Seafood Market to buy grouper for some damn thing Melanie's cooking up tomorrow. How 'bout I meet you at Factory Creek Landing. It'll be on the right, just after Ollie's and just before the bridge. It isn't fancy, but they make some mean shrimp."

"What time?"

"It's six-forty now, so how 'bout seven-thirty. I want to go by the shop and pick up the Harley."

"On one condition. I'm buying."

"You're a tough woman, Tempe."

"Don't mess with me."

"Are we still on for tomorrow?"

"If it's O.K. with you. I don't want t—"

"Yeah. Yeah. Have you told her?"

"Not yet. But she'll figure it out once you meet. See you in an hour."

I tossed my bag onto my bed, then went up to the bridge. The sun was dropping, its last rays tinting the world a warm crimson. It flamed the marsh to my right and tinted a white ibis standing in the grass. The bridge to Beaufort stood out black against the pink, like the backbone of some ancient monster arching across the sky. The boats in the city marina winked across the river at our little pier.

Though the day had cooled, the air still felt like satin. A breeze lifted a strand of hair and wrapped it softly across my face.

"What's the agenda?"

Katy had joined me. I checked my watch.

"We're meeting Sam Rayburn for dinner in half an hour."

"*The* Sam Rayburn? I thought he was dead."

"He is. This one is the mayor of Beaufort and an old friend."

"How old?"

"Older than I am. But he's still ambulatory. You'll like him."

"Wait a minute." She pointed a finger at me, and I could see thought working in her eyes. Then a synapse. "Is this the monkey guy?"

I smiled and tipped my head.

"Is that where we're going tomorrow? No, don't answer. Of course it is. That's why I had to get the shots."

"You had it checked, didn't you?"

"Cancel the bed at the sanitarium," she said, holding out her arm. "I'm certified tuberculosis-free."

When we arrived at the restaurant Sam's motorcycle was parked in the lot. Last summer it had joined the Lotus, the sailboat, and the ultralight as the newest addition to a long list of playthings. I am never sure if these toys are Sam's way of fending off middle age, or his attempts at integration into the activities of people after years of focusing on the activities of primates.

Though he is a decade older, Sam and I have been friends for more than twenty years. When we met I was a college sophomore, Sam a second-year graduate student. We were drawn to each other, I suspect, because our lives to that point had been so different.

Sam is a Texan, the only child of Jewish boardinghouse owners. At fifteen his father was killed defending a cash box that held twelve dollars. Following her husband's death, Mrs. Rayburn sank into a depression from which she never emerged. Sam shouldered the burden of running the business while finishing high school and caring for his mother. Upon her death seven years later, he sold the boardinghouse and joined the marines. He was restless, angry, and interested in nothing.

Life in the military only fed Sam's cynicism. In boot camp he found the antics of his fellow recruits profoundly annoying, and drew deeper and deeper into himself. During his tour in Vietnam he spent hours watching birds and animals, using them as an escape from the horror around him. He was appalled by the carnage of war, and felt tremendous guilt about his role in it. The animals seemed innocent by contrast, not motivated by elaborate schemes designed to kill others of their own kind. He was especially drawn to the monkeys, to the orderliness of their society and the way they resolved disputes with minimal physical injury. For the first time Sam found himself truly fascinated.

Sam returned to the States and enrolled at the University of Illinois at Champaign-Urbana. He finished a bachelor's degree in three years, and when I met him was the teaching assistant for the section of introductory zoology to which I was assigned. He had a reputation among undergraduates for a quick temper, a harsh tongue, and being easily annoyed. Particularly by the slow-witted and the ill-prepared. He was meticulous and demanding, but scrupulously fair in his evaluation of student work.

As I got to know Sam I found that he liked few people, but was tenaciously loyal to those he admitted into his small circle. He once told me that, having spent so many years among primates, he felt he no longer fit in human society. The monkey perspective, as he called it, had shown him the ridiculousness of human behavior.

Sam eventually switched to physical anthropology, did fieldwork in Africa, and completed his doctorate. After stints at several universities, he ended up in Beaufort in the early 1970s as scientist in charge of the primate facility.

Though age has mellowed Sam, I doubt that it will ever change his discomfiture at social interaction. It isn't that he doesn't want to participate. He does. His seeking the office of mayor proves that. Life just doesn't operate for Sam the way it does for others. So he buys bikes and wings for flying. They provide stimulation and excitement, but remain predictable and manageable. Sam Rayburn is one of the most complex and most intelligent people I have ever met.

His mayoral honor was at the bar, watching a basketball game and drinking draft beer.

I made the introductions and, as usual, Sam took charge, ordering a refill for himself, Diet Coke for me and Katy, then herding us to a booth at the back of the restaurant.

My daughter wasted no time in confirming her suspicions regarding tomorrow's plans, then pummeled Sam with questions.

"How long have you directed this primate center?"

"Longer than I care to think about. I worked for someone else until about ten years ago, then bought the damn company for myself. Just about went to the poorhouse, but I'm glad I did it. Nothing beats being your own boss."

"How many monkeys live on the island?"

"Right now about forty-five hundred."

"Who owns them?"

"The FDA. My company owns the island and manages the animals."

"Where do they come from?"

"They were brought to Murtry Island from a research colony in Puerto Rico. Your mom and I both did work there, somewhere back in the early Bronze Age. But they're originally from India. They're rhesus."

"*Macaca mulatta.*" Katy pronounced the genus and species in a lilting, singsong voice.

"Very good. Where did you learn primate taxonomy?"

"I'm a psych major. A lot of research is done using rhesus. You know, like Harry Harlow and his progeny?"

Sam was about to comment when the waitress arrived with plates of fried clams and oysters, boiled shrimp, hush puppies, and slaw. We all concentrated on spooning sauces onto our plates, squeezing lemons, and peeling a starter batch of shrimp.

"What are the monkeys used for?"

"The Murtry population is a breeding colony. Some yearlings are removed and sent to the Food and Drug Administration, but if an animal isn't trapped by the time it reaches a certain body weight, it's there for life. Monkey heaven."

"What else is out there?" My daughter had no reservations about chewing and talking at the same time.

"Not much. The monkeys are free-ranging so they go where they want. They set up their own social groups and have their own rules. There are feeder stations, and corrals for trapping, but outside camp the island is really theirs."

"What's camp?"

"That's what we call the area right at the dock. There's a field station, a small veterinary clinic, mostly for emergencies, some storage sheds for monkey chow, and a trailer where students and researchers can stay."

He dipped an oyster in cocktail sauce, tipped back his head, and dropped it in his mouth.

"There was a plantation on the island back in the nineteenth century." Small drops of red clung to his beard. "Belonged to the Murtry family. That's where the island gets its name."

"Who's allowed out there?" She peeled another shrimp.

"Absolutely no one. These monkeys are virus-free and worth mucho dinero. Anyone, and I mean anyone, who sets foot on the island is cleared through me, and has to have a shitload of immunizations, including a negative TB test within the last six months."

Sam looked a question at me, and I nodded.

"I didn't think anyone caught TB anymore."

"The test isn't for your protection, young lady. The monks are very susceptible to TB. An outbreak can destroy a colony quicker than you can say jackshit."

Katy turned to me. "Your students had to do the shot bit?"

"Every time."

Early in my career, before I was lured into forensics, my research involved the use of monkeys to study the aging process in the skeleton. I'd taught all the primatology courses at UNCC, including a field school on Murtry Island. I'd brought students out for fourteen years.

"Hm," said Katy, popping a clam into her mouth. "This is going to be O.K."

At seven-thirty the next morning we stood on a dock at the northern tip of Lady's Island, eager to go to Murtry. The drive had been like traveling through a terrarium. A heavy mist covered everything, blurring edges and throwing the world slightly out of focus. Though Murtry was less than a mile out, I looked across the water into nothingness. Closer in, an ibis startled and lifted off, its long, slender legs trailing behind.

The staff had arrived and were loading the facility's two open boats. They finished shortly and took off. Katy and I sipped coffee, waiting for Sam's signal. At last he whistled and gave a come-on gesture. We crumpled our Styrofoam cups, threw them into an oil drum turned trash barrel, and hurried down to the lower dock.

Sam helped each of us board, then untied the line and jumped in. He nodded to the man at the wheel, and we putted out into the inlet.

"How long is the ride?" Katy asked Sam.

"The tide's up, so we'll take Parrot Creek, then the back creek and cut through the marsh. Shouldn't be more than forty minutes."

Katy sat cross-legged on the bottom of the boat.

"You'd do better to stand and lean against the side," Sam suggested. "When Joey throttles down, this thing jumps. The vibration's enough to rattle your vertebrae."

Katy got up and he handed her a rope.

"Hang on to this. Do you want a life vest?"

Katy shook her head. Sam looked at me.

"She's a strong swimmer," I assured him.

Just then Joey opened the engine and the boat surged to life. We raced across open water, the wind snapping hair and clothes and ripping the words from our lips. At one point Katy tapped Sam's shoulder and pointed to a buoy.

"Crab pot," yelled Sam.

Farther on, he showed her an osprey nest atop a channel marker. Katy nodded vigorously.

Before long we left open water and entered the marsh. Joey stood with feet spread, eyes fixed straight ahead as he twisted and turned the wheel, piloting the boat through narrow ribbons of water. There couldn't have been more than ten feet of clearance in any of the alleys. We leaned hard left, then hard right, twisting through the cut, our spray showering the grass to either side.

Katy and I clung to the boat and to each other, our bodies pitching with the centrifugal force of hard turns, laughing and enjoying the thrill of speed and the beauty of the day. Much as I love Murtry Island, I think I have always loved the crossing more.

By the time we reached Murtry the mist had burned away. Sunlight warmed the dock and dappled the sign at the entrance to the island. A breeze teased the foliage overhead, sending splotches of shadow and light dancing and changing shape across the words: GOVERNMENT PROPERTY. KEEP OUT. ABSOLUTELY NO ADMITTANCE.

When the boats were unloaded and everyone was inside the field station, Sam introduced Katy to the staff. I knew most of them, though there were a few new faces. Joey had been hired two summers earlier. Fred and Hank were still in training. As he made introductions, Sam gave a quick rundown of the operation.

Joey, Larry, Tommy, and Fred were technicians, their primary duties being day-to-day maintenance of the facility and transport of supplies. They did painting and repair, cleaned the corrals and feeder stations, and kept the animals supplied with water and chow.

Jane, Chris, and Hank were more directly involved with the monkeys, monitoring the groups for various types of data.

"Like what?" Katy asked.

"Pregnancies, births, deaths, veterinary problems. We keep close tabs on the population. And there are research projects. Jane's involved in a serotonin study. She goes out each day to record certain types of behavior, to see which monkeys are more aggressive, more impulsive. Then we run that data against their serotonin levels. We're also looking at their rank. Her monkeys wear telemetric collars that send out a signal so she can find them. You'll probably spot one."

"Serotonin is a chemical in the brain," I offered.

"Yes," said Katy. "A neurotransmitter thought to be correlated with aggression."

Sam and I exchanged smiles. Atta girl!

"How do you gauge whether a monkey is impulsive?" Katy asked.

"He takes more risks. Makes longer leaps, for example, high up in the trees. Leaves home at an earlier age."

"He?"

"This is a pilot study. No girls."

"You may see one of my boys in camp," said Jane, strapping a box with a long antenna to her waist. "J-7. He's in O group. They hang around here a lot."

"He's the klepto?" Hank asked.

"Yeah. He'll snatch anything that isn't nailed down. He got another pen last week. And Larry's watch. I thought Larry'd have a stroke chasing him."

When everyone had stowed his or her gear, checked assignments, and gone out, Sam took Katy on a tour of the island. I tagged along, watching my daughter become a monkey spotter. As we meandered along the trails, Sam pointed out the feeder stations, and described the groups that frequented each. He talked about territory, and dominance hierarchies, and maternal lines while Katy held binoculars to her face and scanned the trees.

At feeder station E Sam threw dried corn kernels against the corrugated metal roof.

"Hold still and watch," he said.

Soon we heard the swish of foliage and saw a group move in. Within minutes monkeys surrounded us, some remaining in the trees, others dropping to the ground and darting forward to pick up corn.

Katy was enthralled.

"That's F group," said Sam. "It's small, but it's run by one of the highest-ranking females on the island. She's a ball buster."

By the time we got back to camp Sam had helped Katy design a simple project. She organized her notes while he got a bag of corn for her, then she headed back out. I watched her disappear into a tunnel of oak trees, the binoculars banging against her hip.

Sam and I sat on the screened porch and talked for a while, then he went to work and I got out the CAT scan draft. Though I tried, I found it hard to focus. Sinus patterns held little appeal when I could look up and see sunshine on a tidal estuary and smell air laced with salt and pine.

The staff came in at noon, Katy among them. After sandwiches and Fritos, Sam went back to his data, and Katy returned to the woods.

I resettled with my paper, but it was still no go. I drifted off after page three.

I woke to a familiar sound.

Thunk! Rat a tat a tat a tat a tat. Thunk! Rat a tat a tat tat tat.

Two monkeys had dropped from the trees and were running across the porch roof. Being as inconspicuous as possible, I opened the screen door and eased myself out and onto the steps. O group had entered camp and was resting in the branches above the field station. The pair that had wakened me now leaped from the field station to the trailer and settled on opposite ends of the roof.

"That's him." I hadn't heard Sam come up behind me. "Look."

He handed me the binoculars.

"I can make out the tattoos," I said, reading the chest of each monkey. "J-7 and GN-9. J-7 has a collar."

I passed back the glasses and Sam took another look.

"What the hell's he got? You don't suppose the little shit's still toting Larry's watch?"

Another handoff.

"It's shiny. Looks like gold when the sun hits it."

Just then GN-9 lunged and gave a full, openmouthed threat. J-7 screeched and flew off the roof, launching himself from branch to branch until he was out of sight behind the trailer. His treasure slid down the roof and into the gutter.

"Let's find out."

Sam dragged a ladder from under the field house and propped it against the trailer. He brushed away spiderwebs, tested his weight on the first rung, then climbed up.

"What the hell?"

"What?"

"Sonofabitch."

"What is it?"

He rotated something in his hand.

"I'll be goddamned."

"What is it?" I tried to see what the monkey had dropped, but Sam's body obscured my view.

Sam stood motionless at the top of the ladder, his head bent.

"Sam, what is it?"

Without a word he climbed down and held the object out for my inspection. I knew instantly what it was and what it meant, and felt the sunshine go out of the day.

I met Sam's eyes and we stared at each other in silence.

16

I STOOD WITH THE THING IN MY HAND, UNWILLING TO BELIEVE what my eyes were telling me.

Sam spoke first.

"That's a human jaw."

"Yes." I watched lacy shadows slide across his face.

"Probably an old Indian burial."

"Not with this dental work." I rotated the mandible and sunlight glinted off gold.

"That's what got J-7's attention," he said, staring at the crowns.

"And this is flesh," I added, pointing to a brown glob clinging to the joint.

"What does that mean?"

I raised the jaw and sniffed. It had the dank, cloying odor of death.

"In this climate, depending on whether the body was buried or left on the surface, I'd say this person has been dead less than a year."

"How the fuck can that be?" A vein throbbed in his forehead.

"Don't yell at me. Apparently everyone who comes to this island does not clear through you!"

I glanced away from him.

"Where the hell did he get it?"

"He's your monkey, Sam. You figure it out."

"You damn well better believe I will."

He strode toward the field station, took the stairs two at a time, and disappeared inside. Through the open windows I heard him call to Jane.

For a moment I stood there, hearing the click of palmetto fronds and feeling surreal. Had death actually penetrated my island of tranquillity?

"No!" cried a voice in my head. "Not here!"

I heard the whirp of the spring as the screen door flew open. Sam emerged with Jane and called to me.

"Come on, Quincy. Let's round up the usual suspects. Jane knows where O group goes when it's not in camp, so we should be able to pick up J-7's collar. Maybe the little bugger will give something up."

I didn't move.

"Son of a buck, I'm sorry. I just don't like body parts showing up on my island. You know my temper."

I did. But it wasn't Sam's outburst that held me back. I smelled the pine and felt the warm breeze on my cheek. I knew what was out there and didn't want to find it.

"C'mon."

I took a deep breath, as enthused as a woman on her way to a meeting requested by an oncologist.

"Wait."

I went into the field station and rooted in the kitchen until I found a plastic tub. I sealed the jaw inside, hid the container in a cabinet in the back room, then left a note for Katy.

We took a trail behind the field station and followed Jane toward the center of the island. She led us to an area where the trees were the size of offshore rigs, the foliage a solid canopy overhead. The ground was a plush of humus and pine needles, the air heavy with the scent of decaying vegetation and animal matter. A swish in the branches told me monkeys were present.

"Someone's here," said Jane, turning on her receiver.

Sam searched the trees with his binoculars, trying to make out tattoo codes.

"It's A group," he said.

"Hunh!"

A juvenile crouched on a branch above me, shoulders down, tail in the air, eyes fixed on my face. The sharp, throaty bark was his way of saying "back off!"

When I met his gaze the monkey sat back, ducked his head, then raised it diagonally across his body. He repeated the bob several times, then spun and did a cannonball into the next tree.

Jane adjusted dials then closed her eyes to listen, face tense with concentration. After a while she shook her head and continued up the path.

Sam scanned the treetops as Jane stopped again and rotated clockwise, totally focused on the sounds in her headset. Finally,

"I've got a very faint signal."

She veered in the direction in which the cannonballer had disappeared, paused, pivoted again.

"I think he's over near Alcatraz." She pointed toward ten o'clock.

While most of the trapping pens on the island are designated by letter, a few of the older ones have names like O.K. Corral or Alcatraz.

We moved toward Alcatraz, but just south of the corral Jane left the path and cut into the woods. The vegetation was thicker here, the ground spongy underfoot. Sam turned to me.

"Watch yourself near the pond. Alice had a mess of babies last season, and I suspect she's not feeling sociable."

Alice is a fourteen-foot alligator who has lived on Murtry for as long as anyone can remember. No one recalls who named her. The staff respects her right to be there and leaves her to her pond.

I gave Sam a thumbs-up sign. While they do not frighten me, gators have never been creatures whose company I sought.

We weren't twenty feet off the trail when I noticed it, faint at first, just a variation on the dark, organic forest smell. Initially I wasn't sure, but as we picked our way closer the odor grew stronger, and a cold band tightened on my chest.

Jane cut north, away from the pond, and Sam followed, binoculars trained on the overhead branches. I held back. The smell was coming from straight ahead.

I circled a fallen sweet gum and stopped. I could see a belt of brush and scrub palm bordering the pond. The forest grew silent as

Jane and Sam pulled away, the rustling of their feet fading with each step.

The odor of decaying flesh is like no other. I'd smelled it on the jaw, and now the sweet, fetid scent tainted the afternoon air, telling me my quarry was near. Barely breathing, I pivoted as Jane had done, eyes closed, every fiber fixed on sensory input. Same motion, different focus. While Jane was tracking with her ears, I hunted with my nose.

The smell was coming from the direction of the pond. I moved toward it, my nose following the odor and my eyes on reptile alert. Overhead a monkey barked, then a stream of urine trickled to the ground. Branches stirred and leaves fluttered earthward. The stench grew stronger with each step.

I drew within ten feet, stopped, and trained my binoculars on the thicket of scrub palm and yaupon holly that separated me from the pond. An iridescent cloud formed and re-formed just outside its border.

I crept forward, carefully testing with each footfall. At the edge of the bushes the smell of putrefaction was overpowering. I listened. Silence. I scanned the underbrush. Nothing. My heart raced and sweat poured down my face.

Move your ass, Brennan. It's too far from the pond for alligators.

I pulled a bandanna from my pocket, covered my mouth and nose, and squatted to see what the flies found so attractive.

They rose as one, whining and darting around me. I waved them away, but they returned immediately. Sweeping back flies with one hand, I wrapped the bandanna around the other and lifted the yaupon branches. Insects bounced off my face and arms, buzzing and swarming in agitation.

The flies had been drawn to a shallow grave, hidden from view by the thick leaves. Staring from it was a human face, the features shifting and changing in the shadowy light. I leaned close, then drew back in horror.

What I saw was no longer a face, but a skull stripped bare by scavengers. What appeared as eyes and nose and lips were, in fact, mounds of tiny crabs, parts of a seething mass that covered the skull and fed on its flesh.

As I looked around I realized there had been other opportunists.

A mangled segment of rib cage lay to my right. Arm bones, still connected by tendrils of dried ligament, peeked from the undergrowth five feet away.

I released the bush and sat back on my heels, immobilized by a cold, sick feeling. On the edge of my vision I saw Sam approaching. He was speaking, but his words didn't penetrate. Somewhere, a million miles away, a motor grew louder then stopped.

I wanted to be somewhere else. To be some*one* else. Someone who had not spent years smelling death and seeing its final degradation. Someone who did not work day after day reassembling the human carnage left by macho pimps, enraged partners, wired cokeheads, and psychopaths. I had come to the island to escape the brutality of my life's work. But even here, death had found me. I felt overwhelmed. Another day. Another death. Death du jour. My God, how many such days would there be?

I felt Sam's hand on my shoulder and looked up. His other hand was cupped across his nose and mouth.

"What is it?"

I inclined my head toward the bush and Sam bent it backward with his boot.

"Holy shit."

I agreed.

"How long has it been here?"

I shrugged.

"Days? Weeks? Years?"

"The burial has been a bonanza for your island fauna, but most of the body looks undisturbed. I can't tell what condition it's in."

"Monkeys didn't dig this up. They won't have anything to do with meat. Must be the damn buzzards."

"Buzzards?"

"Turkey vultures. They love to chow down on monkey carcasses."

"I'd also question the raccoons."

"Yeah? Coons love the yaupon, but I didn't think they'd eat carrion."

I looked again at the grave.

"The body is on its side, with the right shoulder just below the surface. No doubt the smell attracted scavengers. The vultures and raccoons probably dug and ate, then pulled out the arm and the jaw when decomposition weakened the joints." I indicated the ribs. "They chewed off a section of the thorax and dragged that out, too. The rest of the body was probably too deep, or just too hard to get at, so they left it."

Using a stick, I dragged the arm closer. Though the elbow was still connected, the ends of the long bones were missing, their spongy interiors exposed along rough, gnarled edges.

"See how the ends are chewed off? That's animals. And this?" I indicated a small round hole. "That's a tooth puncture. Something small, probably a raccoon."

"Son of a buck."

"And of course the crabs and bugs did their share."

He rose, did a half turn, and kicked the dirt with the heel of his boot.

"Jesus H. Christ. Now what?"

"Now you call your local coroner, and he, or she, calls his, or her, local anthropologist." I rose and brushed dirt from my jeans. "And everybody talks to the sheriff."

"This is a goddam nightmare. I can't have people crawling all over this island."

"They don't have to crawl all over the island, Sam. They just have to come out, recover the body, maybe run a cadaver dog around to see if anyone else is buried here."

"How the—? Shit. This is impossible." A bead of sweat trickled down his temple. His jaw muscles bunched and unbunched.

For a moment neither of us spoke. The flies whined and circled.

Sam finally broke the silence. "You've got to do it."

"Do what?"

"Whatever has to be done. Dig this stuff up." He swept an arm in the direction of the grave.

"No way. Not my jurisdiction."

"I don't give a flying rat's ass whose jurisdiction it is. I'm not going to have a bunch of yo-yos running around out here, sabotaging my island, fucking up my work schedule, and very possibly infecting my monkeys. It's out of the question. It's not going to happen. I'm the bloody mayor, and this is my island. I'll sit on the goddam dock with a goddam shotgun before I let that happen."

The vein was back in his forehead, and the tendons in his neck stood out like guy wires. His finger jabbed the air to emphasize each point.

"That was an Academy Award performance, Sam, but I'm still not doing it. Dan Jaffer is at USC in Columbia. He does the anthropology cases in South Carolina, so that's probably who your coroner will call. Dan is board-certified and he's very good."

"Dan fucking Jaffer could have fucking TB!"

There seemed no point, so I didn't answer.

"You do this all the time! You could dig the guy out and turn everything over to this Jaffer character."

Still no point.

"Why the hell not, Tempe?" He glared at me.

"You know I'm in Beaufort on another case. I've promised these guys I'll work with them, and I have to be back in Charlotte on Wednesday."

I didn't give him the real answer, which was that I wanted nothing to do with this. I wasn't mentally ready to equate my island sanctuary with ugly death. Since first seeing the jaw, broken images had been floating through my brain, shards of cases past. Strangled women, butchered babies, young men with slashed throats and dull, unseeing eyes. If slaughter had come to the island, I wanted no part of it.

"We'll talk about this at camp," said Sam. "Don't mention bodies to anyone."

Ignoring his dictatorial manner, I tied my bandanna to the holly bush, and we headed back.

When we drew close to the trail I could see a battered pickup near the point at which we'd cut into the woods. The truck was loaded with bags of monkey chow and had a three-hundred-gallon water tank chained to the rear. Joey was inspecting the tank.

Sam called to him.

"Hold up a minute."

Joey wiped the back of his hand across his mouth and folded his arms. He wore jeans and a sweatshirt with the sleeves and neck cut out. His greasy blond hair hung like linguini around his face.

Joey watched us approach, his eyes hidden by sunglasses, his mouth a tight line across his face. His body looked taut and tense.

"I don't want anyone going near the pond," Sam said to Joey.

"Alice get another monkey?"

"No." Sam didn't elaborate. "Where's that chow going?"

"Feeder seven."

"Leave it and come right back."

"What about water?"

"Fill the tanks and get back to camp. If you see Jane, send her in."

Joey's shades moved to my face and rested there for what seemed a long time. Then he got into the pickup and pulled away, the tank clanking behind.

Sam and I walked in silence. I dreaded the scene about to take place, and resolved not to let him bully me. I recalled his words, saw his face as he uncovered the grave. Then something else. Just before Sam joined me, I thought I'd heard a motor. Had it been the pickup? I wondered how long Joey had been parked on the trail. And why right there?

"When did Joey start working for you?" I asked.

"Joey?" He thought a moment. "Almost two years ago."

"He's reliable?"

"Let's just say Joey's compassion exceeds his common sense. He's one of these bleeding-heart types, always talking about animal rights and worrying about disturbing the monkeys. He doesn't know jackshit about animals, but he's a good worker."

When we got to camp I found a note from Katy. She'd finished her observation and gone to the dock to read. While Sam got out the phone, I walked down to the water. My daughter sat in one of the boats, shoes off, legs stretched in front of her, her sleeves and pants legs rolled as high as they would go. I waved and she returned the gesture, then pointed at the boat. I wagged my head and held up both hands, indicating it wasn't time to leave. She smiled and resumed reading.

When I entered the field station Sam was at the kitchen table, talking on a cell phone. I slid onto the bench opposite him.

"When will he be back?" he asked into the mouthpiece. He looked more agitated than I'd ever seen him.

Pause. He tapped a pencil against the table, reversing from tip, to end, to tip as he slid it lengthwise through his fingers.

"Ivy Lee, I need to talk to him now. Can't you raise him somehow?"

Pause. Tap. Tap. Tap.

"No, a deputy will not do. I need Sheriff Baker."

Long pause. Tap. Ta— The lead snapped and Sam threw the pencil into a trash basket on the far side of the kitchen.

"I don't care what he said, keep trying. Have him call me here at the island. I'll wait."

He slammed down the receiver.

"How can both the sheriff and the coroner be out of contact?" He ran two hands through his hair.

I turned sideways on the bench, brought my feet up, and leaned against the wall. Through the years I'd learned that the best way to deal with Sam's temper was to ignore it. It came and went like a flash fire.

He got up and paced the kitchen, punching one hand into the palm of the other. "Where the hell is Harley?"

He looked at his watch.

"Four-ten. Terrific. In twenty minutes everyone will be here, wanting to get back to town. Hell, they're not even supposed to be here on Saturday. This is a make-up day for bad weather."

He kicked a piece of chalk across the room.

"I can't make them stay here. Or maybe I should? Maybe I should tell them about the body, say 'nobody leaves the island,' then take each suspect into the back room and grill him, like Hercule fucking Poirot!"

More pacing. Watch checking. Pacing. Finally he dropped onto the opposite bench and rested his forehead on his fists.

"Are you finished with your tantrum?"

No response.

"May I make a suggestion?"

He didn't look up.

"Here it is anyway. The body is on the island because someone doesn't want it found. Obviously they didn't count on J-7."

I spoke to the top of his head.

"I see several possibilities. One. It was brought here by one of your employees. Two. An outsider dropped in by boat, possibly a local who knows your routine. The island is unguarded after the crews leave, right?"

He nodded without raising his head.

"Three. It could be one of the drug traffickers who cruise around these waters."

No response.

"Aren't you a deputy wildlife officer?"

He looked up. His forehead glistened with sweat.

"Yes."

"If you can't raise the coroner or Sheriff Baker, and you won't trust a deputy, call your wildlife buddies. They have jurisdiction offshore, right? Calling them won't arouse suspicion and they can get someone out here to seal off the site until you talk to the sheriff."

He slapped the tabletop. "Kim."

"Whoever. Just ask them to keep it cool until you've talked with Baker. I've already told you what he's going to do."

"Kim Waggoner works for the South Carolina Department of Natural Resources. She's helped me out in the past when I've had law enforcement problems out here. I can trust Kim."

"Will she stay all night?" While I've never been a timid woman, holding murderers or drug dealers at bay was not a job I would want.

"No problem." He was already dialing. "Kim is an ex-marine."

"She can handle intruders?"

"She eats nails for breakfast."

Someone answered and he asked for Officer Waggoner.

"Wait till you see her," he said, covering the mouthpiece with his hand.

By the time the staff reconvened everything had been arranged. The crew took Katy in their boat, while Sam and I stayed behind. Kim arrived shortly after five and was everything Sam had promised. She wore jungle fatigues, combat boots, and an Australian bush hat, and packed enough munitions to hunt rhino. The island would be safe.

On the drive back to the marina, Sam again asked me to do the recovery. I repeated what I'd told him earlier. Sheriff. Coroner. Jaffer.

"I'll talk to you tomorrow," I said as he pulled up to the walkway. "Thanks for taking us out today. I know Katy loved it."

"No problemo."

We watched a pelican glide over the water, then fold its wings and dive headlong into a trough. It reappeared with a fish, the afternoon light metallic on its wet scales. Then the pelican tacked and the fish dropped, a silvery missile plummeting to the sea.

"Jesus Christ. Why did they have to pick my island?" Sam sounded tired and discouraged.

I opened the car door. "Let me know what Sheriff Baker says."

"I will."

"You do understand why I can't do the scene, don't you?"

"Scene. Christ."

When I slammed the door and leaned in the open window he started with a new argument.

"Tempe, think about it. Monkey island. Buried corpse. The local mayor. If there's a leak the press will go crazy with this, and you know how sensitive the animal rights issue is. I don't need the media discovering Murtry."

"That could happen no matter who works the case."

"I know. It's—"

"Let it go, Sam."

As I watched him drive off, the pelican circled back and swooped low above the boat. A new fish glistened in its beak.

Sam had that same tenacity. I doubted he would let it go, and I was right.

After dinner at Steamers Oyster Bar, Katy and I visited a gallery on Saint Helena. We meandered the rooms of the creaky old inn, inspecting the work of local Gullah artists, appreciating another perspective on a place we thought we knew. But as I critiqued collages, paintings, and photos, I remembered bones and crabs and dancing flies.

Katy bought a miniature heron carved from bark and painted periwinkle blue. On the way home we stopped for coffee ice cream, then ate it on the bow of the *Melanie Tess,* talking and listening to the lines and halyards of the surrounding sailboats clicking in the breeze. The moon spread a shimmering triangle outward from the marsh. As we chatted I watched the pale yellow light ripple on the undulating blackness.

My daughter confided her ambition to be a criminal profiler, and shared her misgivings about attaining that goal. She marveled at the beauty of Murtry and described the antics of the monkeys she'd observed. At one point I considered telling her of the day's discovery, but held back. I didn't want to sully the memory of her visit to the island.

I went to bed at eleven and lay for a long time listening to the creak of mooring lines and willing myself to sleep. Eventually I drifted off, taking the day with me and weaving it into the fabric of the last few weeks. I rode in a boat with Mathias and Malachy, desperately trying to keep them on board. I brushed crabs from a corpse, watched the seething mass re-form as fast as I scattered it. The corpse's skull morphed into Ryan's face, then into the charred features of Patrice Simonnet. Sam and Harry shouted at me, their words incomprehensible, their faces hard and angry.

When the phone woke me I felt disoriented, unsure where I was or why. I stumbled to the galley.

"Good morning." It was Sam, his voice sounding strained and edgy.

"What time is it?"

"Almost seven."

"Where are you?"

"At the sheriff's office. Your plan isn't going to work."

"Plan?" My brain fought to patch into the conversation.

"Your guy is in Bosnia."

I peeked through the blinds. At the inner dock, a grizzled old man sat on the deck of his sailboat. As I released the slats he tipped back his head and drained a can of Old Milwaukee.

"Bosnia?"

"Jaffer. The anthropologist at USC. He's gone to Bosnia to excavate mass graves for the UN. No one is sure when he'll be back."

"Who's covering his casework?"

"It doesn't matter. Baxter wants you to do the recovery."

"Who's Baxter?"

"Baxter Colker is the Beaufort County coroner. He wants you to do it."

"Why?"

"Because I want you to do it."

That was straightforward enough.

"When?"

"As soon as possible. Harley's got a detective and a deputy lined up. Baxter is meeting us here at nine. He has a transport team on call. When we're ready to leave Murtry, he'll phone over and they'll meet us at the Lady's Island dock to take the body to Beaufort Memorial. But he wants you to do the digging. Just tell us what equipment you need and we'll get it."

"Is Colker a forensic pathologist?"

"Baxter's an elected official and has no medical training. He runs a funeral home. But he's conscientious as hell and wants this thing done right."

I thought for a minute.

"Does Sheriff Baker have any idea who might be buried out there?"

"There's a lot of drug shit that goes on down here. He's going to talk to the folks over at U.S. Customs and the local DEA people. Also the wildlife agents. Harley tells me they were staking out the marshes in the Coosaw River last month. He thinks one of the drug brethren is our best bet, and I agree. These guys value life about as much as a used Q-Tip. You will help us, won't you?"

Reluctantly, I agreed. I told him what equipment to gather and he said he'd get right on it. I was to be ready at ten.

For several minutes I stood there, unsure what to do about Katy. I could explain the situation and leave it up to her. After all, there was no reason she couldn't go with us to the island. Or, I could simply tell her that something had come up and Sam had asked me for help. Katy could spend the day here, or leave for Hilton Head earlier than planned. I knew the second was a better idea, but decided to tell her anyway.

I ate a bowl of Raisin Bran and washed the dish and spoon. Unable to sit still, I threw on shorts and a T-shirt, and went outside to check the lines and water tank. While there I realigned the chairs on the bridge. Inside again, I made my bed and straightened the towels in the head. I rearranged the pillows on the salon sofa and picked fluff from the carpet. I wound the clock and checked the time. Only seven-fifteen. Katy wouldn't be up for hours. Putting on running shoes, I quietly let myself out.

I drove down Route 21 east across Saint Helena to Harbor Island, then Hunting Island, and turned in at the state park. The narrow blacktop wound through a slough still and dark as an underground lake. Palmetto palms and live oaks rose from the murky bottom. Here and there a shaft of sunlight sliced through the canopy, turning the water a honey gold.

I parked near the lighthouse and crossed a boardwalk to the beach. The tide was out and the wet sand glistened like a mirror. I watched a sandpiper skitter between tidal pools, its long filament legs disappearing into an inverted image of itself. The morning was cool, and goose bumps formed on my arms and legs as I went through my warm-up.

I ran east beside the Atlantic Ocean, my feet sinking only slightly into the packed sand. The air was absolutely calm. I passed a formation of pelicans bobbing on the gently rolling water. The broom sedge and sea oats stood motionless on the dunes.

As I jogged I studied the ocean's offerings. Driftwood, rippled and smoothed and covered in barnacles. Tangled seaweed. The shiny brown shell of a horseshoe crab. A mullet, its eyes and innards gnawed clean by crabs and gulls.

I ran until my lungs burned. Then I ran some more. When I got back to the boardwalk, my trembling legs could barely carry me up the stairs. But mentally I felt rejuvenated. Maybe it was the dead fish, or even the horseshoe crab. Maybe I'd simply raised my endorphin level. But I no longer dreaded the day ahead. Death occurred every minute of every day in every place on the globe. It was part of the cycle of life, and that included Murtry Island. I would unearth this corpse and deliver it to those in charge. That was my job.

When I slipped back onto the boat Katy was still asleep. I made coffee, then went to shower, hoping the sound of the pump wouldn't disturb her. When I'd dressed, I toasted two English muffins, spread them with butter and blackberry jam, and took them to the salon. Friends tell me that physical exertion is an appetite depressant. Not for me. Exercise makes me want to devour my body weight in food.

I clicked on the TV, surfed the channels, and chose one of the half dozen evangelists offering Sunday morning advice. I was listening to the Reverend Eugene Highwater describe the "endless bounty provided the righteous" when Katy stumbled in and threw herself onto the couch. Her face was creased and puffy from sleep, and her hair looked like one of the seaweed tumbles I'd passed on the beach. She wore a Hornets T-shirt that hung to her knees.

"Good morning. You're lovely today."

No response from my daughter.

"Coffee?"

She nodded, eyes still shut.

I went to the kitchen, filled a mug, and brought it to her. Katy rolled to a semi-upright position, tentatively raised her lids, and reached for the coffee.

"I stayed up till two reading."

She took a sip, then held the mug out as she stood and folded her feet under her, Indian style. Her newly opened eyes fell on the Reverend Highwater.

"Why are you listening to that twit?"

"I'm trying to find out how you get this endless bounty stuff."

"Write him a check and he'll send you a four-pack."

Charity was not on the list of my daughter's early morning virtues.

"Who was the moron that called at dawn?"

Nor was delicacy.

"Sam."

"Oh. What did he want?"

"Katy, something happened yesterday that I didn't tell you about."

Her eyes went to full attention and fixed on mine.

I hesitated, then launched into an account of the previous day's discovery. Avoiding details, I described the body, and how J-7 had led us to it, then told her of my phone conversation with Sam.

"So you're going back out there today?" She raised her mug to drink.

"Yes. With the coroner and a team from the sheriff's office. Sam is picking me up at ten. I'm sorry about our day. You're welcome to come along, of course, but I understand if you'd rather not."

For a long time she said nothing. The reverend blustered on about Jeee-sus.

"Do they have any idea who it is?"

"The sheriff is thinking drugs. Traffickers use the rivers and inlets around here to bring stuff in. He suspects a deal went bad and someone ended up with a body to off-load."

"What will you do out there?"

"We'll remove the body, collect samples, and take a lot of pictures."

"No, no. I mean, tell me exactly what you'll do. I might be able to use it for a paper or something."

"Step by step?"

She nodded and settled back into the cushions.

"It looks pretty routine. We'll clear the vegetation, then set up a grid with a reference point for drawings and measurements." The St-Jovite basement flashed through my mind. "When we're done with surface collection I'll open the grave. Some recovery teams excavate in levels, looking for layering and whatnot. I don't really think that's necessary in these situations. When someone digs a hole, drops in a body, and covers it up, there isn't going to be any stratigraphy. But I'll keep one side of the trench clean so I'll have a profile as I go down into the grave. That way I can see if there are tool marks in the soil."

"Tool marks?"

"A shovel, or maybe a spade or a pick that's left an imprint in the dirt. I've never seen one, but some of my colleagues swear they have. They claim you can take impressions then make molds and match them to suspect tools. What I *have* seen are footwear impressions in the bottom of graves, especially if there's a lot of clay and silt. I'll definitely check for those."

"From the guy that dug it?"

"Yeah. When the hole reaches a certain depth the digger may jump in and work from there. If so, he can leave shoe prints. I'll also take soil samples. Sometimes soil from a grave can be matched to dirt found on a suspect."

"Or on his closet floor."

"Exactly. And I'll collect bugs."

"Bugs?"

"This burial is going to be lousy with bugs. It's shallow to begin with, and the turkey vultures and raccoons have partially exposed the body. The flies are having a jamboree out there. They'll be useful for determining PMI."

"PMI?"

"Postmortem interval. How long the person's been dead."

"How?"

"Entomologists have studied carrion-eating insects, mostly flies and beetles. They've found that different species arrive at a body in regular sequence, then each goes through its life cycle just as predictably. Some fly species arrive within minutes. Others show up later. The adults lay their eggs, and the eggs hatch into larvae. That's what maggots are, fly larvae."

Katy gave a grimace.

"After a certain period the larvae abandon the body and encase themselves in a hard outer shell called a pupa. Eventually they hatch as adults and fly off to start the whole thing over again."

"Why don't all the bugs arrive at the same time?"

"Different species have different game plans. Some come to munch on the corpse. Others prefer to dine on the eggs and larvae of their predecessors."

"Gross."

"There's a niche for everyone."

"What will you do with the bugs?"

"I'll collect samples of larvae and pupal casings, and try to net some adult insects. Depending on the state of preservation, I may also use a probe to take thermal readings from the body. When maggot masses form they can raise the internal temperature of a corpse appreciably. That's also useful for PMI estimation."

"Then what?"

"I'll preserve all the adults and half the larvae in an alcohol solution. The other larvae I'll place in containers with liver and vermiculite. The entomologist will raise them to hatching and identify what they are."

I wondered where Sam would come up with nets, ice cream containers, vermiculite, and a thermal probe on a Sunday morning. Not to mention the screens, trowels, and other excavating equipment I'd requested. That was his problem.

"What about the body?"

"That will depend on its condition. If it's fairly intact I'll simply lift it out and zip it in a body bag. A skeleton will take longer since I'll have to do a bone inventory to be sure I have everything."

She thought about this.

"What's the best-case scenario?"

"All day."

"What's the worst-case scenario?"

"Longer."

Frowning, she ran her fingers through her hair, then tied it into a loose knot on her neck.

"You keep your appointment on Murtry. I think I'll hang here then catch a ride to Hilton Head."

"Your friends won't mind picking you up early?"

"Nah. It's on the way."

"Good choice." I meant it.

It went as I'd described to Katy, but for one major variation. There was stratigraphy. Below the body with the crab face I was shocked to find a second decomposing corpse. It lay on the bottom of the four-foot pit, facedown, arms tucked below its belly, at a twenty-degree angle to the body above.

Depth has its benefits. Though the upper remains had been reduced to bone and connective tissue, those below retained a large amount of flesh and soupy innards. I worked until dark, meticulously screening every particle of dirt, taking soil, flora, and insect samples, and transferring the corpses to body bags. The sheriff's detective took videos and stills.

Sam, Baxter Colker, and Harley Baker watched from a distance, occasionally commenting or stepping forward for a better look. The deputy searched the surrounding woods with a Sheriff's Department dog specially trained to alert to the smell of decomposition. Kim looked for physical evidence.

All to no avail. Except for the two bodies, nothing turned up. The victims had been stripped naked and dumped, robbed of everything that linked them to their lives. And as hard as I studied the details, neither the body positions nor anything I observed in the grave contour or fill revealed if the victims had been buried simultaneously, or if the upper corpse had followed at a later date.

It was almost eight when we watched Baxter Colker slam the door of the transport van and lock the handle in place. The coroner, Sam, and I were gathered beside the blacktop, above the dock where we'd moored the boats.

Colker looked like a stick figure in his bow tie and neatly pressed suit, his trousers belted high above the waist. While Sam had warned me of the Beaufort County coroner's fastidiousness, I'd been unprepared for business attire at an exhumation. I wondered what the man wore to dinner parties.

"Well, that does her," he said, wiping his hands on a linen handkerchief. Hundreds of tiny veins had burst and coalesced in his cheeks, giving his face a bluish cast. He turned to me.

"I guess I'll see you at the hospital tomorrow." It was more a statement than a question.

"Whoa. Hold on. I thought these cases were going to the forensic pathologist in Charleston."

"Well, now, I can send these cases up to the medical college, ma'am, but I know what that gentleman is going to tell me." Colker had been "ma'aming" me all day.

"That's Axel Hardaway?"

"Yes, ma'am. And Dr. Hardaway is going to tell me that I need an anthropologist because he doesn't know beans about bones. That's what he's going to tell me. And I understand Dr. Jaffer, the regular anthropologist, isn't available. Now, where does that leave these poor folks?" He waved a bony hand at the van.

"No matter who does the skeletal analysis, you're still going to want a full autopsy on the second body."

Something startled in the river, breaking the moonlight into a thousand little pieces. A breeze had picked up and I could smell rain in the air.

Colker knocked on the side of the van and an arm appeared in the window, waved, and the van pulled away. Colker watched it for a moment.

"Those two souls are going to overnight at Beaufort Memorial, today being Sunday. In the meantime I'll get hold of Dr. Hardaway and see what his preference is. May I ask where you're staying, ma'am?"

As I was telling him, the sheriff joined us.

"I want to thank you again, Dr. Brennan. You did a fine job out there."

Baker stood a foot taller than the coroner, and Sam and Colker together did not equal his body mass. Under his uniform shirt the sheriff's chest and arms looked as if they'd been forged from iron. His face was angular, his skin the color of strong coffee. Harley Baker looked like a heavyweight contender and spoke like a Harvard grad.

"Thank you, Sheriff. Your detective and deputy were very helpful."

When we shook hands mine looked pale and slender inside his. I suspected his grip could crush granite.

"Thank you again. I'll see you tomorrow with Detective Ryan. And I'll take good care of your bugs."

Baker and I had already discussed the insects, and I'd given him the name of an entomologist. I'd explained how to ship them and how to store the soil and plant samples. Everything was now on its way to the county government center in the care of the Sheriff's Department detective.

Baker shook hands with Colker and gave Sam a friendly punch on the shoulder.

"I know I'll see your sorry face," he said to Sam as he strode away. A minute later his cruiser passed us on its way to Beaufort.

Sam and I drove back to the *Melanie Tess,* stopping for carryout on the way. We spoke little. I could smell death on my clothes and hair, and I wanted to shower, eat, and fall into an eight-hour coma. Sam probably wanted me out of his car.

By nine forty-five my hair was wrapped in a towel and I smelled of White Diamonds moisturizing mist. I was raising the cover of my carryout box when Ryan called.

"Where are you?" I asked, squeezing ketchup onto my fries.

"An enchanting little place called the Lord Carteret."

"What's wrong with it?"

"There's no golf course."

"We're to meet with the sheriff at nine tomorrow." I inhaled the fry.

"Zero nine hundred hours, Dr. Brennan. What are you eating?"

"A salami sub."

"At ten P.M.?"

"It was a long day."

"My day wasn't exactly a walk in the park." I heard a match, then a long exhalation of breath. "Three flights, then the drive from Savannah out here to Tara, and then I couldn't even raise this yokel of a sheriff. He was out on some damn thing all day, and no one would say where he was or what he was doing. Very hush-hush. He and Aunt Bee probably work deep cover for the CIA."

"Sheriff Baker is solid. " I slurped a spoonful of slaw.

"You know him?"

"I spent the day with him."

Hush puppy.

"That chewing sounds different."

"Hush puppy."

"What's a hush puppy?"

"If you chip in I'll get you one tomorrow."

"Yahoo. What is it?"

"Deep-fried cornmeal."

"What were you and Baker doing all day?"

I gave him a brief account of the body recovery.

"And Baker suspects the hookah boys?"

"Yes. But I don't think so."

"Why not?"

"Ryan, I'm exhausted, and Baker's expecting us early. I'll tell you tomorrow. Can you find the Lady's Island Marina?"

"My first guess would be Lady's Island."

I gave him directions and we hung up. Then I finished my dinner and fell into bed, not bothering with pajamas. I slept naked and like a rock, dreaming nothing that I could recall for a solid eight hours.

At eight o'clock on Monday morning traffic was heavy on the Woods Memorial Bridge. The sky was overcast, the river choppy and slate green. The news on the car radio predicted light rain and a high of seventy-two for the day. Ryan looked out of place in his wool trousers and tweed jacket, like an arctic creature blown to the tropics. He was already perspiring.

As we crossed into Beaufort, I explained jurisdiction in the county. I told Ryan that the Beaufort Police Department functions strictly within the city limits, and described the other three municipalities, Port Royal, Bluffton, and Hilton Head, each with its own force.

"The rest of Beaufort County is unincorporated, so it's Sheriff Baker's bailiwick," I summed up. "His department also provides services to Hilton Head Island. Detectives, for example."

"Sounds like Quebec," said Ryan.

"It is. You just have to know whose turf you're on."

"Simonnet phoned her calls to Saint Helena. So that's Baker."

"Yes."

"You say he's solid."

"I'll let you form your own opinion."

"Tell me about the bodies you dug up."

I did.

"Jesus, Brennan, how do you get yourself into these things?"

"It is my job, Ryan." The question irked me. Everything about Ryan irked me lately.

"But you were on holiday."

Yes. On Murtry. With my daughter.

"It must be my rich fantasy life," I snapped. "I dream up corpses, then poof, there they are. It's what I live for."

I clamped my teeth and watched tiny drops gather on the windshield. If Ryan needed conversation he could talk to himself.

"I may need a little guidance here," he said as we passed the campus of USC-Beaufort.

"Carteret will take a hard left and turn into Boundary. Go with it."

We curved west past the condominiums at Pigeon Point, and eventually drove between the redbrick walls that enclose the National Cemetery on both sides of the road. At Ribaut I indicated a left turn.

Ryan signaled, then headed south. On our left we passed a Maryland Fried Chicken, the fire station, and the Second Pilgrim Baptist Church. On our right sprawled the county government center. The vanilla stucco buildings house the county administrative offices, the courthouse, the solicitors' offices, various law enforcement agencies, and the jail. The faux columns and archways were intended to create a low-country flavor, but instead the complex looks like an enormous Art Deco medical mall.

At Ribaut and Duke I pointed to a sand lot shaded by live oaks and Spanish moss. Ryan pulled in and parked between a Beaufort City Police cruiser and the county Haz Mat trailer. Sheriff Baker had just arrived and was reaching for something in the back of his cruiser. Recognizing me, he waved, slammed the trunk, and waited for us to join him.

I made introductions and the men shook hands. The rain had dwindled to a fine mist."Sorry to have to put one through your basket," said Ryan. "I'm sure you're busy enough without foreigners dropping in."

"No problem at all," Baker replied. "I hope we can do something for you."

"Nice digs," said Ryan, nodding toward the building housing the Sheriff's Department.

As we crossed Duke, the sheriff gave a brief explanation of the complex.

"In the early nineties the county decided it wanted all its agencies under one roof, so it built this place at a cost of about thirty million dollars. We've got our own space, so does the city of Beaufort, but we share services such as communications, dispatch, records."

A pair of deputies passed us on their way to the lot. They waved and Baker nodded in return, then he opened the glass door and held it for us.

The offices of the Beaufort County Sheriff's Department lay to the right, past a glass case filled with uniforms and plaques. The city police were to the left, through a door marked AUTHORIZED PERSONNEL ONLY. Next to that door another case displayed pictures of the FBI's ten most wanted, photos of local missing persons, and a poster from the Center for Missing and Exploited Children. Straight ahead a hallway led past an elevator to the building's interior.

We entered the sheriff's corridor to see a woman hanging an umbrella on a hall tree. Though well past fifty, she looked like an escapee from a Madonna video. Her hair was long and jet-black, and she wore a lace slip over a peacock mini-dress with a violet bolero jacket over that. Platform clogs added three inches to her height. She spoke to the sheriff.

"Mr. Colker just phoned. And some detective called 'bout half a dozen times yesterday with his balls on fire 'bout something. It's on your desk."

"Thank you, Ivy Lee. This is Detective Ryan." Baker indicated the two of us. "And Dr. Brennan. The department will be assisting them in a matter."

Ivy Lee looked us over.

"You want coffee, sir?"

"Yes. Thank you."

"Three, then?"

"Yes."

"Cream?"

Ryan and I nodded.

We entered the sheriff's office and everyone sat. Baker tossed his hat onto a bank of file cabinets behind his desk.

"Ivy Lee can be colorful," he said, smiling. "She did twenty with the Marines, then came home and joined us." He thought a moment. "That's about nineteen years now. The lady runs this place with the efficiency of a hydrogen fuel cell. Right now she's doing some . . ." He searched for a phrase. ". . . fashion experimentation."

Baker leaned back and laced his fingers behind his head. His leather chair wheezed like a bagpipe.

"So, Mr. Ryan, tell me what you need."

Ryan described the deaths in St-Jovite, and explained the calls to Saint Helena. He had just outlined his conversations with the Beaufort-Jasper Clinic obstetrician and with Heidi Schneider's parents when Ivy Lee knocked. She placed a mug in front of Baker, set two others on a table between Ryan and me, and left without a word.

I took a sip. Then another.

"Does she make this?" I asked. If not the best coffee I'd ever tasted, it was right near the top of the list.

Baker nodded.

I drank again and tried to identify the flavors. I heard a phone in the outer office, then Ivy Lee's voice.

"What's in it?"

"It's a 'don't ask don't tell' policy with regard to Ivy Lee's coffee. I give her an allowance each month, and she buys the ingredients. She claims no one knows the recipe but her sisters and her mama."

"Can they be bribed?"

Laughing, Baker lay his forearms on the desk and leaned his weight on them. His shoulders were wider than a cement truck.

"I wouldn't want to offend Ivy Lee," he said. "And definitely not her mama."

"Good policy," agreed Ryan. "Don't offend the mamas." He flipped the elastic from a corrugated brown folder, searched the contents, and withdrew a paper.

"The number phoned from St-Jovite traces to four-three-five Adler Lyons Road."

"You're right about that being Saint Helena," said Baker.

He swiveled to the metal cabinets, slid open a drawer, and pulled a file. Laying the folder on his desk, he perused its one document.

"We ran the address, and there's no police history. Not a single call in the past five years."

"Is it a private home?" asked Ryan.

"Probably. That part of the island is pretty much trailers and small homes. I've been living here off and on all of my life and I had to use a map to find Adler Lyons. Some of the dirt roads out on the islands are little more than driveways. I might know them to see them, but I don't always know their names. Or if they even have names."

"Who owns the property?"

"I don't have that, but we'll check it out later. In the meantime, why don't we just drop in for a friendly visit."

"Suits me," said Ryan, replacing his paper and snapping the elastic into place.

"And we can swing by the clinic if you think that would be useful."

"I don't want to jam you up with this. I know you're busy." Ryan rose. "If you prefer to point us in the right direction, I'm sure we'll be fine."

"No, no. I owe Dr. Brennan for yesterday. And I'm sure Baxter Colker isn't through with her yet. In fact, would you mind waiting while I check something?"

He disappeared into an adjacent office, returned immediately with a message slip.

"As I suspected, Colker called again. He's sent the bodies up to Charleston, but he wants to talk to Dr. Brennan." He smiled at me. His cheekbones and brow ridges were so prominent, his skin so shiny black, his face looked ceramic in the fluorescent light.

I looked at Ryan. He shrugged and sat back down. Baker dialed a number, asked for Colker, then handed me the phone. I had a bad feeling.

Colker said exactly what I anticipated. Axel Hardaway would perform the autopsies on the Murtry bodies, but refused to do any skeletal analysis. Dan Jaffer couldn't be reached. Hardaway would process the remains at the med school facility following any protocol I specified, then Colker would transport the bones to my lab in Charlotte if I would do the examinations.

Reluctantly, I agreed, and promised to speak directly with Hardaway. Colker gave me the number and we hung up.

"*Allons-y,*" I said to the others.

"*Allons-y,*" echoed the sheriff, reaching for his hat and placing it on his head.

* * *

We took Highway 21 out of Beaufort to Lady's Island, crossed Cowan's Creek to Saint Helena, and continued for several miles. At Eddings Point Road we turned left, and drove past miles of weather-beaten frame houses and trailers set on pilings. Plastic stretched across windows and porches sagged under the weight of moth-eaten easy chairs and old appliances. In the yards I could see junked auto frames and parts, makeshift sheds, and rusted septic tanks. Here and there a hand-lettered sign offered collards, butter beans, or goats.

Before long the blacktop made a hard left and sandy roads took off ahead and to the right. Baker turned and we entered a long, shady tunnel. Live oaks lined the road, their bark mossy, their branches arching overhead like the dome on a green cathedral. To either side ran narrow moats of algae-coated water.

Our tires scrunched softly as we passed more mobile homes and run-down houses, some with plastic or wooden whirligigs, others with chickens scratching in the yards. Save for the model years of the beat-up cars and pickups, the area looked much as it must have in the nineteen-thirties. And forties. And fifties.

Within a quarter mile Adler Lyons joined us from the left. Baker turned and drove almost to the end and stopped. Across the way I could see mossy gravestones shaded by live oaks and magnolias. Here and there a wooden cross gleamed white in the murky shadows.

To our right stood a pair of buildings, the larger a two-story farmhouse with dark green siding, the smaller a bungalow, once white, its paint now gray and peeling. Behind the houses I observed trailers and a swing set.

A low wall separated the compound from the road. It was built of cinder blocks laid sideways and stacked, so the centers formed rows and layers of small tunnels. Each hollow was packed with vines and creepers, and purple wisteria meandered the length of the wall. At the driveway entrance a rusted metal sign said PRIVATE PROPERTY in bright orange letters.

The road continued less than a hundred feet past the wall, then ended in a stand of marsh grass. Beyond the weeds lay water the color of dull pewter.

"That should be four-three-five," said Sheriff Baker, shifting into park and indicating the larger home. "This was a fishing camp years ago." He tipped his head toward the water. "That's Eddings Point Creek out there. It empties into the sound not too far up. I'd forgotten about this property. It was abandoned for years."

The place had definitely seen better times. The siding on the farmhouse was patched and covered with mildew. The trim, once white, was now blistered and flaking to reveal a pale blue underlayer. A screened porch ran the width of the first floor, and dormer windows projected from the third, their upper borders mimicking in miniature the angle of the roof.

We got out, rounded the wall, and headed up the drive. Mist hung in the air like smoke. I could smell mud and decomposing leaves, and from far off, the hint of a bonfire.

The sheriff stepped onto the stoop while Ryan and I waited on the grass. The inner door stood open, but it was too dark to see past the screen. Baker moved to the side and knocked, rattling the door in its frame. Overhead, birdsong mingled with the click of palmetto fronds. From inside, I thought I heard a baby cry.

Baker knocked again.

In a moment we heard footsteps, then a young man appeared at the door. He had freckles and curly red hair, and wore denim overalls with a plaid shirt. I had a feeling we were about to interview Howdy Doody.

"Yeah?" He spoke through the screen, his eyes moving among the three of us.

"How are you doing?" asked Baker, greeting him with the Southern substitute for "hello."

"Fine."

"Good. I'm Harley Baker." His uniform made clear this was not a social call. "May we come in?"

"Why?"

"We'd just like to ask you a few questions."

"Questions?"

"Do you live here?"

Howdy nodded.

"May we come in?" Baker repeated.

"Shouldn't you have a warrant or something?"

"No."

I heard a voice, and Howdy turned and spoke over his shoulder. In a moment he was joined by a middle-aged woman with a broad face and perm-frizzed hair. She held an infant to one shoulder, and alternately patted and rubbed its back. The flesh on her upper arm jiggled with each movement.

"It's a cop," he said to her, stepping back from the screen.

"Yes?"

While Ryan and I listened, Baker and the woman exchanged the same B-movie dialogue we'd just heard. Then,

"There's no one here right now. You come back some other time."

"You're here, ma'am," replied Baker.

"We're busy with the babies."

"We're not going away, ma'am," said the Beaufort County sheriff.

The woman made a face, shifted the baby higher on her shoulder, and pushed open the screen door. Her flip-flops made soft popping sounds as we followed her across the porch and into a small foyer.

The house was dim and smelled slightly sour, like milk left overnight in a glass. Straight ahead, a staircase rose to the second floor, to the right and left archways opened on to large rooms filled with sofas and chairs.

The woman led us to the room on the left and indicated a grouping of rattan couches. As we sat she whispered something to Howdy, and he disappeared up the stairs. Then she joined us.

"Yes?" she asked quietly, looking from Baker to Ryan.

"My name is Harley Baker." He set his hat on the coffee table and leaned toward her, hands on his thighs, arms bent outward. "And you are?"

She placed an arm across the baby's back, cradled its head, and raised the other, palm toward him. "I don't mean to be unpolite, Sheriff, but I got to know what you want."

"Do you live here, ma'am?"

She hesitated, then nodded. A curtain rippled in a window behind me and I felt a damp breeze on my neck.

"We're curious about some calls made to this house," Baker went on.

"Phone calls?"

"Yes, ma'am. Last fall. Would you have been here at that time?"

"There's no phone here."

"No phone?"

"Well, just an office phone. Not for personal use."

"I see." He waited.

"We don't get phone calls."

"We?"

"There are nine of us in this house, four next door. And of course the trailers. But we don't talk on no phones. It's not allowed."

Upstairs, another baby started to cry.

"Not allowed?"

"We're a community. We live clean and don't cause no trouble. No drugs, none of that. We keep to ourselves and follow our beliefs. There's no law against that, is there?"

"No, ma'am, there isn't. How large is your group?"

She thought a minute. "We're twenty-six here."

"Where are the others?"

"Some's gone off to jobs. Those that integrate. The rest are at morning meeting next door. Jerry and I are watching the babies."

"Are you a religious group?" Ryan asked.

She looked at him, back to Baker.

"Who are they?" She raised her chin toward Ryan and me.

"They're homicide detectives." The sheriff stared at her, his face hard and unsmiling. "What is your group, ma'am?"

She fingered the baby's blanket. Somewhere in the distance I heard a dog bark.

"We want no problems with the law," she said. "You can take my word on that."

"Are you expecting trouble?" Ryan.

She gave him an odd look, then glanced at her watch. "We are people wanting peace and health. We can't take no more of the drugs and crime, so we live out here by ourselves. We don't hurt no one. I don't have no more to say. You talk to Dom. He'll be here soon."

"Dom?"

"He'll know what to tell you."

"That would be good." Baker's dark eyes impaled her again. "I wouldn't want everyone to have to make that long trip into town."

Just then I heard voices and watched her gaze slide off Baker's face and out the window. We all turned to look.

Through the screen I saw activity at the house next door. Five women stood on the porch, two holding toddlers, a third bending to set a child onto the ground. The tot took off on wobbly legs, and the woman followed across the yard. One by one a dozen adults emerged and disappeared behind the house. Seconds later a man came out and headed in our direction.

Our hostess excused herself and went to the foyer. Before long we heard the screen door, then muted voices.

I saw the woman climb the stairs, then the man from next door appeared in the archway. I guessed he was in his mid-forties. His blond hair was going gray, his face and arms deeply tanned. He wore khakis, a pale yellow golf shirt, and Topsiders without socks. He looked like an aging Kappa Sigma.

"I'm so sorry," he said. "I didn't realize we had visitors."

Ryan and Baker started to rise.

"Please, please. Don't get up." He crossed to us and held out a hand. "I'm Dom."

We all shook, and Dom joined us on one of the sofas.

"Would you like some juice or lemonade?"

We all declined.

"So, you've been talking to Helen. She says you have some questions about our group?"

Baker nodded once.

"I suppose we're what you'd call a commune." He laughed. "But not what the term usually conjures up. We're a far cry from the counterculture hippies of the sixties. We are opposed to drugs and polluting chemicals, and committed to purity, creativity, and self-awareness. We live and work together in harmony. For instance, we've just finished our morning meeting. That's where we discuss each day's agenda and collectively decide what has to be done and who will do it. Food preparation, cleaning chores, housekeeping mostly." He smiled. "Mondays can be long since that's the day we air grievances." Again the smile. "Although we rarely have grievances."

The man leaned back and folded his hands in his lap. "Helen tells me you're interested in phone calls."

The sheriff introduced himself. "And you are Dom . . . ?"

"Just Dom. We don't use surnames."

"We do," said Baker, his voice devoid of humor.

There was a long pause. Then,

"Owens. But he's long dead. I haven't been Dominick Owens in years."

"Thank you, Mr. Owens." Baker made a note in a tiny spiral notebook. "Detective Ryan is investigating a homicide in Quebec and has reason to believe the victim knew someone at this address."

"Quebec?" Dom's eyes widened, revealing tiny white creases in his tan skin. "Canada?"

"Calls were made to this number from a home in St-Jovite," said Ryan. "That's a village in the Laurentian Mountains north of Montreal."

Dom listened, a puzzled look on his face.

"Does the name Patrice Simonnet mean anything to you?"

He shook his head.

"Heidi Schneider?"

More head shaking. "I'm sorry." Dom smiled and gave a light shrug. "I told you. We don't use last names. And members often change their given names. In the group one is free to choose whatever name one likes."

"What is the name of your group?"

"Names. Labels. Titles. *The* Church of Christ. *The* People's Temple. *The* Righteous Path. Such egomania. We choose not to use one."

"How long has your group lived here, Mr. Owens?" Ryan.

"Please call me Dom."

Ryan waited.

"Almost eight years."

"Were you here last summer and fall?"

"On and off. I was traveling quite a bit."

Ryan took a snapshot from his pocket and placed it on the table.

"We're trying to track the whereabouts of this young woman."

Dom leaned forward and examined the photo, his fingers smoothing the edges. They were long and slender, with tufts of golden hair between the knuckles.

"Is she the one that was killed?"

"Yes."

"Who's the boy?"

"Brian Gilbert."

Dom studied the faces a long time. When he looked up his eyes had an expression I couldn't read.

"I wish I could help you. Really, I do. Perhaps I could ask at this evening's experiential session. That's when we encourage self-exploration and movement toward inner awareness. It would be an appropriate setting."

Ryan's face was rigid as his eyes held Dom's.

"I'm not in a ministerial mood, Mr. Owens, and I'm not particularly concerned with what you consider appropriate times. Here's chapter and verse. I know calls were made to this number from the house where Heidi Schneider was murdered. I know the victim was in Beaufort last summer. I'm going to find the connection."

"Yes, of course. How terrible. It is this kind of violence that causes us to live as we do."

He closed his eyes, as though seeking holy guidance, then opened them and gazed intently at each of us.

"Let me explain. We grow our own vegetables, raise chickens for eggs, we fish, and gather mollusks. Some members work in town and contribute wages. We have a set of beliefs that forces us to reject society, but we wish no harm to others. We live simply and quietly."

He took a long breath.

"While we have a core of longtime members, there are many that come and go. Our lifestyle is not for everyone. It's possible your young woman visited with us, perhaps during one of my absences. You have my word. I will speak to the others," said Dom.

"Yes," said Ryan. "So will I."

"Of course. And please let me know if there is anything else that I can do."

At that moment a young woman burst through the screen door, a toddler on her hip. She was laughing and tickling the child. He giggled and batted at her with pudgy fingers.

Malachy's pale little hands skittered across my mind.

When she saw us, the woman hunched and gave a grimace.

"Oops. Sorry." She laughed. "I didn't know anyone was here." The toddler thumped her head, and she scratched a finger on his stomach. He squealed and kicked his legs.

"Come in, Kathryn," said Dom. "I think we're finished here."

He looked a question at Baker and Ryan. The sheriff retrieved his hat and we all rose.

The child turned toward Dom's voice, spotted him, and began to wriggle. When Kathryn set him down, he teetered forward with outstretched arms, and Dom bent to scoop him up. His arms looked milky white around Dom's sun-darkened neck.

Kathryn joined us.

"How old is your baby?" I asked.

"Fourteen months. Aren't you, Carlie?" She extended a finger and Carlie grabbed for it, then held his arms out toward her. Dom returned the baby to its mother.

"Excuse us," Kathryn said. "He needs a nappy change."

"Before you go, may I ask you one question?" Ryan produced the photo. "Do you know either of these people?"

Kathryn studied the snapshot, holding it beyond Carlie's reach. I watched Dom's face. His expression never changed.

Kathryn shook her head, then handed back the photo. "No. Sorry." She fanned the air and wrinkled her nose. "Gotta go."

"The woman was pregnant," Ryan offered.

"Sorry," said Kathryn.

"He's a beautiful baby," I said.

"Thank you." She smiled and disappeared into the back of the house.

Dom looked at his watch.

"We'll be in touch," said Baker.

"Yes. Good. And good luck."

Back in the car, we sat and studied the property. I'd cracked the passenger-side window, and mist blew in and settled on my face. The flash of Malachy had depressed me, and the damp, gray weather mirrored my mood perfectly.

I scanned the road in both directions, then looked again at the houses. I could see people working in a garden behind the bungalow. Seed packets stuck on sticks identified the contents of each patch. Otherwise, there were no signs of life.

"What do you think?" I asked no one in particular.

"If they've been here eight years they've kept a very low profile," said Baker. "I haven't heard a thing about them."

We watched Helen leave the green house and walk to one of the trailers.

"But they're about to be discovered," he added, reaching for the ignition.

For several miles, no one spoke. We were crossing the bridge into Beaufort when Ryan broke the silence.

"There's got to be a link. It can't be coincidence."

"Coincidences do happen," said Baker.

"Yes."

"One thing bothers me," I said.

"What's that?"

"Heidi quit going to the clinic here in her sixth month. Her parents said she showed up in Texas in late August. Right?"

"Right."

"But the phone calls continued to the number here until December."

"Yes," said Ryan. "That's a problem."

19

THE MIST CHANGED TO RAIN AS WE DROVE TO THE BEAUFORT-Jasper Comprehensive Health Clinic. It turned the tree trunks dark and shiny and painted a sheen on the blacktop. When I cracked the window I could smell wet grass and earth.

We located the doctor with whom Ryan had spoken, and he showed her the photo. She thought she recognized Heidi as the patient she'd treated the previous summer, but couldn't be sure. The pregnancy was normal. She'd written the standard prenatal prescriptions. Beyond that, she could tell us nothing. She had no recollection of Brian.

At noon Sheriff Baker left us to handle a domestic situation on Lady's Island. We agreed to meet at his office at six, by which time he hoped to have information on the Adler Lyons property.

Ryan and I stopped for barbecue at Sgt.White's Diner, then spent the afternoon showing Heidi's snapshot around town, and asking about the commune on Adler Lyons Road.

By four o'clock we knew two things: No one had heard of Dom Owens or his followers. No one remembered Heidi Schneider or Brian Gilbert.

We sat in Ryan's rental car and stared up Bay Street. On my right customers entered and left the Palmetto Federal Banking Center. I looked across to the stores we'd just canvassed. The Cat's Meow.

Stones and Bones. In High Cotton. Yes. Beaufort had embraced the world of tourism.

The rain had stopped but the sky was still dark and heavy. I felt tired and discouraged, and no longer sure about the Beaufort–St-Jovite connection.

Outside Lipsitz Department Store a man with greased hair and a face like bread dough waved a Bible and screamed about Jesus. March was the off season for sidewalk salvation, so he had the stage to himself.

Sam had told me about his war with the street preachers. For twenty years they'd been coming to Beaufort, descending on the city like pilgrims on hajj. In 1993 His Honor had the Reverend Isaac Abernathy arrested for harassing women in shorts, calling them whores and bellowing about eternal damnation. Suits were filed against the mayor and the city, and the ACLU jumped to the defense of the evangelists, the issue being one of First Amendment rights. The case was pending review by the Fourth Circuit Court of Appeals in Richmond, and the preachers still came.

I listened to the man rant about Satan and heathens and Jews, and felt tiny hairs rise on the back of my neck. I resent those who see themselves as God's spokesmen and next of kin, and am disturbed by people interpreting the Gospel to push a political agenda.

"What do you think of Southern civilization?" I asked Ryan, my eyes never leaving the preacher.

"Sounds like a good idea."

"Well, well. Stealing material from Gandhi," I said, turning to him in surprise. It was one of my favorite Gandhi quotes.

"Some homicide detectives *can* read." There was an edge to his voice.

Guilty, Brennan. Apparently the reverend isn't the only one harboring cultural stereotypes.

I watched an old woman circle wide to avoid the preacher, and wondered what sort of salvation Dom Owens promised his followers. I checked my watch.

"We're moving toward the dinner hour," I said.

"Could be a good time to catch folks mixing up tofu burgers."

"We can't meet Baker for another ninety minutes."

"You up for a surprise visit, skipper?"

"Beats sitting here."

Ryan was reaching for the ignition when his hand stopped. I followed his gaze and saw Kathryn coming up the sidewalk, Carlie on her back. An older woman with long, dark braids walked beside her. The damp breeze blew their skirts backward, molding fabric to hips and legs. They paused and Kathryn's companion spoke to the preacher, then the pair continued in our direction.

Ryan and I exchanged glances, then got out and crossed to the women. They stopped speaking when we approached, and Kathryn smiled at me.

"How's it going?" she asked, brushing back a tangle of curls.

"Not so good," I said.

"No luck finding your missing girl?"

"No one remembers her. I find that odd, since she spent at least three months here."

I watched for a reaction, but her expression didn't change.

"Where did you ask?" Carlie stirred and Kathryn reached over her shoulder to adjust his carrier.

"Shops, food stores, pharmacies, gas stations, restaurants, the library. We even tried Boombears."

"Yeah. That's a cool idea. If she was expecting she might have gone to a toy store."

The baby whimpered, then raised his arms and arched backward, pressing his feet against his mother's back.

"Guess who's up?" said Kathryn, reaching back to calm her son. "And no one knew her from that picture?"

"No one."

Carlie's whimpers grew more strident, and the older woman moved behind Kathryn and slid the baby from the carrier.

"Oh, sorry. This is El." Kathryn indicated her companion.

Ryan and I introduced ourselves. El nodded, but said nothing as she tried to calm Carlie.

"Could we buy you ladies a Coke or a cup of coffee?" Ryan asked.

"Nah. That stuff will mess up your genetic potential." Kathryn crinkled her nose, then broke into a smile. "But I could go for juice. So could Carlie." She rolled her eyes and reached for her baby's hand. "He can be a handful when he's not happy. Dom's not picking us up for another forty minutes, right, El?"

"We should wait for Dom." The woman spoke so softly I could hardly make out her words.

"Oh, El, you know he'll be late. Let's get some juice and sit outside. I don't want to ride back with Carlie fussing all the way."

El opened her mouth, but before she could speak Carlie twisted and let out a wail.

"Juice," said Kathryn, taking the baby and bouncing him on her hip. "Blackstone's has lots of choices. I've seen their menu in the window."

We entered the deli and I ordered a Diet Coke. The others asked for juice, then we took our drinks to an outside bench. Kathryn pulled a small blanket from her shoulder bag, spread it at her feet, and set Carlie on it. Then she dug out bottled water and a small yellow mug. The cup had a round bottom and a removable cover with a drinking spout. She filled it halfway with her Very Berry, added water, and handed it to Carlie. He made a two-handed grab and started sucking on the spout. I watched, remembering, and the sensation I'd had on the island washed over me again.

I felt out of sync with the world. The bodies on Murtry. Thoughts of infant Katy. Ryan in Beaufort, with his gun and badge and Nova Scotia speech. The world seemed strange around me, the space in which I moved transported from another place or time, yet somehow present and jarringly real.

"Tell me about your group," I said, forcing my thoughts back to the moment.

El looked at me but didn't speak.

"What do you want to know?" Kathryn asked.

"What is it you believe in?"

"Knowing our own minds and bodies. Keeping our cosmic and molecular energy clear."

"What is it you do?"

"Do?" The question seemed to puzzle her. "We grow our own food, and we don't eat anything polluting." She gave a slight shrug of the shoulders. As I listened to her, I thought of Harry. Purification through diet. ". . . we study. We work. We sing and play games. Sometimes we have lectures. Dom is incredibly smart. He's completely clear—"

El tapped her on the arm and pointed to Carlie's cup. Kathryn retrieved it, wiped the spout on her skirt, and held it out to her son. The baby grabbed the mug and pounded it on his mother's foot.

"How long have you lived with the group?"

"Nine years."

"How old are you?" I couldn't keep the amazement out of my voice.

"Seventeen. My parents joined when I was eight."

"And before that?"

She bent and redirected the cup to Carlie's mouth. "I remember I cried a lot. I was alone a lot. I was always sick. My parents fought all the time."

"And?"

"When they joined the group we underwent a transformation. Through purification."

"Are you happy?"

"The point of life is not happiness." El spoke for the first time. Her voice was deep and whispery, with just the trace of an accent I couldn't place.

"What is?"

"Peace and health and harmony."

"Can't that be attained without withdrawing from society?"

"We think not." Her face was bronzed and deeply lined, her eyes the color of mahogany. "In society, too many things divert us. Drugs. Television. Possessions. Interpersonal greed. Our own beliefs stand in the way."

"El says things a lot better than I do," said Kathryn.

"But why the commune?" asked Ryan. "Why not blow it all off and join an order?"

Kathryn gave El a "take it away" gesture.

"The universe is one organic whole composed of many interdependent elements. Every part is inseparable from and interacts with every other part. While we live apart, our group is a microcosm of that reality."

"Would you care to explain that?" Ryan.

"By living apart from the world we reject the slaughterhouses and chemical plants and oil refineries, the beer cans, and the tire heaps, and the raw sewage. By living together as a group we support each other, we feed each other both spiritually and physically."

"All for one."

El gave him a brief smile. "All the old myths have to be eliminated before true consciousness is possible."

"All of them?"

"Yes."

"Even his?" Ryan tipped his head in the direction of the preacher.

"All of them."

I circled the conversation back.

"Kathryn, if you wanted information on someone, where would you ask?"

"Look," she said, smiling, "you're not going to find her." She retrieved Carlie's cup again. "She's probably on the Riviera right now, smearing sunblock on her babies."

I looked at her a long time. She didn't know. Dom hadn't told her. She'd missed the introductions and had no idea why we were asking about Heidi and Brian. I took a deep breath.

"Heidi Schneider is dead, Kathryn. So is Brian Gilbert."

She looked at me as if I were crazy.

"Dead? She can't be dead."

"Kathryn!" El's voice was sharp.

Kathryn ignored her.

"I mean, she's so young. And she's pregnant. Or was." Her voice was plaintive, like a child's.

"They were murdered less than three weeks ago."

"You're not here to take her home?" Her eyes shifted from Ryan to me. I could see tiny yellow flecks in the green irises. "You're not her parents?"

"No."

"They're dead?"

"Yes."

"Her babies?"

I nodded.

Her hand went to her mouth, then fluttered to her lap, like a butterfly unsure where to light. Carlie tugged her skirt, and the hand dropped to stroke his head.

"How could someone do something like that? I mean, I didn't know them, but, how could someone kill a whole family? Kill babies?"

"We all pass through," said El, placing an arm around the girl's shoulders. "Death is merely a transition in the process of growth."

"A transition to what?" asked Ryan.

There was no answer. At that moment a white van pulled to the curb in front of the People's Bank on the far side of Bay Street. El squeezed Kathryn's shoulders and nodded toward it. Then she gathered Carlie, rose, and extended her hand. Kathryn took it and got to her feet.

"I wish you the best of luck," said El, and the two women set off toward the van.

I watched them a moment, then downed the last of my Coke. As I looked for a trash can something under the bench caught my eye. The cover to Carlie's cup.

I dug a card from my purse, scribbled a number, and snatched up the lid. Ryan looked amused as I bolted from the bench.

She was just climbing into the van.

"Kathryn," I called from the middle of the street.

She looked up, and I waved the cover in the air. Behind her the clock on the bank said five-fifteen.

She spoke into the van then walked toward me. When she reached out I gave her the lid with my card tucked inside.

Her eyes met mine.

"Call me if you'd like to talk."

She turned without a word, walked back to the van, and got in. I could see Dom's blond head silhouetted behind the wheel as they disappeared up Bay Street.

Ryan and I showed the snapshot at another pharmacy and several fast-food restaurants, then drove to Sheriff Baker's office. Ivy Lee told us his domestic situation had turned into a standoff. An unemployed sanitation worker was barricaded in his house with his wife and three-year-old daughter, threatening to shoot everyone. Baker would not be joining us that evening.

"Now what?" I asked Ryan. We were standing in the Duke Street parking lot.

"I don't think Heidi was making the night scene, so we're not going to accomplish anything running around to bars and clubs."

"No."

"Let's call it a day. I'll drive you back to the Love Boat."

"It's the *Melanie Tess.*"

"Tess. Is that something you eat with corn bread and greens?"

"Ham hocks and yams."

"Do you want the ride?"

"Sure."

We rode in silence most of the way. I'd found Ryan annoying all day and couldn't wait to be free of him. We were on the bridge when he broke the silence.

"I doubt she'd go to beauty parlors or tanning salons."

"That's amazing. I can see why you made detective."

"Maybe we should focus on Brian. Maybe he worked for a time."

"You've already run him. There's no tax record, right?"

"Nothing."

"He could have been paid in cash."

"That narrows the possibilities."

We turned in at Ollie's.

"So where do we go from here?" I asked.

"I never got that hush puppy."

"I meant the investigation. You're on your own for dinner. I'm going to go home, take a shower, and make myself a scrumptious plate of instant macaroni. In that order."

"Jesus, Brennan, that stuff has more preservatives than Lenin's cadaver."

"I've read the label."

"You might as well swallow industrial waste. You'll mess up your"—he mimicked Kathryn—"genetic potential."

Some half-forgotten thought started to seep into my mind, formless, like the morning's mist. I tried to reel it in, but the harder I concentrated the faster it dissolved.

"—Owens better keep his skivvies up. I'm going to be on his ass like flies on a Tootsie Roll."

"What sort of gospel do you suppose he preaches?"

"Sounds like some combination of ecological Armageddon and self-improvement through Wheaties."

When he pulled up at the pier the sky was beginning to clear over the marsh. Streaks of yellow lit the horizon.

"Kathryn knows something," I said.
"Don't we all."
"You can be a real pain in the ass, Ryan."
"Thank you for noticing. What makes you think she's holding out?"
"She said babies."
"So?"
"Babies."
I saw thought working in his eyes. Then,
"Son of a bitch."
"We never told her Heidi was carrying twins."

Forty minutes later I heard a knock at the port-side entrance. I was wearing the Hornets T-shirt Katy had left, no panties, and a towel fashioned into a pretty slick turban. I peered through the blinds.

Ryan stood on the dock holding two six-packs and a pizza the size of a manhole cover. He'd abandoned his jacket and tie, and rolled his shirtsleeves to just below the elbows.

Shit.

I released the slats and pulled back. I could turn off the light and refuse to answer. I could ignore him. I could tell him to go away.

I peeked out again and found myself looking directly into Ryan's eyes.

"I know you're in there, Brennan. I'm a detective, remember?"

He dangled a six-pack in front of me. "Diet Coke."

Damn.

I didn't dislike Ryan. In fact, I enjoyed his company more than that of most people. More than I cared to admit. I liked his commitment to what he did, and the compassion he showed to victims and their families. I liked his intelligence and wit. And I liked the story of Ryan, the college kid gone wild, beaten up by a biker cokehead, then converted to the other side. Tough kid turned tough cop. It had a kind of poetic symmetry.

And I definitely liked the way he looked, but my better judgment told me not to get involved.

Oh hell. It beat noodles and synthetic cheese.

I dropped to my stateroom, grabbed a pair of cutoffs, and ran a brush through my hair.

I raised the blinds and slid back the screen to allow him in. He handed down the drinks and pizza, then turned and climbed aboard backward.

"I have my own Coke," I said, closing the screen.

"One can never have too much Coke."

I pointed to the galley and he set the pizza on the table, detached a beer for himself and a Diet Coke for me, then placed the other cans in the refrigerator. I got out plates, napkins, and a large knife while he opened the pizza box.

"You think that's more nourishing than pasta?"

"It's a veggie supreme."

"What's that?" I pointed to a brown chunk.

"Side order of bacon. I wanted all the food groups."

"Let's take it into the salon," I suggested.

We spread the food on the coffee table and settled on the couch. The smell of marsh and wet wood floated in and mingled with the aroma of tomato sauce and basil. We ate and talked about the murders, and weighed the likelihood that the victims in St-Jovite had a connection to Dom Owens.

Eventually, we drifted to more personal topics. I described the Beaufort of my childhood, and shared memories of my summers at the beach. I talked about Katy, and about my estrangement from Pete. Ryan told stories of his early years in Nova Scotia, and disclosed his feelings about a recent breakup.

The conversation was easy and natural, and I revealed more about myself than I would ever have imagined. In the silences we listened to the water and the rustling of the spartina grass in the marsh. I forgot about violence and death and did something I hadn't done in a very long time. I relaxed.

"I can't believe I'm talking so much," I said, as I began to gather plates and napkins.

Ryan reached for the empty cans. "Let me help."

Our arms brushed and I felt heat race across my skin. Wordlessly, we gathered the dinner mess and brought it to the kitchen.

When we returned to the couch Ryan stood over me a moment, then sat close, placed both hands on my shoulders, and turned my body away from him. As I was about to object he began massaging the muscles at the base of my neck, across my shoulders, and down my arms to just above the elbows. His hands slid down my back, then worked their way upward, each thumb moving in small circles along the edge of a shoulder blade. When he reached my hairline his fingers made the same rotating motions in the hollows below my skull.

My eyes closed.

"Mmmmm."

"You're very tense."

This was too good to ruin with talk.

Ryan's hands dropped to the small of my back, and his thumbs kneaded the muscles paralleling my spine, pressing higher inch by inch. My breathing slowed and I felt myself melt.

Then I remembered Harry. And my lack of underwear.

I turned to face him, to pull the plug, and our eyes met. Ryan hesitated a moment, then cupped my face in both his hands, and pressed his lips to mine. He ran his fingers along my jawline and backward through my hair, then his arms circled my shoulders and he pulled me close. I started to push away, then stopped, my hands flat on his chest. He felt lean and taut, his muscles molded to his bones.

I felt the heat of his body and smelled his skin, and my nipples hardened under my thin cotton shirt. Collapsing against his chest, I closed my eyes and kissed back.

He held me hard against him and we kissed a long time. When my arms went around his neck he slid his hand under my shirt and danced his fingers across my skin. His stroke felt cobweb light, and shivers raced up my back and across the top of my skull. I arched against his chest and kissed him harder, opening and closing my mouth to the rhythm of his breathing.

He dropped his hand and ran his fingers around my waist and up my stomach, circling my breasts with the same feathery touch. My nipples throbbed and fire surged through my body. He thrust his tongue into my mouth and my lips closed around it. His hand cupped my left breast, then gently bounced it up and down. Then he squeezed the nipple between his thumb and finger, compressing and releasing in time to the sucking of our mouths.

I ran my fingers along his spine and his hand traveled downward to the curve of my waist. He caressed my belly, circled my navel, then hooked his fingers inside the waistband of my shorts. Current shot through my lower torso.

Eventually, our lips separated and Ryan kissed my face and ran his tongue inside my ear. Then he eased me back against the cushions, and lay beside me, the off-the-chart blue eyes boring into mine. Shifting onto his side, he took me by the hips, and pulled me to him. I could feel his hardness, and we kissed again.

After a while he disengaged, crooked his knee, and pressed his thigh between my legs. I felt an explosion in my loins and found it hard to breathe. Again Ryan put one hand below the T-shirt and slid it upward to my breast. He made circular movements with his palm, then ran his thumb across my nipple. I arched my back and moaned as the sensation obliterated the world around me. I lost all sense of time.

Moments or hours later his hand dropped, and I felt a tugging on my zipper. I buried my nose in his neck and knew one thing with certainty. Regardless of Harry, I wouldn't say no.

Then the phone shrilled.

Ryan's hands went to my ears and he kissed me hard on the mouth. I responded, clutching the hair at the back of his head, cursing Southern Bell. We ignored it through four rings.

When the answering machine clicked on the voice was soft and hard to hear, as though its owner were speaking from the end of a long tunnel. We both lunged, but it was too late.

Kathryn had hung up.

THERE WAS NO SALVAGING THE SITUATION AFTER KATHRYN'S CALL. While Ryan was up for giving it a go, rational thought had returned and I was not in a good mood. Not only had I missed the opportunity to talk with Kathryn but I knew I'd have to live with Detective Dick's new sense of sexual prowess. While the orgasm was overdue and would certainly have been welcome, I suspected the cost was already too high.

I hustled Ryan out and fell into bed, ignoring teeth and my nightly routine. My last image before drifting off came to me from the seventh grade: Sister Luke lecturing on the wages of sin. I supposed my romp with Ryan would goose these wages well above minimum.

I woke to sunshine and the cry of gulls, and an immediate flashback to my roll on the couch. I cringed and covered my face with both hands, feeling like a teen who'd given it up in a Pontiac.

Brennan, what were you thinking?

That was not the issue. The problem lay in what I'd been thinking *with*. Edna St. Vincent Millay had written a poem about that. What was it called? "I Being Born a Woman and Distressed."

Sam called at eight to say the Murtry case was going nowhere. No one had seen anything unusual. No strange boats had been spotted approaching or leaving the island in the past few weeks. He wanted to know if I'd heard from Hardaway.

I told him I hadn't. He said he was going to Raleigh for a few days and wanted to be sure I was taken care of.

Oh, yeah.

He explained how to close up the boat and where to leave the key, and we said good-bye.

I was scraping pizza into the garbage when I heard a knock at the port entrance. I had a feeling who was there and ignored it. The banging continued, relentless as a National Public Radio fund drive, and after a while I couldn't take it. I raised the blinds to see Ryan standing exactly where he'd been the night before.

"Good morning." He held out a bag of doughnuts.

"Expanding into food delivery?" I lowered the screen. One innuendo and I knew I'd rip his throat out.

He climbed in, grinned, and offered high-calorie, low-food-value treats. "They go well with coffee."

I went to the galley, poured two cups, and added milk to mine.

"It's a beautiful day out there." He reached for the milk carton.

"Mm."

I helped myself to a chocolate-glazed and leaned against the sink. I had no intention of resettling on the couch.

"I've already spoken to Baker," said Ryan.

I waited.

"He'll meet with us at three."

"I'll be on the road at three." I reached for another doughnut.

"I think we should make another social call," said Ryan.

"Yes."

"Maybe we can get Kathryn alone."

"That seems to be your specialty."

"Are you going to keep this up all day?"

"I'll probably sing when I'm on the road."

"I didn't come out here intending to seduce you."

That piqued me even more.

"You mean I'm not in my sister's league?"

"What?"

We drank in silence, then I refilled my mug and pointedly replaced the pot. Ryan watched, then crossed to Mr. Coffee and poured himself a second cup.

"Do you think Kathryn actually has something to tell us?" he asked.

"She probably phoned to invite me for tuna casserole."

"Now who's being a pain in the ass?"

"Thanks for noticing." I rinsed my mug and placed it upside down on the counter.

"Look, if you're embarrassed about last night . . ."

"Should I be?"

"Of course not."

"What a relief."

"Brennan, I'm not going to go berserk in the autopsy room or grope you on a stakeout. Our personal relationship will in no way affect our professional behavior."

"Small chance. Today I'm wearing underwear."

"See." He grinned.

I went aft to gather my things.

Half an hour later we were parked in front of the farmhouse. Dom Owens sat on the porch talking with a group of people. Through the screen it was impossible to tell anything about the others but gender. All four were male.

A crew was at work in the garden behind the white bungalow, and two women pushed children on the swings by the trailers while several others hung laundry. A blue van was parked in the driveway, but I saw no sign of the white one.

I scanned the figures at the swing set. I didn't see Kathryn, though I thought one of the infants looked like Carlie. I watched a woman in a floral skirt push the baby back and forth in smooth metronomic arcs.

Ryan and I walked to the door and I knocked. The men stopped talking and turned in our direction.

"May I help you?" said a high-pitched voice.

Owens held up a hand. "It's fine, Jason."

He rose, crossed the porch, and pushed open the screen door.

"I'm sorry, but I don't think I ever got your names."

"I'm Detective Ryan. This is Dr. Brennan."

Owens smiled and stepped out onto the stoop. I nodded and took my turn at shaking hands. The men on the porch grew very still.

"What can I do for you today?"

"We're still trying to determine where Heidi Schneider and Brian Gilbert spent last summer. You were going to raise the question during family hour?" Ryan's voice held no warmth.

Owens smiled again. "Experiential session. Yes, we did discuss it. Unfortunately, no one knew anything about either of them. I'm so sorry. I had hoped we could be of help."

"We'd like to speak to your people, if we may."

"I'm sorry, but I can't encourage that."

"And why is that?"

"Our members live here because they seek peace and refuge. Many want nothing to do with the filth and violence of modern society. You, Detective Ryan, represent the world they have rejected. I cannot violate their sanctuary by asking them to speak to you."

"Some of your members work in town."

Owens tipped his head and looked to heaven for patience. Then he gave Ryan another smile.

"One of the skills we nurture is encapsulation. Not everyone is equally gifted, but some of our members learn to function in the secular yet remain sealed off, untouched by the moral and physical pollution." Again the patient smile. "While we reject the profanity of our culture, Mr. Ryan, we are not fools. We know that man does not live by spirit alone. We also need bread."

While Owens talked I checked the gardeners. No Kathryn.

"Is everyone here free to come and go?" I asked, turning back to Owens.

"Of course." He laughed. "How could I stop them?"

"What happens if someone wants to leave for good?"

"They go." He shrugged and spread his hands.

For a moment no one spoke. The creak of the swings carried across the yard.

"I thought your young couple might have stayed with us briefly, perhaps during one of my absences," Owens offered. "Though not common, that has happened. But I'm afraid that is not the case. No one here has any recollection of either of them."

Just then Howdy Doody appeared from behind the neighboring

house. When he spotted us he hesitated, then turned and hurried back in the direction from which he'd come.

"I'd still like to speak to a few folks," said Ryan. "There could be something someone knows that they just don't think is important. That happens all the time."

"Mr. Ryan, I will not have my people harassed. I asked about your young couple and no one knew them. What more is there to say? I'm afraid I really can't have you disturbing our routine."

Ryan cocked his head and made a clucking sound. "I'm afraid you're going to have to, Dom."

"And why is that?"

"Because I'm not going to go away. I have a friend named Baker. You do remember him? And he has friends who give him things called warrants."

Owens and Ryan locked eyes, and for a moment no one spoke. I heard the men on the porch rise, and in the distance a dog barked. Then Owens smiled and cleared his throat.

"Jason, please ask everyone to come to the parlors." His voice was low and even.

Owens stood back and a tall man in a red warm-up suit slipped past him and angled toward the neighboring property. He was soft and overweight, and looked a little like Julia Child. I watched him stop to stroke a cat, then continue toward the garden.

"Please come in," said Owens, opening the screen. We followed him to the same room we'd occupied the day before and sat on the same rattan couch. The house was very quiet.

"If you'll excuse me, I'll be right back. Would you care for anything?"

We told him no, and he left the room. Overhead, a fan hummed softly.

Soon I heard voices and laughter, then the creak of the screen door. As Owens' flock filtered in I studied them one by one. I sensed Ryan doing the same.

Within minutes the room was full, and I could conclude only one thing. The assembly looked totally unremarkable. They might have been a Baptist study group on its annual summer picnic. They joked and laughed and looked anything but oppressed.

There were babies, adults, and at least one septuagenarian, but no adolescents or children. I did a quick count: seven men, thirteen women, three kids. Helen had said there were twenty-six living at the commune.

I recognized Howdy and Helen. Jason leaned against a wall. El stood near the archway, Carlie on her hip. She stared at me intently. I smiled, remembering our meeting in Beaufort the previous afternoon. Her expression didn't change.

I scanned the other faces. Kathryn was not present.

Owens returned and the room fell silent. He made introductions, then explained why we were there. The adults listened attentively, then turned to us. Ryan handed the photo of Brian and Heidi to a middle-aged man on his left, then outlined the case, avoiding unnecessary detail. The man looked at the picture and passed it on. As the snapshot circulated I studied each face, watching for subtle changes of expression that might indicate recognition. I saw only puzzlement and empathy.

When Ryan finished, Owens again addressed his followers, soliciting input on the couple or the phone calls. No one spoke.

"Mr. Ryan and Dr. Brennan have requested permission to interview you individually." Owens looked from face to face. "Please feel free to talk to them. If there is a thought you harbor, please share it with honesty and compassion. We did not cause this tragedy, but we are part of the cosmic whole and should do what is in our power to set this dislocation in order. Do it in the name of harmony."

Every eye was on him, and I felt a strange intensity in the room.

"Those of you who cannot speak should feel no guilt or shame." He clapped his hands. "Now. Work and be well! Holistic affirmation through collective responsibility!"

Spare me, I thought.

When they'd gone Ryan thanked him.

"This is not Waco, Mr. Ryan. We have nothing to hide."

"We were hoping to speak with the young woman we met yesterday," I said.

He looked at me a moment then said, "Young woman?"

"Yes. She came in with a child. Carlie, I believe?"

He looked at me so long I thought perhaps he didn't remember. Then the Owens smile.

"That would be Kathryn. She had an appointment today."

"An appointment?"

"Why are you concerned with Kathryn?"

"She seems close to Heidi's age. I thought they might have known each other." Something told me not to discuss our juice party in Beaufort.

"Kathryn wasn't here last summer. She'd gone to visit with her parents."

"I see. When will she be back?"

"I'm not certain."

The screen door opened and a tall man appeared in the hallway. He was scarecrow thin, and had a white streak across his right eyebrow and lashes, giving him an oddly lopsided look. I remembered him. During the assembly he'd stood near the hall, playing with one of the toddlers.

Owens held up one finger, and scarecrow nodded and pointed to the back of the house. He wore a bulky ring that looked out of place on his long, bony finger.

"I'm sorry, but there are things I must do," said Owens. "Talk with whomever you like, but please, respect our desire for harmony."

He ushered us to the door and extended a hand. If nothing else, Dom was a great shaker. He said he was glad we had stopped by and wished us luck. Then he was gone.

Ryan and I spent the rest of the morning talking to the faithful. They were pleasant, and cooperative, and totally harmonious. And they knew zilch. Not even the whereabouts of Kathryn's appointment.

By eleven-thirty we knew nothing more than when we'd arrived.

"Let's go thank the reverend," said Ryan, taking a set of keys from his pocket. They hung from a large plastic disk, and were not the ones for the rental car.

"What the hell for?" I asked. I was hungry and hot and ready to move on.

"It's good manners."

I rolled my eyes, but Ryan was already halfway across the yard. I watched him knock on the screen door, then speak to the man with the pale eyebrow. In a moment Owens appeared. Ryan said something and extended his hand and, like marionettes, the three men squatted then rose quickly. Ryan spoke again, turned, and walked toward the car.

* * *

After lunch we tried a few more pharmacies, then drove back to the government center. I showed Ryan the records offices, then we crossed the grounds to the law enforcement building. A black man in a tank top and fedora was crisscrossing the lawn on a small tractor, his bony knees projecting like legs on a grasshopper.

"How y'all doin'? he said, putting one finger to his brim.

"Good." I breathed in the smell of fresh-cut grass and wished it were true.

Baker was on the phone when we entered his office. He gestured us to chairs, spoke a few more words, and hung up.

"So, how's it going?" he asked.

"It isn't," said Ryan. "Nobody knows squat."

"How can we help?"

Ryan lifted his jacket, pulled a Ziploc bag from the pocket, and laid it on Baker's desk. Inside was the red plastic disk.

"You can run this for prints."

Baker looked at him.

"I accidentally dropped it. Owens was kind enough to pick it up for me."

Baker hesitated a moment, then smiled and shook his head. "You know it may not be usable."

"I know. But it may tell us who this puke is."

Baker laid the bag aside. "What else?"

"How about a wiretap?"

"No way. You haven't got enough."

"Search warrant?"

"What's your probable cause?"

"Phone calls?"

"Not enough."

"Didn't think so."

Ryan let out a breath and stretched his legs.

"Then I'll do it the hard way. I'll start with deeds and tax records, see who owns the country club on Adler Lyons. I'll check the utilities, find out who pays the bills. I'll talk to the postal boys, see if anyone gets *Hustler* or orders from J. Crew. I'll run Owens for a Social Security number, former wife, that sort of thing. I assume he has a driver's license, so that should take me somewhere. If the reverend's ever taken an illegal piss, I'll nail him. Maybe I'll do a little surveillance, see what cars go in and out of the compound, run the tags. Hope you don't mind my hanging around for a while."

"You are welcome in Beaufort for as long as it takes, Mr. Ryan. I'll assign a detective to help you. And, Dr. Brennan, what are your plans?"

"I'm heading out shortly. I have classes to prepare for and Mr. Colker's cases from Murtry to look at."

"Baxter will be glad to hear that. He called to say that Dr. Hardaway would like to speak with you as soon as possible. In fact, he's rung us three times today. Would you like to use my phone to call up there?"

No one can say I can't take a hint.

"Please."

Baker asked Ivy Lee to get Hardaway on the line. In a moment the phone rang and I picked it up.

The pathologist had finished with what he felt he could do. He was able to determine the gender of the corpse in the bottom of the grave, and that the race was probably white. The victim had died of what he thought were incised injuries, but the body was too badly decomposed to determine their exact nature.

The burial had been shallow enough that insects had gained access, probably using the body above as a conduit. The open wounds had also encouraged colonization. The skull and chest contained the largest maggot masses he'd ever seen. The face was not recognizable and he was unable to estimate an age. He thought he might have some usable prints.

In the background Ryan and Baker discussed Dom Owens.

Hardaway went on. The upper body was largely skeletonized, though some connective tissue remained. He could do little with it, and asked me to do a full analysis.

I told him to send me the skull, the hip blades, the clavicles, and the chest ends of the third through fifth ribs from the bottom body. I would need the entire skeleton from the upper burial. I also asked for a series of X-rays on each victim, a copy of his report, and a full set of autopsy photos.

Last, I explained how I preferred to have the bones processed.

Hardaway was familiar with the routine and said both sets of remains and all documents would arrive in my lab in Charlotte on Friday.

I hung up and looked at my watch. If I had any hope of getting everything done before my conference trip to Oakland, I had to get moving.

Ryan and I crossed to the lot, where I had left my car that morning. The sun was hot and the shade felt good. I opened the door and leaned my arm on the upper edge.

"Let's have dinner," said Ryan.

"Sure. Then I'll put on pasties and we'll take pics for the *New York Times.*"

"Brennan, for two days now you've been treating me like I'm gum on the sidewalk. Actually, now that I think about it, you've had some kind of burr up your ass for a couple of weeks. Fine. I can live with that."

He took my chin in his hands and looked straight into my eyes.

"But I want you to know one thing. That was not just a chemical event last night. I care about you and I was enjoying the hell out of being close. I'm not sorry it happened. And I can't say I won't try again. Remember, I might be the wind, but you control the kite. Drive safely."

With that he released my chin and walked to his car. Unlocking the door, he threw his jacket on the passenger seat and turned back to me.

"By the way, you never told me why you doubt the Murtry victims are dealers."

For a moment I could only stare. I wanted to stay, but I also wanted to be continents away from him. Then my mind snapped back.

"What?"

"The bodies from the island. Why do you question the drug burn theory?"

"Because they're both girls."

21

DURING THE DRIVE I PLAYED SOME TAPES, BUT THE NEWS FROM Lake Wobegon didn't hold my attention. I had a million questions and very few answers. Had Anna Goyette returned home? Who were the women buried on Murtry Island? What would their bones tell me? Who killed Heidi and her babies? Was there a connection between St-Jovite and the commune on Saint Helena? Who was Dom Owens? Where had Kathryn gone? Where the hell had Harry gone?

My mind spun off thoughts of all I had to do. And wanted to do. I hadn't read a word about Élisabeth Nicolet since leaving Montreal.

By eight-thirty I was back in Charlotte. In my absence the grounds at Sharon Hall had put on their finest springtime attire. Azaleas and dogwoods were in full bloom, and a few Bradford pears and flowering crabapples still retained blossoms. The air smelled of pine needles and bark chips. Inside, my arrival at the Annex was a replay of the week before. The clock was ticking. The message light was flashing. The refrigerator was empty.

Birdie's bowls were in their usual place under the bay window. Odd that Pete hadn't emptied them. Disorderly with everything else, my estranged husband was fastidious about foodstuffs. I did a quick patrol to see if the cat was skulking under a chair or in a closet. No Bird.

I called Pete, but, as before, he wasn't in. Neither was Harry at the condo in Montreal. Thinking perhaps she'd gone home, I tried her number in Texas. No answer.

After unpacking, I fixed a tuna sandwich and ate it with dill pickles and chips while I watched the end of a Hornets' game. At ten I turned off the TV and tried Pete again. Still no answer. I considered driving over to collect Birdie, but decided to let it go until morning.

I showered, then propped myself in bed with the Bélanger photocopies and escaped into the world of nineteenth-century Montreal. The hiatus had not improved Louis-Philippe, and within an hour my lids were drooping. I turned off the light and curled into a tuck position, hoping a good long rest would bring order to my mind.

Two hours later I was sitting bolt upright, my heart hammering, my brain struggling to know why. I clutched the blanket to my chest, barely breathing, straining to identify the threat that had sent me into full alert.

Silence. The only light in the room came from my bedside clock.

Then the sound of shattering glass sent the hairs straight up on my arms and neck. My adrenals went to high tide. I had a flashback to another break-in, reptilian eyes, a knife flashing in moonlight. A single thought crackled in my brain.

Not again!

Crash! Thud!

Yes, again!

The noise wasn't outside! It was downstairs! It was in my house! My mind sprinted through options. Lock the bedroom. Check it out. Call the police.

Then I smelled smoke.

Shit!

I threw back the covers and fumbled across the room, digging below the terror for elements of rational thought. A weapon. I needed a weapon. What? What could I use? Why did I refuse to keep a gun?

I stumbled to the dresser and felt for a large conch I'd collected on the Outer Banks. It wouldn't kill, but the point would penetrate flesh and do damage. Turning the sharp end forward, I wrapped my fingers inside and braced my thumb against the outer surface.

Hardly breathing, I crept toward the door, my free hand sliding over familiar surfaces as if seeking guidance in Braille. Dresser. Doorjamb. Hallway.

At the top of the stairs I froze and peered downward into the blackness. Blood pounded in my ears as I clutched the shell and listened. Not a sound from below. If there was someone there I should stay upstairs. Phone. If there was fire downstairs, I needed to get out.

I took a breath and placed one foot on the top stair, waited. Then the second. Third. Knees bent, shell raised to shoulder level, I crept toward the first floor. The acrid smell grew stronger. Smoke. Gasoline. And something else. Something familiar.

At the bottom I stopped, my mind playing back a scene from Montreal less than a year ago. That time he'd been inside, a killer, waiting to attack.

That isn't going to happen again! Call 911! Get out!

I rounded the banister and looked into the dining room. Blackness. I doubled back toward the parlor. Darkness, but strangely altered.

The far end of the room looked bronzed in the surrounding gloom. The fireplace, the Queen Anne chairs, all the furnishings and pictures glimmered gently, like objects in a mirage. Through the kitchen door I could see orange light dancing on the front of the refrigerator.

Eeeeeeeeeeeeeeeeeeeeeeeeeeeeeeeeeee!

My chest constricted as the silence was split by a high-pitched wail. I jerked and the shell struck plaster. Trembling, I pressed backward against the wall.

The sound was from the smoke detector!

I watched for signs of movement. Nothing but darkness and the eerie flickering.

The house is on fire. Move!

My heart drumming, my breath coming in short gasps, I lunged toward the kitchen. A fire crackled in the center of the room, filling the air with smoke and reflecting off every shiny surface.

My shaking hand found the switch and I threw on the light. My eyes darted left and right. The burning bundle lay in the middle of the floor. The flames hadn't spread.

I put down the shell and, holding the hem of my nightie across my mouth and nose, I bent low and circled to the pantry. I pulled the small extinguisher from the top shelf. My lungs drew in smoke and tears blurred my vision, but I managed to squeeze the handle. The extinguisher only hissed.

Damn!

Coughing and gagging, I squeezed again. Another hiss, then a stream of carbon dioxide and white powder burst from the spout.

Yes!

I aimed the nozzle at the flames and in less than a minute the fire was out. The alarm still screamed, the sound like shards of metal piercing my ears and dragging across my brain.

I opened the back door and the window above the sink, then crossed to the table. No need to open that one. The panes were shattered, and glass and splintered wood covered the sill and floor. Tiny gusts of wind played with the curtains, tugging them in and out of the jagged opening.

Circling the thing on the floor, I turned on the ceiling fan, grabbed a towel, and fanned smoke from the room. Slowly, the air began to clear.

I wiped my eyes and made an effort to control my breathing.

Keep fanning!

The alarm shrieked on.

I stopped waving the towel and looked around the room. A cinder block lay beneath the table, another rested against the cabinet below the sink. Between them were the charred remains of the bundle that had been burning. The room reeked of smoke and gasoline. And another odor I knew.

With shaky legs, I crossed to the smoldering heap. I was staring, not comprehending, when the alarm stopped. The silence seemed unnatural.

Dial 911.

It wasn't necessary. As I reached for the phone I heard a distant siren. It grew louder, very loud, then stopped. In a moment a fireman appeared at my back door.

"You O.K., ma'am?"

I nodded and folded my arms across my chest, self-conscious about my state of undress.

"Your neighbor called." His chin strap dangled.

"Oh." I forgot my nightie. I was back in St-Jovite.

"Everything under control?"

Another nod. St-Jovite. Almost a synapse.

"Mind if I make sure?"

I stepped back.

He sized it up in one look.

"Pretty mean prank. Know who might have heaved this through your window?"

I shook my head.

"Looks like they broke the glass with the cinder blocks, then chucked that thing in." He walked over to the smoldering mound. "They must've soaked it in gasoline, lit it, and pitched it."

I heard his words but couldn't speak. My body had locked up as my mind tried to rouse some shapeless notion sleeping in the core of my brain.

The firefighter slipped a shovel from his belt, snapped open the blade, and poked at the heap on my kitchen floor. Black flecks shot upward, then rejoined the rubble below. He slid the blade below the object, flipped it over, and leaned in.

"Looks like a burlap sack. Maybe a seed bag. Damned if I can tell what's inside."

He scraped the object with the tip of the shovel and more charred particles spiraled up. He prodded harder, rolling the thing from side to side.

The smell grew stronger. St-Jovite. Autopsy room three. Memory broke through and I went cold all over.

With trembling hands I opened a drawer and withdrew a pair of kitchen scissors. No longer concerned about my nightie, I squatted and cut the burlap.

The corpse was small, its back arched, its legs contracted by the heat of the flames. I saw a shriveled eye, a tiny jaw with blackened teeth. Anticipation of the horror that the sack held made me begin to feel faint.

No! Please no!

I leaned in, my mind recoiling from the smell of burned flesh and hair. Between the hind legs I saw a curled and blackened tail, its vertebrae protruding like thorns on a stem.

Tears slid down my cheeks as I cut further. Near the knot I saw hairs, scorched now, but white in spots.

The half-full bowls.

"Nooooooooooooooooo!"

I heard the voice, but did not connect it to myself.

"No! No! No! Birdie. Please God, no!"

I felt hands on my shoulders, then on my hands, taking the scissors, gently pulling me to my feet. Voices.

Then I was in the parlor, a quilt around me. I was crying, shaking, my body in pain.

I don't know how long I'd been sobbing when I looked up to see my neighbor. She pointed at a cup of tea.

"What is it?" My chest heaved in and out.

"Peppermint."

"Thanks." I drank the tepid liquid. "What time is it?"

"A little past two." She wore slippers and a trench coat that didn't cover her flannel gown. Though we'd waved to each other across the lawn, or exchanged hellos on the walk, I hardly knew her.

"I'm so sorry you had to get up in the middle of the nigh—"

"Please, Dr. Brennan. We're neighbors. I know you'd do the same for me."

I took another sip. My hands were icy, but trembled less.

"Are the firemen still here?"

"They left. They said you can fill out a report when you feel better."

"Did they take—" My voice broke and I felt tears behind my eyes.

"Yes. Can I get you anything else?"

"No, thank you. I'll be fine. You've been very kind."

"I'm sorry about your damage. We put a board across the window. It's not elegant, but it will keep the wind out."

"Thank you so much. I—"

"Please. Just get some sleep. Perhaps this won't seem so bad in the morning."

I thought of Birdie and dreaded the morning. In desperate hope I picked up the phone and dialed Pete's number. No answer.

"You will be O.K.? Shall I help you upstairs?"

"No. Thank you. I'll manage."

When she'd gone I crawled into bed and cried myself to sleep with great, heaving sobs.

I awoke with the feeling that something was wrong. Changed. Lost. Then full consciousness, and with it, memory.

It was a warm spring morning. Through the window I could see blue sky and sunlight and smell the perfume of flowers. But the beauty of the day could not lift my depression.

When I called the fire department I was told the physical evidence had been sent to the crime lab. Feeling leaden, I went through the morning motions. I dressed, applied makeup, brushed my hair, and headed downtown.

The sack contained nothing but the cat. No collar. No tags. A hand-lettered note was found inside one of the cinder blocks. I read it through the plastic evidence bag.

Next time it won't be a cat.

"Now what?" I asked Ron Gillman, director of the crime lab. He was a tall, good-looking man with silver-gray hair and an unfortunate gap between his front teeth.

"We've already checked for prints. Zippo on the note and blocks. Recovery will be out to your place, but you know as well as I do they won't find much. Your kitchen window is so close to the street the perps probably pulled up, lit the bag, then threw everything in from the sidewalk. We'll look for footprints, and we'll ask around, of course, but at one-thirty in the morning it's not too likely anyone was awake in that neighborhood."

"Sorry I don't live on Wilkinson Boulevard."

"You get into enough trouble wherever you are."

Ron and I had worked together for years. He knew about the serial murderer who had broken into my Montreal condo.

"I'll have recovery go over your kitchen, but since these guys never went inside, there won't be any trace. You didn't touch anything, I assume."

"No." I hadn't gone near the kitchen since the night before. I couldn't bear the sight of Birdie's dishes.

"Are you working on anything that could piss folks off?"

I told him about the murders in Quebec and about the bodies from Murtry Island.

"How do you think they got your cat?"

"He may have run out when Pete went in to feed him. He does that." A stab of pain. "Did that."

Don't cry. Don't you dare cry.

"Or . . ."

"Yes?"

"Well, I'm not sure. Last week I thought someone might have broken into my office at school. Well, not exactly broken in. I may have left the door unlocked."

"A student?"

"I don't know."

I described the incident.

"My house keys were still in my purse, but I suppose she could have made an impression."

"You look a little shaken up."

"A little. I'm fine."

For a moment he said nothing. Then,

"Tempe, when I heard about this I assumed it was a disgruntled student." He scratched the side of his nose. "But this could be more than a prank. Watch yourself. Maybe tell Pete."

"I don't want to do that. He'd feel obligated to baby-sit me, and he doesn't have time for that. He never did."

When we'd finished talking, I gave Ron a key to the Annex, signed the incident report, and left.

Though traffic was light, the drive to UNCC seemed longer than usual. An icy fist had hold of my innards and refused to let go.

All day the feeling was there. Through task after task I was interrupted by images of my murdered cat. Kitten Birdie sitting upright, forepaws flapping like a baby sparrow's. Birdie, flat on his back beneath the sofa. Rubbing figure eights around my ankles. Staring me down for cereal leavings. The sadness that had plagued me in recent weeks was deepening into unshakable melancholy.

After office hours I crossed campus to the athletic complex and changed into running gear. I pushed myself as hard as I could, hoping physical exertion would relieve the ache in my heart and the tension in my body.

As I pounded around the track my mind shifted gears. Ron Gillman's words replaced the images of my dead pet. Butchering an animal is cruel but it's amateur. Was it merely an unhappy student? Or could Birdie's death be a real threat? From whom? Was there a link to the mugging in Montreal? To the Murtry investigation? Had I been drawn into something far bigger than I knew?

I kicked it hard and with each lap the tightness drained from my body. After four miles I collapsed on the grass. Breath rasping, I watched a miniature rainbow shimmer in the spray of a lawn sprinkler. Success. My mind was blank.

When my pulse and breathing had slowed, I returned to the locker room, showered, and dressed in fresh clothes. Feeling better, I climbed the hill to the Colvard Building.

The sensation was short-lived.

My phone was flashing. I punched in the code and waited.

Damn!

I'd missed Kathryn again. As before, she'd left no information, only a statement that she'd called. I rewound the message and listened a second time. She sounded breathless, her words tense and clipped.

I played the message again and again, but could make nothing of the background noise. Kathryn's voice was muffled, as though she were speaking from inside a small space. I imagined her cupping the receiver, whispering, furtively checking her surroundings.

Was I being paranoid? Had last night's incident sent my imagination into overdrive? Or was Kathryn in real danger?

The sun through the venetian blinds threw bright stripes across my desk. Down the hall, a door slammed. Slowly, an idea took shape.

I reached for the phone.

"THANKS FOR MAKING TIME FOR ME THIS LATE IN THE DAY. I'M surprised you're still on campus."

"Are you implying that anthropologists work harder than sociologists?"

"Never," I laughed, settling into the black plastic chair he indicated. "Red, I'd like to pick your brain. What can you tell me about local cults?"

"What do you mean by cult?"

Red Skyler slouched sideways behind his desk. Though his hair had gone gray, the russet beard explained the origin of the nickname. He squinted at me through steel-rimmed glasses.

"Fringe groups. Doomsday sects. Satanic circles."

He smiled and gave me a "carry on" gesture.

"The Manson Family. Hare Krishna. MOVE. The People's Temple. Synanon. You know. Cults."

"You're using a very loaded term. What you call a cult someone else may see as a religion. Or family. Or political party."

I had a flashback to Daisy Jeannotte. She, too, had objected to the word, but there the similarity ended. In that interview I sat across from a tiny woman in a huge office. Now I faced a large man in a space so small and crowded I felt claustrophobic.

"All right. What's a cult?"

"Cults are not just groups of crazies who follow weird leaders.

At least the way I use the term, they are organizations with a set of common features."

"Yes." I leaned back in my chair.

"A cult forms around a charismatic individual who promises something. This individual professes some special knowledge. Sometimes the claim is access to ancient secrets, sometimes it's an entirely new discovery to which he or she alone is privy. Sometimes it's a combination of both. The leader offers to share the information with those who follow. Some leaders offer utopia. Or a way out. Just come along, follow me. I'll make the decisions. All will be fine."

"How does that differ from a priest or rabbi?"

"In a cult it's this charismatic leader who eventually becomes the object of devotion; in some cases he's actually deified. And as that happens, the leader comes to hold extraordinary control over the lives of his followers."

He removed his glasses and rubbed each lens with a square of green material he took from his pocket. Then he replaced them, wrapping each bow behind an ear.

"Cults are totalistic, authoritarian. The leader is supreme and delegates power to very few. The leader's morality becomes the only acceptable theology. The only acceptable behavior. And, as I said, veneration is eventually centered on him, not on supreme beings or on abstract principles."

I waited.

"And often there is a double set of ethics. Members are urged to be honest and loving to each other but to deceive and shun outsiders. Established religions tend to follow one set of rules for everybody."

"How does a leader gain such control?"

"That's another important element. Thought reform. Cult leaders use a variety of psychological processes to manipulate their members. Some leaders are fairly benign, but others are not and really exploit the idealism of their followers."

Again I waited for him to go on.

"The way I see it, there are two broad types of cults, both of which use thought reform. The commercially packaged 'awareness programs'"— he gestured quotation marks—"use very intense persuasion techniques. These groups keep members by getting them to buy more and more courses.

"Then there are the cults that recruit followers for life. These groups use organized psychological and social persuasion to produce extreme attitudinal changes. As a result they come to exert enormous control over the lives of their members. They are manipulative, deceptive, and highly exploitative."

I digested that.

"How does thought reform work?"

"You begin by destabilizing a person's sense of self. I'm sure you discuss this in your anthropology classes. Separate. Deconstruct. Reconstruct."

"I'm a physical anthropologist."

"Right. Cults cut newcomers off from all other influences, then get them to question everything they believe in. Persuade them to reinterpret the world and their own life history. They create a whole new reality for the person, and in so doing they create a dependence on the organization and its ideology."

I thought back to the cultural anthropology courses I'd taken in graduate school.

"But you're not talking about rites of passage. I know in some cultures kids are isolated for a period in their lives and subjected to training, but the process is meant to reinforce ideas the child has grown up with. You're talking about getting people to reject the values of their upbringing, to toss out everything they believe in. How is that done?"

"The cult controls the recruit's time and environment. Diet. Sleep. Work. Recreation. Money. Everything. It creates a sense of dependency, of powerlessness apart from the group. As it does that it instills the new morality, the system of logic to which the group adheres. The world according to the leader. And it is definitely a closed system. No feedback allowed. No criticism. No complaints. The group suppresses old behaviors and attitudes and, bit by bit, replaces them with its own behaviors and attitudes."

"Why does anyone go along with that?"

"The process is so gradual the person isn't aware of what's happening. You're taken through a series of tiny steps, each one seemingly unimportant. Other members grow their hair. You grow your hair. Others speak softly, so you lower your voice. Everyone listens docilely to the leader, asking no questions, so you do the same. There is a sense of approval by the group and of acceptance into it. The new recruit is totally unaware of the double agenda that's operating."

"Don't they eventually see what's happening?"

"Usually new members are encouraged to break all contact with friends and family, to cut themselves off from their former networks. Sometimes they're taken to isolated places. Farms. Communes. Chalets.

"This isolation, both physical and social, strips them of their normal support systems and increases their sense of personal powerlessness and need for group acceptance. It also eliminates the normal sounding boards we all use for evaluating what we're being told. The person's confidence in his or her own judgment and perception deteriorates. Independent action becomes impossible."

I thought of Dom and his group on Saint Helena.

"I can see how a cult has control if you live under its roof twenty-four hours a day, but what if members work outside the headquarters?"

"Easy. Members are given instructions to do chants or meditation whenever they're not working. Lunch hour. Coffee break. The mind is occupied by cult-directed behaviors. And outside the job all their time is devoted to the organization."

"But what is the appeal? What drives someone to reject his past and turn himself over to a sect?"

I couldn't wrap my mind around this. Were Kathryn and the others automatons, controlled in their every move?

"There is a system of rewards and punishments. If the member behaves, talks, and thinks appropriately he or she is loved by the leader and by the peer group. And, of course, he or she will be saved. Enlightened. Taken to another world. Whatever the ideology promises."

"What *do* they promise?"

"You name it. Not all cults are religious. The public has that idea because back in the sixties and seventies a lot of groups registered as churches for the tax break. Cults come in all shapes and sizes and promise all kinds of benefits. Health. Overthrow of the government. A trip to outer space. Immortality."

"I still don't see why anyone but a nutcase would fall for such crap."

"Not at all." He shook his head. "It's not just marginal people who get sucked in. In some studies approximately two thirds of the respondents came from normal families and were demonstrating age-appropriate behavior when they entered a cult."

I looked at the tiny Navajo rug beneath my feet. The mental itch was back. What was it? Why couldn't I bring it to the surface?

"Has your research shed light on why people seek out these movements?"

"Often they don't. These groups seek you. And as I've said, these leaders can be incredibly charming and persuasive."

Dom Owens fit that description. Who was he? An ideologue forcing his whims on malleable followers? Or just a health-fad prophet trying to grow organic butter beans?

Again I thought of Daisy Jeannotte. Was she right? Had the public become overly fearful of Satan worshipers and doomsday prophets?

"How many cults exist in the U.S.?" I asked.

"Depending on your definition"—he gave a wry smile and spread his hands—"anywhere from three to five thousand."

"You're kidding."

"One of my colleagues estimates that over the past two decades as many as twenty million people have had some involvement with a cult. She believes that at any given time the number is two to five million people."

"Do you agree?" I was astounded.

"It's awfully hard to know. Some groups inflate their numbers by counting as a member anyone who ever attended a meeting or requested information. Others are very secretive, and keep as low a profile as possible. The police discover some groups only indirectly, if there's a problem, or if a member leaves and files a complaint. The small ones are particularly hard to track."

"Ever hear of Dom Owens?"

He shook his head. "What's the name of his group?"

"They don't use one."

Down the hall a printer whirred to life.

"Are there any organizations in the Carolinas that the police are monitoring?"

"Not my area, Tempe. I'm a sociologist. I can tell you how these groups work, but not necessarily who's at the plate at any given time. I can try to find out if it's important."

"I just don't get it, Red. How can people be so gullible?"

"It's seductive to think that you're elite. Chosen. Most cults teach their members that only they are enlightened and everyone else in the world is left out. Lesser in some way. It's powerful stuff."

"Red, are these groups violent?"

"Most aren't, but there are the exceptions. There was Jonestown, Waco, Heaven's Gate, and the Solar Temple. Obviously their members didn't fare too well. Remember the Rajneesh cult? They attempted to poison the water supply in some town in Oregon, and made threatening moves toward the county officials. And Synanon? Those fine citizens placed a diamondback in the mailbox of a lawyer who brought suit against them. The guy barely survived."

I vaguely recalled the incident.

"What about small groups, the ones with less profile?"

"Most are harmless, but some are sophisticated and potentially dangerous. I can think of only a few that have crossed the line in recent years. Does this have to do with a case?"

"Yeah. No. I'm not sure." I picked at a hangnail on my thumb.

He hesitated. "Is it Katy?"

"What?"

"Is Katy involved with . . ."

"Oh no, nothing like that. Really. It's related to a case. I came across this commune in Beaufort and they got me thinking."

The border of my nail began to bleed.

"Dom Owens."

I nodded.

"Things aren't always what they seem."

"No."

"I can make a few calls if you'd like."

"I'd appreciate that."

"Do you want a Band-Aid?"

I dropped my hands and stood.

"No, thanks. I really won't keep you any longer. You've been very helpful."

"Any more questions, you know where I am."

* * *

Back in my office, I sat and watched shadows lengthen across the room, the feeling of an unformed thought still teasing my mind. The building was heavy with after-hours quiet.

Was it Daisy Jeannotte? I'd forgotten to ask Red if he knew her. Was that it?

No.

What was it that kept calling from the labyrinth of my neural wiring? Why couldn't I drag it into consciousness? What link did my id see that I did not?

My eyes fell on the small collection of mystery writers I keep on campus for exchange with colleagues. What did these authors call it? The "Had-I-But-Known" technique. Was that it? Was tragedy approaching because of a subconscious message I couldn't manage to retrieve?

What tragedy? Another death in Quebec? More killings in Beaufort? Harm to Kathryn? Another attack on me, with more serious consequences?

Somewhere a phone rang and rang, then stopped abruptly as the messaging service cut in. Silence.

I tried Pete's number again. No answer. He was probably off on another deposition trip. It didn't matter. I knew Birdie wasn't there.

I got up and started filing papers, sorted through a stack of reprints, then switched to shelving books. I knew it was avoidance, but couldn't help myself. The thought of going home was unbearable.

Ten minutes of restless activity. Don't think. Then,

"Oh hell, Birdie!"

I slammed a copy of *Baboon Ecology* onto the desk and slumped into my chair.

"Why did you have to be there? I'm so sorry. I'm so very, very sorry, Bird."

I lay my head on the blotter and sobbed.

THURSDAY WAS DECEPTIVELY PLEASANT.

In the morning I had two small surprises. The call to my insurance carrier went well. Both repairmen I phoned were available and would start work immediately.

During the day I taught my classes and revised the CAT scan paper for the physical anthropology conference. Late in the afternoon Ron Gillman reported that the Crime Scene Recovery unit had found nothing useful in the debris from my kitchen. No surprise there. He'd asked patrol to keep an eye on my place.

I also heard from Sam. He had no news, but was becoming increasingly convinced the bodies had been dropped on his island by dope dealers. He was taking it as a personal challenge and had dug out an old twelve gauge and stashed it under a bunk in the field station.

On the way home from the university I stopped at the Harris Teeter superstore across from the Southpark Shopping Center and bought all of my favorite foods. I worked out at the Harris YMCA and arrived at the Annex around six-thirty. The window had been fixed and a workman was just finishing sanding the floor. Every surface in the kitchen was coated in fine white dust.

I cleaned the stove and counters, then fixed crab cakes and a goat cheese salad and ate them while watching a rerun of "Murphy Brown." The Murph was tough. I resolved to be more like her.

During the evening I revised the CAT scan paper again, watched a Hornets' game, and thought about my taxes. I resolved to do that, too. But not this week. At eleven I fell asleep with the copies of Louis-Philippe's journal spread across the bed.

Friday was scripted by Satan. It was then I got my first inkling of the horror about to unfold.

The Murtry victims arrived from Charleston early in the morning. By nine-thirty I was gloved and goggled and had the cases spread out in my lab. One table held the skull and bone samples Hardaway had removed during his autopsy of the lower corpse. The other held a full skeleton. The technicians at the medical university had done an excellent job. All the bones looked clean and undamaged.

I started with the body from the bottom of the pit. Though putrefied, it had retained enough soft tissue to allow a full autopsy. Sex and race were evident, so Hardaway wanted my help only in assessing age. I left the pathologist's report and photos until later since I didn't want to bias my conclusions by knowing his.

I popped the X-rays onto the light box. Nothing unusual. In the cranial views I could see that all thirty-two teeth were erupted, their roots fully formed. There were no restorations or missing teeth. I noted this on a case form.

I walked to the first table and looked at the skull. The gap at the cranial base was fused. This was not an adolescent.

I studied the rib ends and the surfaces where the halves of the pelvis join in front, the pubic symphyses. The ribs had moderately deep indentations where cartilage had connected them to the breastbone. Wavy ridges ran across the pubic symphyseal faces, and I could see tiny nodules of bone along the outer border of each.

The throat end of each collarbone was fused. The upper edge of each hip blade retained a thin line of separation.

I checked my models and histograms, and wrote down my estimate. The woman was twenty to twenty-eight years of age when she died.

Hardaway wanted a full analysis on the subsurface burial. Again I started with the X-rays. Again they were unremarkable, except for the perfect dentition.

I already suspected this victim was also female, as I'd told Ryan. As I'd laid out the bones, I'd noted the smooth skull and delicate facial architecture. The broad, short pelvis with its distinctly feminine pubic area confirmed my initial impression.

This woman's age indicators were similar to those of the first victim, though her pubic symphyses showed deep ridges across their entire surfaces and lacked the little nodes.

I estimated this victim had died slightly younger, probably in her late teens or early twenties.

For the question of ancestry, I returned to the cranium. The mid-face region was classic, especially the nasal features: high bridge between the eyes, narrow opening, prominent lower border and spine.

I took measurements that I would analyze statistically, but I knew the woman was white.

I measured the long bones, fed the data into the computer, and ran the regression equations. I was entering a height estimate into the case form when the phone rang.

"If I stay here one more day I'm going to need complete linguistic retraining," Ryan said, then added, "y'all."

"Catch a bus north."

"I thought it was just you, but now I see it's not your fault."

"It's hard to overcome one's roots."

"Yo."

"Have you learned anything new?"

"I saw a great bumper sticker this morning."

I waited.

"Jesus loves you. Everyone else thinks you're an asshole."

"Is that what you called to tell me?"

"That was the bumper sticker."

"We are a religious people."

I looked at the clock. Two-fifteen. I realized I was famished and reached for the banana and Moon Pie I'd brought from home.

"I've spent some time observing Dom's little ashram. Not very useful. Thursday morning three of the faithful piled into a van and drove off. Other than that I saw no traffic in or out."

"Kathryn?"

"Didn't see her."

"Did you run the plates?"

"Yes, ma'am. Both vans are registered to Dom Owens at the Adler Lyons address."

"Does he have a driver's license?"

"Issued by the great Palmetto State in 1988. No record of a previous license. Apparently the reverend just walked in and took the exam. He pays his insurance right on time. In cash. No record of claims. No record of traffic arrests or citations."

"Utilities?" I tried not to crinkle the cellophane.

"Phone, electric, and water. Owens pays cash."

"Does he have a Social Security number?"

"Issued in 1987. But there's no record of any activity. Never paid in, never requested benefits of any kind."

"Eighty-seven? Where was he before that?"

"An insightful question, Dr. Brennan."

"Mail?"

"These folks are not great correspondents. They get the usual personal greetings addressed to 'Occupant,' and the utility bills, of course, but that's it. Owens has no box, but there could be a drop under another name. I staked the post office briefly, but didn't recognize any of the flock."

A student appeared in the doorway and I shook my head.

"Were there prints on your key chain?"

"Three beauties, but no hits. Apparently Dom Owens is a choirboy."

Silence stretched between us.

"There are kids living at that place. What about Social Services?"

"You're not half bad, Brennan."

"I watch a lot of television."

"I checked with Social Services. A neighbor called about a year and a half ago, worried about the kids. Mrs. Joseph Espinoza. So they sent a caseworker out to investigate. I read the report. She found a clean home with smiling, well-nourished young'uns, none of which was of school age. She saw no cause for action, but recommended a follow-up visit in six months. That was not done."

"Did you talk to the neighbor?"

"Deceased."

"How about the property?"

"Well, there is one thing."

Several seconds passed.

"Yes?"

"I spent Wednesday afternoon going through property deeds and tax records."

He went quiet again.

"Are you trying to annoy me?" I prompted.

"That piece of land has a colorful history. Did you know there was a school out there from the early 1860s until the turn of the century? One of the first public schools in North America established exclusively for black students."

"I didn't know that." I opened a Diet Coke.

"And Baker was right. The property was used as a fishing camp from the thirties until the mid-seventies. When the owner died it passed to her relatives in Georgia. I guess they weren't big on seafood. Or maybe they got fed up with the property taxes. Anyway, they sold the place in 1988."

This time I waited him out.

"The purchaser was one J. R. Guillion."

It took a nanosecond for the name to register.

"Jacques Guillion?"

"*Oui, madame.*"

"The same Jacques Guillion?" I said it so loudly a student turned in the corridor to peer in at me.

"Presumably. The taxes are paid . . ."

"With an official check from Citicorp in New York."

"You got it."

"Holy shit."

"Well put."

I was unnerved by the information. The owner of the Adler Lyons property also held title to the burned-out house in St-Jovite.

"Have you talked to Guillion?"

"Monsieur Guillion is still in seclusion."

"What?"

"He hasn't been located."

"I'll be damned. There really is a link."

"Looks that way."

A bell rang.

"One other thing."

The hall filled with the commotion of students passing between classes.

"Just to be perverse I sent the names out to Texas. Came up empty on the Right Reverend Owens, but guess who's a rancher?"

"No!"

"Monsieur J. R. Guillion. Two acres in Fort Bend County. Pays his taxes . . ."

"With official bank checks!"

"Eventually I'll head out that way, but for now I'm letting the local sheriff snoop around. And the gendarmerie can flush Guillion. I'm going to hang here a few more days and turn the heat up on Owens."

"Locate Kathryn. Sh called here, but I missed her again. I'm sure she knows something."

"If she's here, I'll find her."

"She could be in danger."

"What makes you say that?"

I thought of describing my recent conversation about cults, but since I'd only been fishing I wasn't sure if I'd learned anything relevant. Even if Dom Owens was leading some type of cult, he was not Jim Jones or David Koresh, of that I was certain.

"I don't know. Just a feeling. She sounded so edgy when she called."

"My impression of Miss Kathryn is that all her lobes may not be firing."

"She is different."

"And her friend El doesn't look like a candidate for Mensa. Are you keeping busy?"

I hesitated, then told him about my own attack.

"Sonofabitch. I'm sorry, Brennan. I liked that cat. Any idea who did it?"

"No."

"Have they put a unit on your place?"

"They're doing drive-bys. I'm fine."

"Stay out of dark alleys."

"The cases from Murtry arrived this morning. I'm pretty tied up in the lab."

"If those deaths are drug-related, you could be pissing off some heavy characters."

"That's breaking news, Ryan." I tossed the banana peel and Moon Pie wrapper into the trash. "The victims are both young, white, and female, just as I thought."

"Not your typical trafficker profile."

"No."

"Doesn't rule it out. Some of these guys use women like condoms. The ladies might have been at the wrong place at the wrong time."

"Yes."

"Cause of death?"

"I haven't finished yet."

"Go get 'em, tiger. But remember, we're going to need you on the St-Jovite cases when I nail these bastards."

"What bastards?"

"Don't know yet, but I will."

When we disconnected I stared at my report. Then I got up and paced the lab. Then I sat. Then I paced some more.

My mind kept throwing up images from St-Jovite. Doughy white babies, eyelids and fingernails a delicate blue. A bullet-pierced skull. Slashed throats, hands scored with defense wounds. Scorched bodies, their limbs twisted and contorted.

What linked the Quebec deaths to the point of land on Saint Helena Island? Why babies and fragile old women? Who was Guillion? What was in Texas? Into what form of malignancy had Heidi and her family stumbled?

Concentrate, Brennan. The young women in this lab are just as dead. Leave the Quebec murders to Ryan and finish these cases. They deserve your attention. Find out when they died. And how.

I pulled on another pair of gloves and examined every bone of the second victim's skeleton under magnification. I found nothing to tell me what caused her death. No blunt instrument trauma. No gunshot entry or exit. No stab wound. No hyoid fracture to indicate strangulation.

The only damage I observed was caused by animals scavenging on her corpse.

As I replaced the last foot bone, a tiny black beetle crawled from under a vertebra. I stared at it, remembering an afternoon when Birdie had tracked a June bug in my kitchen in Montreal. He'd played with the creature for hours before finally losing interest.

Tears burned my eyelids, but I refused to give in.

I collected the beetle and put it in a plastic container. No more death. I would release the bug when I left the building.

O.K., beetle. How long have these ladies been dead? We'll work on that.

I looked at the clock. Four-thirty. Late enough. I flipped through my Rolodex, found a number, and dialed.

Five time zones away a phone was answered.

"Dr. West."

"Dr. Lou West?"

"Yes."

"A.k.a. Kaptain Kam?"

Silence.

"Of Spam fame?"

"It's tuna fish. Is that you, Tempe?"

In my mind's eye I saw him, thick silver hair and beard framing a face permanently tanned by the Hawaiian sun. Years before I'd met him, a Japanese ad agency spotted Lou and cast him as spokesman for a brand of canned tuna. His earring and ponytail were perfectly suited to the sea captain image they wanted. The Japanese loved Kaptain Kam. Though we teased him unmercifully, no one I knew had ever seen the ads.

"Ready to give up bugs and hawk tuna full time?"

Lou holds a doctorate in biology and teaches at the University of Hawaii. In my opinion he is the best forensic entomologist in the country.

"Not quite." He laughed. "The suit itches."

"Do it in the buff."

"I don't think the Japanese are ready for that."

"When has that ever stopped you?"

Lou and I, and a handful of other forensic specialists, teach a course on body recovery at the FBI Academy in Quantico, Virginia. It's an irreverent group, composed of pathologists, entomologists, anthropologists, botanists, and soil experts, most with academic backgrounds. One year a zealously conservative agent suggested to the entomologist that his earring was inappropriate. Lou listened solemnly, and the next day the small gold loop was replaced by an eight-inch Cherokee feather with beads, fringe, and a small silver bell.

"I've got your bugs."

"They came through intact?"

"Unscathed. And you did a great job collecting. In the Carolinas the insect assemblage associated with decomposition includes over five hundred and twenty species. I think you sent me most of them."

"So what can you tell me?"

"You want the whole rundown?"

"Sure."

"First of all, I think your vics were killed during the day. Or at least the bodies were exposed during daylight hours for a while before burial. I found larviposition by *Sarcophaga bullata.*"

"Give that to me in English."

"It's a species of flesh fly. You collected empty *Sarcophaga bullata* puparial cases and intact puparia from both bodies."

"And?"

"The *Sarcophagidae* aren't too spunky after sundown. If you drop a body right next to them they might larviposit, but they're not very active at night."

"Larviposit?"

"Insects use larviposition or oviposition. Some lay eggs, some lay larvae."

"Insects lay larvae?"

"First instar larvae. That's the very first larval stage. The *Sarcophagidae* as a group larviposit. It's a strategy that gives them a head start on the rest of the maggots, and also provides some protection against predators that feed on eggs."

"Then why don't all these insects larviposit?"

"There's a downside. The females can't produce nearly as many larvae as they can eggs. It's a trade-off."

"Life is compromise."

"Indeed. I also suspect the bodies were exposed outside, at least for a short period. The *Sarcophagidae* aren't quite as willing to enter buildings as some other groups. The *Calliphoridae,* for example."

"That makes sense. They were either killed on the island or the bodies were transported there by boat."

"In any event, I'd guess they were killed during the day, then spent some time outside and aboveground before being buried."

"What about the other species?"

"You want the whole party?"

"Definitely."

"For both corpses burial would have delayed the normal insect invasion. Once the top body was exposed by the scavengers, however, the *Calliphoridae* would have found it irresistible for egg laying."

"*Calliphoridae*?"

"Blowflies. They usually arrive within minutes of death, along with their friends the flesh flies. They're both strong fliers."

"Bully."

"You collected at least two species of blowflies, *Cochliomyia* . . ."

"Maybe we should stick to common names."

"O.K. You collected first, second, and third instar larvae and intact and empty puparial cases for at least two species of blowflies."

"Which means what?"

"O.K., class. Let's review the life cycle of the fly. Like us, adult flies are concerned with finding suitable places to rear their young. A dead body is perfect. Protected environment. Lots to eat. The perfect neighborhood to raise the kids. Corpses are so attractive, blowflies and flesh flies may arrive within minutes after death. The female will either oviposit immediately, or feed for a while on the fluids seeping from the remains, and then lay her eggs."

"Nice."

"Hey, the stuff is very rich in protein. If there's trauma to the corpse, they'll go for that, if not they'll settle for orifices—eyes, nose, mouth, anus . . ."

"I get the picture."

"Blowflies lay huge clusters of eggs that can completely fill natural body openings and wound sites. You say it's been cool there, so there may not have been quite as many in your grave."

"When the eggs hatch, the maggots take center stage."

"Exactly. Act two. Maggots are really pretty cool. On the front end they have a pair of mouth hooks that they use for feeding and locomotion. They breathe through little flat structures on the back end."

"They breathe through their asses."

"In a sense. Anyway, eggs laid at the same time hatch at the same time and the maggots mature together. They also feed together, so you can get these enormous maggot masses moving around the body. The group feeding behavior results in the dissemination of bacteria and the production of digestive enzymes which permit maggots to consume most of the soft tissues of a corpse. It's all highly efficient.

"Maggots mature rapidly, and when they reach maximum size they undergo a dramatic change in behavior. They stop feeding and look for drier digs, usually away from the body."

"Act three."

"Yep. The larvae burrow in and their outer skins harden and form protective encasements called puparia. They look like tiny footballs. The maggots stay inside the pupal casings until their cells have reorganized, then emerge as adult flies."

"That's why the empty puparial cases are significant?"

"Yes. Remember the flesh flies?"

"The *Sarcophagidae.* The larvipositers."

"Very good. They're usually the first to emerge as adults. It takes them anywhere from sixteen to twenty-four days to mature, given temperatures around eighty degrees Fahrenheit. They'd be slowed under the conditions you describe."

"Yes. It wasn't that warm."

"But the empty puparial casings mean some of the flesh flies had finished their development."

"Flown the pupae, as it were."

"It takes the blowfly about fourteen to twenty-five days to mature, probably longer in the wet environment on your island."

"Those estimates tally."

"You also collected what I'm pretty sure are *Muscidae* larvae, maggots of the housefly and its relatives. Typically these species don't show up for five to seven days after death. They prefer to wait for what we call the late fresh or early bloat stages. Oh, and there were cheese skippers."

Cheese skippers are maggots that jump. Though not always easy, I've learned to ignore them while working on putrefied bodies.

"My personal favorites."

"Everybody's got to make a living, Dr. Brennan."

"I suppose one has to admire an organism that can jump ninety times its body length."

"Have you measured?"

"It's an estimate."

"A particularly useful critter for estimating PMI is the black soldier fly. They don't usually show up until twenty days after death, and they're fairly consistent, even with buried remains."

"They were present?"

"Yes."

"What else?"

"The beetle assemblage was more limited, probably due to the wet habitat. But the typical predator forms were there, no doubt munching happily on the maggots and soft-bodied forms."

"So what's your estimate?"

"I'd say we're talking about three to four weeks."

"Both bodies?"

"You measured four feet to the bottom of the pit, three feet to the top of the lower body. We've already discussed the preburial larviposition by the flesh flies, so that explains the puparial cases you found on and above the deeper body. Some held adults, half in and half out. They must have been trapped by the soil while trying to exit. The *Piophilidae* were there, also."

"Lou?"

"Cheese skippers. I also found some coffin flies in the soil sample you took from above the lower body, and some larvae on the body itself. These species are known to burrow down to corpses to deposit their eggs. The soil disturbance in the grave and the presence of the upper body would have facilitated their access. I forgot to mention I found coffin flies on the upper body."

"Were the soil samples useful?"

"Very. You don't want to hear about all the critters that chow down on maggots and decompositional materials, but I found one form that's helpful with PMI. When I processed the soil I collected a number of mites which support a minimum time since death of three weeks."

"So you're saying three to four weeks for both bodies."

"That's my preliminary estimate."

"This is very helpful, Lou. You guys amaze me."

"Does all this square with the condition of the remains?"

"Perfectly."

"There's one other thing I want to mention."

What he told me next sent an icy wind rocketing through my soul.

"I'M SORRY, LOU. GO OVER THAT AGAIN."

"It's not new. The increase in drug-related deaths in recent years has prompted research into testing for pharmaceuticals in carrion-feeding insects. I don't have to tell you that bodies aren't always found right away, so investigators may not have the specimens they need for tox analysis. You know, blood, urine, or organ tissues."

"So you test for drugs in maggots?"

"You can, but we've had better luck with the puparial casings. Probably because of the longer feeding time compared to the larvae. We've also played with beetle exuviae and frass . . ."

"Which is?"

"Cast-off beetle skins and fecal matter. We're finding the highest drug levels in the fly puparia, though. That probably reflects feeding preference. While beetles prefer dried integument, flies go for soft tissues. That's where drug concentrations are likely to be greatest."

"What's been found?"

"The list is pretty long. Cocaine, heroin, methamphetamine, amitriptyline, nortriptyline. Most recently we've been working with 3,4-methylenedioxymethamphetamine."

"Street name?"

"Ecstasy is the most common one."

"And you're finding these substances in puparial casings?"

"We've isolated both the parent drugs and their metabolites."

"How?"

"The extraction method is similar to that used on regular pathology samples, except that you have to break down the tough chitin/protein matrix in the insect puparia and exuviae so the toxins can be released. You do that by crushing the casings, then using either a strong acid or base treatment. After that, and a pH adjustment, you just use routine drug-screening techniques. We do a base extraction followed by liquid chromatography and mass spectrometry. The ion breakdown indicates what's in your sample and how much."

I swallowed.

"And you're telling me you found flunitrazepam in the puparial casings I sent?"

"The ones associated with the upper body contained flunitrazepam and two of its metabolites, desmethylflunitrazepam and 7-aminoflunitrazepam. The concentration of the parent drug was much greater than the metabolites."

"Which is consistent with acute rather than chronic exposure."

"Exactamundo."

I thanked Lou and hung up.

For a moment I just sat there. The shock of discovery had curdled my stomach and I felt I might throw up. Or maybe it was the Moon Pie.

Flunitrazepam.

The word had finally roused the stored memory.

Flunitrazepam.

Rohypnol.

That was the wake-up call my brain had been sounding.

With trembling hands I dialed the Lord Cartaret Motel. No answer. I redialed and left my number on Ryan's pager.

Then I waited, my sympathetic nervous system broadcasting a low-level alert, telling me to fear. Fear what?

Rohypnol.

When the phone rang I lunged for it.

A student.

I cleared the line and waited some more, feeling a dark, cold dread.

Rohypnol. The date rape drug.

Glaciers formed. Ocean levels rose and fell. Somewhere a star spun planets from dust.

Eleven minutes later Ryan called.

"I think I've found another link."

"What?"

Slow down. Don't let the shock interfere with your thinking.

"The Murtry Island and St-Jovite murders."

I told him about my conversation with Lou West.

"One of the women on Murtry had massive amounts of Rohypnol in her tissue."

"So did the bodies in the upstairs bedroom at St-Jovite."

"Yes."

Another memory had slammed to the surface when Lou spoke the name of the drug.

Boreal forest. Aerial views of a smoldering chalet. A meadow, shrouded bodies arranged in a circle. Uniformed personnel. Stretchers. Ambulances.

"Do you remember the Order of the Solar Temple?"

"The wing nut worshipers that offed themselves en masse?"

"Yes. Sixty-four people died in Europe. Ten in Quebec."

I fought to steady my voice.

"Some of those chalets were wired to explode and burn."

"Yeah. I've thought of that."

"Rohypnol was found in both locations. Many of the victims had ingested the drug shortly before they died."

Pause.

"You think Owens is rezoning for the Temple?"

"I don't know."

"Think they're dealing?"

Dealing what? Human lives?

"I suppose it's a possibility."

For several moments neither of us spoke.

"I'll run this past the guys who worked Morin Heights. Meantime, I'm going to shove a deadbolt up Dom Owens' ass."

"There's more."

The line hummed softly.

"Are you listening?"

"Yes."

"West estimates the women died three to four weeks ago."

My breath sounded loud in the receiver.

"The fire in St-Jovite was on March tenth. Tomorrow's the first."

I listened to the hum as Ryan did the math.

"Holy Christ. Three weeks ago."

"I have a feeling something terrible is going to happen, Ryan."

"Roger that."

Dial tone.

In looking back I always have the sense events accelerated after that conversation, gathered speed and grew more frantic, eventually forming a vortex that sucked everything into itself. Including me.

That evening I worked late. So did Hardaway. He called as I was pulling his autopsy report from the envelope.

I gave him the profile for the subsurface body, and my age estimate for the deeper one.

"That squares," he said. "She was twenty-five."

"You've got an ID?"

"We were able to lift one readable print. Got nothing from the local or state files, so they sent it up to the FBI. Nothing in their AFIS.

"Screwiest thing, though. Don't know what made me do it, probably 'cause I know you work up there. When the guy at the bureau suggested we try the RCMP I said, what the hell, fire it through. Damned if she doesn't pop up Canadian."

"What else did you find out about her?"

"Hang on."

I heard the creak of springs, then the rustle of paper.

"The sheet came through late today. Name's Jennifer Cannon. White race. Height five foot five, weight one hundred thirty pounds. Hair brown. Eyes green. Single. Last seen alive . . ." There was a pause while he calculated. ". . . two years, three months ago."

"Where's she from?"

"Let's see." Pause. "Calgary. Where's that?"

"Out west. Who reported her missing?"

"Sylvia Cannon. It's a Calgary address, so it must be the mother."

I gave Hardaway the pager number and asked him to phone Ryan.

"When you speak to him, please have him call me. If I'm not here I'll be at home."

I boxed and locked up the Murtry bones. Then I stuffed my diskette and case forms, Hardaway's autopsy report and photos, and the CAT scan paper into my briefcase, secured the lab, and left.

The campus was deserted, the night still and moist. Unseasonably warm, the broadcasters would call it. The air was heavy with the smell of grass just cut and rain about to fall. I heard the faint rumble of distant thunder, and pictured the storm rolling down from the Smokies and across the Piedmont.

On the way home I stopped for take-out at the Selwyn Pub. The after-work crowd was dispersing, and the younger set from Queens College had not yet arrived to take over the premises for the evening. Sarge, the rascally Irish co-owner, sat on his usual corner stool dispensing opinions on sports and politics, while Neal the bartender dispensed any one of a dozen draft beers. Sarge wanted to discuss the death penalty, or rather have his say about the death penalty, but I was not in the mood for banter. I took my cheeseburger and left quickly.

The first drops were patting the magnolias as I slipped my key into the Annex lock. Nothing greeted me but a soft, steady ticking.

It was almost ten when I heard from Ryan.

Sylvia Cannon had not lived at the address provided in the missing person report for over two years. Nor was she residing at the one given the post office for forwarding.

Neighbors at the earlier address remembered no husband and only one daughter. They described Sylvia as quiet and reclusive. A loner. No one knew where she had worked, or where she had gone. One woman thought there was a brother in the area. The Calgary PD were trying to locate her.

Later in bed, up under the eaves, I listened to rain tick on the roof and leaves. Thunder rumbled and lightning popped, now and then backlighting the silhouette of Sharon Hall. The ceiling fan brought in a cool mist, and with it the smell of petunias and wet window screen.

I adore storms. I love the raw power of the spectacle: Hydraulics! Voltage! Percussion! Mother Nature has dominion and everyone awaits her whim.

I enjoyed the show as long as I could, then got up and crossed to the dormer. The curtain felt damp and water was already pooling on the sill. I closed and latched the left window, took hold of the right, and breathed deeply. The thundershower cocktail triggered a flood of childhood recollections. Summer nights. Lightning bugs. Sleeping with Harry on Gran's porch.

Think about that, I told myself. Listen to those memories, not the voices of the dead clamoring in your brain.

Lightning flashed and my breath froze in my throat. Was something moving under the hedge?

Another flicker.

I stared, but the shrubs looked still and empty.

Could I have imagined it?

My eyes searched the dimness. Green lawn and hedges. Colorless walks. Pale petunias against the darkness of pine chips and ivy.

Nothing moved.

Again the world lit up and a loud crack split the night.

A white form burst from the bushes and tore across the lawn. I strained to see, but the image was gone before my eyes could focus.

My heart beat so frantically I could feel it in my skull. I threw back the window and leaned into the screen, searching the darkness where the thing had disappeared. Water soaked my nightgown and goose bumps spread across my body.

I scanned the yard, trembling.

Stillness.

Forgetting the window, I turned and raced down the stairs. I was about to throw open the back door when the phone shrilled, sending my heart pounding into my throat.

Oh, God. What now?

I grabbed the receiver.

"Tempe, I'm sorry."

I looked at the clock.

One-forty.

Why was my neighbor calling?

"... he must have gotten in there on Wednesday when I showed the place. It's empty, you know. I went over just now to check on things, with the storm and all, and he came tearing out. I called, but he just took off. I thought you'd want to know..."

I dropped the receiver, threw open the kitchen door, and rushed outside.

"Here, Bird," I called. "Come on, boy."

I stepped off the patio. In seconds my hair was drenched and my nightie clung like wet Kleenex.

"Birdie! Are you there?"

Lightning flared, illuminating walkways, bushes, gardens, and buildings.

"Birdie!" I screamed. "Bird!"

Raindrops pounded brick and slapped at leaves above my head.

I shouted again.

No response.

Over and over I called his name, a madwoman, prowling the grounds of Sharon Hall. Before long I was shaking uncontrollably.

Then I saw him.

He was huddled under a bush, head down, ears forward at an odd angle. His fur was wet and clumped, revealing ribbons of pale skin, like cracks on an old painting.

I walked over to him and squatted. He looked like he'd been dipped then rolled. Pine needles, bark chips, and minced vegetation clung to his head and back.

"Bird?" I said in a soft voice, holding out my arms.

He raised his head and searched my face with round yellow eyes. Lightning flicked. Birdie rose, arched his back, and said, "Mrrrrp."

I turned my palms up. "Come on, Bird," I whispered.

He hesitated, then crossed to me, pressed his body sideways against my thigh, and repeated himself. "Mrrrrrp."

I scooped my cat up, hugged him close, and ran for the kitchen. Birdie draped his front paws over my shoulder and pressed himself to me, like a baby monkey clinging to its mother. I felt his claws through my rain-soaked gown.

Ten minutes later I'd finished rubbing him down. White fur

coated several towels and drifted in the air. For once there'd been no protest.

Birdie wolfed down a bowl of Science Diet and a saucer of vanilla ice cream. Then I carried him up to bed. He crawled under the covers and stretched full length against my leg. I felt his body tense then relax as he extended his paws, then settled into the mattress. His fur was still damp but I didn't care. I had my cat back.

"I love you, Bird," I said to the night.

I fell asleep to a duet of muffled purring and pelting rain.

THE NEXT DAY WAS SATURDAY SO I DIDN'T GO TO THE UNIVERSITY. I planned to read Hardaway's findings, then write my reports on the Murtry victims. After that I would purchase flowers at the garden center and transplant them to the large pots I keep on my patio. Instant gardening, one of my many talents. Then a long talk with Katy, quality time with my cat, the CAT scan paper, and an evening with Élisabeth Nicolet.

That's not how it turned out.

When I woke Birdie was already gone. I called but got no response, so I threw on shorts and a T-shirt and went downstairs to find him. The trail was easy. He'd emptied his dish and fallen asleep in a patch of sunlight on the couch in the living room.

The cat lay on his back, hind legs splayed, front paws dangling over his chest. I watched him a moment, smiling like a kid on Christmas morning. Then I went to the kitchen, made coffee and a bagel, collected the *Observer,* and settled at the kitchen table.

A doctor's wife was found stabbed to death in Myers Park. A child had been attacked by a pit bull. The parents were demanding the animal be destroyed, and the owner was indignant. The Hornets beat Golden State 101 to 87.

I checked the weather. Sunshine and a high of seventy-four predicted for Charlotte. I scanned world temperatures. On Friday the mercury had climbed to forty-eight degrees in Montreal. There is a reason for Southern smugness.

I read the entire paper. Editorials. Want ads. Pharmacy flyers. It's a weekend ritual I enjoy, but one I'd had to forgo in the past few weeks. Like a junkie on a binge I absorbed every printed word.

When I'd finished I cleared the table and went to my briefcase. I stacked the autopsy photos to my left and lay Hardaway's report in front of me. My pen gave out with the first notation. I rose and went to the living room to find another.

When I saw the figure on the front stoop my heart slipped in an extra beat. I had no idea who it was or how long it had been there.

The figure turned, stepped up against the outer wall, and leaned into the window. Our eyes met and I stared in disbelief.

Immediately, I crossed and opened the door.

She stood with hips thrust forward, hands clutching the straps of a backpack. The hem of her skirt billowed around her hiking boots. The morning sun caught her hair, outlining her head in a copper glow.

Sweet Jesus, I thought. Now what?

Kathryn spoke first.

"I need to talk. I—"

"Yes, of course. Please, come in." I stood back and held out a hand. "Let me take your pack."

She stepped inside, slipped off the backpack, and dropped it to the floor, her eyes never leaving my face.

"I know this is a terrible imposition, and I—"

"Kathryn, don't be silly. I'm glad to see you. I was just so surprised my brain locked up for a second."

Her lips parted but no words came out.

"Would you like something to eat?"

The answer was in her face.

I put my arm around her and took her to the kitchen table. She complied meekly. I stacked the photos and report to the side and sat her down.

As I toasted a bagel, spread it with cream cheese, and poured orange juice, I stole glances at my visitor. Kathryn stared at the tabletop, her hands smoothing nonexistent wrinkles from the mat I'd placed in front of her. Her fingers arranged and rearranged the fringe, straightening each clump and laying it parallel to the next.

My stomach was tied in a granny knot. How had she gotten here? Had she run away? Where was Carlie? I held my questions while she ate.

When Kathryn had finished and declined seconds, I cleared the dishes and rejoined her at the table.

"So. How did you find me?" I patted her hand and smiled encouragingly.

"You gave me your card." She dug it from her pocket and laid it on the table. Then her fingers went back to the place mat. "I called the number in Beaufort a couple of times, but you were never there. Finally some guy answered and said you'd gone back to Charlotte."

"That was Sam Rayburn. I was staying on his boat."

"Anyway, I decided to leave Beaufort." She raised her eyes to mine, then quickly dropped them. "I hitched up here and went to the university, but it took longer than I'd figured. When I got to campus you were gone. I crashed with someone, then this morning she dropped me here on her way to work."

"How did you know where I live?"

"She looked you up in some kind of book."

"I see." I was sure my home address was not listed in the faculty directory. "Well, I'm glad you're here."

Kathryn nodded. She looked exhausted. Her eyes were red and a dark crescent underscored each lower lid.

"I would have returned your calls but you left no number. When Detective Ryan and I visited the compound on Tuesday we didn't see you."

"I was there, but . . . " Her voice faded out.

I waited.

Birdie appeared in the doorway then withdrew, deflected by the tension. The clock chimed the half-hour. Kathryn's fingers worked the fringe.

Finally, I could take it no longer.

"Kathryn, where's Carlie?" I placed my hand on hers.

She raised her eyes to mine. They looked flat and empty.

"They're taking care of him." Her voice was small, like a child answering an accusation.

"Who is?"

She pulled her hand free, rested her elbows on the table, and rubbed small circles on each of her temples. Her eyes were back on the place mat.

"Is Carlie on Saint Helena?"

Another nod.

"Did you want to leave him there?"

She shook her head and her hands slid upward so the palms pressed against her temples.

"Is the baby all right?"

"He's my baby! Mine!"

The vehemence took me by surprise.

"I can take care of him." When she raised her head a tear glistened on each cheek. Her eyes bored into mine.

"Who says you can't?"

"I'm his mother." Her voice trembled. With what? Exhaustion? Fear? Resentment?

"Who is taking care of Carlie?"

"But what if I'm wrong? What if it's all true?" Her gaze went back to the tabletop.

"What if *what* is true?"

"I love my baby. I want the best for him."

Kathryn's answers were unrelated to my questions. She was probing her own dark places, reworking a familiar discourse with herself. Only this time it was in my kitchen.

"Of course you do."

"I don't want my baby to die." Her fingers trembled as they caressed the tassels on the mat. It was the same movement I'd seen her use to stroke Carlie's head.

"Is Carlie sick?" I asked, alarmed.

"No. He's perfect." The words were almost inaudible. A tear dropped to the mat.

I looked at the small, dark spot, feeling completely inept.

"Kathryn, I don't know how to help you. You have to tell me what's going on."

The phone rang, but I ignored it. From the other room I heard a click, my message, then a beep followed by a tinny voice. More clicks, then silence.

Kathryn didn't move. She seemed paralyzed by the thoughts that tortured her. Across the silence I felt her pain, and waited.

Seven spots darkened the blue linen. Ten. Thirteen.

After what seemed an eternity Kathryn raised her head. She wiped each cheek and brushed back her hair, then intertwined her fingers and placed her hands carefully in the center of the mat. She cleared her throat twice.

"I don't know what it's like to live a normal life." She gave a self-deprecating smile. "Until this year I didn't know that I wasn't."

She dropped her eyes.

"I guess it had to do with having Carlie. I never doubted anything before he was born. It never occurred to me to ask questions. I was home-schooled so what I knew—" Again the smile. "What I know of the world is limited." She thought for a moment. "What I know of the world is what they want me to know."

"They?"

She clutched her hands so tightly the knuckles grew white.

"We're never supposed to talk about group matters." She swallowed. "They're my family. They've been my world since I was eight years old. He's been my father and counselor and teacher and—"

"Dom Owens?"

Her eyes flew to mine. "He's a brilliant man. He knows all about health and reproduction and evolution and pollution and how to keep the spiritual and biological and cosmic forces in balance. He sees and understands things the rest of us don't have a clue about. It's not Dom. I trust Dom. He would never hurt Carlie. He does what he does to protect us. He's watching out for us. I'm just not sure—"

She closed her eyes and tipped her face upward. A small vessel throbbed in the side of her neck. Her larynx rose and fell, then she took a deep breath, lowered her chin, and looked directly into my eyes.

"That girl. The one you were looking for. She was there."

I had to strain to hear her.

"Heidi Schneider?"

"I never knew her last name."

"Tell me what you remember about her."

"Heidi joined somewhere else. Texas, I think. She lived on Saint Helena for about two years. She was older than me, but I liked her.

She was always willing to talk or to help me out. She was funny." She paused. "Heidi was supposed to procreate with Jason—"

"What?" I thought I'd heard incorrectly.

"Her procreation partner was Jason. But she was in love with Brian, the guy she was with when she joined. He's the one in your snapshot."

"Brian Gilbert." My mouth felt dry.

"Anyway, she and Brian used to sneak off to be together." Her eyes went to a point somewhere in the distance. "When Heidi got pregnant she was terrified because the baby wouldn't be sanctified. She tried to hide it, but eventually they found out."

"Owens?"

Her eyes refocused on mine and I could see real fear.

"It doesn't matter. It affects everyone."

"What does?"

"The order." She rubbed her palms on the mat then reclasped her hands. "Some things I can't talk about. Do you want to hear this?" She looked at me and I could see that her eyes were starting to water again.

"Go on."

"One day Heidi and Brian didn't show up for morning meeting. They were gone."

"Where?"

"I don't know."

"Do you think Owens sent someone to find them?"

Her eyes slid to the window, and she bit down on her lower lip.

"There's more. One night last fall Carlie woke up fussy, so I went downstairs to get him milk. I heard movement in the office, then a woman speaking, real quiet like she didn't want anyone to hear. She must have been on the phone."

"Did you recognize her voice?"

"Yes. It was one of the women who worked in the office."

"What did she say?"

"She was telling someone that someone else was O.K. I didn't hang around to hear more."

"Go on."

"About three weeks ago the same thing happened, only this time I overheard people arguing. They were really angry, but the door was closed, so I couldn't make out their words. It was Dom and this same woman."

She wiped a tear from her cheek with the back of her hand. She still did not look at me.

"The next day she was gone and I never saw her again. She and another woman. They just disappeared."

"Don't people come and go from the group?"

Her eyes locked on to mine.

"She worked in the office. I think she was the one taking the calls you were asking about." I could see her chest rise and fall as she fought back the tears. "She was Heidi's best friend."

I felt the knot tighten in my stomach. "Was her name Jennifer?"

Kathryn nodded.

I took a deep breath. Stay calm for Kathryn's sake.

"Who was the other woman?"

"I'm not sure. She hadn't been there long. Wait. Maybe her name was Alice. Or Anne."

My heart changed speed. Oh, God. No.

"Do you know where she came from?"

"Somewhere up North. No, maybe it was Europe. Sometimes she and Jennifer spoke a different language."

"Do you think Dom Owens had Heidi and her babies killed? Is that why you're afraid for Carlie?"

"You don't understand. It isn't Dom. He's just trying to protect us and get us across." She gazed at me intently, as though trying to reach inside my head. "Dom doesn't believe in Antichrists. He just wants to transport us out of the destruction."

Her voice had grown tremulous and short gasps punctuated the spaces between her words. She rose and crossed to the window.

"It's the others. It's her. Dom wants us all to live forever."

"Who?"

Kathryn paced the kitchen like a caged animal, her fingers twisting the front of her cotton blouse. Tears slid down her face.

"But not now. It's too soon. It can't be now." Pleading.

"What's too soon?"

"What if they're wrong? What if there isn't enough cosmic energy? What if there's nothing out there? What if Carlie just dies? What if my baby dies?"

Fatigue. Anxiety. Guilt. The mix won over and Kathryn began to weep uncontrollably. She was growing incoherent and I knew I would learn nothing further.

I went to her and hugged her with both arms. "Kathryn, you need rest. Please, come and lie down for a while. We'll talk later."

She made a sound I couldn't interpret, and allowed herself to be led upstairs to the guest room. I got towels and went down to the parlor for her pack. When I returned, she lay on the bed, one arm thrown across her forehead, eyes shut, tears sliding into the hair at her temples.

I left the pack on the dresser and pulled the window shades. As I was closing the door she spoke softly, eyes still closed, lips barely moving.

Her words frightened me more than anything I had heard in a long time.

"'ETERNAL LIFE'? THOSE WERE HER EXACT WORDS?"

"Yes." I clutched the phone so tightly the tendons in my wrist ached.

"Give it to me again."

"'What if they go and we're left behind?' 'What if I deny Carlie eternal life?'"

I waited while Red considered Kathryn's words. When I switched hands I could see a print where my palm had sweated onto the plastic.

"I don't know, Tempe. It's a tough call. How can we ever know when a group will turn violent? Some of these marginal religious movements are extremely volatile. Others are harmless."

"Are there no predictors?"

What if my baby dies?

"There are a number of factors that feed back on each other. First there's the sect itself, its beliefs and rituals, its organization and, of course, its leader. Then there are the outside forces. How much hostility is directed toward the members? How stigmatized are they by society? And the mistreatment doesn't have to be real. Even perceived persecution can cause an organization to become violent."

He just wants to transport us out of the destruction.

"What types of beliefs push these groups over the line?"

"That's what concerns me about your young lady. Sounds like she's talking about a voyage. About going somewhere for eternal life. That sounds apocalyptic."

He's just trying to protect us and get us across.

"The end of the world."

"Exactly. The last days. Armageddon."

"That's not new. Why does an apocalyptic worldview encourage violence? Why not just hunker in and wait?"

"Don't get me wrong. It doesn't always. But these groups believe the last days are imminent, and they see themselves as having a key role in the events that are about to unfold. They're the chosen ones who will give birth to the new order."

She was terrified because the baby wouldn't be sanctified.

"So what develops is a kind of dualism in their thinking. They are good, and all others are hopelessly corrupt, totally lacking in moral virtue. Outsiders come to be demonized."

"You're with me or you're against me."

"Exactly. According to these visions the last days are going to be characterized by violence. Some groups go into a sort of survivalist mode, stockpiling weapons and setting up elaborate surveillance systems against the evil social order that's out to get them. Or the Antichrist, or Satan, or whatever they see as the perceived threat."

Dom doesn't believe in Antichrists.

"Apocalyptic beliefs can be especially volatile when embodied in a charismatic leader. Koresh saw himself as the Lord's appointed."

"Go on."

"You see, one of the problems for a self-appointed prophet is that he has to constantly reinvent himself. There's no institutional support for his long-term authority. There are also no institutional restraints on his behavior. The leader runs the show, but only as long as his disciples follow. So these guys can be very volatile. And they can do whatever they choose within their sphere of power.

"Some of the more paranoid respond to perceived threats to their authority by becoming oppressively dictatorial. They make increasingly bizarre demands, insisting their followers comply in order to show loyalty."

"Such as?"

"Jim Jones had tests of faith, as he called them. Members of the

People's Temple would be forced to sign confessions or suffer public humiliations to prove their devotion. One little ritual required the participant to drink unidentified liquids. When told it was poison, the testee wasn't supposed to show fear."

"Charming."

"Vasectomy is another favorite. It's said that the leadership of Synanon required some of the male members to go under the knife."

Her procreation partner was Jason.

"What about arranging marriages?"

"Jouret and DiMambro, Jim Jones, David Koresh, Charles Manson. They all used controlled coupling. Diet, sex, abortion, dress, sleep. It really doesn't matter what the idiosyncrasy is. As a leader conditions his followers to abide by his rules he breaks down their inhibitions. Eventually this unquestioning acceptance of bizarre behaviors may habituate them to the idea of violence. At first it's small acts of devotion, seemingly harmless requirements like hairstyles or meditation at midnight, or sex with the messiah. Later his demands may become more lethal."

"Sounds like the deification of insanity."

"Well put. The process has another advantage for the leader. It weeds out the less committed, since they get fed up and leave."

"O.K., fine. You have these fringe groups living a life orchestrated by some nutcase. What makes them turn violent at any given time? Why today and not next month?"

It's too soon. It can't be now.

"Most outbreaks of violence involve what sociologists refer to as 'escalating boundary tensions.' "

"Don't feed me jargon, Red."

"O.K. These fringe groups usually are concerned with two things, getting members and keeping members. But if a leader feels threatened the emphasis often shifts. Sometimes recruitment stops and existing members are monitored more closely. The demand for commitment to eccentric rules may intensify. The theme of doom may become more pronounced. The group can grow increasingly isolated and increasingly paranoid. Tensions with the surrounding community, or with the government, or law enforcement may escalate."

"What could possibly threaten these megalomaniacs?"

"A member who leaves could be seen as a defector."

We woke up and Heidi and Brian were gone.

"The leader might feel he's losing control. Or if the cult exists in more than one place, and he can't always be there, he might feel his authority is slipping during his absences. More anxiety. More isolation. More tyranny. It's a paranoid spiral. Then all it takes is some external factor to pull the pin."

"How disruptive would the outside event have to be?"

"It varies. At Jonestown it took only the visit by a congressman and his press entourage, and their attempt to return to the U.S. with a handful of defectors. At Waco it took a military-style raid by the Bureau of Alcohol, Tobacco, and Firearms, and the eventual insertion of CS gas and the breaching of the compound walls by armored vehicles."

"Why the difference?"

"That has to do with ideology and leadership. The settlement at Jonestown was more internally volatile than the community at Waco."

My fingers felt cold on the handset.

"Do you think Owens has a violent agenda?"

"He definitely bears watching. If he's holding your friend's baby against her will that should get you a warrant."

"It's unclear whether she agreed to leave him there. She's very reluctant to talk about the cult. She's been raised by these people since she was eight years old. I've never seen anyone so torn. But the fact that Jennifer Cannon was living at the Owens compound when she was killed should do it."

For a while neither of us spoke.

"Could Heidi and Brian have sent Owens over the edge?" I asked. "Could he have ordered someone to kill them and their babies?"

"Could be. And don't forget, he's had some other blows. Sounds like Jennifer Cannon may have concealed those phone calls from Canada, then refused to go along with something Owens wanted when he found out. And of course there's you."

"Me?"

"Brian gets Heidi pregnant against cult orders. Then the couple splits. Then the thing with Jennifer. Then you and Ryan show up. Odd coincidence in names, by the way."

"What?"

"The congressman who showed up in Guyana. His name was Ryan."

"Give me a prediction, Red. Based on what I've told you, what do you see in your crystal ball?"

There was a long pause.

"From what you've told me Owens may fit the profile of a charismatic leader with a messianic self-image. And it sounds like his followers have accepted that vision. Owens may feel he's losing control over his members. He may see your investigation as an additional threat to his authority."

Another pause.

"And this Kathryn is talking about crossing over to eternal life."

I heard him take a deep breath.

"Given all of that, I'd say there is a high potential for violence."

I disconnected and dialed Ryan's pager. While I waited for him to phone back I returned to the Hardaway report. I'd just pulled it from the envelope when the phone rang. Had I not been so agitated it might have been amusing. I seemed destined never to read that document.

"You must have hit the floor running this morning." Ryan's voice sounded tired.

"I'm always up early. I have a visitor."

"Let me guess. Gregory Peck."

"Kathryn showed up this morning. She says she spent the night at UNCC and found me through the faculty directory."

"Not smart to list your home address."

"I don't. Jennifer Cannon lived at the Saint Helena compound."

"Damn."

"Kathryn overheard an argument between Jennifer and Owens. The next day Jennifer was gone."

"Good stuff, Brennan."

"It gets better."

I told him about Jennifer's access to the phone and her friendship with Heidi. He came back with his own shocker.

"When you talked to Hardaway you asked when Jennifer Cannon was last seen alive. What you didn't ask was where. It wasn't Calgary. Jennifer hadn't lived there since she went off to school.

According to the mother they kept in close contact until shortly before she disappeared. Then her daughter's calls became less frequent, and when they spoke Jennifer seemed evasive.

"Jennifer called home at Thanksgiving two years ago, then nothing. The mother phoned the school, contacted her daughter's friends, even visited the campus, but she never discovered where Jennifer had gone. That's when she filed the missing person report."

"And?"

I heard him draw a deep breath.

"Jennifer Cannon was last seen leaving the McGill University campus."

"No."

"Yes. She didn't take her finals or withdraw from her classes. She just packed up and left."

"Packed up?"

"Yeah. That's why the police didn't pursue the case too vigorously. She packed her belongings, closed her bank account, left a note for her landlord, and vanished. It didn't look like an abduction."

My mind threw up an image, then resisted bringing it into focus. A face with bangs. A nervous gesture. I forced my lips to form the words.

"Another young woman disappeared from the compound at the same time Jennifer Cannon did. Kathryn didn't know her since she was a newcomer." I swallowed. "Kathryn thought the girl's name might have been Anne."

"I don't follow."

"Anna Goyette was"—I corrected myself—"is a McGill student."

"Anna is a common name."

"Kathryn heard Jennifer and this girl speak a foreign language."

"French?"

"I'm not sure Kathryn would know French if she heard it."

"You think the second Murtry victim could be Anna Goyette?"

I didn't answer.

"Brennan, just because some girl showed up on Saint Helena who may have been called Anna doesn't mean it was a McGill class reunion. Cannon left the university over two years ago. Goyette is nineteen. She wasn't there yet."

"True. But everything else fits."

"I don't know. And even if Jennifer Cannon lived with Owens it doesn't mean he killed her."

"They fight. She disappears. Her body turns up in a shallow grave."

"Maybe she was into dope. Or her friend Anne was. Maybe Owens found out and threw them out. They've got nowhere to go so they squeeze their business associates. Or they take off with a bag of the merchandise."

"Is that what you think happened?"

"Look, all we know for sure is that Jennifer Cannon left Montreal a couple of years ago and her body turned up on Murtry Island. She may have spent time with the community on Saint Helena. She may have argued with Owens. If so, those facts may or may not be relevant to her death."

"They're sure as hell germane to the question of her whereabouts for the past several years."

"Yes."

"What are you going to do?"

"First I'm going to visit Sheriff Baker to see if this gets us a warrant. Then I'm going to light a fire under the boys in Texas. I want to know about every cell this Owens has ever shed. Then it's back out to Happy Acres for some high-visibility surveillance. I want to see what color the guru sweats, and I don't have much time. They want me in Montreal on Monday."

"I think he's dangerous, Ryan."

He listened without interrupting as I outlined my conversation with Red Skyler. When I'd finished there was a long silence as Ryan integrated the sociologist's words with what we'd just discussed.

"I'll call Claudel and get a status on Anna Goyette."

"Thanks, Ryan."

"Keep an eye on Kathryn," he said solemnly.

"I will."

I didn't get that opportunity. When I went upstairs, Kathryn was gone.

"DAMN!" I SAID TO THE EMPTY AIR.

Birdie had followed me up the stairs. He froze at my outburst, lowered his head, and regarded me with a steady gaze.

"Damn!"

No one answered.

Ryan was right. Kathryn was not stable. I knew I couldn't assure her safety, or that of her baby, so why did I feel responsible?

"She split, Bird. What can you do?"

The cat had no suggestions, so I followed my usual pattern. When anxious, I work.

I returned to the kitchen. The door was ajar and wind had scattered the autopsy photos.

Or had it? Hardaway's report lay exactly as I'd left it.

Had Kathryn viewed the pictures? Had the grisly tableau sent her fleeing in panic?

Feeling another surge of guilt, I sat down and sorted through the stack.

Cleaned of its shroud of maggots and sediment, Jennifer Cannon's body was better preserved than I'd expected. Though decomposition had ravaged her face and viscera, wounds were clearly evident in the bloated and discolored flesh.

Cuts. Hundreds of them. Some circular, others linear, measuring one to several centimeters. They clustered near her throat, in her thorax, and ran the length of her arms and legs. All over her body I could see what looked like superficial scratches, but skin slippage made these lesions difficult to observe. The mottling of hematoma was everywhere.

I examined several close-ups. While the chest wounds had smooth, clean edges, the other cuts looked jagged and uneven. A deep gash circled her upper right arm, exposing torn flesh and splintered bone.

I moved to the cranial photos. Though sloughing had begun, most of the hair was still in place. Oddly, the posterior views showed bone gleaming through the tangled mat, as though a section of scalp were missing.

I'd seen that pattern before. Where?

I finished with the photos and opened Hardaway's report.

Twenty minutes later I leaned back and closed my eyes.

Probable cause of death: exsanguination due to stabbing. The smooth-bordered chest wounds were made by a blade that had severed critical vessels. Due to decomposition, the pathologist was uncertain as to the cause of the other lacerations.

I passed the rest of the day in a state of agitation. I wrote my reports on Jennifer Cannon and the other Murtry victim, then turned to the CAT scan data, stopping frequently to listen for Kathryn.

Ryan phoned at two to say that the Jennifer Cannon link had convinced a judge, and a search warrant was being issued for the Saint Helena compound. He and Baker were heading out as soon as they had the paper.

I told him about Kathryn's disappearance, and listened to his assurances that I was not to blame. I also told him about Birdie.

"At least there's some good news."

"Yeah. Any word on Anna Goyette?"

"No."

"Texas?"

"Still waiting. I'll let you know what goes down here."

As I hung up, I felt fur brush my ankle, and looked down to see Birdie worming figure eights between my feet.

"Come on, Bird. How 'bout a treat?"

My cat is inordinately fond of canine chew toys. I've explained that these products are for dogs, but he will not be dissuaded.

I dug a small rawhide bone from a kitchen drawer and sailed it into the living room.

Birdie raced across the room, pounced, then rolled onto his prey. He righted himself, positioned the object between his front paws, and began gnawing on his kill.

I watched, wondering about the appeal of slimy hide.

The cat chewed a corner, then turned the toy and dragged his teeth the length of one edge. The object fell sideways and Bird nudged it back and sank a canine into the leather.

I watched, transfixed.

Was that it?

I went to Birdie, squatted, and pried his quarry from him. The cat placed his front paws on my knee, stood on hind legs, and tried to retrieve his prize.

My pulse quickened as I stared at the mangled leather.

Sweet Jesus.

I thought of the puzzling wounds in Jennifer Cannon's flesh. Superficial scratches. Jagged tears.

I ran to the living room for my lens, then raced to the kitchen and rifled through Hardaway's photos. I selected the head views and studied each under magnification.

The balding was not due to decomposition. The strands that remained were firmly rooted. The detached segment of skin and hair was neatly rectangular, its edges torn and ragged.

Jennifer Cannon's scalp had been ripped from her skull.

I thought of what that meant.

And I thought of something else.

Could I have been so thick? Could a preconceived mind-set have blinded me to the obvious?

I grabbed my keys and purse and flew out the door.

Forty minutes later I was at the university. The bones of the unidentified Murtry victim stared accusingly from my lab table.

How could I have been so careless?

"Never assume a single source of trauma." My mentor's words floated back across the decades.

I'd fallen into the trap. When I saw the destruction on the bones

I'd thought raccoons and vultures. I hadn't looked closely. I hadn't measured.

Now I had.

While there was extensive damage on the skeleton due to postmortem scavenging, other injury had gone before.

The two holes in the occipital bone were the most telling. They measured five millimeters each, with a distance between them of thirty-five. These punctures were not made by a turkey vulture, and the pattern was too large for a raccoon.

The dimensions suggested a large dog. So did parallel scratches on the cranial bones, and similar perforations in the clavicle and sternum.

Jennifer Cannon and her companion had been attacked by animals, probably large dogs. Teeth had torn their flesh and scored their bones. Some bites had been powerful enough to pierce the thickness at the back of the skull.

My mind made a leap.

Carole Comptois, the Montreal victim who had been hung by her wrists and tortured, had also been mauled.

That's reaching, Brennan.

Yes.

It's ridiculous.

No, I told myself. It's not.

Up to now my skepticism had done nothing for these victims. I'd been slack about the animal damage. I'd doubted the link between Heidi Schneider and Dom Owens, and I'd failed to see his connection to Jennifer Cannon. I hadn't helped Kathryn or Carlie, and I'd done nothing to locate Anna Goyette.

From now on, if necessary, I *would* reach. If there was a remote possibility that Carole Comptois and the women on Murtry Island were linked, I would consider it.

I phoned Hardaway, not expecting him to be working late on Saturday. He wasn't. Neither was LaManche, the pathologist who had done the Comptois autopsy. I left messages for both.

Frustrated, I took out a tablet and began to list what I knew.

Jennifer Cannon and Carole Comptois were both from Montreal. Each died following an animal attack.

The skeleton buried with Jennifer Cannon also bore the marks of animal teeth. The victim died with levels of Rohypnol indicative of acute intoxication.

Rohypnol was isolated in two of the victims found with Heidi Schneider and her family in St-Jovite.

Rohypnol was found in bodies at the murder/suicide sites of the Order of the Solar Temple.

The Solar Temple operated in Quebec and Europe.

Phone calls were made from the house in St-Jovite to Dom Owens' commune on Saint Helena. Both properties were owned by Jacques Guillion, who also owned property in Texas.

Jacques Guillion is Belgian.

One of the St-Jovite victims, Patrice Simonnet, was Belgian.

Heidi Schneider and Brian Gilbert joined Dom Owens' group in Texas and returned there for the birth of their babies. They left Texas and were murdered. In St-Jovite.

The St-Jovite victims died approximately three weeks ago.

Jennifer Cannon and the unidentified victim on Murtry died three to four weeks ago.

Carole Comptois died a little less than three weeks ago.

I stared at the page. Ten. Ten people dead. Again the odd phrase ricocheted through my brain. Death du jour. Death of the day. We'd found them day by day, but they'd all died around the same time. Who would be next? Into what circle of hell had we stumbled?

When I got home I went directly to the computer to revise my report on the Murtry skeleton to include injury due to animal attack. Then I printed and read what I'd written.

As I finished, the clock chimed the full Westminster refrain, then gave six low bongs. My stomach growled a reminder that I'd eaten nothing since the bagel and coffee.

I went to the patio and snipped basil and chives. Then I cut chunks of cheese, took two eggs from the fridge, and scrambled everything together. I toasted another bagel, poured a Diet Coke, and returned to the desk in the living room.

When I reviewed the list I'd made at the university, an unsettling thought popped into my mind.

Anna Goyette had also disappeared a little less than three weeks ago.

My appetite vanished. I left the desk and crossed to the couch. I lay down and allowed my mind to drift, willing associations to rise to the surface.

I went through names. Schneider. Gilbert. Comptois. Simonnet. Owens. Cannon. Goyette.

Nothing.

Ages. Four months. Eighteen. Twenty-five. Four score.

No pattern.

Places. St-Jovite. Saint Helena.

A connection?

Saints. Could that be a link? I made a note. Ask Ryan where the Guillion property is located in Texas.

I chewed my thumbnail. What was taking Ryan so long?

My eyes drifted over the shelves that line six of the eight sunroom walls. Floor-to-ceiling books. It's the one thing I can never bring myself to discard. I really needed to sort and eliminate. I had dozens of texts I'd never open again, some dating to my undergraduate days.

University.

Jennifer Cannon. Anna Goyette. Both were students at McGill.

I thought of Daisy Jeannotte, and the odd words she'd spoken about her teaching assistant.

My eyes wandered to the computer. My screen saver sent vertebrae in a sinuous snake dance around the monitor. Long bones replaced the spinal column, then ribs, a pelvis, and the screen went black. The performance began anew with a slowly rotating skull.

E-mail. When Jeannotte and I had exchanged addresses I'd asked her to contact me if Anna returned. I hadn't checked my messages in days.

I logged on, downloaded my mail, and skimmed the names of the senders. There was nothing from Jeannotte. My nephew, Kit, had sent three messages. Two last week, one this morning.

Kit never sent me e-mail.

I opened the most recent communication.

From: khoward
To: tbrennan
Subject: Harry

Aunt Tempe:
I called but you must not be there. I am ferociously worried about Harry.
Please call.

Kit

From age two Kit had called his mother by name. Though his parents disapproved, the boy refused to change. Harry simply sounded better to his ear.

As I worked my way backward through my nephew's messages, I experienced a mix of emotions. Fear for Harry's safety. Annoyance at her cavalier attitude. Compassion for Kit. Guilt at my own inconsideration. His must have been the call I ignored while talking with Kathryn.

I went to the hall and hit the button.

Hi, Aunt Tempe. It's Kit. I'm calling about Harry., When I call your condo in Montreal she doesn't answer, and I have no idea where she's gone. I know she was there until a few days ago. Pause. *Last time we talked she sounded strange, even for Harry.* Nervous laugh. *Is she still in Quebec? If not, do you know where she is? I'm worried. I've never heard her sound like this before. Please give me a call. Bye.*

I pictured my nephew, with his green eyes and sandy hair. It was hard to believe Howard Howard had made any genetic contribution to Harry's son. Six foot two and thin as a ladder, Kit was an exact replica of my father.

I replayed the message and considered whether something was amiss.

No, Brennan.

But why was Kit so concerned?

Call him. She's fine.

I hit the speed dial button. No answer.

I tried my number in Montreal. Ditto. I left a message.

Pete. He hadn't heard from Harry.

Of course not. He was as fond of my sister as he was of nail fungus. She knew that.

Enough, Brennan. Back to the victims. They need you.

I turned my thoughts from my sister. Harry had gone off before. I had to assume she was all right.

I went back to the sofa and lay down. When I woke I was in my clothes, the portable phone ringing on my chest.

"Thanks for calling, Aunt Tempe. I—Maybe I'm jumping the gun, but my mother sounded very depressed the last time I talked to her. And now she's disappeared. It's not like Harry. To sound so down, I mean."

"Kit, I'm sure she's fine."

"You're probably right, but, well, we'd made these plans. She's always complaining that we never spend time together anymore, so I promised to take her out on the boat next week. I've pretty much finished the renovations, so Harry and I were going to sail around the Gulf for a few days. If she's changed her mind, she could at least call."

I experienced the usual anger at my sister's thoughtlessness.

"She'll get in touch, Kit. When I left she was pretty caught up in her workshop. You know how your mother is."

"Yeah." He paused. "But that's just it. She sounded so . . ." He searched for a word. "Flat. Not like Harry."

I remembered my last evening with Harry.

"Maybe it's part of the new persona. A lovely, exterior calm." My words even sounded false to me.

"Yeah. I guess. Did she mention she was going someplace else?"

"No. Why?"

"Something she said made me think she might have a trip planned. But, like, it wasn't her idea, or she didn't want to? Oh hell, I don't know."

He let out a sigh. In my mind's eye I saw my nephew run a hand backward through his hair, then rub the top of his head. Kit frustration.

"What did she say?" Despite my resolve, I felt the beginnings of anxiety.

"I don't remember exactly, but get this. It wouldn't matter what she wore or how she looked. Does that sound like my mother?"

No. It didn't.

"Aunt Tempe, do you know anything about this outfit she's hooked up with?"

"Just the name. Inner Life Empowerment, I think. Would you feel better if I made some inquiries?"

"Yeah."

"And I'll call my neighbors in Montreal and see if they've seen her. O.K.?"

"Yeah."

"Kit. Remember when she met Striker?"

There was a pause.

"Yeah."

"What happened?"

"She set off for a balloon rally, went missing for three days, then turned up married."

"Remember how freaked you were?"

"Yeah. But she didn't give up her curling iron. Just have her call me. I've left messages on the machine up there but, hell, maybe she's pissed off about something. Who knows?"

I clicked off and looked at the clock. Twelve-fifteen. I tried Montreal. Harry didn't answer, so I left another message. As I lay in the dark my mind positioned itself for cross-examination.

Why *hadn't* I checked out ILE?

Because there was no reason to do so. She took the course through a legitimate institution, and there was no cause for alarm. Besides, to research each of Harry's schemes would take a full-time investigator.

Tomorrow. I'll make some calls tomorrow. Not tonight. I shut down the inquisition.

I mounted the stairs, stripped, and slid under the covers. I needed sleep. I needed a respite from the turmoil that dominated my conscious thought.

Overhead, the ceiling fan hummed softly. I thought of Dom Owens' parlor, and, though I fought them, the names drifted back.

Brian. Heidi. Brian and Heidi were students.

Jennifer Cannon was a student.

Anna Goyette.

My stomach turned over.

Harry.

Harry had registered for her first seminar at the North Harris County Community College. Harry was a student.

The others had been killed or had disappeared while in Quebec.

My sister was in Quebec.

Or was she?

Where the hell was Ryan?

When he finally called my trepidation escalated to real fear.

"GONE? WHAT DO YOU MEAN, GONE?"

I'd slept fitfully, and when Ryan woke me at dawn, I felt headachy and out of sorts.

"When we arrived with the warrant the place was deserted."

"Twenty-six people just vanished?"

"Owens and a female companion gassed up the vans around seven yesterday morning. The attendant remembered because it wasn't their normal routine. Baker and I got to the commune around five P.M. Sometime in between the padre and his disciples took the big powder."

"They just drove off?"

"Baker's put out an APB, but so far the vans haven't been spotted."

"For God's sake." I wasn't believing this.

"Actually, it's worse."

I waited.

"Another eighteen people have vanished in Texas."

I felt myself go cold.

"Turns out there was another little band on the Guillion property out there. The Fort Bend County Sheriff's Department has been monitoring them for several years and weren't all that adverse to taking a closer look. Unfortunately, when the team showed up, the brethren had split. They bagged one old man and a cocker spaniel hiding under the porch."

"What's his story?"

"The guy's in custody, but he's either senile or feebleminded and hasn't given much up."

"Or cagey as hell."

I watched the gray outside my window lighten.

"Now what?"

"Now we toss the Saint Helena compound and hope the state boys can discover where Owens has led the faithful."

I glanced at the clock. Seven-ten and already I was at the thumbnail.

"How's your end?"

I told Ryan about the tooth marks on the bones, and about my suspicions concerning Carole Comptois.

"Not the right MO."

"What MO? Simonnet was shot, Heidi and her family were slashed and stabbed, and we don't know how the two in the upstairs bedroom died. Cannon and Comptois were both attacked by animals and knives. That's not a common occurrence."

"Comptois was killed in Montreal. Cannon and friend were found twelve hundred miles south of there. Did this dog catch a shuttle?"

"I'm not saying it's the same dog. Just the same pattern."

"Why?"

I'd been asking myself that question all night. And who?

"Jennifer Cannon was a McGill student. So is Anna Goyette. Heidi and Brian were also in school when they joined Owens' group. Can you find out if Carole Comptois had any university ties? Took a course or worked at a college?"

"She was a hooker."

"Maybe she won a scholarship," I snapped. His negative attitude was irritating me.

"O.K., O.K. Don't get your bra in a twist."

"Ryan . . ." I hesitated, not wanting to give reality to my fear by shaping it into words.

He waited.

"My sister registered for her seminar at a community college in Texas."

The line was quiet.

"Her son called me yesterday because he can't contact her. Neither can I."

"She may be hunkered in as part of the training. You know, like a retreat. Maybe she's laid a grid map over her soul and she's combing it inch by inch. But if you're really worried, call the college."

"Yeah."

"Just because she enrolled in the Lone Star State doesn't m—"

"I realize I'm being absurd, but Kathryn's words frightened me, and now Dom Owens is out there planning God knows what."

"We'll nail his ass."

"I know."

"Brennan, how do I say this?" He drew a long breath, let it out. "Your sister is going through a transition, and right now she's open to new relationships. She may have met someone and gone off for a few days."

Without her curling iron? Anxiety lodged like a cold, dense mass inside my chest.

When we disconnected I tried Harry again. In my mind's eye I saw the phone ringing in my empty condo. Where could she be at seven on a Sunday morning?

Sunday. Damn! I couldn't call the college until tomorrow.

I made coffee then rang Kit, even though it was an hour earlier in Texas.

He was polite but groggy, and didn't follow my line of questioning. When he finally began to comprehend, he was unsure if his mother's course had been a regular college offering. He thought he remembered literature, and promised to drop by her house to check.

I couldn't sit still. I opened the *Observer*, then the Bélanger journals. I even tried the Sunday morning evangelists. Neither crime nor Louis-Philippe nor Jeeee-zus could hold my attention. I was a mental cul-de-sac with no outlet.

Not really in the mood, I threw on running gear and headed out. The sky was clear, the air soft and balmy as I followed Queens Road West, then cut over on Princeton to Freedom Park. Sweat droplets changed to rivulets as my Nikes pounded past the lagoon.

Little ducks glided single file behind their mother, their quacks drifting on the Sunday morning air.

My thoughts remained jumbled and useless, the players and events of the past weeks running in circles around my brain. I tried to focus on the steady beat of my sneakers, the rhythm of my breath, but I kept hearing Ryan's phrase. New relationships. Is that what he and Harry had called their Hurley's night? Is that what I'd danced into with my adventure with Ryan on the *Melanie Tess*?

I traversed the park, ran north past the medical clinic, then snaked my way through the narrow streets of Myers Park. I passed flawless gardens and parklike lawns, here and there tended by an equally impeccable homeowner.

I'd just crossed Providence Road when I nearly collided with a man in tan slacks, a pink shirt, and a rumpled seersucker sports jacket that looked like a Sears original. He carried a battered briefcase and a canvas bag bulging with slide carousels. It was Red Skyler.

"Slumming in southeast?" I asked, trying to catch my breath. Red lived on the opposite side of Charlotte, near the university.

"My lecture at Myers Park Methodist is today." He gestured at the gray stone complex across the street. "I've come early to set my slides."

"Right." I was slick with sweat, and my hair hung in stringy, wet clumps. I pinched my T-shirt and flapped it away from my skin.

"How is your case progressing?"

"Not well. Owens and his followers have gone to ground."

"They're in hiding?"

"Apparently. Red, can I follow up on something you said?"

"Of course."

"When we discussed cults, you mentioned two broad types. We talked so much about one I forgot to ask about the other."

A man passed with a black Standard poodle. Both needed a trim.

"You said you would include some of the commercially packaged awareness programs in your definition."

"Yes. If they rely on thought reform to get and keep members." He set the bag on the sidewalk and scratched the side of his nose.

"I think you said these groups fill their ranks by persuading participants to buy more and more courses?"

"Yes. Unlike the cults we discussed, these programs don't intend to keep people forever. They exploit participants as long as they're willing to buy more courses. And bring in others."

"So why do you consider them cults?"

"The coercive influence that these so-called self-improvement programs exert is amazing. It's the same old thing, behavioral control through thought reform."

"What goes on in these awareness training programs?"

Red glanced at his watch.

"I finish at ten forty-five. Let's meet for breakfast and I'll share what I know."

"It's known as large group awareness training."

As he spoke Red spread red-eye gravy over his grits. We were at Anderson's, and through the window I could see the hedges and brick of Presbyterian Hospital.

"They're packaged to sound like seminars, or college courses, but the sessions are scripted to get participants emotionally and psychologically aroused. That part isn't mentioned in the brochure. Neither is the fact that attendees will be brainwashed into accepting an entirely new worldview." He forked a piece of country ham.

"How do they work?"

"Most programs last four or five days. The first day is devoted to establishing the leader's authority. Lots of humiliation and verbal abuse. The next day pounds in the new philosophy. The trainer convinces participants their lives are crap and that the only way out is to accept the new way of thinking."

Grits.

"Day three is typically filled with exercises. Trance inducement. Memory regression. Guided imagery. The trainer gets everyone to dredge up disappointments, rejections, bad memories. It really lays people out emotionally. Then the following day there's a lot of warm fuzzy group sharing, and the leader morphs from the hard taskmaster to the loving mommy or daddy. It's the beginning of the pitch for the next series of courses. The last day is fun and happy, with lots of hugs and dancing and music and games. And the hard sell."

A couple in khakis and identical golf shirts slid into the booth to our right. He was seashell, she was foam green.

"The damaging thing is that these courses can be incredibly stressful, both physically and psychologically. Most people have no idea how intense it's going to be. If they did, they wouldn't sign up."

"Don't participants talk about the program afterward?"

"They're told to be vague, that to discuss the experience would spoil it for others. They're instructed to rave about how their lives have changed, but to conceal how confrontational and unnerving the process was."

"Where do these groups recruit?" I feared I already knew the answer.

"Everywhere. On the street. Door to door. At schools, businesses, health clinics. They advertise in alternative newspapers, New Age magazines—"

"What about colleges and universities?"

"Very fertile ground. On bulletin boards, in dorms and eating halls, at student activity sign-up days. Some cults assign members to hang around campus counseling centers looking for students who come in alone. The schools don't condone or encourage these outfits, but there's little they can do. The administrations have the flyers removed from bulletin boards, but the ads go right back up."

"But this is a separate animal, right? These awareness seminars are unrelated to the type of cults we discussed before?"

"Not necessarily. Some programs are used to recruit members to background organizations. You take the course, then you're told that you've performed so well you've been singled out to go to a higher level, or meet the guru, or whatever."

The words hit me like a blow to the chest. Harry's dinner at the leader's house.

"Red, what sort of people fall for these things?" I hoped my voice sounded calmer than I felt.

"My research shows that there are two important factors." He ticked them off on greasy fingers. "Depression and broken affiliations."

"What do you mean?"

"Someone who is in transition is often lonely and confused, and therefore vulnerable."

"In transition?"

"Between high school and college, college and a job. Recently separated. Recently fired."

Red's words blurred into the breakfast clatter. I had to talk to Kit.

When I refocused Red was eyeing me strangely. I knew I had to say something.

"I think my sister may have signed on to one of these group training courses. Inner Life Empowerment."

He shrugged. "There are so many. It's not one that I know."

"Now she's gone incommunicado. No one can raise her."

"Tempe, most of these programs are fairly benign. But you should talk to her. The effects can be very damaging for certain individuals."

Like Harry.

The usual mix of fear and aggravation seethed inside me.

I thanked Red and paid the bill. On the sidewalk I remembered another question.

"Have you ever heard of a sociologist named Jeannotte? She studies religious movements."

"Daisy Jeannotte?" One eyebrow rose, sending lopsided furrows across his forehead.

"I met her at McGill several weeks ago and I'm curious about how she's viewed by her colleagues."

He hesitated. "Yes. I'd heard she was in Canada."

"Do you know her?"

"I knew her years ago." His voice had gone flat. "Jeannotte is not considered mainstream."

"Oh?" I searched his face but it was blank.

"Thank you for the ham and grits, Tempe. I hope you got your money's worth." His grin looked strained.

I touched his arm. "What aren't you telling me, Red?"

The grin faded. "Is your sister a pupil of Daisy Jeannotte?"

"No. Why?"

"Jeannotte was at the center of a controversy some years back. I don't know the real story, and I don't want to spread gossip. Just be cautious."

I wanted to ask more, but with that he nodded and set off toward his car.

I stood in the sunshine with my mouth open. What the hell did that mean?

When I got home Kit had left a message. He'd located a course catalog, but there was nothing that sounded like Harry's workshop in the North Harris County Community College listings. He had found an Inner Life Empowerment flyer on his mother's desk, however. The paper had a thumbtack hole, and he suspected it had come from a bulletin board. He'd called the number. It was no longer in service.

Harry's course had nothing to do with the college!

Red's words intertwined with Ryan's, heightening my feeling of dread. New relationships. In transition. Unaffiliated. Vulnerable.

For the rest of the day I skittered from task to task, my concentration destroyed by worry and indecision. Then, as shadows lengthened across my patio, I took a call that jarred me into more organized thinking. I listened in shock as the story unfolded, then I made a decision.

I dialed my department head to tell him that I would be leaving earlier than planned. Since I'd scheduled an absence for the physical anthropology conference my students would miss only one additional class period. I was sorry, but I had to go.

When we disconnected I went upstairs to pack. Not for Oakland, but for Montreal.

I had to find my sister.

I had to stop the madness that was rolling in like Piedmont thunder.

29

AS THE PLANE TOOK OFF I CLOSED MY EYES AND LEANED INTO THE seat, too exhausted from another restless night to notice my surroundings. Normally I enjoy feeling the acceleration as I rise and watch the world grow small, but not at that moment. The words of a frightened old man rebounded through my brain.

I stretched, and my foot tapped the package I'd placed beneath the seat. Hand-carried. Always in view. Chain of custody could be important.

Beside me, Ryan flipped through the USAirways magazine. Unable to get a flight from Savannah, he'd driven to Charlotte for the six thirty-five. At the airport he'd elaborated on the statement taken in Texas.

The old man had fled to protect his dog.

Like Kathryn, I thought, afraid for her baby.

"Did he say exactly what they intend to do?" I asked Ryan in a low whisper. The attendant demonstrated seat belts and oxygen.

Ryan shook his head. "The guy's a zomboid. He was at the ranch because they gave him a place to stay and let him keep his dog. He wasn't really tuned in to the credo, but he picked up enough." The magazine dropped to his lap.

"He's rambling on about cosmic energy and guardian angels and fiery inhalation."

"Annihilation?"

Ryan shrugged. "He says the people he lives with don't belong to this world. Seems they've been battling the forces of evil and now it's time to go. Only he couldn't bring Fido."

"So he hid under the porch."

Ryan nodded.

"Who are these forces of evil?"

"He's not sure."

"And he can't say where the righteous are going?"

"North. Remember, Gramps is not at the top of the bell curve."

"He's never heard of Dom Owens?"

"No. His troop leader was someone named Toby."

"No last name."

"Last names are of this world. But that's not who frightens him. Apparently Toby and the cocker got along. It's some woman that scares the shit out of him."

What had Kathryn said? "It's not Dom. It's her." A face flashed in front of me.

"Who is she?"

"He doesn't have a name, but he says this chick told Toby that the Antichrist had been destroyed and doomsday was at hand. That's when the wagon train rolled."

"And?" I felt numb.

"The dog wasn't invited."

"Nothing else?"

"He says the lady is definitely mother superior."

"Kathryn also spoke of a woman."

"Name?"

"I didn't ask. It just didn't sink in at the time."

"What else did she say?"

I repeated what I could remember.

Ryan placed a hand on mine.

"Tempe, we really don't know anything about this Kathryn except that she's spent her life with the encounter culture. She shows up at your place claiming she found you through the university. You say your address isn't listed. That same day forty-three of her closest friends take a hike in two states and the lady does her own vanishing act."

True. Ryan had voiced misgivings about Kathryn earlier.

"You never found out who pulled the cat trick?"

"No." I withdrew my hand and went to work on the thumbnail.

For a while neither of us spoke. Then I remembered something else.

"Kathryn also made reference to an Antichrist."

"How?"

"She said Dom didn't believe in Antichrists."

Ryan was quiet a long time. Then,

"I talked to the guys who worked the Solar Temple deaths in Canada. Do you know what went down in Morin Heights?"

"Just that five people died. I was in Charlotte, and the American media focused mostly on Switzerland. The Canadian end got very little press."

"I'll tell you what happened. Joseph DiMambro sent a team of assassins to kill a baby." He paused to let that sink in. "Morin Heights was the kickoff for the fireworks overseas. Seems this kid's birth hadn't been approved by Big Daddy, so he viewed him as the Antichrist. Once the tyke was dead the faithful were free to make the crossing."

"Jesus Christ. Do you think Owens really is one of these Solar Temple fanatics?"

Ryan shrugged again. "Or it could be some sort of copycat shuck. It's hard to know what the Adler Lyons babble means until the psychologists work it out."

A treatise had been found at the compound on Saint Helena. And a map of Quebec Province.

"But I don't give a hog's tit which looney is in the lead if innocent people are trailing along to their deaths. I'm going to catch this bastard and gut him and fry him up myself."

His jaw muscles bunched as he picked up the magazine.

I closed my eyes and tried to rest, but the images wouldn't settle.

Harry, buoyant and full of life. Harry in sweats and no makeup.

Sam, unnerved by the invasion of his island.

Malachy. Mathias. Jennifer Cannon. Carole Comptois. A charred cat. The contents of the package at my feet.

Kathryn, eyes pleading. As if I could help her. As if I could take her life and somehow make it better.

Or was Ryan right? Had I been set up? Was Kathryn sent for

some sinister purpose of which I was unaware? Was Owens responsible for the slaughtered cat?

Harry had spoken of order. Her life sucked and the order was going to pull her clear. So had Kathryn. She said the order affects everyone. Brian and Heidi had broken it. What order? Cosmic order? An order from on high? The Order of the Solar Temple?

I felt like a moth in a jar, batting against the glass with random thought after random thought, but unable to escape the cognitive restraints of my own jumbled thinking.

Brennan, you're making yourself crazy! There's nothing you can do at thirty-seven thousand feet.

I decided to break free by dropping back a hundred years.

I opened my briefcase, pulled out a Bélanger diary, and skipped to December of 1844, hoping the holidays had put Louis-Philippe in a better mood.

The good doctor enjoyed Christmas dinner at the Nicolet house, liked his new pipe, but did not approve of his sister's plan for a return to the stage. Eugénie had been invited to sing in Europe.

What he lacked in humor, Louis-Philippe made up for in tenacity. His sister's name was written often in the early months of 1845. He apparently expressed his views frequently. But, much to the doctor's annoyance, Eugénie would not be dissuaded. She was leaving in April, would do concerts in Paris and Brussels, then spend the summer in France, returning to Montreal at the end of July.

A voice ordered trays and chair backs into full upright and locked position for landing in Pittsburgh.

An hour later, again airborne, I skimmed through the spring of 1845. Louis-Philippe was busy with hospital and city affairs, but made weekly visits to his brother-in-law. Alain Nicolet, it appears, did not travel to Europe with his wife.

I wondered how Eugénie's tour had gone. Apparently Uncle Louis-Philippe had not, since she was mentioned little during those months. Then an entry caught my eye.

July 17, 1845. Due to irregular circumstances, Eugénie's stay in France would be prolonged. Arrangements had been made, but Louis-Philippe was vague as to their nature.

I stared at the whiteness outside my window. What "irregular circumstances" had kept Eugénie in France? I calculated. Élisabeth was born in January. Oh, boy.

Throughout the summer and fall Louis-Philippe made only brief reference to his sister. Letter from Eugénie. Doing well.

As our wheels touched pavement at Dorval Airport, Eugénie reappeared. She, too, had returned to Montreal. April 16, 1846. Her baby was three months old.

There it was.

Élisabeth Nicolet was born in France. Alain could not be her father. But who was?

Ryan and I deplaned in silence. He checked his messages while I waited for the baggage. When he returned his face told me the news was not good.

"They found the vans near Charleston."

"Empty."

He nodded.

Eugénie and her baby faded into another century.

The sky was nickel and a light rain blew across the headlights as Ryan and I drove east along Highway 20. According to the pilot, Montreal was a balmy thirty-eight degrees Fahrenheit.

We rode in silence having already agreed on our courses of action. I wanted to rush home, to find my sister and relieve myself of a building sense of foreboding. Instead, I would do as Ryan asked. Then I would pursue a plan of my own.

We parked in the lot at Parthenais and Ryan and I picked our way toward the building. The air smelled of malt from the Molson brewery. Oil filmed the pools of rainwater collecting on the uneven pavement.

Ryan got off on the first floor and I continued to my office on the fifth. After removing my coat, I dialed an inside extension. They'd gotten my message and we could begin as soon as I was ready. I went at once to the lab.

I gathered scalpel, ruler, glue, and a two-foot length of rubber eraser material and set them on my worktable. Then I opened my carry-on package, unwrapped and inspected the contents.

The skull and mandible of the unknown Murtry victim had

made the trip undamaged. I often wonder what the airport scanner operators think when my skeletal parts go through. I placed the skull on a cork ring in the middle of the table. Then I squeezed glue into the temporomandibular joint and fixed the jaw in place.

While the Elmer's dried, I found a chart of facial tissue thicknesses for white American females. When the jaw felt firm I slid the skull onto a holder, adjusted the height, and secured it with clamps. The empty orbits stared directly into my eyes as I measured and cut seventeen tiny rubber cylinders and glued them onto the facial bones.

Twenty minutes later I took the skull to a small room down the corridor. A plaque identified the section as Section d'Imagerie. A technician greeted me and indicated that the system was up and running.

Wasting no time, I placed the skull on a copy stand, captured images of it with a video camera, and sent them to the PC. I evaluated the digitized views on the monitor and chose a frontal orientation. Then, using a stylus and drawing tablet attached to the computer, I connected the rubber markers projecting from the skull. As I directed the crosshairs around the screen a macabre silhouette began to emerge.

When satisfied with the facial contour, I moved on. Using the bony architecture as a guide I sampled eyes, ears, noses, and lips from the program's database, and fitted predrawn features onto the skull.

Next I tested hair, and added what I thought would be the least distracting style. Knowing nothing of the victim, I decided it was better to be vague than wrong. When I was happy with the components I'd added to the captured cranial image, I used the stylus to blend and shadow to make the reconstruction as lifelike as possible. The whole process took less than two hours.

I leaned back and looked at my work.

A face gazed from the monitor. It had drooping eyes, a delicate nose, and broad, high cheekbones. It was pretty in a robotic, expressionless way. And somehow familiar. I swallowed. Then with a touch of the stylus I modified the hair. Blunt cut. Bangs.

I drew in a breath. Did my reconstruction resemble Anna Goyette? Or had I simply created a generic young female and given the hair a familiar cut?

I returned the hair to the original style and evaluated the likeness. Yes? No? I had no idea.

Finally, I touched a command on the drop-down menu, and four frames appeared on the screen. I compared the series, looking for hints of inconsistency between my merged image and the skull. First, the unaltered cranium and jaw. Next, a peel image, with bare bone on the skull's left, fleshed features on the right. Third, the face I'd created superimposed in ghostly translucence over bone and tissue markers. Last, the finished facial approximation. I clicked the final image to full screen and stared at it a long time. I still wasn't sure.

I printed, then stored the image, and hurried to my office. As I left the building I dropped copies of the sketch on Ryan's desk. The attached note consisted of two words: Murtry, *Inconnue.* Unknown. I had other things on my mind.

When I climbed out of the taxi the rain had eased, but the temperature had plummeted. Thin membranes were forming on puddles and crystallizing on wires and branches.

The apartment was as dim and still as a crypt. Dropping my coat and bags in the hall, I went directly to the guest room. Harry's makeup lay scattered across the dresser. Had she used it this morning or last week? Clothes. Boots. Hair dryer. Magazines. My search turned up nothing to indicate where Harry had gone or when she had left.

I'd expected that. What I'd not expected was the alarm that gripped me as I rummaged from room to room.

I checked the machine. No messages.

Calm down. Maybe she phoned Kit.

Negative.

Charlotte?

No word from Harry, but Red Skyler had called there to say he'd contacted the Cult Awareness Network. They had nothing on Dom Owens, but there was a file on Inner Life Empowerment. According to CAN, the outfit was legit. ILE operated in several states, offering insight seminars that were useless but nontoxic. Confront the intimate you and the intimate other. Crap, but probably harmless and I shouldn't be too concerned. If I wanted more information I could call him or CAN. He left both numbers.

I hardly listened to the other voices. Sam, wanting news. Katy reporting her return to Charlottesville.

So ILE was not dangerous and Ryan was probably right. Harry had gone off again. Anger made my cheeks feel warm.

Like a robot I hung my coat and rolled my suitcase to the bedroom. Then I sat on the edge of the bed, kneaded my temples, and let my thoughts roll. The digits on my clock slowly marked the minutes.

These last few weeks had been some of the most difficult of my career. The torture and mutilation these victims had endured far surpassed what I normally saw. And I couldn't remember when I'd worked so many deaths in so short a period of time. How were the murders on Murtry linked to those in St-Jovite? Was Carole Comptois killed by the same monstrous hand? Had the slaughter in St-Jovite been merely the beginning? At this moment was some maniac scripting a bloodbath too terrible to contemplate?

Harry would have to deal with Harry.

I knew what I was going to do. At least I knew where I would start.

It was raining again and the McGill campus was covered with a thin, frozen crust. The buildings stood out as black silhouettes, their windows the only light in the dreary, wet dusk. Here and there a figure moved in an illuminated square, a tiny puppet in a shadow-box theater.

A porous ice shell crumbled to the steps as I gripped the handle to Birks Hall. The building was empty, abandoned by occupants fearing the storm. No raincoats on hooks, no boots melting along walls. The printers and copy machines were still, the only sound the tick of raindrops high above on leaded glass.

My steps echoed hollowly as I climbed to the third floor. From the main corridor I could see that Jeannotte's door was closed. I didn't really think she'd be here, but had decided it was worth a try. She didn't expect me, and people say odd things when caught outside their normal routines.

When I turned the corner I saw yellow light spilling from below the door. I knocked, unsure what to expect.

When the door opened my jaw dropped in amazement.

30

HER EYES WERE RED ALONG THE RIMS, HER SKIN PALE AND DRAWN. She tensed when she recognized me, but said nothing.

"How are you, Anna?"

"O.K." She blinked and her lids made the bangs hop.

"I'm Dr. Brennan. We met several weeks ago."

"I know."

"When I returned they told me you were ill."

"I'm fine. I was gone for a while."

I wanted to ask her where she'd been, but held back. "Is Dr. Jeannotte here?"

Anna shook her head. She did a slow-motion hair tuck, absently circling her ear.

"Your mother was worried about you."

She shrugged, the movement sluggish and barely noticeable. She didn't question my knowledge of her home life.

"I've been working on a project with your aunt. She was also concerned."

"Oh." She looked down so I couldn't see her face.

Hit her with it.

"Your friend said you might be involved with something that's upsetting you."

Her eyes came back to mine. "I have no friends. Who are you talking about?" Her voice was small and flat.

"Sandy O'Reilly. She was replacing you that day."

"Sandy wants my hours. Why are you here?"

Good question.

"I wanted to talk to you and to Dr. Jeannotte."

"She's not in."

"Could you and I talk?"

"There's nothing you can do for me. My life is my own business." The listlessness chilled me.

"I appreciate that. But, actually, I thought you might be able to help me."

Her glance slid down the corridor then back to me.

"Help you how?"

"Would you like some coffee?"

"No."

"Could we go somewhere else?"

She looked at me a long time, her eyes flat and empty. Then she nodded, took a parka from the hall tree, and guided me down the stairs and out a back door. Bending into the frigid rain we trudged uphill to the center of campus, and circled to the back of the Redpath Museum. Anna took a key from her pocket, opened a door, and led me into a dim corridor. The air smelled faintly of mildew and decay.

We climbed to the second floor and sat on a long wooden bench, surrounded by the bones of creatures long dead. Above us hung a beluga whale, casualty of some Pleistocene misfortune. Dust motes drifted in the fluorescent light.

"I don't work in the museum anymore, but I still come here to think." She gazed at the Irish elk. "These creatures lived millions of years and thousands of miles apart and now they're fixed at this one point in the universe, forever motionless in time and place. I like that."

"Yes." That was one way to view extinction. "Stability is a rare thing in today's world."

She gave me an odd look, then turned back to the skeletons. I watched her profile as she studied the collection.

"Sandy talked about you, but I didn't really listen." She spoke without turning to face me. "I'm not sure who you are or what you want."

"I'm a friend of your aunt."

"My aunt is a nice person."

"Yes. Your mother thought you might be in trouble."

She gave a wry smile. Obviously this was not a happy subject for her.

"Why do you care what my mother thinks?"

"I care that Sister Julienne was distressed by your disappearance. Your aunt is not aware that you've taken off before."

Her eyes left the vertebrates and swung to me. "What else do you know about me?" She flicked her hair. Perhaps the cold had revived her. Perhaps escape from her mentor's presence. She seemed slightly more animated than she'd been in Birks.

"Anna, your aunt begged me to find you. She didn't want to pry, she simply wanted to reassure your mother."

She looked uncertain. "Since you seem to have made me your pet project, you must also know that my mother is crazy. If I'm ten minutes late she calls the cops."

"According to the police your absences lasted a bit longer than ten minutes."

Her eyes narrowed slightly.

Good, Brennan. Put her on the defensive.

"Look, Anna, I don't want to meddle. But if there's anything I can do to help you, I'm more than willing to try."

I waited but she said nothing.

Turn it around. Maybe she'll open up.

"Perhaps you can help me. As you know I work with the coroner, and some recent cases really have us baffled. A young woman named Jennifer Cannon vanished from Montreal several years ago. Her body was found last week in South Carolina. She was a McGill student."

Anna's expression did not change.

"Did you know her?"

She was as silent as the bones around us.

"On March seventeenth a woman named Carole Comptois was murdered and dumped on Île des Sœurs. She was eighteen."

A hand slid to her hair.

"Jennifer Cannon wasn't alone." The hand dropped to her lap, floated back to her ear. "We haven't identified the person buried with her."

I withdrew the composite sketch and held it out. She took it, her eyes avoiding mine.

The paper trembled slightly as she stared at the face I'd created.

"Is this for real?"

"Facial approximation is an art, not a science. One can never be certain about the accuracy."

"You did this from a skull?" There was a tremor in her voice.

"Yes."

"The hair is wrong." Barely audible.

"You recognize the face?"

"Amalie Provencher."

"Do you know her?"

"She works in the counseling center." She kept her eyes averted.

"When did you last see her?"

"It's been a couple of weeks. Maybe longer, I'm not sure. I was gone."

"Is she a student?"

"What did they do to her?"

I hesitated, uncertain how much to reveal. Anna's mood swings made me suspect she was either unstable or taking drugs. She didn't wait for my answer.

"Did they murder her?"

"Who, Anna? Who are 'they'?"

Finally, she looked at me. Her pupils glistened in the artificial light.

"Sandy told me about your conversation. She was right, and she was wrong. There is a group here on campus, but they have nothing to do with Satan. And I have nothing to do with them. Amalie did. She got the job in the counseling center because they told her to."

"Is that where you met?"

She nodded, ran a knuckle under each eye, and wiped them on her pants.

"When?"

"I don't know. Awhile back. I was pretty bummed, so I thought I'd try counseling. When I went to the center Amalie always made a point of chatting with me, acting really concerned. She'd never talk about herself or her problems. She really listened to what I had to say. We had a lot in common, so we became friends."

I remembered Red's words. Recruiters are instructed to learn about potential members, to convince them of their common ground and earn their trust.

"She'd talk about this group she belonged to, said it turned her life around. I finally went to one of the meetings. It was O.K." She shrugged. "Someone spoke and we ate and did breathing exercises and stuff. It didn't really grab me, but I went back a couple of times because everyone acted as if they really liked me."

Love bombing.

"Then they invited me to the country. That sounded cool, so I went. We played games and listened to lectures and chanted and did exercises. Amalie loved it, but it wasn't for me. I thought it was a lot of gobbledygook, but you couldn't disagree. Plus they never left me alone. I wasn't allowed a minute to myself.

"They wanted me to stay for a longer workshop, and when I said no, they got kind of huffy. I had to get pretty bitchy to get a ride back to town. I avoid Amalie now, but I see her from time to time."

"What's this group called?"

"I'm not sure."

"Do you think they killed Amalie?"

She wiped her palms on the sides of her thighs.

"There was a guy I met out there. He signed up through a course someplace else. Anyway, after I left he stayed, so I didn't see him for a long time. Maybe a year. Then I ran into him at a concert on Île Notre Dame. We saw each other for a while, but that didn't work out." Another shrug. "By then he'd left the group, but he had some spooky stories about what went on. Mostly, he wouldn't talk about it, though. He was pretty freaked."

"What was his name?"

"John something."

"Where is he now?"

"I don't know. I think he moved away." She wiped tears from her lower lashes.

"Anna, is Dr. Jeannotte connected with this group?"

"Why do you ask that?" Her voice broke on the last word. I could see a small blue vein pulsing in her neck.

"When I first met you, in her office, you seemed very nervous around Dr. Jeannotte."

"She's been wonderful to me. She's a lot better for my head than meditation and heavy breathing." She snorted. "But she's also demanding, and I worry all the time that I'll mess up."

"I understand you spend a lot of time with her."

Her eyes went back to the skeletons. "I thought you were concerned about Amalie and these dead people."

"Anna, would you be willing to talk to someone else? What you've told me is important, and the police will definitely want to follow up on it. A detective named Andrew Ryan is investigating these homicides. He's a very kind man, and I think you'll like him."

She gave me a confused look and whipped hair behind both ears.

"There's nothing I can tell you. John could, but I really don't know where he's gone."

"Do you remember where this seminar took place?"

"Some kind of farm. I rode in a van and didn't pay much attention because they had us playing games. Coming back, I just slept. They kept us up a lot and I was exhausted. Except for John and Amalie, I never saw any of them again. And now you say she's—"

Downstairs a door opened, then a voice rolled up the stairs.

"Who's there?"

"Great. Now I'll lose the key," Anna whispered.

"Are we not supposed to be here?"

"Not exactly. When I stopped working in the museum I just sort of kept the key."

Terrific.

"Go along with me," I said, rising from the bench.

"Is someone there?" I called out. "We're here."

Footfalls on the stairs, then a security guard appeared in the doorway. His knitted cap stopped just above his eyes, and a water-soaked parka barely covered his paunch. He was breathing hard, and his teeth looked yellow in the violet light.

"Oh, God, are we glad to see you." I overacted. "We were sketching *Odocoileus virginianus* and lost track of time. Everyone left early because of the ice, and I guess they forgot about us. We got locked in." I gave a silly-me smile. "I was about to call security."

"You can't be in here now. The museum's closed," he rasped.

Obviously my performance had been wasted.

"Of course. We really need to be on our way. Her husband will be crazy wondering where she is." I gestured at Anna, who was nodding like a box turtle.

The guard shifted watery eyes from Anna to me, then tipped his head toward the stairs.

"Let's go, then."

We wasted no time.

Outside, rain was still falling. The drops were thicker now, like the Slushes my sister and I had bought from summer vendors. Her face rose from a niche in my mind. Where are you, Harry?

At Birks Hall Anna gave me a funny look.

"*Odocoileus virginianus*?"

"It popped into my head."

"There is no white-tailed deer in the museum."

Did the corners of her mouth pucker, or was it merely the cold? I shrugged.

Reluctantly, Anna gave me her home number and address. We parted, and I assured her that Ryan would call soon. As I hurried down University something made me turn back. Anna stood in the archway of the Gothic old building, motionless, like her Cenozoic comrades.

When I got home I dialed Ryan's pager. Minutes later the phone rang. I told him that Anna had surfaced and outlined our conversation. He promised to inform the coroner so a search could begin for Amalie Provencher's medical and dental records. He rang off quickly, intending to contact Anna before she left Jeannotte's office. He would phone later to fill me in on what he'd learned during the day.

I ate a supper of salad niçoise and croissants, took a long bath, and slipped into an old sweat suit. I still felt chilled, and decided to light a fire. I'd used the last of my starter logs so I wadded newspaper into balls and overlaid them with kindling. Ice was ticking against the windows as I lit the pile and watched it catch.

Eight-forty. I got the Bélanger journals and turned on "Seinfeld," hoping the rhythm of the dialogue and laughter would have a soothing effect. Left on their own I knew my thoughts would run like cats in the night, rooting and snarling, and raising my anxiety to a level where sleep would be impossible.

No go. Jerry and Kramer did their best, but I couldn't concentrate.

My eyes drifted to the fire. The flames had dwindled to a few sparse tongues curving around the bottom log. I went to the hearth, separated a section of paper, tore and balled up several pages, and stuffed them into the embers.

I was poking the logs when recall kicked in.

Newspapers!

I'd forgotten about the microfilm!

I went to the bedroom, pulled out the pages I'd copied at McGill, and took them back to the sofa. It took only a moment to locate the article in *La Presse.*

The story was as brief as I remembered it. April 20, 1845. Eugénie Nicolet was sailing for France. She would sing in Paris and Brussels, summer in the south of France, and return to Montreal in July. The members of her entourage were listed, as were her upcoming concert dates. There was also a brief summary of her career, and comments as to how she would be missed.

My coins had taken me through April 26. I skimmed everything I'd printed, but Eugénie's name did not reappear. Then I went back through, strip-searching every story and announcement.

The article appeared on April 22.

Someone else would appear in Paris. This gentleman's talent lay not in music, but in oratory. He was on a speaking tour, denouncing the selling of human beings and encouraging commerce with West Africa. Born in the Gold Coast, he'd been educated in Germany and held a professorship in philosophy at the University of Halle. He'd just completed a series of lectures at the McGill School of Divinity.

I backpedaled through history. Eighteen forty-five. Slavery was in full swing in the United States, but had been banned in France and England. Canada was still a British colony. Church and missionary groups were begging Africans to stop exporting their brothers and sisters, and encouraging Europeans to engage in legal commerce with West Africa as an alternative. What did they call it? The "legitimate trade."

I read the passenger's name with growing excitement.

And the name of the vessel.

Eugénie Nicolet and Abo Gabassa had made the crossing on the same ship.

I got up to poke the fire.

Was that it? Had I stumbled on the secret hidden for a century and a half? Eugénie Nicolet and Abo Gabassa? An affair?

I slipped on shoes, went to the French doors, flipped the handle, and pushed. The door was frozen shut. I leaned hard with my hip and the seal cracked.

My woodpile was frozen, and it took me some time to hack a log free with a garden trowel. When I finally got back inside I was shivering and covered with tiny pellets. A sound stopped me dead as I crossed to the hearth.

My doorbell doesn't ring, it twitters. It did so now, then stopped abruptly, as if someone had given up.

I dropped the log, raced to the security box, and hit the video button. On the screen I saw a familiar figure disappearing through the front door.

I grabbed my keys, ran to the lobby, and opened the door to the vestibule. The outer door was settling into place. I depressed the tongue and pulled it wide.

Daisy Jeannotte lay sprawled across my steps.

31

Before I could reach her, she moved. Slowly, she drew in her hands, rolled, and pushed to a sitting position, her back to me.

"Are you hurt?" My throat was so dry my words came out high and stretched.

She flinched at the sound of my voice, then turned.

"The ice is treacherous. I slipped, but I'm quite fine."

I reached out and she allowed me to help her up. She was trembling, and didn't look fine at all.

"Please, come inside and I'll make some tea."

"No. I can't stay. There's someone waiting for me. I shouldn't be out on such a dreadful night but I had to speak to you."

"Please come in where it's warmer."

"No. Thank you." Her tone was as cold as the air.

She retied her scarf, then looked directly into my eyes. Behind her, bullets of ice sliced through a cone of streetlight. The tree limbs looked shiny black through the sodium vapor.

"Dr. Brennan, you must leave my students alone. I've tried to be helpful to you, but I do believe you are abusing my kindness. You cannot pursue these young people in this manner. And to give my number to the police for the purpose of harassing my assistant is simply unthinkable."

A gloved hand wiped her eye, leaving a dark smear trailing across her cheek.

Anger flared like a kitchen match. My arms were wrapped around my midriff, and through the flannel I felt my nails dig into my flesh.

"What the hell are you talking about? I'm not *pursuing* Anna." I spat the word back at her. "This isn't some goddam research project! People are dead! Ten for certain, God knows how many others."

Pellets bounced off my forehead and arms. I didn't feel them. Her words enraged me, and I vented all the anguish and frustration that had built in me over the past few weeks.

"Jennifer Cannon and Amalie Provencher were McGill students. They were murdered, Dr. Jeannotte. But not just murdered. No. That wasn't enough for these people. These maniacs threw them to animals, then watched their flesh torn and their skulls pierced right into their brains."

I ranted on, no longer in control of my voice. I noticed a passing couple quicken their pace, despite the glassy sidewalk.

"A family was slashed and mutilated and an old woman shot in the head not two hundred kilometers from here. Babies! They slaughtered two little babies! An eighteen-year-old girl was torn apart, stuffed in a trunk, and dumped right in this city. They're dead, Dr. Jeannotte, murdered by a group of loonies who think they're the posse for all morality."

I felt flushed, despite the freezing cold.

"Well, let me tell you something." I jabbed a trembling finger. "I'm going to find these self-righteous, malevolent bastards and put them out of business, no matter how many altar boys, or guidance counselors, or Bible-toting swamis I have to harass! And that includes your students! And that may include you!"

Jeannotte's face looked ghostly in the darkness, the smeared mascara transforming it into a macabre mask. A lump had formed above her left eye, throwing it into shadow and causing the right to look strangely light.

I dropped my finger and rewrapped the arm around my body. I had said too much. My outburst spent, the cold was causing me to shiver.

The street was deserted and utterly silent. I could hear the rasping of my breath.

I don't know what I expected to hear, but it was not the question that came from her lips. "Why do you use such imagery?"

"*What?*" Was she questioning my prose?

"Bibles and swamis and altar boys. Why do you make these references?"

"Because I believe these murders were committed by religious fanatics."

Jeannotte held herself completely still. When she spoke her voice was icier than the night, and her words chilled me more than the weather.

"You are out of your depth, Dr. Brennan. I'm warning you to leave this alone." The colorless eyes bore into mine. "If you persist, I will be forced to take action."

A car crept down the alley opposite my building and stopped. As it turned onto the street, the headlights made a wide arc, sweeping the block and momentarily illuminating Jeannotte's face.

I tensed, and my nails dug deeper into my sides.

Oh, God.

It was not an illusion created by shadow. Jeannotte's right eye was eerily pale. Stripped of makeup, the brow and lashes flared white in the passing beams.

She may have seen something in my face, for she pulled her scarf forward, turned, and picked her way down the steps. She did not look back.

When I got inside, the message light was flashing. Ryan. I phoned him back with shaky hands.

"Jeannotte's involved," I said, wasting no time. "She was just here telling me to back off. Seems your call to Anna really irked her. Listen, when we went back to Saint Helena, do you remember the man with the white streak?"

"Yeah. Skinny guy, scarecrow-thin, tall. He came in to talk to Owens." Ryan sounded exhausted.

"Jeannotte has the same pattern of depigmentation, same eye. It's not obvious because she hides it with makeup."

"Same hair streak?"

"I couldn't tell, but she probably uses dye. Look, these two must be related. The trait's just too unusual to be a coincidence."

"Siblings?"

"I didn't pay much attention at the time, but I think the guy on Saint Helena was too young to be her father and too old to be her son."

"If she's from the Tennessee mountains there are limited genetic possibilities."

"Funny." I was not in the mood for redneck jokes.

"Could be whole clans that share the gene."

"This is serious, Ryan."

"You know, different stripes in different hollers." He imitated Jeff Foxworthy. "If your stripe is the same as your sister's, then you may be—"

Stripes. Something about stripes pulled at me.

"What did you say?"

"Hollers, it's what you folk—"

"Will you stop it! I just thought of something else. Do you remember what Heidi Schneider's father said about their visitor?"

The line was quiet.

"He said the guy looked like a skunk. A goddam skunk."

"Shit. So maybe Daddy wasn't being poetic."

In the background a phone rang and rang. No one answered it.

"You think Owens sent Streak to Texas?" Ryan asked.

"No, not Owens. Kathryn and the old man both talked about a woman. I think it's Jeannotte. She probably directs the show from here and has lieutenants at her other camps. I also think she recruits on campus through some sort of seminar network."

"What else can you tell me about Jeannotte?"

I related everything I knew, including her behavior toward her assistant, and asked what he'd learned in his conversation with Anna.

"Not much. I think there's a shitload she's keeping bottled up. This kid makes Zelda look stable."

"She could be on drugs."

The ringing started up again.

"Are you alone there?" Save for the phones, the squad room sounded unnaturally quiet.

"Everyone's been pulled out for this friggin' storm. Are you having problems?"

"Like what?"

"Don't you listen to the news? The ice is really screwing things up. They've closed the airport, and a lot of the minor roads are impassable. Power lines are cracking like dry spaghetti, and stretches of the south shore are cold and dark. The city fathers are starting to worry about old folks. And looters."

"I'm fine so far. Did Baker's men find anything to tie Saint Helena to the group in Texas?"

"Not really. The old guy with the dog talked a lot about meeting his guardian angel. Seems Owens and his disciples had the same idea. It's all through their journals."

"Journals?"

"Yeah. Apparently some of the faithful had the creative urge."

"And?"

I heard him inhale, then exhale slowly.

"Tell me, goddamit!"

"According to some expert down there, it's definitely apocalyptic and it's now. They're heading for the big one. Sheriff Baker's taking no chances. He's called in the feds."

"And they found no clue as to destination? The earthly destination, I mean."

"To meet their guardian angel and make the crossing to a better place. That's the kind of crap we're dealing with. But they're well organized. Apparently the trip has been planned for a long time."

"Jeannotte! You've got to find Jeannotte! It's her! She's the guardian angel!"

I knew I sounded frantic, but I couldn't help myself.

"O.K. I agree. It's time to drive Miss Daisy hard. When did she leave your place?"

"Fifteen minutes ago."

"Where was she going?"

"I don't know. She said she was meeting someone."

"O.K., I'll find her. Brennan, if you're right about this, the little professor is a very dangerous woman. Do *not,* I repeat, do not do anything on your own. I know you're worried about Harry, but if she's been sucked into this thing it may take professionals to get her out. Do you understand?"

"May I brush my teeth? Or is that considered risky?" I snapped. His paternalism did not bring out the best in me.

"You know what I mean. Find yourself some candles. I'll get back to you as soon as I learn anything."

I hung up and walked to the French doors. I wanted more space around me and slid the curtain aside. The courtyard looked like a mythological garden, the trees and shrubs fashioned of spun glass. Filmy nets covered the upstairs balconies and clung to the brick chimneys and walls.

I located candles, matches, and a flashlight, then dug my radio and headphones from my gym bag and placed everything on the kitchen counter. Back in the living room, I settled on the couch and clicked to the CTV news.

Ryan was right. The storm was big news. Lines were down throughout the province and Hydro-Québec could not say when power would be restored. Temperatures were dropping and more precipitation was on the way.

I threw on a jacket and made three trips for logs. If the electricity failed, I would have heat. Next, I got extra blankets and placed them on the bed. When I returned to the living room a grim-looking newscaster was listing events that would not take place.

It was a familiar ritual, and oddly comforting. When snow threatens in the South, schools close, public activities cease, and frenzied homeowners strip store shelves. Usually the blizzards never come, or if snow falls, it disappears the following day. In Montreal storm preparations are methodical, not frantic, dominated by an air of "we will cope."

My preparations occupied me for fifteen minutes. The TV held my attention for another ten. A brief respite. When I clicked off, my agitation returned full force. I felt stuck, a bug on a pin. Ryan was right. There was nothing I could do, and my powerlessness made me all the more restless.

I went through my nighttime routine, hoping to keep bad thoughts at bay a little longer. No go. When I crawled into bed, the neural floodgates overflowed.

Harry. Why hadn't I listened to her? How could I have been so self-absorbed? Where had she gone? Why hadn't she called her son? Why hadn't she called me?

Daisy Jeannotte. Who had she been going to meet? What crazed course was she mapping? How many innocent souls did she intend to take with her?

Heidi Schneider. Who had felt so threatened by Heidi's babies as to resort to brutal infanticide? Were these deaths the herald of more bloodshed?

Jennifer Cannon. Amalie Provencher. Carole Comptois. Were their murders part of the madness? What demonic mores had they violated? Had their deaths been the choreography of some hellish ritual? Had my sister suffered the same fate?

When the phone rang I jumped and knocked the flashlight to the floor.

Ryan, I prayed. It's Ryan and he's got Jeannotte.

My nephew's voice came across the line.

"Oh hell, Aunt Tempe. I think I've really screwed up. She called. I found it on the other cassette."

"What other cassette?"

"I've got one of these old answering machines with the tiny tapes. The one I had wasn't rewinding right so I put in a new one. I didn't think about it until a friend came by just now. I was pretty hacked off at her because we were supposed to go out last week, but when I went to get her she wasn't home. When she dropped by tonight I told her to kiss off, and she insisted she'd left a message. We got into a hassle so I got out the old tape and played it. She was on there, all right, but so was Harry. Right at the end."

"What did your mother say?"

"She sounded pissed off. You know how Harry is. But she sounded scared at the same time. She was at some farm or something and wanted to split but no one would drive her back to Montreal. So I guess she's still in Canada."

"What else did she say?" My heart was pounding so hard I thought my nephew would hear it.

"She said things were getting creepy and she wanted out. Then the tape quit or she was cut off or something. I'm not sure. The message just ended."

"When did she call?"

"Pam phoned Monday. Harry's message was after that."

"There's no date indicator?"

"This thing was made during the Truman years."

"When did you change the tape?"

"I think maybe Wednesday or Thursday. I'm not sure. But before the weekend, I know that."

"Think, Kit!"

The line buzzed.

"Thursday. When I got home from the boat I was tired and the tape wouldn't rewind, so I popped the cassette and pitched it. That's when I put in the new one. Shit, that means she phoned at least four days ago, maybe even six. God, I hope she's all right. She sounded pretty panicky, even for Harry."

"I think I know who she's with. She'll be fine." I didn't believe my own words.

"Let me know as soon as you talk to her. Tell her I feel bad about this. I just didn't think."

I went to the window and pressed my face to the glass. The coating of ice turned the streetlights into tiny suns, and my neighbors' windows into glimmering rectangles. Tears ran down my cheeks as I thought of my sister, somewhere in that storm.

I dragged myself back to bed, turned on the lamp, and settled in to await Ryan's call.

Now and then the lights dimmed, flickered, then returned to normal. A millennium passed. The phone sat mute.

I drifted off.

It was the dream that provided the final epiphany.

32

I STAND GAZING AT THE OLD CHURCH. IT IS WINTER AND THE trees are bare. Though the sky is leaden, the branches send spiderwebs of shadow crawling across the weathered gray stone. The air smells of snow, and the prestorm silence is thick around me. In the distance I see a frozen lake.

A door opens and a figure is silhouetted against the soft yellow of lamplight. It hesitates, then walks in my direction, head lowered against the wind. The figure draws near, and I see she is female. Her head is veiled and she wears a long black gown.

As the woman comes closer the first powdery flakes appear. She carries a candle, and I realize her crouching is to protect the flame. I wonder how it survives.

The woman stops and beckons with her head. Already the veil is flecked with snow. I strain to recognize her face, but it moves in and out of focus, like pebbles at the bottom of a deep pool.

She turns and I follow.

The woman pulls farther and farther ahead. I feel alarm and try to catch up, but my body does not respond. My legs are weighted and I cannot hurry. I see her disappear through the door. I call out, but there is no sound.

Then I am inside the church and everything is dim. The walls are stone, the floor dirt. Huge carved windows disappear into darkness overhead. Through them I see tiny flakes wafting like smoke.

I can't remember why I've come to the church. I feel guilty, because I know it is important. Someone has sent me, but I can't recall who.

As I walk through the dusklike gloom I look down and see that my feet are bare. I am ashamed because I don't know where I've left my shoes. I want to leave, but don't know the way. I feel if I abandon my task I won't be able to leave.

I hear muffled voices and turn in that direction. There is something on the ground but it is obscure, a mirage I can't identify. I move toward it and the shadows congeal into separate objects.

A circle of wrapped cocoons. I stare down at them. They are too small to be bodies, but are shaped like bodies.

I go to one and loosen a corner. There is a muffled buzzing. I pull back the cloth and flies billow out and float to the window. The glass is frosted with vapor and I watch the insects swarm across it, knowing they are wrong in the cold.

My eyes drop back to the bundle. I don't hurry because I know it isn't a corpse. The dead are not packaged and arrayed in this manner.

Only it is. And I recognize the face. Amalie Provencher stares at me, her features a cartoon portrait in shades of gray.

Still, I cannot hurry. I move from bundle to bundle, unbinding fabric and sending flies rising into the shadows. The faces are white, the eyes fixed, but I do not recognize them. Except for one.

The size tells me before I open the shroud. It is so much smaller than the others. I don't want to see, but it is impossible to stop.

No! I try denial, but it doesn't work.

Carlie lies on his stomach, hands curled into upturned fists.

Then I see two others, tiny, side by side in the circle.

I cry out, but again there is no sound.

A hand closes around my arm. I look up and see my guide. She is changed, or just more clearly visible.

It is a nun, her habit frayed and covered with mold. When she moves I hear the click of beads and smell wet earth and decay.

I rise and see cocoa skin covered with oozing, red sores. I know it is Élisabeth Nicolet.

"Who are you?" I think the question, but she answers.

"All in robe of darkest grain."

I don't understand.

"Why are you here?"

"I come a reluctant bride of Christ."

Then I see another figure. She stands in a recess, the dim snowfall light obscuring her features and turning her hair a lackluster gray. Her eyes meet mine and she speaks, but the words are lost.

"Harry!" I scream, but my voice is thin and weak.

Harry doesn't hear. She extends both arms and her mouth moves, a black oval in the specter that is her face.

Again I shout, but no sound emerges.

She speaks again and I hear her, though her words are distant, like voices drifting across water.

"Help me. I am dying."

"No!" I try to run, but my legs won't move.

Harry enters a passageway I haven't noticed. Above it I see an inscription. GUARDIAN ANGEL. She becomes shadow, merges with the darkness.

I call but she won't look back. I try to go to her, but my body is frozen, nothing moves but the tears down my cheeks.

My companion transforms. Dark feathered wings sprout from her back, and her face grows pale and deeply creviced. Her eyes congeal into chunks of stone. As I stare into them the irises go clear and color drains from the brows and lashes. A white streak appears in her hair and races backward, separating a flap of scalp and throwing it high into the air. The tissue flutters to the floor and flies swarm from the window and settle on it.

"The order must not be ignored." The voice comes from everywhere and nowhere.

The dreamscape shifts to the low country. Long rays of sun slant through Spanish moss, and giant shadows dance between the trees. It is hot and I am digging. I sweat as I scoop mud the color of dried blood and fling it to a mound behind me.

The blade hits something and I scrape the edges, carefully revealing the form. White fur clotted with brick-red clay. I follow the arch of the back. A hand with long, red nails. I work my way up the arm. Cowboy fringe. Everything shimmers in the intense heat.

I see Harry's face and scream.

* * *

Heart pounding and bathed in sweat, I sat upright. It took me a moment to reconnect.

Montreal. Bedroom. Ice storm.

The light still burned and the room was quiet. I checked the clock. Three forty-two.

Calm down. A dream is just a dream. It reflects fears and anxieties, not reality.

Then another thought. Ryan's call. Had I slept through it?

I threw back the quilt and moved to the living room. The answering machine was dark.

Back in the bedroom, I took off my damp clothes. As I dropped the sweatpants to the floor I could see fingernail-shaped moons in the flesh of my palms. I dressed in jeans and a heavy sweater.

More sleep did not seem likely, so I went to the kitchen and set water to boil. I felt queasy from the dream. I didn't want to bring it back, but the vision had knocked something loose in my mind, and I needed to make sense of it. I took my tea to the sofa.

My dreams as a rule are not particularly wondrous nor frightening or grotesque. They are of two types.

Most commonly, I cannot dial the phone, see the road, catch the plane. I must take an exam but have never attended the class. Piece of cake: anxiety.

Less frequently the message is more baffling. My subconscious sifts material that my conscious mind has amassed, and weaves it into surreal tableaux. I am left to interpret what my psyche is saying.

Tonight's nightmare was clearly of the cryptic type. I closed my eyes to see what I could decode. Images flashed, like glimpses through a picket fence.

Amalie Provencher's computer face.

The dead babies.

A winged Daisy Jeannotte. I remembered my words to Ryan. Was she truly an angel of death?

The church. It resembled the convent at Lac Memphrémagog. Why was my brain beaming that to me?

Élisabeth Nicolet.

Harry, beckoning for help, then disappearing into a dark tunnel. Harry, dead with Birdie. Was Harry at serious risk?

A reluctant bride. What the hell did that mean? Was Élisabeth held against her will? Was that part of her saintly truth?

I had no time to sort it further, for just then the doorbell sounded. Friend or foe, I wondered as I stumbled to the security panel and picked up the handset.

Ryan's tall, lanky frame filled the screen. I buzzed him in and watched through the peephole as he trudged up the corridor. He looked like a survivor of the Trail of Tears.

"You look exhausted."

"It's been a long one and we're still in overtime. I'm on my own, thanks to the storm."

Ryan wiped his boots and unzipped his parka. Ice cascaded to the floor when he pulled off his tuque. He didn't question why I was dressed at four o'clock in the morning, and I didn't ask why he was dropping in at that hour.

"Baker's found Kathryn. She had a last-minute change of mind and bailed on Owens."

"The baby?" My heart raced.

"He's there too."

"Where?"

"Got coffee?"

"Yeah, sure."

Ryan threw his hat on the hall table and followed me to the kitchen. He talked as I ground beans and measured water.

"She's been in hiding with some guy named Espinoza. Remember the neighbor who called Social Services about Owens?"

"I thought the neighbor was dead."

"She is. This is her son. He's one of the faithful, but he holds a day job and lives down the road in Mama's house."

"How did Kathryn get Carlie?"

"He was already there. Ready for this? Someone drove the vans to Charleston while the group went to ground in the Espinoza house. They were all on the island the whole time. Then, when the heat cooled they left."

"How?"

"They split up and everybody boogied to a different tune. Some were picked up by boat, others were smuggled in pickups and car trunks. Seems Owens has quite an underground. And like schmucks, we just focused on the vans."

I handed him a steaming mug.

"Kathryn was supposed to go with Espinoza and some other guy, but she talked him into staying put."

"Where's the other guy?"

"Espinoza turns into igneous rock on that topic."

"Where did everyone go?" My throat felt tight. I already knew the answer.

"I think they're here."

I said nothing.

"Kathryn isn't sure where they were heading, but she knows it involved a border crossing. They're traveling in twos and threes and they've got directions for roads that aren't patrolled."

"Where?"

"She thinks she heard talk of Vermont. The highway patrol and INS have been alerted, but it's probably too late. They've had almost three days and Canada isn't exactly Libya when it comes to border security."

Ryan sipped his coffee.

"Kathryn claims she didn't pay much attention because she never thought they'd really go. But she is clear on one thing. When they find this guardian angel, everyone will die."

I began wiping the counter, though it was already clean.

For a long time neither of us spoke. Then,

"Any word from your sister?"

My stomach constricted anew. "No."

When he spoke again his voice had softened.

"Baker's boys found something in the Saint Helena compound."

"What?" Fear shot through me.

"A letter to Owens. In it someone named Daniel is discussing Inner Life Empowerment." I felt a hand on my shoulder. "It looks like the organization was a front, or else Owens' followers infiltrated the courses. That part's not clear, but what is clear is that they used ILE to recruit."

"Oh, my God."

"The letter's dated about two months ago, but there's nothing to indicate where it came from. The wording's vague, but it sounds like there was some sort of quota to be met, and this Daniel is promising he'll deliver."

"How?" I could hardly speak.

"He doesn't say. There's nothing else that makes reference to ILE. Just that one letter."

The dream slammed back in vivid detail and I felt ice slide through my veins.

"They've got Harry!" I said with trembling lips. "I have to find her!"

"We will."

I told him about Kit's call.

"Shit."

"How can these people remain invisible for years, then we turn over their rock and they slither away and vanish?" My voice was quavery.

Ryan set down his mug and turned me around with both hands. I was squeezing the sponge so hard it made small hissing sounds.

"There's no trail because these people have a tremendous source of clandestine income. They deal exclusively in cash but don't seem to be involved in anything illegal."

"Except murder!" I wanted to pace but Ryan held me firmly.

"What I'm saying is these assholes can't be tied to drugs or theft or credit card scams. There's no money trail and no evidence of crime, and that's usually where the break comes." His eyes were hard. "But they've fucked up badly by coming into my backyard and I'm going to nail the rabid little pricks."

I ripped free of his grasp and threw the sponge across the kitchen.

"What did Jeannotte say?"

"I tried her office, then staked her pad. No-show at either place. Don't forget I'm working this alone, Brennan. This storm has shut down the province."

"What did you find out about Jennifer Cannon and Amalie Provencher?"

"The university is pulling the usual student-privacy crap. They won't release a thing without a court order."

That did it. I pushed past him and went to the bedroom. I was pulling on wool socks when he appeared in the doorway.

"What do you think you're doing?"

"I'm going to get some answers from Anna Goyette, then I'm going to find my sister."

"Whoa, scout. There's a blanket of polar ice out there."

"I'll manage."

"In a five-year-old Mazda?"

I was shaking so badly I couldn't lace my boots. I stopped, untangled the knot, and crisscrossed the cord carefully through the prongs. Then I did the other foot, stood, and turned to Ryan.

"I am not going to sit here and allow these fanatics to murder my sister. They may be consumed with suicidal obsession, but they are not taking Harry with them. With or without you I'm going to find her, Ryan. And I'm going to do it *now*!"

For a full minute he simply stared. Then he breathed deeply, exhaled through his nose, and opened his mouth to speak.

It was then the lights flared, dimmed, and died.

33

THE FLOOR OF RYAN'S JEEP WAS WET WITH MELTED SLUSH. THE wipers slapped back and forth, now and then skipping on a patch of ice. In the fans of cleared windshield I could see millions of silvery slivers slicing through the beams from our headlights.

Centre-Ville was dark and deserted. No street or building lights, no neon signs, no traffic signals. The only cars I saw were police cruisers. Yellow tape cordoned off sidewalks adjacent to high-rises to prevent injuries from falling ice. I wondered how many people would really try to go to work today. Now and then I heard a crack, then a frozen sheet exploded on the pavement. The landscape brought to mind news clips of Sarajevo, and I pictured my neighbors hunkered in cold, dark rooms.

Ryan was blizzard driving, shoulders tense, fingers tightly clutching the wheel. He kept the speed low and even, accelerating gradually and easing off the gas well in advance of intersections. Even so we fishtailed often. Ryan was right to drive his Jeep. The cruisers we saw were sliding more than rolling.

We crawled up rue Guy and turned east onto Docteur-Penfield. Above us I could see Montréal General glowing under the power of its own generator. My fingers strangled the armrest on the right, and my left hand was in a fist.

"It's colder than crap. Why isn't this snow?" I snapped. Tension and fear were showing.

Ryan's eyes never left the road.

"According to the radio there's some sort of inversion working, so it's warmer in the clouds than on the ground. The stuff is forming as rain, but freezing when it gets down here. The weight of the ice is taking out whole power stations."

"When is it going to let up?"

"The weather guy says the system is stuck and going nowhere."

I closed my eyes and focused on sound. Defroster. Wipers. Whistling wind. My pounding heart.

The car swerved and my lids flew open. I unclenched a hand and punched the radio.

The voice was solemn but reassuring. Much of the province was without electricity, and Hydro-Québec had three thousand employees on the job. Crews would work around the clock, but no one could say when the lines would be repaired.

The transformer serving Centre-Ville had blown because of overload, but was being given top priority. The filtration plant was down and residents were advised to boil their water.

Tough without power, I thought.

Shelters had been set up, and police would start going door to door at dawn to locate stranded seniors. Many roads were closed and motorists were advised to stay home.

I clicked the radio off, desperately wishing I were at home. With my sister. The thought of Harry set something pounding behind my left eye.

Ignore the headache and think, Brennan. You'll be of no use if you become distracted.

The Goyettes lived in an area known as the Plateau, so we cut north, then east on avenue des Pins. Uphill, I could see lights at Royal Victoria Hospital. Below us McGill was a black swatch, beyond that the city and waterfront, where the only thing visible was Place Ville-Marie.

Ryan turned north on St-Denis. Normally teaming with shoppers and tourists, the street was abandoned to the ice and wind. A translucence blanketed everything, obliterating the names of boutiques and bistros.

At Mont-Royal we headed east again, turned south on Christophe Colomb, and a decade later pulled up at the address

Anna had given me. The building was a typical Montreal three-flat, bayed in front, with narrow metal stairs sweeping to the second floor. Ryan nosed the Jeep toward the curb and left it in the street.

When we got out the ice stung my cheeks like tiny cinders and brought tears to my eyes. Head down, we climbed to the Goyette flat, slipping and sliding on the frozen steps. The bell was encased in solid gray, so I pounded on the door. In a moment the curtain moved and Anna's face appeared. Through the frosted pane I could see her head wag from side to side.

"Open the door, Anna!" I shouted.

The head shaking intensified, but I was not in a mood to negotiate.

"*Open the goddam door!*"

She went still, and a hand flew to her ear. She stepped back and I expected her to disappear. Instead, I heard the sound of a key, then the door opened a crack.

I didn't wait. I pushed hard and Ryan and I were inside before she could react.

Anna backed away and stood with arms crossed, hands clutching the sleeves of her jacket. An oil lamp sputtered on a small wooden table, sending shadows twitching high up the walls of the narrow hallway.

"Why can't you all just leave me alone?" Her eyes looked huge in the flickering light.

"I need your help, Anna."

"I can't do it."

"Yes, you can."

"I told her the same thing. I can't do it. They'll find me." Her voice trembled and I saw real fear on her face. The look sent a shaft straight to my heart. I'd seen it before. A friend, terrified by a stalker. I'd convinced her the danger wasn't real and she died because of it.

"Told who?" I wondered where her mother was.

"Dr. Jeannotte."

"She was here?"

A nod.

"When?"

"Several hours ago. I was sleeping."

"What did she want?"

Her eyes flicked to Ryan, then dropped to the floor.

"She asked odd questions. She wanted to know if I'd been seeing anyone from Amalie's group. I think she was going to the country, to the place I did the workshop. I—she hit me. I never had someone hit me like that. She was like a crazy person. I'd never seen her that way."

I heard anguish and shame in her voice, as if the attack were somehow her fault. She looked so small standing in the dark that I went to her and wrapped my arms around her.

"Don't blame yourself, Anna."

Her shoulders began to heave and I stroked her hair. It shimmered in the flickering lamplight.

"I would have helped her, but I honestly don't remember. I—it was one of my bad times."

"I know, but I want you to go back to that time and think hard. Think of everything you remember about where you were."

"I've tried. It just isn't there."

I wanted to shake her, to jar loose the information that would save my sister. I remembered a course in child psychology. No abstracts, ask specific questions. Gently, I pushed her to arm's length and raised her chin with my hand.

"When you went to the workshop did you leave from school?"

"No. They picked me up here."

"Which way did you turn off from your street?"

"I don't know."

"Do you remember how you left town?"

"No."

Abstract, Brennan.

"Did you cross a bridge?"

Her eyes narrowed, then she nodded.

"Which one?"

"I don't know. Wait, I remember an island with lots of tall buildings."

"Île des Sœurs," said Ryan.

"Yes." Her eyes opened wide. "Someone made a joke about nuns living in the condos. You know, *sœurs.* Sisters."

"The Champlain Bridge," said Ryan.

"How far was the farm?"

"I—"

"How long were you in the van?"

"About forty-five minutes. Yeah. When we got there the driver bragged that he'd made it in less then an hour."

"What did you see when you got out of the van?"

Again I saw doubt in her eyes. Then, slowly, as if she were describing a Rorschach spatter,

"Right before we got there I remember a big tower with lots of wires and antennae and disks. And then a tiny little house. Someone probably built it for their kids to wait for the school bus. I remember thinking it was made of gingerbread and decorated with frosting."

At that moment a face materialized behind Anna. It wore no makeup and looked shiny and pale in the flickering light.

"Who are you? Why do you come in the middle of the night?" The English was heavily accented.

Without waiting for an answer the woman grabbed Anna's wrist and pulled the girl behind her.

"You leave my daughter alone."

"Mrs. Goyette, I believe people are going to die. Anna may be able to help save them."

"She is not well. Now go." She pointed at the door. "I order you or I will call the police."

The ghostly face. The dim light. The tunnel-like hall. I was back in the dream, and suddenly I remembered. I knew, and I had to get there!

Ryan started to speak but I cut him off.

"Thank you. Your daughter has been very helpful," I managed.

Ryan glared as I pushed past him and out the door. I nearly fell in my plunge down the stairs. I no longer felt the cold as I stood at the Jeep, impatient for Ryan to speak to Mrs. Goyette, snug his tuque, then pick his way to ground level.

"What the hell—"

"Get me a map, Ryan."

"That little loony may be—"

"Do you have a goddam map of this province?" I hissed.

Without a word Ryan circled the Jeep and we both got in. He took a map from a holder on the driver's-side door, and I dug a flashlight from my pack. As I unfolded the province he started the engine, then got out to scrape the windshield.

I located Montreal, then followed the Champlain Bridge across the St. Lawrence and on to 10 East. With a numb finger I traced the route I had taken to Lac Memphrémagog. In my mind's eye I saw the old church. I saw the grave. I saw the signpost, half covered in snow.

I moved my finger along the highway, estimating driving time. The names wavered in the flashlight beam.

Marieville. St-Grégoire. Ste-Angèle-de-Monnoir.

My heart stopped when I saw it.

Please, God, let us be in time.

I lowered the window and screamed into the wind.

The grating stopped and the door opened. Ryan threw the scraper into the back and slid behind the wheel. He pulled off his gloves and I handed him the map and flashlight. Wordlessly, I pointed to a small dot on the square I'd folded upward. He studied it, his breath like fog in the yellow beam.

"Holy shit." An ice crystal melted and ran from his lash. He swiped at the eye.

"It makes sense. Ange Gardien. It's not a person, it's a place. They're going to meet *at* Ange Gardien. It should be about forty-five minutes from here."

"How did you think of it?" he asked.

I didn't want to go into the dream. "I remembered the sign from my drive to Lac Memphrémagog. Let's go."

"Brennan—"

"Ryan, I'll say this one more time. I am going to get my sister." I fought to keep my voice steady. "I am going with or without you. You can take me home or you can take me to Ange Gardien."

He hesitated, then,

"Fuck!" He got out, flipped his seat forward, and dug around in back. As he slammed the door I saw him drop something into his pocket and yank the zipper. Then he resumed scraping.

In a minute he was back. Without a word he clicked his seat belt, put the Jeep in gear, and accelerated. The wheels spun but we went nowhere. He changed to reverse, then quickly back to first. The car rocked as Ryan shifted from first gear to reverse and back again. The Jeep broke free and we moved slowly up the block.

I said nothing as we crept south on Christophe Colomb, then west on Rachel. At St-Denis Ryan turned south, reversing the route we'd just driven.

Damn! He was taking me home. My blood went cold as I thought of the drive to Ange Gardien.

I closed my eyes and leaned back to prepare myself. You have chains, Brennan. You will put them on and drive as Ryan is doing. Dickhead Ryan.

Silence intruded on my lecture. I opened my eyes to pitch-black. Ice no longer pelted the windshield.

"Where are we?"

"Ville-Marie Tunnel."

I said nothing. Ryan raced through the tunnel like a starship threading a wormhole in space. When he took the exit for the Champlain Bridge I felt both relief and apprehension.

Yes! Ange Gardien.

Ten light-years later we were crossing the St. Lawrence. The river looked unnaturally dense, the buildings of Île des Sœurs black against the predawn sky. Though their scoreboards were out I knew the players. Nortel. Kodak. Honeywell. So normal. So familiar in my world at the end of the second millennium. I wished I were approaching their well-ordered offices instead of the madness that lay ahead.

The atmosphere in the Jeep was tense. Ryan focused on the road and I worked the thumbnail. I stared out the window, avoiding thoughts of what might await us.

We crawled through a cold and forbidding landscape, a vista beamed from a frozen planet. As we moved east the ice increased visibly, robbing the world of texture and hue. Edges were blurred and objects seemed to blend together like parts of a giant plaster sculpture.

Guideposts, signs, and billboards were obliterated, erasing messages and boundaries. Here and there through the darkness wisps of smoke could be seen curling from chimneys, otherwise everything seemed frozen in place. Just over the Richelieu River the road curved, and I saw a beached car, belly-up like a loggerhead turtle. Stalactites hung from the bumpers and tires.

We'd been driving almost two hours when I spotted the sign. It was dawn, and the sky was changing from black to murky gray. Through the ice I could see an arrow and the letters *nge Gardi.*

"There."

Ryan released the gas and eased onto the exit. When it ended at a T-intersection he pumped the brake and the Jeep crunched to a stop.

"Which way?"

I grabbed the scraper, got out, and struggled to the sign, slipping once and cracking my knee. As I hacked away, the wind stood my hair on end and drove icy granules into my eyes. Overhead it hissed through branches and rattled power lines with an odd clacking sound.

I chopped at the ice as though demented. Eventually the blade snapped, but I jabbed on until the plastic was completely shattered. Using the wooden handle I scraped and clawed until finally, I could see letters and an arrow.

As I scrambled back to the Jeep something in my left knee felt terribly wrong.

"That way." I pointed. I didn't apologize for the scraper.

When Ryan turned, the rear spun out and we swerved wildly. My feet flew forward and I grabbed the armrests.

Ryan regained control and my teeth unclenched.

"There's no brake on your side."

"Thanks."

"This is the Rouville district. There's an SQ post not far from here. We'll go there first."

Though I begrudged the lost time, I didn't argue. If we walked into a hornet's nest I knew we might need backup. And, while Ryan's Jeep was good on ice, it had no radio.

Five minutes later I saw the tower. Or what was left of it. The metal had cracked under the weight of the ice, and beams and girders lay twisted and scattered like parts of a giant Erector set.

Just beyond the collapsed tower, a road took off to the left. Ten yards down I could see Anna's gingerbread hut.

"It's here, Ryan! Turn here!"

"We're doing this my way or not at all." He continued without slowing.

I was frantic. Any argument.

"It's getting light. What if they've decided to act at dawn?" I thought of Harry, drugged and helpless while zealots lit fires and prayed to their god. Or loosed wild dogs onto sacrificial lambs.

"We're going to check in first."

"We could be too late!" My hands trembled. I couldn't bear it. My sister could be ten yards away. I felt my chest begin to heave and turned my back to him.

A tree decided it.

We hadn't gone a quarter mile when an enormous pine blocked our way. It had fallen, bringing up a twelve-foot root wad and dragging power lines across the road. We would not be continuing in that direction.

Ryan struck the wheel with the heel of his hand.

"Jesus Christ in a peach tree!"

"It's pine." My heart hammered.

He stared at me, unamused. Outside, the wind moaned and threw ice against the windows. I saw Ryan's jaw muscles bunch, relax, bunch again. Then,

"We do this my way, Brennan. If I say wait in the Jeep, that's where your ass will be. Is that clear?"

I nodded. I would have agreed to anything.

We did an about-face and hung a right at the toppled tower. The road was narrow and littered with trees, some uprooted, others snapped where their trunks had failed. Ryan wove in and out among them. To either side poplars, ashes, and birches formed inverted U's, their crowns bent toward earth by the burden of ice.

A split-log fence began just beyond the gingerbread shelter. Ryan slowed and crept along it. At several places toppled trees had crushed the rails. Then I spotted the first living thing since Montreal.

The car was nose-down in a gully, wheels spinning, enveloped in a cloud of exhaust. The driver's door was open and I could see one booted leg planted on the ground.

Ryan braked and shifted to park.

"Stay here."

I started to object, thought better of it.

He got out and walked to the car. From where I sat the occupant could have been male or female. As Ryan and the driver exchanged words I lowered the window, but I couldn't make out what was said. Ryan's breath spurted like jets of mist. In less than a minute he was back in the Jeep.

"Not the most helpful character."

"What did he say?"

"*Oui* and *non.* He lives just up the road, but the cretin wouldn't notice if Genghis Khan moved in next door."

We moved on to where the fence ended at a gravel drive. Ryan pulled in and switched off the engine.

Two vans and a half dozen cars were scattered in front of a ramshackle lodge. They looked like rounded humps, frozen hippos in a river of gray. Ice dripped from the eaves and sills of the building and turned the windows milky, eliminating any view of the inside.

Ryan turned to me.

"Now listen. If this is the right place we're going to be about as welcome as a cottonmouth." He touched my cheek. "Promise me you'll stay here."

"I—"

His fingers slid to my lips.

"Stay here." His eyes were blindingly blue in the dreary dawn light.

"This is bullshit," I said into his fingertips.

He withdrew the hand and pointed at me.

"Wait in the car."

He pulled on gloves and stepped into the storm. When he slammed the door I reached for my mittens. I would wait two minutes.

What happened next comes back as disjointed images, shards of memory fragmented in time. I saw, but my mind did not accept the whole. It collected the memory and stored it away as separate frames.

Ryan had taken a half dozen steps when I heard a pop and his body jerked. His hands flew up and he started to turn. Another pop and another spasm, then he dropped to the ground and lay still.

"Ryan!" I yelled as I threw open the door. When I jumped out pain shot up my leg and my knee buckled. "Andy!" I screamed at his inert form.

Then lightning burst inside my skull and I was engulfed in darkness thicker than the ice.

34

MY NEXT CONSCIOUS SENSATION WAS ALSO OF BLACKNESS. Blackness and pain. I sat up slowly, unable to see any form to the darkness. Fierce pain shot into my head and I thought I would vomit. More pain as I raised my knees and hung my head between them.

In a moment the queasiness passed. I listened. Nothing but the pounding of my own heart. I looked at my hands but they were lost to the darkness. I inhaled. Rotten wood and damp earth. Gingerly, I reached out.

I was sitting on a dirt floor. Behind me and to both sides I could feel a wall of rough, round stones. Six inches above my head my hand met wood.

My breath came in short, rapid gasps as I fought panic.

I was trapped! I had to get out!

Nooooooooo!

The scream was in my mind. I hadn't entirely lost my self-control.

I closed my eyes and tried to control the hyperventilation. Clasping my hands, I tried to concentrate on one thing at a time.

Breathe in. Breathe out. In. Out.

Slowly the panic receded. I got to my knees and stretched a hand straight out in front of me. Nothing. The pain in my left knee brought me to tears, but I crawled forward into the inky void. Two feet. Six. Ten.

As I moved unobstructed my terror receded. A tunnel was better than a stone cage.

I sat back and tried to connect with a functioning portion of my brain. I had no idea where I was, how long I'd been there, or how I'd arrived.

I began to reconstruct.

Harry. The lodge. The car.

Ryan! God, my God, oh, God!

Please, no! Please, please, not Ryan.

My stomach roiled again and a bitter taste rose to my mouth. I swallowed.

Who shot Ryan? Who brought me in here? Where was Harry?

My head pounded and I was becoming stiff with cold. This was no good. I had to do something. I took a deep breath and rolled back to my knees.

Step by throbbing step I crept along the tunnel. I'd lost my gloves, and the frigid clay numbed my hands and jarred my injured patella. The pain kept me focused until I touched the foot.

As I recoiled my head cracked wood and the start of a scream froze in my throat.

Goddam it, Brennan, get ahold of yourself. You are a crime scene professional, not a hysterical onlooker.

I crouched, still paralyzed with dread. Not of the tomblike space, but of the thing with which I shared it. Generations were born and died as I waited for a sign of life. Nothing spoke, nothing moved. I breathed deeply, then inched forward and touched the foot again.

It wore a leather boot, small, with laces like mine. I found its partner and followed the legs upward. The body was lying on its side. Cautiously, I rolled it over and continued my exploration. Hem. Buttons. Scarf. My throat constricted as my fingertips recognized the clothing. Before I touched the face I knew.

But it couldn't be! It didn't make sense.

I pulled off the scarf and felt the hair. Yes. Daisy Jeannotte.

Jesus, God! What was going on?

Keep moving! a portion of my brain commanded.

I dragged myself forward on one knee and one hand, bracing a palm against the wall. My fingers touched cobwebs and things I didn't want to consider. Debris crumbled and trickled to earth as I moved slowly along the tunnel.

After several more feet the gloom lightened almost imperceptibly. My hand struck something and I followed it. Wooden rails. Trestles. When I looked up I could see a faint rectangle of amber light. Steps leading up.

I eased up the stairs, testing for sound at each riser. Three steps brought me to the ceiling. My hands identified the borders of a cover, but when I pushed it didn't budge.

I pressed my ear to the wood and the barking of dogs sent adrenaline to every part of my being. The sound seemed far off and muffled, but I could tell the animals were excited. A human voice yelled some command, then silence, then the yapping started again.

Directly overhead, no sounds of movement, no voices.

I pressed with my shoulder and the panel shifted slightly, but didn't give. When I examined the strips of light I could see a shadow at the midpoint of the right side. I tried poking it with my fingertips, but the gap was too narrow. Frustrated, I inserted my fingers farther up and slid them along the crack. Splinters pierced my flesh and tore at my nails, but I could not reach the retaining point. The opening around the edges wasn't wide enough.

Damn!

I thought of my sister and dogs and Jennifer Cannon. I thought of me and dogs and Jennifer Cannon. My fingers were so cold I could no longer feel them, and I slid them into my pockets. My right knuckle struck something hard and flat. Puzzled, I withdrew the object and held it up to the crack.

The broken scraper blade!

Please!

With a silent prayer, I inserted an edge. The blade fit! Trembling, I wiggled it toward the retaining point. The scraping seemed loud enough to be heard for miles.

I froze and listened. No movement overhead. Barely breathing, I nudged the shard farther. Inches short of what I hoped was a latch it snagged, popped from my hand, and fell into darkness.

Damn! Damn! Sonofabitch!

I bumped down the stairs on my hands and bum, and seated myself on the ground. Cursing my clumsiness, I began a miniature grid search across the dank clay. Within moments my fingers came down on the broken scraper.

Back up the stairs. By now movement sent searing pain firing up and down my leg. Using both hands I reinserted the blade and pushed up on the latch. No go. I withdrew and repositioned the shard, then swiped it sideways along the crack.

Something clicked. I listened. Silence. I pushed with my shoulder and the trapdoor lifted. Grabbing the panel along its edges, I eased it up, then lowered it quietly to the floor above. Heart racing, I raised my head and peeked around.

The room was lit by a single oil lamp. I could tell it was a pantry of some sort. Shelves lined three walls, some of which held boxes and cans. Stacks of cartons filled the corners ahead and to my left and right. When I looked to my rear a chill far greater than any caused by the weather overcame me.

Dozens of propane tanks lined the wall, their enamel luminous in the soft light. An image flitted through my mind, a wartime propaganda photo of armaments stockpiled in orderly rows. With shaking hands I eased myself down, and perched on the top step.

What could I do to stop them?

I glanced down the steps. A square of yellowish light fell across the cellar floor, just reaching Daisy Jeannotte's face. I looked at the cold, still features.

"Who are you?" I muttered. "I thought this was your show."

Total stillness.

I drew a few steadying breaths, then ascended into the pantry. Relief at escaping the tunnel alternated with fear of what I would encounter next.

The pantry opened onto a cavernous kitchen. I hobbled to a door on the far side, pressed my back against the wall, and sifted sounds. The creak of wood. The hiss of wind and ice. The click of frozen branches.

Barely breathing, I eased around the doorjamb and entered a long, dark hall.

The storm sounds faded. I could smell dust and wood smoke and old carpet. I limped forward, supporting myself against the wall. Not a sliver of light penetrated to this part of the house.

Where are you, Harry?

I came to a door and leaned close. Nothing. My knee trembled and I wondered how much farther I could go. Then I heard muffled voices.

Hide! the brain cells screamed.

The knob turned and I slipped into blackness.

The room smelled dank and sweet, like flowers left to die in a vase. Suddenly, the hair on my arms and neck stood straight. Was that movement? Again, I held my breath and sorted sounds.

Something was breathing!

Mouth dry, I swallowed and strained for the tiniest motion. Save for the steady rhythm of inhaling and exhaling, the room was devoid of sound. Slowly, I crept forward until objects emerged from the darkness. A bed. A human form. A nightstand with water glass and adjacent vial of pills.

Two more steps and I could see long blond hair on a patchwork quilt.

Could it be? Could my prayers possibly be answered this quickly?

I stumbled forward and turned the head to expose the face.

"Harry!" God, yes. It was Harry.

Her head rolled and she gave a low moan.

I was reaching for the vial of pills when an arm caught me from behind. It wrapped around my throat, crushing my windpipe and cutting off my air. A hand clamped across my mouth.

My legs thrashed and I clawed to break free. Somehow I got hold of the wrist and twisted the hand off my face. Before it arced back I saw the ring. A black rectangle with a carved ankh and crenulated border. As I thrashed and clawed I remembered a bruise in soft, white flesh. I knew I was in hands that would not hesitate to end my life.

I tried to scream but Malachy's killer had me in a grip that compressed my throat and muffled my mouth. Then my head was yanked sideways and pressed against a bony scarecrow chest. In the murky gloom I saw one pale eye, a white hair streak. Light-years passed as I struggled for air. My lungs burned, my pulse pounded, and I slipped in and out of consciousness.

I heard voices, but the world was receding. The pain in my knee faded as a numbness overtook my mind. I felt myself being dragged. My shoulder struck something. Softness underfoot. Hard again. We banged through another doorway, the arm a vise on my trachea.

Hands grabbed me and something rough slid over my wrists. My arms shot up, but the pressure on my head and throat was released and I could breathe! I heard a moan from my own throat as my lungs gulped precious air.

As I reestablished contact with my body, the pain returned.

My throat ached and my breath was labored. My shoulders and elbows were stretched from the traction, and my hands felt cold and numb above my head.

Forget your body. Use your brain.

The room was large, the kind you see in inns and lodges. It had a wide plank floor and heavy log walls, and was lit only by candle-light. I was roped to an overhead beam, my shadow a Giacometti figure with arms held high.

I turned my head and the ovoid shadow skull elongated in the flickering light. Double doorway straight ahead. Stone fireplace to my left. Picture window to my right. I stored the blueprint.

Hearing voices behind me, I threw one shoulder forward, retracted the other, and pushed with my toes. My body twisted, and for a split second I saw them before the ropes spun me back. I recognized the streaked hair and eye of the man. But who was the other?

The voices paused, then continued in hushed tones. I heard footsteps, followed by quiet. I knew I wasn't alone. I held my breath and waited for them.

When she stepped in front of me I was startled but not shocked. Today the braids were coiled on her head, not hanging down as they had been when she had walked the streets of Beaufort with Kathryn and Carlie.

She reached out and wiped a tear from my cheek.

"Are you frightened?" Her eyes looked cold and hard.

Fear will rouse her like a junkyard dog!

"No, Ellie. Not of you or your band of zealots." The pain in my throat made it hard to talk.

She ran the finger down my nose and across my lips. It felt rough against my skin. "Not Ellie. *Je suis Elle.* I am She. The female force."

I recognized the deep, breathy voice.

"The high priestess of death!" I spat.

"You should have left us alone."

"You should have left my sister alone."

"We need her."

"Didn't you have enough others? Or does each kill excite you so much?"

Keep her talking. Buy time.

"We punish the intractable."

"Is that why you killed Daisy Jeannotte?"

"Jeannotte." Her voice grew harsh with contempt. "That vicious, meddling old fool. Finally, she'll let him be."

What's the right thing to say to keep the conversation going?

"She didn't want her brother to die."

"Daniel will live forever."

"Like Jennifer and Amalie?"

"Their weakness was going to hold us back."

"So you take the weak and watch them torn to bits?"

Her eyes narrowed into something I couldn't interpret. Bitterness? Regret? Anticipation?

"I brought them out of the famine and showed them how to survive. They chose cataclysm."

"What was Heidi Schneider's sin? Loving her husband and babies?"

The eyes hardened.

"I revealed the way and she brought poison into the world! Evil in duplicate!"

"The Antichrist."

"Yes!" she hissed.

Think! What were her words in Beaufort?

"You say death is a transition in the growth process. Do you nurture by slaughtering babies and old women?"

"The corrupt cannot be permitted to pollute the new order."

"Heidi's babies were four months old!" Fear and anger made my voice crack.

"They were perversion!"

"They were babies!" I struggled and tried to lunge at her, but the ropes held firm.

Beyond the doorway I could hear the sound of others moving

around. I thought of the children at the Saint Helena compound, and felt my chest heave.

Where was Daniel Jeannotte?

"How many children will you and your henchman kill?"

The corners of her eyes pinched almost imperceptibly.

Keep her talking.

"Are you going to ask all your followers to die?"

Still she said nothing.

"Why do you need my sister? Have you lost your ability to motivate followers?" My voice sounded tremulous and two octaves too high.

"She will take the place of another."

"She doesn't believe in your Armageddon."

"Your world is ending."

"The last I looked it was doing fine."

"You kill redwoods to make toilet paper and pour poisons into the rivers and oceans. Is that doing fine?" She thrust her face so close to mine I could see vessels throbbing at her temples.

"Kill yourself if you must, but let the others make their own choices."

"There must be perfect balance. The number has been revealed."

"Really? And is everyone else here?"

She drew back her head but didn't speak. I saw something spark in her eye, like light skipping off broken glass.

"They're not all coming, Elle."

The eyes never faltered.

"Kathryn's not going to die for you. She's miles from here, safe with her baby."

"You lie!"

"You're not going to hit your cosmic quota."

"The signs have been sent. The apocalypse is now and we will rise from the ashes!"

Her eyes were black holes in the flickering light. I recognized the look for what it was. Madness.

I was about to respond when I heard the snarling and yapping of dogs. The sound was coming from deep inside the lodge.

I yanked desperately, but the ropes only tightened. My breathing turned to frenzied gasping. It was reflex, unthinking struggle.

I couldn't do it! I couldn't get free! And what if I did? I was there among them.

"Please," I begged.

Elle stared, her eyes unfeeling.

A sob escaped me as the barking grew louder. I continued to thrash. I would not submit passively, however hopeless my resistance.

What had the others done? I saw the torn flesh and punctured skulls. The barking turned to growls. The dogs were very near. Fear beyond control overcame me.

I twisted to see and my eyes swept across the bay window. My heart froze. Had I seen figures moving outside?

Don't draw attention to the window!

I dropped my gaze and rotated back to Elle, still straining, but my thoughts now on the outside. Was there still hope of rescue?

Elle watched me wordlessly. One second passed. Two. Five. I spun myself to the right and stole another peek.

Through the ice and condensation I saw a shadow slide from left to right.

Distract her!

I pivoted back and fixed my eyes on Elle. The window was to her left.

The barking grew louder. Closer.

Say anything!

"Harry doesn't believe in—"

The door burst inward, then I heard deep voices.

"Police!"

Boots chocked on hardwood.

"*Haut les mains!*" Hands up!

Snarling and yelping. Shouts. A scream.

Elle's mouth turned to an oval, then to a thin, dark line. She drew a gun from the folds of her dress and aimed it at something behind me.

The instant her eyes left me I wrapped my fingers around the ropes, threw my hips forward, kicked out with my feet, and arched toward her. Pain screamed through my shoulders and wrists as my body swung out, my arms in full extension. I flexed my hips and brought my boots up, hitting her arm with the full force of my weight. The gun flew across the room and out of my field of vision.

My feet slammed to the floor and I scrabbled backward to relieve the pressure on my upper limbs. When I looked up, Elle stood frozen, an SQ muzzle trained on her chest. One dark braid had fallen and looped her forehead like a brocade sash.

I felt hands on my back and heard voices speak to me. Then I was free and strong arms half dragged, half carried me to a couch. I smelled wintry air and wet wool. English Leather.

"*Calmez-vous, madame. Tout va bien.*"

My arms were lead, my knees were jelly. I wanted to sink back and sleep forever but I struggled to stand.

"*Ma soeur!* I have to find my sister!"

"*Tout est bien, madame.*" Hands pressed me back into the cushions.

More boots. Doors. Shouted commands. I saw Elle and Daniel Jeannotte handcuffed and led away.

"Where's Ryan? Do you know Andrew Ryan?"

"Take it easy, you're going to be fine." English.

I tried to pry myself loose.

"Is Ryan all right?"

"Relax."

Then Harry was beside me, eyes enormous in the dreamlike gloom.

"I'm scared," she murmured in a thick, slurry voice.

"It's O.K." I wrapped my deadened arms around her. "I'm taking you home."

Her head dropped onto my shoulder, and I rested mine against it. I held her a moment, then released her. Summoning up memories of religious education from my childhood, I closed my eyes, clasped my hands in front of my chest, and wept quietly as I prayed to God for the life of Andrew Ryan.

35

ONE WEEK LATER I WAS SITTING ON MY PATIO IN CHARLOTTE, thirty-six exam booklets stacked to my right, the thirty-seventh on a lap table in front of me. The sky was Carolina blue, the yard a deep, rich green. In the adjacent magnolia, a mockingbird strove for a personal best.

"Brilliantly average job," I said, marking a C+ on the blue cover and circling it several times. Birdie looked up, stretched, and slithered from the chaise.

My knee was healing well. The small hairline fracture in my left patella had been nothing compared with the injuries to my psyche. After the terror in Ange Gardien I'd spent two days in Quebec, recoiling at every sound and every shadow, barking dogs in particular. Then I returned to Charlotte to hobble through the remainder of the semester. I filled the days with relentless activity, but the nights were difficult. In the dark my mind loosened, releasing visions the daytime had locked away. Some nights I slept with the lamp on.

The phone rang and I reached for the handset. It was the call I'd been expecting.

"*Bonjour,* Dr. Brennan. *Comment ça va?*"

"*Ça va bien,* Sister Julienne. More important, how is Anna?"

"I think the medication is helping." Her voice went low. "I don't know anything about bipolar disorder, but the doctor gave me a great deal of material and I am learning. I had never understood her depression. I thought Anna was moody because that's what her mother said. Sometimes she'd be down, then suddenly she'd be full of energy and feeling good about herself. I didn't know that was, what is it called . . . ?"

"A manic phase?"

"*C'est ça.* She seemed to go up and down so quickly."

"I'm so glad she's better."

"Yes, God be praised. Professor Jeannotte's death hit her hard. Please, Dr. Brennan, for Anna's sake, I must know what went on with that woman."

I took a deep breath. What to say?

"Professor Jeannotte's troubles stemmed from her love for her brother. Daniel Jeannotte spent his life organizing one cult group after another. Daisy believed he was well intentioned and wrongly scorned by mainstream society. Her career in American academia was compromised following complaints to her university by parents of students she had steered to Daniel's conferences and workshops. She took a leave from teaching to do research and write, and resurfaced in Canada. For years she continued to be supportive of her brother.

"When Daniel hooked up with Elle, Daisy began to lose confidence. She thought Elle was a psychopath, and a struggle developed between the two women for Daniel's allegiance. Daisy wanted to protect her brother, but was afraid of something catastrophic.

"Jeannotte knew that Daniel and Elle's group was active on campus, though the university had tried to drive them off. So when Anna had her encounter with them, Daisy wanted to monitor them through Anna.

"Daisy was never a recruiter for the group. She learned that cult members had infiltrated the counseling center, looking for students to befriend. My sister was recruited that way at a community college in Texas. This agitated Daisy all the more because she feared being blamed because of the episode in her past."

"Who is this Elle?"

"Her real name is Sylvie Boudrais. What we know is patchy. She's forty-four, born in Baie Comeau of an Inuit mother and québécois father. Her mother died when she was fourteen, her father was an alcoholic. The old man beat her regularly and forced her into prostitution when she was fourteen. Sylvie never finished high school, but she tests in the stratosphere for IQ.

"Boudrais disappeared after dropping out of school, then showed up in Quebec City sometime in the mid-seventies offering psychic healing for a moderate fee. She acquired a small following, and eventually became the leader of a group that took up residence in a hunting lodge near Ste-Anne-de-Beaupré. There was constant money pressure, and problems developed because of underaged members. A fourteen-year-old turned up pregnant, and the parents went to the authorities.

"The group disbanded and Boudrais moved on. She did a brief stint with a sect called the Celestial Pathway in Montreal, but left. Like Daniel Jeannotte, she wandered from group to group, turning up in Belgium around 1980, where she preached a combination of shamanism and New Age spiritualism. She established a band of followers, including a very wealthy man named Jacques Guillion.

"Boudrais had met Guillion early through the Celestial Pathway, and saw him as the answer to a group's cash flow problems. Guillion fell under her spell, and was eventually persuaded to sell his properties and turn over his assets."

"No one objected?"

"The taxes were paid and Guillion had no family, so no questions arose."

"*Mon Dieu.*"

"In the mid-eighties the group left Belgium for the U.S. They established a commune in Fort Bend County, Texas, and Guillion shuttled back and forth to Europe for several years, probably transferring money. He last entered the U.S. two years ago."

"What happened to him?" Her voice was small and tremulous.

"The police think he's buried somewhere on the ranch."

I heard the swish of fabric.

"Jeannotte's brother met Boudrais in Texas and was captivated. By then she was calling herself Elle. That's also where Dom Owens came into the picture."

"He is the man from South Carolina?"

"Yes. Owens was a small-time dabbler in mysticism and organic healing. He visited the Fort Bend ranch and was infatuated with

Elle. He invited her to the South Carolina compound on Saint Helena, and she seized control of his group."

"But it all sounds so harmless. Herbs and spells and holistic medicine. How did it come to violence and death?"

How does one explain madness? I didn't want to discuss the psychiatric evaluation lying on my desk, or the rambling suicide notes found at Ange Gardien.

"Boudrais read extensively, especially philosophy and ecology. She was convinced the earth would be destroyed, and before that happened she would take her followers away. She believed herself to be the guardian angel of those devoted to her, and the lodge at Ange Gardien was the jumping-off point. "

There was a long pause. Then,

"Did they really believe it?"

"I don't know. I don't think Elle was willing to trust entirely to the power of her oratory. She relied in part on drugs."

Another pause.

"Do you think they believed enough to be willing to die?"

I thought of Kathryn. And Harry.

"Not all of them."

"It is mortal sin to orchestrate the loss of life, or even to hold another living soul as a captive."

A perfect bridge.

"Sister, did you read the information I sent regarding Élisabeth Nicolet?"

The pause at her end was longer. It ended with a deep sigh.

"Yes."

"I've done a lot of research on Abo Gabassa. He was a well-respected philosopher and public speaker, known all over Europe, Africa, and North America for his efforts to end the slave trade."

"I understand that."

"He and Eugénie Nicolet sailed for France on the same ship. Eugénie returned to Canada with an infant daughter." I took a breath. "The bones don't lie, Sister Julienne. And they are not judgmental. From the moment I looked at Élisabeth's skull, I knew she was a person of mixed race."

"That doesn't mean she was a prisoner."

"No, it does not."

Another pause. Then she spoke slowly.

"I agree that an illegitimate child would not have been well received in the Nicolet circle. And in those days a mixed-race black baby might have been impossible. Perhaps Eugénie viewed the convent as the most humane solution."

"Perhaps. Élisabeth may not have chosen her own fate, but that doesn't diminish her contribution. According to all accounts, her work during the smallpox epidemic was heroic. Thousands may have been spared by her efforts.

"Sister, are there any saints from North America whose bloodlines included Native American, African, or Asian ancestry?"

"Why, I'm not sure." I heard something new in her voice.

"What an extraordinary role model Élisabeth could be to people of faith who suffer prejudices because they were not born Caucasian."

"Yes. Yes, I must speak to Father Ménard."

"May I ask you a question, Sister?"

"*Bien sûr.*"

"Élisabeth appeared to me in a dream and spoke a line I cannot place. When I asked who she was she said, 'All in robe of darkest grain.' "

"'Come pensive nun devout and pure; Sober steadfast and demure; All in robe of darkest grain; Flowing with majestic train.' John Milton's *Il Penseroso.*"

"The brain is an amazing archive," I said, laughing. "It's been years since I read that."

"Would you like to hear my favorite?"

"Of course."

It was a lovely thought.

When we hung up I looked at my watch. Time to go.

During the drive I turned the radio on and off, tried to identify a rattle in the dashboard, and just drummed my fingers.

The traffic signal at Woodlawn and the Billy Graham Parkway took a lifetime.

This was your idea, Brennan.

Right. But does that make it a good one?

I arrived at the airport and went directly to baggage claim.

Ryan was draping a garment bag over his left shoulder. His right arm was in a sling and he moved with an uncharacteristic stiffness. But he looked good. Very good.

He's here to recover. That's all.

I waved and called to him. He smiled and pointed to an athletic bag circling toward him on the carousel.

I nodded and began sorting my keys, deciding which should go to another chain.

"*Bonjour*, y'all."

I gave him a minimal-contact hug, the kind people use when picking up in-laws. He stepped back, and the too-damn-blue eyes looked me up and down.

"Nice outfit."

I was wearing jeans and a shirt that didn't bunch too high with the crutches.

"How was your trip?"

"The flight attendant took pity and moved me up front."

I'll bet she did.

On the ride home I asked about the state of his injuries.

"Three fractured ribs and one perforated a lung. The other bullet preferred muscle. It was no big deal, except for some blood loss."

The no big deal had taken four hours of surgery.

"Are you in pain?"

"Only when I breathe."

When we got to the Annex, I showed Ryan the guest room and went to the kitchen to pour iced tea.

Minutes later he joined me on the patio. Sunlight was slanting through the magnolia, and a troupe of song sparrows had replaced the mockingbird.

"Nice outfit," I said, handing him a glass.

Ryan had changed to shorts and a T-shirt. His legs were the color of uncooked cod, and athletic socks bagged around his ankles.

"Been wintering in Newfoundland?"

"Tanning causes melanoma."

"I'll need shades for the glare."

Ryan and I had already reviewed the events in Ange Gardien.

We'd discussed it at the hospital, then later by phone as more information came to light.

Ryan had used his cell phone to call the Rouville district SQ post while I was outside scraping the road sign. When we didn't appear there the dispatcher sent a truck to clear the road so a unit could investigate. The officers found Ryan unconscious and called in backup and ambulances.

"So your sister is through with cosmic healing?"

"Yeah." I smiled and shook my head. "She came down here for a few days, then headed back to Texas. It won't be long before she becomes enthused by some other alternative agenda."

We sipped our tea.

"Have you read the psychiatric stuff?"

"Delusional misidentification with significant components of grandiosity and paranoia. What the frig does that mean?"

That same question had already sent me to the psychiatric literature.

"The Antichrist delusion. People see themselves or others as demonic. In Elle's case, she projected the delusion onto Heidi's babies. She'd read about matter and antimatter, and believed everything has to be in balance. She said one of the babies was the Antichrist, the other some type of cosmic backup. Is she still talking?"

"Like a DJ on uppers. She admits to sending the hit team to St-Jovite to kill the kids. Simonnet tried to intervene, so they shot her. Then the killers downed the drugs and started the fire."

I thought of the old lady whose bones I'd examined.

"Simonnet must have tried to protect Heidi and Brian. All those calls to Saint Helena, then the rescue mission to Texas after Daniel Jeannotte showed up at the Schneider home." My fingers made oval prints in the condensation on my tea glass. "Why do you suppose Simonnet kept phoning after Heidi and Brian left Saint Helena?"

"Heidi kept in contact with Jennifer Cannon, and Simonnet phoned for reports. When Elle found out, she had Cannon killed."

"The same exorcism by dogs, knives, and scalding liquid she'd ordered when Carole Comptois got pregnant."

The image still made me shudder.

"Was Comptois still working as a hooker?"

"She'd given it up. Ironically, she was introduced to Elle by a former customer. Though Comptois lived with the group off and on, apparently she maintained outside interests, since her baby's father was not a member and therefore not an approved sperm donor. That's why Elle ordered the exorcism."

"Why Amalie Provencher?"

"That's unclear. Amalie may have gotten in the way of the elimination of Jennifer."

"Elle believed she needed the psychic strength of fifty-six souls to muster the energy for the final crossing. She hadn't counted on losing Comptois. That's why she needed Harry."

"Why fifty-six?"

"It has something to do with the fifty-six Aubrey holes at Stonehenge."

"What are Aubrey holes?"

"Small pits that were dug and filled in immediately. They were probably used to predict lunar eclipses. Elle has woven all kinds of esoterica into her delusions."

I took a sip of tea.

"She was obsessed with the idea of balance. Matter and antimatter. Controlled coupling. Exactly fifty-six people. She chose Ange Gardien not just because of the name, but because it's equidistant from there to the communes in Texas and South Carolina. It's an amazing coincidence, isn't it?"

"What's that?"

"My sister lives in Texas. I work in Quebec, and have lifelong ties to the Carolinas. Everywhere I turned, Elle's influence was there. Her reach was awesome. How many lives do you suppose these cults affect?"

"There's no telling."

The sound of Vivaldi drifted from my neighbor's patio.

"How did your friend Sam take the news that one of his employees brought bodies to Murtry?"

"He wasn't thrilled." I remembered Joey's nervousness by the water truck when we emerged from the burial location. "Joey Espinoza had been working for Sam for almost two years."

"Right. He was an Owens follower, but lived in his mother's house. She's the one who phoned Social Services. Well, it turns out he's also Carlie's father. That's why Kathryn fled to him when things got ugly. It seems she didn't know anything about the murders."

"Where are they now?"

"She and the baby are with some cousin of hers. Joey is discussing the recent past with Sheriff Baker."

"Has anyone been charged?"

"Elle and Daniel have each been charged with three counts of first-degree murder for the deaths of Jennifer Cannon, Amalie Provencher, and Carole Comptois."

Ryan picked up a magnolia leaf and trailed it across his thigh.

"What else was in the evaluation?"

"According to the court-appointed shrink Elle suffers from an elaborate multidelusional psychosis. She's convinced that the apocalypse will occur soon in the form of a giant environmental disaster, and that she's destined to preserve humanity by transporting followers away from the apocalypse."

"Where were they going?"

"She's not saying. But you aren't on her manifest."

"How do people buy into such crap?" Ryan echoed my question to Red Skyler.

"The group recruited people who were disillusioned with their lot and attracted by group acceptance, being accorded a sense of worth and importance, and being given simple answers to all questions, with a little drug therapy thrown in."

A breeze lifted the branches of the magnolia, bringing with it the smell of wet grass. Ryan said nothing.

"Elle may be crazy, but she's smart and extraordinarily persuasive. Even now her followers are loyal. While she's pontificating, they're not saying a word."

"Yeah." He stretched, raised his bandaged arm, and repositioned it on his chest. "She's cunning, all right. She was never after a huge following. She wanted a small but loyal band. That and Guillion's money let her keep a low profile. Until it began to unravel, she made very few mistakes."

"What about the cat? That was brutal but stupid."

"That was Dom Owens. Elle ordered him to stop your meddling. He claims he was not into physically harming people, so he directed some student followers in Charlotte to do something to frighten you off. They devised the cat trick. Got the poor thing from the animal shelter."

"How did they find me?"

"One of them took a bill or something from your office. It had your home address."

Ryan sipped his tea.

"By the way, your St. Paddy's Day adventure in Montreal was also student-inspired."

"How did you know about that?"

He smiled and waggled the teacup. "It seems the protective attitude went both ways between Jeannotte and her students. One of them saw that she was upset, and concluded your visits were the cause. He decided to freelance and deliver a personal message."

I changed the subject. "Do you believe Owens was involved in killing Jennifer and Amalie?"

"He denies it. Claims that after he confronted Jennifer about the phone calls he reported to Elle. Says Elle told him she and Daniel were taking Jennifer and Amalie back to Canada."

"Why was Owens not at Ange Gardien?"

"Owens had decided to bail. He either became afraid over what Elle might do because he had lost track of Joey, Kathryn, and Carlie, or he didn't have confidence in the cosmic crossover. Either way, he had over two hundred thousand dollars of Guillion's money left, so he gathered it up and went west as everyone else headed north. The American feds caught up with him at a naturalist commune in Arizona. Elle would not have had her fifty-four souls even with Harry."

"Hungry?"

"Let's eat."

We made salad, then skewered chicken and vegetables for shish kebabs. Outside the sun had dropped below the horizon, and the deepening dusk filled the trees and grounds with dark shadows. We ate on the patio, talking and watching night settle in. Inevitably, the conversation drifted back to Elle and the murders.

"I guess Daisy Jeannotte felt she could confront her brother and force him to stop the madness."

"Yeah, but Elle spotted Daisy first and had Daniel eliminate her and throw her into the crawl space where they later stashed you. You had been perceived as a lesser threat and had simply been rapped over the head and stuck in the hole. When you responded by getting free and causing more trouble, Elle was outraged and committed you to the same murder-exorcism that she had lavished on Jennifer and Amalie."

"Daniel helped Elle kill Jennifer and Amalie, and he's the main suspect in the Carole Comptois murder. Who were the assassins in St-Jovite?"

"We may never know. No one has told that story yet."

Ryan finished his tea and leaned back. Crickets had taken over for birds. Far off a siren moaned in the night. For a long time we didn't speak.

"Do you remember the exhumation I did in Lac Memphrémagog?"

"The saint."

"One of the nuns in that order is Anna Goyette's aunt."

"Thanks to nuns I still have limited use of my knuckles."

I smiled. Another gender inequality.

I told him about Élisabeth Nicolet.

"They were all captives in one way or another. Harry. Kathryn. Élisabeth."

"Elle. Anna. Prisons take many forms."

"Sister Julienne shared a quote with me. In *Les Misérables* Victor Hugo refers to the convent as an optical device whereby man gains a glimpse of infinity."

The crickets chirped.

"It's not infinity, Ryan, but we're barreling toward the end of a millennium. Do you suppose there are others out there preaching Armageddon and orchestrating rituals of group death?"

For a moment he didn't answer. The magnolia rustled overhead.

"There will always be mystic hustlers who will play upon disillusionment, despair, low self-esteem, or fear to promote their own agendas. But if any of these psycho charlatans get off the bus in my town the reckoning will be swift and certain. Revelation according to Ryan."

I watched a leaf tumble across the brick.

"What about you, Brennan? Will you be there to help me?"

Ryan's form was black against the night sky. I couldn't see his eyes, but I knew they were looking straight toward mine.

I reached over and took his hand.